THE PLYMOUTH LEGACY

THE PLYMOUTH LEGACY IS A NOVEL INTERPRETATION OF HISTORICAL FACTS WRITTEN IN EASY-TO-READ LANGUAGE WHICH COULD HAVE BEEN UTTERED BY THE PILGRIMS THEMSELVES. IT BEGINS WITH THE BIRTH OF MARY (ALLERTON) CUSHMAN IN 1616 AND ENDS WITH HER DEATH IN 1699. A MUST READING FOR YOUNG ADULTS, AND A PLEASURE FOR ADULTS.

THE PLYMOUTH LEGACY

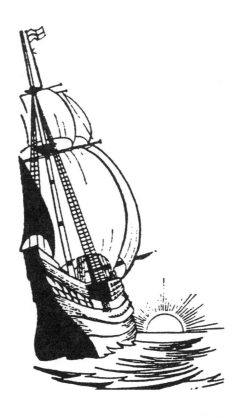

DONALD F. KENT

ALPHA GROUP PUBLICATIONS
BOX 95
BLOOMFIELD, NEW JERSEY 07003

CO-PUBLISHER
PMC PUBLICATIONS
FAIRFIELD, NEW JERSEY

THE PLYMOUTH LEGACY...

AN HISTORICAL NOVEL.

COPYRIGHT © 1997 BY DONALD F. KENT.

ALL RIGHTS RESERVED.

FOR INFORMATION, ADDRESS: ALPHA GROUP PUBLICATIONS,
BOX 95, BLOOMFIELD, NEW JERSEY 07003. USA

CO-PUBLISHED BY: PMC PUBLICATIONS, FAIRFIELD, NJ 07004

ALPHA GROUP BOOKS MAY BE PURCHASED FOR EDUCATIONAL,
BUSINESS, OR SALES PROMOTIONAL USE.
FOR INFORMATION, PLEASE WRITE:
SPECIAL MARKETING DIVISION,
ALPHA GROUP PUBLICATIONS,
BOX 95
BLOOMFIELD, NEW JERSEY 07003

LIBRARY OF CONGRESS CATALOG CARD NUMBER: 96-86532
KENT, DONALD F.
THE PLYMOUTH LEGACY / BY DONALD F. KENT
P. CM.   FIRST EDITION
ISBN 1-881275-27-2

MANUFACTURED IN THE UNITED STATES OF AMERICA
10 9 8 7 6 5 4 3 2 1

*D*edicated to my wife,
Harriet Mary (Cushman) Kent,
and my two sons, Donald and Peter.

*S*pecial thanks to
Ray Burke, Robert Rosier
and Sam Gallucci for their
confidence and cooperation.

NATIONAL MONUMENT TO THE FOREFATHERS

The photograph on the back of the book's jacket is the National Monument to the Forefathers. It is located in Plymouth, Massachusetts and is an impressive tribute to the skilled artisans and the unselfish donors who made this a successful endeavor after years of toil and dedication.

The complete statue is eighty-one feet tall. The main figure which depicts "Faith" is thirty-six feet tall and its fourteen granite sections alone weigh one hundred eight tons. She stands with her left foot on Plymouth Rock, in her left hand she holds a Bible and her uplifted right hand and index finger point to the heavens.

Each of the smaller figures, which average fifteen feet tall, weighs between twenty and twenty-five tons and each is carved out of a single piece of granite.

It is the largest solid granite monument in the United States.

Extracted in part from the writing of *Plymouth's Grand Old Lady* by the Rev. Richard Howland Maxwell.

THE PLYMOUTH LEGACY

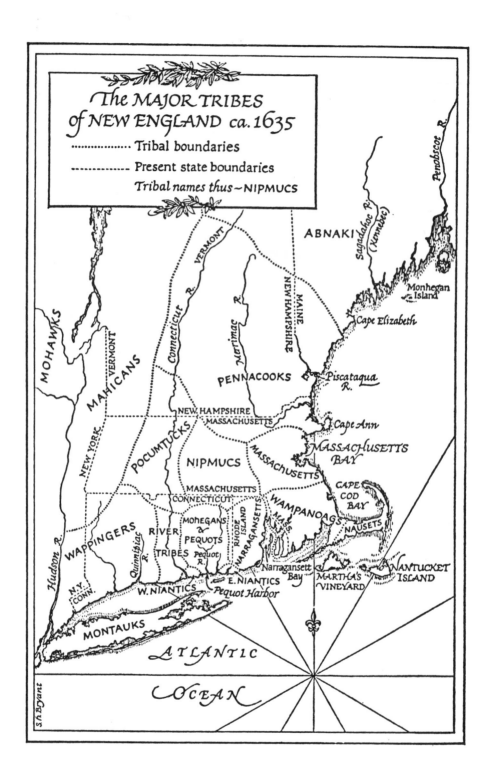

The MAJOR TRIBES of NEW ENGLAND ca. 1635

.... Tribal boundaries

------------- Present state boundaries

Tribal names thus ~ NIPMUCS

Map-Courtesy of Mayflower Quarterly.

A. Crew busy furling fore topsail on Mayflower II

B. Crewman tarring ropes on Mayflower II

C. Mayflower II at pier in Plymouth Harbor

D. Francis Cooke's home in Plimoth Plantation.

E. View of typical homes in Plimoth Plantation.

F. Pilgrim's final resting place-Burial Hill overlooking
Plymouth Harbor.

THE PLYMOUTH
LEGACY

AUTHOR'S NOTES

History was always a boring subject to me when I was attending school. I hated remembering dates and tying dates to events. We studied ancient, medieval as well as contemporary history. Who remembers the Punic Wars? Carthage, as you know, was involved in the Punic Wars and is located in North Africa. I visited the ruins of what was once Carthage...there remains very little to show that this was once a thriving civilization of Carthaginians who dominated the Mediterranean Sea. I saw Agrigento in Sicily with its ruins of a Greek and Roman civilization. The Island of Sicily has been invaded or inhabited at various times.

They were occupied by the Phoenicians, Carthaginians, Greeks, Romans (they stayed for five hundred years), Arabs, Norsemen, Normans and Spanish. Lately, (World War II) the Germans were their guests but were invaded by the British and Americans who then left them.

I could probably guess the origin of Sicily within... let us say...give or take five hundred years. The point is, there is nothing tangible to associate the present with the past. We have our history books that give a fleeting record of civilization. Encyclopedias give a few words about events that could have taken a hundred years to play out its scene in the history of mankind. I guess that there is so much history and the happenings of mankind that we can only expect to get a smattering of what went on before us.

Mankind was lucky when Johanna Gutenberg invented movable type around 1454. They claim that this event was the most important invention through the ages...it was a new means of communication. All this brings me to the point of communication by printing. Many books give facts, figures and dates but in my estimation although a necessary evil ...are still boring. So I have written this book, "The Plymouth Legacy" and it was meant to be a novel. The dialogue is fictional and the rest is historical. The characters portrayed were real.

They earned their place in history over a hundred and fifty years before we became a nation. In our reading of events that happened at that time we marvel at the courage, perseverance and the determination that our forefathers showed.

The following are the main characters in most books written about the Pilgrims: Bradford, Brewster, Carver, Alden, Standish...but there were others...they are mentioned fleetingly, they are given a brief line in history. I have attempted to bring the "unsung" heroic characters to life, particularly Mary Allerton who became the wife of Thomas Cushman. Thomas followed William Brewster as Elder of the First Church of Plymouth. There is Robert Cushman, Thomas's father who, along with William Carver, organized the trip of the Mayflower to the New World.

Thomas and Mary Cushman had eight children. With these humble beginnings eventually produced notable descendants that became famous in all walks of life including two Presidents of the United States; Zachery Taylor and Franklin Delano Roosevelt...

I became interested in the Cushman and Allerton families while doing research into the genealogy of my wife Harriet Mary (Cushman). These families seemed to have established a relationship with almost all the families that came over on the *Mayflower* and had descendants.

It became an interesting experience and I met some wonderful and cooperative people during my search. In researching the book I visited several libraries; the New Jersey Historical Society, the New York Public Library, Rutgers University in New Brunswick and local libraries. I used reference material from numerous books including *Plymouth Plantation* by William Bradford and edited by Samuel Eliot Morison; *Saints and Strangers* by George F. Willison; *Plymouth Colony* by Eugene Aubrey Stratton.

My wife and I made several trips to Plimoth Plantation in Plymouth, Massachusetts and we were amazed at the authenticity of the informants who portrayed some of the original settlers with their accents and their thorough knowledge of life at that time. They wear duplicates of the original costumes of their namesakes. I was especially interested in the part that was played by Thomas Cushman as a youth. After a few minutes one had the feeling of living in that era of 1627. So I had the privilege of using my new-found knowledge of the Pilgrims and their lives.

There is a faithful reproduction of a Wampanoag Indian settlement nearby that gives one an experience that the Pilgrims probably encountered when they first set foot in the New World. The Indians way of life stands in stark contrast to the Pilgrims.

In addition to visiting Plimoth Plantation and the Indian Village of the Wampanoags, we also enjoyed ourselves in seeing the replica of the *Mayflower* (called *Mayflower II*) with its crew that seems hand-picked from history's pages.

Although there were twenty ships in England bearing the name *Mayflower* during the time the original ship came to the New World, only one gained immortality in history. Ironically, the original *Mayflower*, a few years after the death of Captain Jones in 1622, was tied up to a dock in Rotterdam, Holland, decomposing. The sails were in poor shape and there were no bidders on her sale. The owners wanted one-hundred fifty pounds for her.

Thousands of descendants have proven their dedication and loyalty by retaining their roots and giving support with their membership in the General Society of *Mayflower* Descendants of Plymouth and their state and foreign chapters.

As previously mentioned, the dialogue in this book is fictional but could conceivably have been used in the original event or circumstances.

I found discrepancies in dates in the books that I read during my research. For instance, in *Saints and Strangers* by George F. Willison, it gives the date of the marriage of Francis Cooke and Hester Mayhieu in Leyden, Holland in 1613. Other sources gives the date as 1603. In *Saints and Strangers* it shows Francis Cooke's birthday as 1577, another gives the date as 1583, so at his marriage, if it was 1603 he was either twenty-six or twenty and Hester would have been eleven! It also shows that Francis Cooke left England in 1607 to go to Amsterdam and he stayed until 1609 when he went with Reverend Robinson to Leyden along with the congregation that would form their settlement at Green Gate. They applied to the Burgomaster for permission to settle in the city of Leyden on February 12, 1609.

I think that you'll find the story interesting reading as I have found the characters entirely engrossing. Although it is historical, I feel sure that you won't find it boring.

> Note: You will notice that Plymouth is also spelled Plimoth, an earlier version. Leyden is also spelled Leiden.

I believe that you'll find that The Plymouth Legacy, besides being an interesting and easy-to-read book for adults, is also a treasure trove of historical, factual information for teen-agers. When they begin to read the book, they will change their minds about history. They will get a personal look at the exciting daily lives and problems of our first immigrants . . . the Pilgrims of Plymouth.

THE PLYMOUTH LEGACY

PROLOGUE

Isaac Allerton was born in the suburbs of London in 1586. He was of medium build, five feet eight inches tall with brownish-blonde hair, which now at the age of thirty-one years was beginning to recede slightly. He was serious in nature and interested in improving his position in life. He had a dry wit with an active mind which was continually seeking new ways to accomplish his tasks which seemed to occupy most of his time. He had gone to Amsterdam around 1607 with a group of English Separatists under Pastor Richard Clyfton and his assistant John Robinson. There were many disputes among the British churches in Amsterdam, they could never seem to agree with policy. Part of the congregation decided to move to Leyden and Reverend Robinson became Pastor of the Church which they founded. Pastor Clyfton remained in Amsterdam until his death in 1616.

Isaac was a tailor by trade who had learned his profession in London. He was skilled and provided a good livelihood for his family by joining the tailor's guild and becoming a citizen of Leyden. The city fathers took a dim view of "outsiders" taking jobs; therefore, many of the expatriates from England, through necessity, became citizens. The Allertons had moved into a modest brick building on cobblestoned Bell Alley. Leyden was an old city of about eighty thousand residents and it was renown for its famous university which had been founded in 1575.

Isaac married Mary Norris in 1611 in Leyden when she was twenty-two years old. She was born in 1588 in Newbury, Berkshire, England. Like Isaac, she left England to begin a new life with religious freedom in Leyden, Holland. She was well-liked by everyone, trim of figure, outgoing and with a well developed sense of humor. She had large bright hazel eyes that were complimented by her chestnut-brown hair. She was petite, a mere five feet three inches tall.

Their marriage resulted in the birth of a son, named Bartholomew, a year after they were married. Two years after his birth, his sister, Remember was born.

There was a great deal of excitement in the Allerton household on a warm day in June, 1616. Mary Allerton had a rough time delivering her other two children, now this was to be their third and hopefully her final ordeal.

"Isaac, I think it's about time." Mary said.

Mary had been having labor pains for several hours... severe wrenching pains that seemed to tear at her insides. Bridget Robinson and another neighbor, Mary Brewster, shooed Isaac out of the bedroom and continued to assist Mary in delivering her baby. It didn't matter to the parents whether it was a boy or girl, they already had one child of each sex who were being supervised by Elizabeth Tilley, daughter of John Tilley, who lived nearby.

"Mary, we're still with you...relax now, you're an old hand at this...push!...push!" This had been an arduous task, true she had been through this twice before but being a mother required a great sacrifice. Mary continued to strain, then a little pink feminine being came into the world. She let out a wild cry after she was slapped on the bottom. Then the women cleaned the baby, cut the cord and prepared her to meet the family. Every few minutes Bridget wiped the perspiration from the brow of the mother. It was unbearably hot in the bedroom...it had been unseasonably hot the whole week and there was no relief in sight. Bridget opened the door and said, "You can come in now, Mr. Allerton, and see your new daughter!'

Isaac had a big smile on his face as he entered the room. "How are you feeling Mary?"

"I feel better, a little tired...but what do you think of your new daughter—Mary?"

"She looks just like you. I think the children would like to see their new sister. They're outside the door with Elizabeth, anxiously waiting."

Isaac called out, "Come on in and see your new sister!"

The children, Bartholomew aged four and Remember, now two, stood in awe and then silently stood at the foot of the bed. Bartholomew dropped Remember's hand, which he was holding tightly, and said, "She's awfully small...how come she's so wrinkled?"

"You were once that small; just as wrinkled. She will be as pretty as Remember soon," Isaac replied.

They talked for awhile then Isaac said, "I think we should leave your mother now, so she can rest. Mrs. Robinson and Mrs. Brewster will take good care of her."

Bartholomew said, "How about the baby? Who's going to take care of her?"

"They'll take good care of her too." Isaac placed his hands on his children's shoulders and steered them out of the room.

CHAPTER 1

Leyden, Holland

1617-1619

The year was 1617 and the Sabbath was observed as it had been for years. The Allertons attended the Green Gate Meeting House on Bell Alley for the services on Sunday which had become an all day affair. The services started at eight in the morning and lasted until noon. In the afternoon a general meeting was held where Pastor Robinson or the Elder would introduce a subject and members of the congregation, usually the head of a household, would carry on, giving their own view. Green Gate was a large house that had been converted into a meeting house and a parsonage. Pastor Robinson and his wife, Bridget (White), were the parents of three children; John, Bridget and Isaac.

The Elder of the church was William Brewster, whose wife Mary attended Mary Allerton in birthing her child. One of the Deacons was Samuel Fuller; all three, Robinson, Fuller and Brewster were well regarded by the three hundred members of the congregation. The men, women and children were separated into three groups. The children were under the watchful eye of the deacons, who were stern and disciplined them frequently with switches. The boys showed off in front of the girls, who giggled, a common occurrence throughout the ages. If the children were very young they remained in the arms of their mothers. In fact the procedure in the church remained the same for hundreds of years.

The women and men sat in separate sections of the church on hard wooden benches. The women had little to say about the conduct of the services but they did contribute to the praying and in the singing of hymns unaccompanied by any musical instruments—they were started off by a deacon giving the pitch. The quality of the sound left much to be desired. The men in their section were very impressive in their Sunday's best suits. They were vocal in their contribution of ideas to the church and it s governing, although Elder Brewster soon set them in the proper perspective.

Elder William Brewster was a quiet man and he had a very dignified appearance. He was adorned with greyish-white hair and a trim beard. He had alert brown eyes that seemed to dart about, one could feel that he was a highly intelligent person. He was short of stature, being only five feet six inches tall and slightly heavy. He was a sincere, compassionate man filled with a desire to help his fellow man.

One could always count on Brewster as a dependable, loyal friend. He had attended Emmanuel College and was quite proficient in translating Latin Scriptures into English. He had written and printed several articles about the Anglican Church which was printed by the Pilgrim Press in Choir Alley in Leyden and smuggled into Scotland and England. Consequently, the English authorities were attempting to trace the origin of the articles.

Another hardworking person to make his mark in the development of the Mayflower adventure was Robert Cushman. In 1617, Cushman was forty years old. He was five feet seven inches tall and had brown hair, and of average build. Unlike many men at that time, Cushman was clean shaven. He was quick-witted and sincere in his effort to help his fellow congregation members and he served as a deacon. Cushman was born at Canterbury, England in 1578. He was a woolcomber by trade but he had a great potential for leadership. He stuck closely to the Separatist doctrine, but did nothing to induce wrath from the Anglican Church and the royal government. He went to Leyden in 1611 with his wife Sarah (Reder) and his daughter and son. They occupied a small house in Nun's Alley but the next year he purchased a larger house. He was intelligent and although he was not wealthy he was much better off financially than many of his neighbors.

In 1616, the year little Mary Allerton was born, Cushman lost his wife and daughter, leaving him with his nine year old son, Thomas, who was very much like his father with brown hair and brown eyes and similar features. Robert had later married Mary (Clarke) Singleton of Sandwich, England, who was herself a widow. After his second marriage he was to leave in a couple of months with John Carver on their mission to London to seek out the Virginia Company to get their support in getting funds for the expedition to the New World.

Cushman's friend, John Carver, was born in 1566 in Doncaster, Yorkshire and now was about fifty-one years old. He was well educated and quite wealthy. He was quiet, a mysterious person but capable. A merchant by profession, a shrewd buyer, this would be a valuable trait in seeking out and convincing the Virginia Company to invest their money. While in London, he would leave his wife, Catherine, behind with other relatives in Leyden. Catherine Carver was the eldest sister of Bridget Robinson.

Pastor John Robinson, Deacon Robert Cushman and

John Carver were seated in Robinson's living room discussing Cushman's and Carver's role in representing the members of Green Gate in their vision of going to the New World.

Robinson said, "Well, Robert, how will you go about convincing investors to help us in getting funds for the trip?"

"I'll tell them about the profit they can make and the dedication of the people that will undertake to put their future on the line so they, along with the investors, will be successful. The investors will provide half the money to pay for the trip of two vessels that will transport the Pilgrims and for all the foodstuff, clothes and other provisions that they will need. The new settlers will hunt, trap, fish, farm and by other means create credit toward a joint account or the common store. The investors and the settlers will have shares held by each. Each share will be worth about ten pounds and they can be paid in food, provisions or money.

Each settler will also receive, after seven years, a share for each head of household; this to include wife, servants and children. Children ten to sixteen years of age will rate a half share while those younger will be entitled to fifty acres of "unmanured" land. I don't know if we can achieve all that we seek but it will be a good plan for all of us," Cushman said.

Carver said, "Brewster's father has a house that is owned by the Treasurer of the Virginia Company and I understand they are good friends. I'm sure that the treasurer will put in a good word for us when the time comes."

"I wonder how things are in Virginia?" Robinson asked. "How do you think our people will adapt to going from city life to a rather primitive change in habits and living in the wilderness?"

Cushman replied, "John you know our people, you officiated in the baptism of many of the children. I think that you know the answer. If there is any group of people that can survive the change, it's the members of our congregation."

"Robert, you're right. They are an unusual group of people. If God had destined a people to become Pilgrims he couldn't have chosen wiser."

Robinson said, "Have you made arrangements as to where you both will stay when you go to London?"

Carver replied, "I guess that Robert and I will have to depend on the Virginia Company to come up with a solution when we get there."

Cushman laughed and said, "I hope that we don't have to sleep in the office—or worse still—in the streets of London!"

Reverend Robinson joined the laughter and said, "Maybe they can find an empty closet where you both can rest, vertically!"

Carver replied, "I think the closet will be a bit crowded with our luggage."

Cushman said, "Seriously, now, I have never met the people from the Virginia Company and neither has John. I hope that they will be receptive to our needs, and we aren't put in a position where everything will be one-sided. We're giving up a lot to embark in this direction."

Robinson answered, "I know, Robert, all our contact with them has been made by courier. There is no doubt that you and John will be in a tough spot trying to bargain with them. Collectively, they have a lot of money behind them, but then I know you realize that we have a lot to offer them, too. They need us, too!"

Carver, who had been quietly sitting back drinking a tankard of beer, said, "I'm a small town citizen at heart, and to stay in a city the size of London will be quite a novelty. Going to the New World will be a major change for us. At least we have our own homes here... who knows what we will have in store for us. I know that we can turn back now and forget the Virginia Company ever existed and go on with our lives. But, I feel that we have a destiny to fulfill. We will go and do our best and know that God is on our side."

Cushman said, "You're right, John. We will do our best in London, and hopefully we'll do our best in the New World, too. We owe it to our families and friends."

Reverend Robinson replied, "All the people going will be entering the unknown and we can only hope that things will work out all right. It's quite a challenge, but I know that with your spirit, you'll succeed."

CHAPTER 2

Leyden, Holland

1619-1620

One Sunday evening the Allertons were in their living room discussing the move that would change their lives.

Isaac said, "Mary, I know you'll have to sacrifice a lot when we go to the New World. You'll be leaving some of your best friends behind, probably never to see them again. You will go because you're my wife and feel that it's your duty as a wife to go where I go. If you didn't have this obligation would you want to go? I know that you'll tell me the truth."

"Well Isaac, I know that your heart is set on going. You say that we will have a chance at economic opportunity and I know we won't be persecuted for our religion in the New World, but even when I pray, I still wonder if we're making the right decision. How do you children feel about going?"

Isaac laughed, "I guess that they're too young to decide now. I think Bartholomew is putting up a brave front, he doesn't want his sisters and friends to think he's afraid. Remember and Mary are younger and don't realize the changes that we have to undergo...the dangers we will experience."

Isaac said, "To tell you the truth, sometimes I have some doubts about going, but it's not concern for my safety, it's my family I'm thinking about and the problems we'll have on the ship and getting used to rough living. You remember why we left England to come to Holland; we had very few rights, we had no opportunity to improve our income, we had no tolerance from the government for our religious beliefs...we were treated like outcasts, we had no right to express ourselves, we couldn't speak our minds. It's true we have more liberty now than we had in England but there is still something lacking...I think we'll find it in the New World. We'll be creating a future for our children."

A group of men were gathered in the rectory at Green Gate one evening. There were Isaac Allerton, William Bradford, Deacon Samuel Fuller, Elder William Brewster and Reverend John Robinson. They were having an informal talk about the trip to the New World. Bradford brought up the subject which everyone had on their minds. "Where do you think we should finally end up in the Virginia? I understand that it covers a lot of territory."

Deacon Fuller replied, "Virginia? What do you think of another spot...I was thinking of Guiana. I heard it's a hot tropical country and it's a regular Garden of Eden."

Allerton said, "I heard about Guiana too. They say the soil is very fertile and growing crops is easy. Besides you don't need much knowledge of farming to be an expert. I think we would be able to grow abundant crops that we could put to our own use and send the rest back to England."

Brewster while listening to his friends seemed miles away, Bradford said, "What do you think William? What do you think of Guiana as a place to settle?"

"Brewster said, "Oh, I was listening but I have reservations about Guiana. I wonder how the fishing is? Don't forget that would be one of our principal means of support."

Fuller joined in, "I haven't heard about the fishing, but we can settle right next to the ocean and fish to our heart's content."

Brewster said, "Maybe the fish we catch won't be the right type. The water is probably warm and I heard the best fish for eating comes from cold water."

Allerton, who had a tankard of beer, drank some and then said, "If we choose Guiana we would be able to have houses that wouldn't have to be made quite as weatherproof as we would need in Virginia. Besides we could save on clothing. We wouldn't have to wear winter clothing."

Bradford replied, "I can see a couple of drawbacks to moving to Guiana...first, there are probably diseases there we haven't got in England and Holland and they could prove fatal to us. Second...do you believe the Spanish would stand by and see us thrive in an area where their ships roam freely? True, we defeated the Spanish Armada about thirty-two years ago, but they still have plenty of ships that they replaced."

"William, the more I think about it, the more I am convinced you're right. I don't think that we Englishmen are suited for the climate. Having the Spanish around as neighbors doesn't sound too good either. If we go to Virginia at least we'll have other English speaking people there and we can join them." Brewster said.

Deacon Fuller spoke up, "There is also another alternative that we can consider. How about the Dutch Colony they will form near the Hudson River. I'm sure that we can get a patent from the Dutch government to form our own settlement."

Brewster replied, "Well, I'm sure that we could, however, there are certain disadvantages in joining the Dutch. Although they are good people, we'll run into the same problem that we have here. We don't speak their language; that is, some do, but the bulk of us don't and we have different religious beliefs, we can live together, but I don't think it will work out."

Bradford said, "We could go to a place called New England that is part of the Virginia territory. It's a long way from the scrutiny of the English and the Anglican Church will have no authority over us."

Robinson said, "Well gentlemen...we should discuss these same facts that you have suggested with the full congregation and see how they feel. They have the final say. We'll discuss this at our next Sabbath meeting. I'll make a list of the pros and cons of each place you mentioned, then they can decide."

So Pastor Robinson on their next meeting had a short sermon with his congregation so that he could spend some time with them discussing the move to the New World. Robinson addressing the congregation said, "If you have any questions you would like answered, please raise your hand."

"John Tilley, you have a question?"

"I was wondering what the climate is year round where we will settle?"

Robinson replied, "I had the great fortune of meeting Captain John Smith, who has traveled to the New World several times. He has been to Virginia and as far north as New England. He has fallen in love with the country Did you know that he named several places in the New World including "New England" and "Cape Cod?" Well, to get to the point, Captain Smith said that the climate in Virginia is a little warmer than in southern England, but as you travel in New England the weather is very pleasant in the summer but the winters can be very cold with heavy snow and severe weather, the further north you travel."

"Next...Francis Cooke, your question, please."

"Well Reverend. I was wondering about the Indians, will they present much of a problem?"

"I don't think so. We will go and join them in their land where they have lived for centuries. When you have faith and treat the Indians fairly, you shouldn't expect trouble. You will be prepared to fight and have strong defenses but if you want peace and treat the Indians like brothers, as I said, you should expect tranquility."

"Yes, Brother Fuller, your question."

"I don't have a question, Reverend Robinson, but I'd like to address the congregation if I may."

"Go right ahead, Samuel."

"I was thinking of this war going on between the Netherlands and Spain. The other night we were discussing a couple of other places that we could consider settling. The places we mentioned were; Guiana and Dutch territory in the New World and how this area could be affected by the war. Shall I go on, Reverend?"

"Go on, Samuel, you're doing fine."

'We, that is, a group of us, Masters Allerton, Bradford, Brewster, Reverend Robinson and I went to the rectory to discuss our future move. We came to the conclusion that although Guiana and the Dutch territory had some good points they were greatly outweighed by the bad. One strong point against them was the danger of the Spanish fleet attacking these areas; being both Dutch colonies they would be prime targets. As William Bradford said, the English navy defeated the Spanish armada over thirty-two years ago but now they have a strong naval force."

"Thank you, Deacon Fuller. Brethren, you've heard the questions and answers to some of your doubts you have about the New World. I think that we've narrowed down our choice to the following areas; Guiana, Dutch territory, Virginia and New England. We will call each place mentioned and if you will raise your hand and vote we will determine which one the majority has chosen. We'll start now...Guiana... Dutch territory...Virginia...New England...according to your votes you have chosen Virginia with New England a close second. So Jamestown, Virginia will be your new home and I think you'll fit well into the community."

They would attempt to get patents or grants from the Virginia Company in London for land and certain rights such as self-government, jurisdiction, permission to trade with the Indians, fishing rights, etc.

*   *   *

Mrs. Brewster along with Elizabeth Tilley and her teenage daughter, also called Elizabeth, were visiting the Allerton household one sunny afternoon and they were having lunch. The children were playing in another room, laughing and teasing each other.

Mary Brewster said, "I wonder why it's so hard trying to make a living in Leyden? We have many skills that we can use, but they don't seem to hire the English."

Elizabeth replied, "I think that our biggest problem is not being able to speak their language, that is our handicap. Don't you think so Mary?"

Mary Brewster answered, "Well, the men can join the guilds if they become citizens, as you know, but the women can only get employment as domestics at very low wages. The Dutch treat us well, but it's very hard trying to understand their language. I guess that's why we English seem to stick together. I'm a little worried about the future of our children if we remain in Leyden."

Elizabeth replied, "So am I, now that our children are starting to grow into teenagers. Other parents that I've spoken to also feel the same way."

Mary Allerton who had just returned with some food from the kitchen said, "I've heard that there are some problems with the older Dutch children."

Mary Brewster replied, "I'm sorry to say the teen-aged children seem attracted to the Dutch youth who are undisciplined and sort of wild. It appears all the teaching at home and at church will be in vain."

Elizabeth said, "I know that the Dutch like and respect us, but the issue of work, the language and the association of our children creates a very difficult situation. I just hope we weren't too hasty in leaving England. I know we'll be better off in not having our religion challenged, but... well I'll be glad when we leave."

Mary Brewster said, "I guess we all agree that in the long run we'll be better off. I know we'll have a rough time at first but our faith will see us through. God will protect us—I feel it in my heart."

They all said, "Amen."

The incidents the mothers were talking about grew daily and was an added problem handling their children. When the children came home from school, a few of them said that the Dutch boys from another school ridiculed them and called them names.

The parents of the English children told them that they shouldn't pay attention to their insults, but that they should smile at them and speak in a friendly fashion.

The children wanted to know what they should do if they were attacked by the Dutch boys, either by being hit with their fists, or if they threw stones at them. The fathers agreed with the mothers' thoughts that they should be friendly and it would make the Dutch feel ashamed at the way they were acting and eventually, they would improve their ways and try to become friends.

In time, this method seemed to work and the Dutch

boys stopped the teasing and then they seemed to accept the English as friends. The English children came to like the Dutch and sought them out—they led a more exciting way of life! This became a bigger problem for the English... the children became more secretive at home and began to give the parents trouble. They knew that they would eventually move to the New World and leave this all behind them.

They didn't know exactly when they would leave, and they hoped the children wouldn't adopt this bad influence as a way of life, taking it with them to the New World.

The parents knew they couldn't forbid their children to associate with the Dutch, but they could pay more attention to them and lecture them on morality.

CHAPTER 3

London, England

1620

D ue to their tight economic plight, it was a miracle that some were able to put some of their money into a fund to buy shares in their dream for a new home in the colony in Virginia, where they would get a new start. The plans were underway in England; Robert Cushman and John Carver had the overwhelming task of raising funds for the expedition. Having left their families in Leyden, they had worked diligently since 1617 in England trying to interest the Virginia Company in investing money in their mission.

Cushman and Carver were becoming weary. They had to convince the investors to supply the money for shares along with the Pilgrims supplying shares. The Pilgrims would reimburse the investors by the fruits of their labor in the New World sending the furs, dried fish and whatever goods or services need for sale to the Britons. There was to be a time limit for the debt to be paid. They also insisted they would have two days off a week so they wouldn't become slaves to the company.

One day while Bradford was visiting the Allerton's they were discussing the feeling of the Pilgrims and about the doubts many were expressing.

Bradford said, "I've been listening to many complaints and worries on the minds of members of the church."

"Yes, I've heard them too. What have you heard?" Isaac asked.

"Well, they know it's a difficult decision to make. In spite of their faith in God, inwardly they have a feeling they could all die."

"I can see their point. There lies ahead the trip on more or less uncharted seas, the Indians...could our small force handle them? Then there's food. Will we all starve? The weather...the winters are more brutal than which we are accustomed," Isaac said.

"We will have to come up with the right answers for our brethren. I'm sure when Reverend Robinson hears of our concern about their present state of minds and questions, he can come up with logical solutions to calm their anxiety."

Bradford and Allerton went to see Robinson and told him about the problems that were arising. Reverend Robinson said, "I heard from several members and I know about their concern—many want to drop out. I'm going to give a sermon dealing with their problems. The main theme is belief in God and the power of prayer will overcome all obstacles."

On the next Sabbath Reverend Robinson addressing the members of the congregation said, "I know many of you are worrying about the trip to the New World. I understand your worries and concerns. We are capable leaders that will guide you and we have experienced seamen that have sailed this route many times before. You will have ample food and your relations with the Indians...I know will be peaceful. Your strength will come from your inner soul and by prayer. As you know, prayer can accomplish miracles. God will always be there looking out for you."

After the meeting the congregation seemed to have more confidence in their future. Mary Brewster speaking to several ladies said, "You know, I've never said it before, but I confess I was a little worried about the trip but the Reverend, as usual, said the right things. I just know we'll be safe."

The object of Cushman's and Carver's mission to London was to get the funding to outfit two ships with provisions and supplies, and to be self-sufficient for an indefinite period. The ships would be the *Mayflower*, a "fine and sweet ship" according to Robert Cushman. It was about one hundred and eighty tons, ninety feet overall, with a sixty foot keel, a twenty-six foot beam and had eleven feet depth of hold. It had twelve cannon and was about twelve years old. It also had a double-deck with superstructure fore and aft. It had two lookout towers or crow's nests. The cannon was needed as there was always the danger of pirates boarding or taking the ship by force. It was strictly a merchant ship flying the Saint George Cross flag.

The *Mayflower* had been in the service of the wine trade in the Mediterranean and for years hauled fish, timber and turpentine, tar and other products from Norway. The wine had neutralized the filth in the bilge, so it would help the Pilgrims survive the trip without a foul odor.

The second ship, which was purchased by the group at Leyden was the *Speedwell*, about sixty tons and trim, but its seaworthiness was in question. It would require new sails and much needed repair work before it could survive a voyage across the Atlantic. It was being fitted-out and made ready to pick up its passengers at Delft Haven.

Carver, like Cushman, was anxious to get out of England and return to his family. He said to Cushman, "I really don't like the attitude of the government here. Did you hear the latest outrage made against a hero?'

Cushman replied, "There have been so many outrageous acts...which one do you have in mind?"

Carver said, "When Sir Walter Raleigh returned in 1618, after his fifth trip to Roanoke, Virginia, which incidentally he financed himself, he had a minor argument with the Queen; he lost the argument and his head. At least he had a sense of humor to the end. When he knew that he was about to die, he felt the edge of the executioner's ax that was to be used on him and said, "Tis a sharp remedy but a sure one for all ills."

Cushman said, "Yes, it certainly was a tragic end to an illustrious career. But now I'm glad we are making some headway in getting to the New World. Although I sometimes think it's a thankless job and they don't appreciate our efforts in Leyden."

Carver replied, "Yes Robert, I think you're right."

It was about this time, that the leaders at Leyden wanted Brewster to go to England to assist Cushman and Carver. It was a coincidence that Elder Brewster heard rumors that Sir Dudley Carleton, the English ambassador stationed at the Hague, was looking for him for publishing the Perth Assembly, an inflammatory critique of King James I and the bishops. It had been printed at the Pilgrim Press and smuggled in vats into Scotland. Agents of the crown had arrested an associate of his named Brewer, thinking that it was Brewster himself. It was then Brewster decided to leave for England which he thought would be the last place they would look for him. It was just in time!

The government had started a manhunt in the Netherlands especially around Leyden where they raided the Pilgrim Press and found type hidden in the attic. After comparing the ornamental and regular type which was the same as printed material they had confiscated, they were sure Brewster was their man. The only trouble was, they couldn't catch him; was he in Amsterdam...maybe he's in London...no, somebody saw him in Leyden. He was one step ahead of Sir Dudley Carleton and the authorities in England began to look at the hunter as being a little foolish. The more frustrated he became, the more determined he was in catching Brewster.

Elder Brewster had gone to assist Cushman and Carver in trying to handle the association with the Virginia Company. He heard that the crown authorities were getting close in their hunt for him. When he thought he was about to be arrested, he said to Cushman, "Robert, I think I'd better get away from here as fast as I can. I don't want you to get in trouble with me being here. Do you remember what happened to Alexander Leighton? He was a minister from Scotland who also published in the Netherlands. He was tried, sentenced to pay a fine of £10,000 ($500,000), he was also whipped and pilloried in view of the court and he had an ear cut off and his nose split. With all this, he also had the letters SS (Stirrer of Sedition) branded on his forehead, again whipped and was pilloried, later and to top it all off, he will be imprisoned for life in the rotten, stinking Fleet Prison."

Cushman said, 'Yes, I remember the story, although not all the details which you have now told me. I remember Leighton and it is a shame the way they treated him just for expressing himself. I agree with you...the way they treat us, you can't blame people for complaining."

Brewster said, "I will go now Robert, I won't tell you where, so that you won't be burdened with my secret in case you're questioned. You can be assured that I'll join you on the trip to the New World...so goodbye, dear friend." They shook hands...with that he was gone!

*   *   *

Things were in a turmoil in England, serious trouble was brewing. The fate of the expedition of the Pilgrims to the new World was in doubt. All the work that the future Pilgrims had done was starting to unravel; in fact, the whole business was in a mess. Cushman and Carver were thoroughly disgusted at the turn of events. There had been an interchange of letters at Leyden. They were forwarded to a group composed of Samuel Fuller, Edward Winslow, William Bradford and Isaac Allerton. The Leyden Committee, as they were known, was very critical of Cushman and Carver and their handling of the Virginia Company. They were second-guessing Cushman and lost confidence in his management... they were in Holland, he was in England trying his best to handle overbearing, and stubborn members of the Virginia Company, who cared little for the Pilgrims, but were willing to exploit them to make a profit. Cushman understood this, he attempted to keep them interested in the project without yielding too much to their advantage. He wrote, "If you aren't satisfied with my performance I will gladly go back to my old trade. This is a thankless job and all I get from you are complaints. I have enough worries here and I do my job for my many friends at Leyden. If they are also discontented with my work say the word and replace me. I shall return home happy that this load is lifted from my shoulders but discouraged that I left the job incompleted."

The leaders at Leyden were assembled at Bradford's house one day and they were discussing the effort that Carver and Cushman were making in London. Bradford said, "I think that we haven't done justice to our brethren, Deacon Cushman and John Carver. They have a monumental task to undertake in London. We're here in Leyden criticizing them for not doing this or that when they know what the problems are first hand."

Winslow replied , "You're right William, I guess we've

unfairly blamed them when we know in our hearts that the Virginia Company is stubborn and obstinate in their dealings with us. I know we should give them more assistance at this end. I agree they have a tough job, especially when we don't have the money to fund the expedition. I don't think we have to go to the Virginia Company with hat in hand either, after all, they will make a great profit from our effort once we establish a colony. We should send a letter to Cushman and Carver telling them we understand the situation and they are doing a good job, under the circumstances they have to endure."

There were many changes being made. Cushman was informed that a new man would be entering the picture to help them. Most of this was done in Leyden, by the Commission, while he was working with the Virginia Company in London.

Many members of the congregation at Green Gate welcomed their friend, Thomas Weston, who was invited to speak to the leaders who were also organizing the journey to the New World. Weston was familiar with the plans and suggested they break off with their association with the Virginia Company which was awash with dissension and the treasury was almost empty. He knew many merchants in London that would go along with their needs and he would form a stock company which would contribute ample money for their mission. In modern times Weston would be called a "wheeler-dealer", but the Pilgrims were anxious to go to the New World and he had the reputation of getting things done. Due to their naiveté, the pilgrims agreed to his scheme and said they would buy their goods from the Merchant Adventurers

Having spent two years trying to get sponsorship with off-again, on-again tactics by the Virginia Company and the offer by the Dutch of the Netherland Group that if the Pilgrims would go to the Dutch settlement near the Hudson

River, they would provide many things free. Among those items which the Dutch offered and were under consideration were free passage for all passengers, free land on which to settle, cattle and the offer of a couple of Dutch Men-of-War ships to escort them.

Weston found fault with all the offers and dismissed them saying that the acceptance of the Merchant Adventurers was the correct way to go. The Pilgrims, although opposed to gambling in any form, said maybe this could be their salvation. One wonders about Thomas Weston's stake in this venture, it wouldn't be done out of the kindness of his heart or the strong religious belief that Cushman or Carver held.

The congregation was urged to sign a contract outlining the nature of the trip and the agreement for repayment. Weston was appointed the first president of the association. He did not incorporate the business, in fact it remained a voluntary business in all its troubled years of existence.

They were next joined by Christopher Martin who had been appointed by the Merchant Adventurers to work with Cushman and Carver in the position of Treasurer. A few weeks after Martin started to participate with Cushman and Carver they were a little distressed at his behavior.

Carver said, "Robert, I think we have a problem with Martin, the way he's spending money!"

"Yes, he's spending money in Kent and London for everything that takes his fancy. He won't give an accounting of anything he buys. I don't know just how much he's spending, but I know it's a lot, he has spent at least 700 pounds."

"He's acting as though we were bystanders and he was in complete charge," Carver said.

"I was talking to Thomas Weston yesterday and he was saying the same thing. He's thoroughly disgusted with the way Martin's acting."

Cushman had to eliminate two items from the agreement at Weston's urging to benefit the Merchant Adventurers. He didn't have time to contact those in Leyden that had signed the original agreement. Cushman said, "If I didn't make the changes the whole agreement would have collapsed. Some of the Merchant Adventurers wanted their money back if the changes weren't made. One of the investors who had contributed £500, was adamant about this."

The three agents working on the problems of getting all the details wrapped up, were reaching the point of complete frustration. Cushman and Carver because of constant harping and criticism from the leaders at Leyden were at their wits-end trying to resolve the problems. With the ultimate in gross understatement of the situation, Weston said, "Things are not going as well as we expected with a myriad of problems to solve, especially as debts are being incurred."

When Cushman told Weston he needed money to pay some of the debts, he was chastised and was told, "The Pilgrims won't get a penny more!" The Pilgrims were forced to sell butter and other supplies which were needed on the trip, to settle the debt. Most of the money went to Weston who was hounding them for it. The Pilgrims said they would eat plain bread without butter rather than owe Weston a debt.

This continual harassment from Martin and Weston was beginning to wear down Carver and Cushman and their only comfort came to them when they realized that their assignment in London would soon be over. The trip to the New World was fast approaching and they were tying up loose ends.

The *Mayflower* was just about loaded with supplies and the ship itself was checked over from bow to stern and the crew declared the ship seaworthy. The passengers were later curious about their "thorough checking", when the ship almost met with disaster on the trip across the Atlantic.

The *Speedwell,* now at Delft Haven in Holland, was to be its companion ship on the trip to the New World. The crew still wasn't satisfied with the refitting of the ship with new sails and mast. They thought the ship appeared to be top-heavy and not fit for the pounding she would take on the long trip across the Atlantic. They didn't reveal their dissatisfaction with the owners, but their unhappiness with the *Speedwell* was apparent.

This resentment finally boiled over later when the passengers eventually boarded the ship.

CHAPTER 4

Leyden, Holland

1620

Little Mary Allerton was about four years old and she was holding her own with her six-year-old sister and her brother who at eight was growing up to be quite independent. A constant companion for Mary was her rag doll, which was her prized possession. She slept with it at night and it gave her much comfort during the day. She named the doll "Dorothy". She played games with the neighborhood children and in spite of her age she would often lead the others.

One night while sitting with his family at the table at dinner, Bartholomew said, "Are we going on that long trip to another place?"

Isaac said, "Yes, someday soon the whole family will go to the New World. We'll have a new house and a new start. Remember when Mr. Cushman and Mr. Carver went to England? Well, they went to arrange to rent a ship and to take care of other business. It will be a great adventure."

Mrs. Allerton, who was expecting her fourth child,

tried to be optimistic, especially in front of the children, but she was still very nervous about the trip and the future of her unborn child and the whole family.

She said, "Isaac, when do you think we'll be going?"

Isaac replied, "I was talking to Reverend Robinson today and he said he had a letter from Cushman and Carver and all was going well. We bought a ship called the *Speedwell*. It is being refitted in Delft Haven and we will go there when it's ready. We'll travel to England to join up with another ship called the *Mayflower*. This ship is much larger than the *Speedwell* so naturally more people will go on it. We'll use the *Speedwell* in the New World for fishing and trips along the coast."

Remember, who had been sitting quietly, spoke up, "Why can't we go on the *Mayflower* if it's bigger?"

"I don t know if we can change our trip from the *Speedwell* to the *Mayflower*, but we'll find out when we reach England," Isaac said.

While the Allertons cleared the table, the children went to the corner and Remember spoke, "Do you think we'll die on the trip?" Little Mary eyes widened and she looked for assurance from her brother that everything would be all right and they wouldn't drown on their way to the New World.

"You girls are a bunch of 'fraidy cats'...of course we won't die, besides I'll take good care of you." Bartholomew said, in his most bravado manner. He hoped he could calm his fears also, for inwardly he had his doubts, too.

Six weeks later, the Allertons were going strong in preparation for the trip. Like their neighbors that were going too, they sold most of their furniture and their home. They had to travel light.

On the day before departure, the congregation gathered at Green Gate where they were offered a prayer and food and drink. The members who were staying behind, said their farewells amid tears and smiles. Many would follow in later trips, but the majority would never see each other again. They had an agreement that if the mission failed, they would return to Leyden and those remaining behind would help them get back on their feet. They also agreed that if they were successful and members left Leyden to join them in the New World, they would also help them to get established.

The Allertons got up early on July 21st, 1620. Isaac said, "Come on folks, today is the day we will start on that long trip."

Little Mary replied, "Are we going to get there on a little boat?"

"Yes, we'll go on a barge down the canal to the ship."

Mary Allerton asked, "Is it near Rotterdam?"

"It's a little nearer than Rotterdam. We'll go down the canal to Delft Haven, it's about twenty miles from here."

"Are we going to take food with us to eat on the way to the *Speedwell*?" asked Bartholomew.

"Yes, your mother is fixing something to eat and we'll all meet at Green Gate this morning. We will have to hurry and get ready to go."

The Allertons gave their former home a long, last look. The children had all been born here so they were leaving behind many memories. Mary Allerton turned to Isaac and said, "There is no turning back now...I hope we have made the right decision."

Isaac said, "We have. Look to the future, we'll be better off."

They were met at Green Gate by Reverend Robinson and the other members of the congregation who would join them on the long trip to the New World. There was William White with his wife, Susanna, who was pregnant, and their son who was called Resolved. John Tilley and his wife Elizabeth (Comyngs) and their daughter, Elizabeth. His brother Edward and his wife Anne were accompanied by their two small cousins, Humility Cooper and Henry Samson. There was also Tom Blossom with his wife and two sons, and Thomas Tinker with his wife and son. Robert Cushman's wife, Mary, with their stepson, Thomas, who was thirteen at the time. They planned to meet Robert in England where he was up to his neck in financial problems.

The Allertons were also greeted by Edward Winslow and his wife, Elizabeth. Mrs. Carver was to meet her husband, John, in England, where he was still with Cushman. With her, was Desire Minter who was Thomas Minter's daughter.

Mrs. Allerton saw Mary Brewster and said, "Hello Mary, I guess that we're about ready to go. Have you heard from your husband lately?"

Mary Brewster replied, "I haven't heard from him for some time. He's still hiding out and he'll join us in Southhampton, England where we'll meet the *Mayflower*. Since he published the *Perth Assembly*, the English authorities have been trying to find him and put him into prison. I guess he'll be safe but I'm very nervous about his welfare and thinking of the trip before us. I've brought Wrestling and Love along; like all boys of six and nine, they are looking forward to a great adventure. I'm going to leave my daughters, Fear and Patience, behind with their brother Jonathan and they will come over later."

William and Dorothy Bradford decided to leave their son, John, now eight years old, with Reverend Robinson at Leyden.

He was brokenhearted and appealed to his parents to take him along. His cries tore at their heartstrings and it effected Dorothy Bradford deeply.

There were other men that would leave their wives in Leyden and they would follow later. Among those were Francis Cooke and his son, John, who was about Bartholmew

Allerton's age. There were others at the gathering; Thomas Rogers and his son, Joseph, aged twelve, there were John Crackston with his son, John, also John Turner and his two sons. There were others who would leave behind their wives and children; they were Degory Priest, Deacon Samuel Fuller, Moses Fletcher and John Goodman, who would leave his bride of just a few months.

The total that would leave Leyden was forty-six people (now called "Saints") that would go aboard the *Speedwell*. The group was composed of sixteen men, eleven women and nineteen children.

They made the short trip to the canal, laughing children and adults trying to make small talk. Each putting on an air of indifference, they knew this was the beginning of the greatest adventure of their lives. They seemed to take it all in stride; at first glance one would think they were going on holiday. If you looked closely you would see a certain tightness about their lips, a nervous laugh or a little anxiety which was barely discernible.

They boarded a couple of barges that had been brought there to transport the passengers going on the *Speedwell* and their friends in the congregation who would travel to Delft Haven to see them off. Once they were all aboard the barges, they set sail on a clear day with the sun dancing on every changing ripple in the water...it was a nice day for a boat ride and the reality of their trip didn't seem to bother them.

The city of Leyden soon passed from view. The stately spires and the tall buildings were the last to disappear. Now their attention was brought to the beauty of the countryside with the trees growing down to the waters edge, the green grass and the colorful flowers made a picturesque scene.

After a trip of about twenty miles they saw the Port of Delft Haven ahead; there were cranes and other ship building facilities operating and then they saw a ship proudly resting at anchor. Its sails were down and it seemed peaceful with the waves caused by the canal traffic gently rocking it.

Little Mary asked her father, "Is that the ship we will be going on?"

Bartholomew quickly asked, "Is that the *Speedwell?*"

Isaac said, "Yes children I think it is...what a wonderful sight it makes. I guess it will be your home soon."

"How long will it take to where we're going?" Little Mary asked.

"We'll go to Southhampton in England first, we'll meet with the *Mayflower* and then we'll head for the New World," Isaac said.

"Yes, but how long will it take?" Little Mary insisted.

"Oh, I guess we'll be there in two or three months."

"How long is that...two or three months?"

Bartholomew said impatiently, "It's a long time!"

The members of the congregation who were going on the *Speedwell* were united with their friends from Amsterdam. They had traveled fifty miles to get to Delft Haven and some planned to go on the *Speedwell* while others came to see them off. Some of the congregation from Leyden had lived in the city of Amsterdam when they originally came to Holland. They renewed their friendship which was still warm after several years of absence. They hugged and kissed one another and brought their friends up to date on their families and all events.

`Reverend Robinson, with a great amount of assistance, planned a huge feast for all. They had improvised tables and the food was donated by all the families. There was mutton and beef, vegetables and bread and little cakes. Wine and beer were in ample supply and it added to the good fellowship as time went on. They spent the rest of the day saying their farewells and showing great regard for each other.

Reverend Robinson gathered all the people and said; "Friends, some of you will be traveling far from your adopted home. You will experience some danger and hardship but you will be rewarded with the knowledge that you will be instrumental in the building of a new country. In your humble way you will be making history. May God always give you a helping hand and look after you. Let us bend our heads in prayer for a safe journey." After praying, the friends who were not passengers drifted away with tears in their eyes; they had known each other for years.

The ship was under the command of Captain Reynolds who was at the helm when she left the quay lined with friends and relatives waving and wiping away tears, for some this could be the last time they would see each other. The passengers were at the ship's rails vigorously waving to their friends and relatives.

The sails were trimmed and pennants flying as they pulled away, bound for Southampton. The cannons aboard roared a salute while those ashore shot off firearms in response.

They soon faded from view...they were on their way!

The friends and neighbors of the passengers and curious bystanders stayed around the pier until the *Speedwell* sailed westward down the Meuse River and it disappeared around a bend. It soon was nearing the English Channel.

The people that remained stood around in groups discussing the upcoming voyage of the *Speedwell*. Some said they would go later... they probably wouldn't. Others wanted to wait and see how the Pilgrims, as they were now known, made out in the New World. Most agreed that the passengers were indeed courageous to attempt such a voyage across the "wild" Atlantic at this time of year and wondered if they would be attacked by roving renegade ships from foreign nations.

It was commonplace for pirates who spend most of

thier lives at sea, to stop and board the ship then loot them, taking everything of value from the crew and passengers and then leaving. Many times they would simply sink the ships after the looting if they couldn's use the ships. None aboard the ship would survive. There was always the question left to the surviving relatives—did they die during a storm at sea, or were they victims of pirates or an unfriendly foe?

* * *

On the ship, the passengers were excited that they were sailing to join the *Mayflower* and they were smiling and talking with their fellow passengers. They didn't have a care in the world.

The ship seemed to heel over slightly when it finally reached the English Channel and got the full effect of the strong wind.

CHAPTER 5

Southampton, Dartmouth, England

1620

Among the passengers that stood on deck was little Mary Allerton, one hand holding her doll and the other held her brother's hand...he was taking care of her.

Remember spoke, "I'm going to miss all my friends when we go to our new home."

Little Mary agreed, saying, "Me too. I hope we'll see them again. They were such fun. Do you think we'll see them again?"

Bartholmew said, "Sure we'll see them, at least some of them. There are a lot of them going and others will follow us on another ship. We'll see the rest again. They will always be our friends."

Isaac was standing nearby and he whispered to his wife, so the children couldn't hear, "We better get below...the wind is getting stronger and we're beginning to heel over... we'll come up on deck again when the wind calms down."

The incident made many remember the stories about the *Speedwell's* unseaworthiness. Many sailors claimed that the sails that were now installed were too cumbersome and too large for the ship. They had continued along in the English Channel and later passed the cliffs of Dover in the Dover Straits, its stately, chalky, white surface was visible from a great distance. This was about the halfway mark or ninety miles from Southampton, down the coast. They pulled into Southampton's harbor and saw for the first time their companion ship, the *Mayflower*, sitting majestically at anchor, its pennants flying in a gentle breeze. It seemed very impressive to the passengers of the *Speedwell*. It was about three times larger than their ship. The *Speedwell*, in spite of its smaller size, was larger than most ships that had explored the coast and rivers of the New World.

Some that were going to sail on the *Mayflower* had dropped out, they were a little discouraged at the problems they would have to endure. Many from Amsterdam didn't want to go and they wanted their money back. There was no argument, if they wanted their money back, they got it.

Captain Christopher Jones, who commanded the *Mayflower*, was a mariner who had years of experience. He was demanding, but beneath his rough veneer there was a kindly enough man.

He was anxious for his passengers, especially for the women and children. He wanted to leave much earlier in the season because he knew any delay would be a severe setback. For the experienced sailor the rough seas and windy conditions in the fall were bad enough, but for the Pilgrims with none or little experience on ships, this could be devastating. He was concerned about the performance of the *Mayflower* over-loaded with passengers and supplies. The *Speedwell* had dropped out and it was a sad story; the *Speedwell's* run from Delft Haven and its poor handling in a fairly short trip foretold an ominous harbinger of things to come. To recount the story: The Governor of the *Speedwell* was Robert Cushman who was responsible for the allotment of supplies and the well-being of the passengers. On the *Mayflower*, Christopher Martin was appointed Governor. He would have the same responsibility as Cushman.

One night in Southampton another passenger inconspicuously boarded the *Speedwell*. He stayed by himself and didn't speak. He moved furtively among the passengers and went below where he recognized many of the Pilgrims. He approached Isaac Allerton, shook his hand and said, "Isaac, it's good seeing you again!"

"Hello...it's good seeing you too! I'm glad you were able to meet us. You must have a lot of stories to tell. I know you want to see your family...they're with my wife and children over in the corner. Come on, I'll go over with you."

When they joined their families, Isaac said, "Look who I have here!"

"William! You're here at last!" Mary Brewster said, grabbing at her husband. "How are you?"

Brewster who hadn't seen his wife and family for almost a year, greeted them enthusiastically. He hugged and kissed his wife, Mary. His two sons, Wrestling and Love, were next in line. There were tears in the eyes of all as they laughed and cried at the same time. The Allertons joined in welcoming him back with hand shakes and backslapping, then other Saints took part...they really did miss him.

Isaac said, "You haven't changed a bit in the past year, in spite of the hardship you must have undergone."

Brewster smiled at Isaac and said, "Well, it was a little nerve-wracking but I was among friends that were unknown to the authorities."

Mary Allerton said, "It goes without saying your family missed you while you were away, but we all were concerned about your safety."

Brewster said to Isaac, "I wasn't sure if the crown had some agents planted among the Strangers to try to catch me. I guess that I'll be safe now. I'll try to avoid mingling with the Strangers until we're underway."

They finally left Southampton on a clear, mild day on August 5, 1620. Between the two ships, there was a total of one hundred twenty-two passengers, lining the decks amidst the shouting and blowing of horns and whistles. The *Speedwell* with the *Mayflower* in the lead, hoisted sails and both ships started on their long voyage...almost.

The *Speedwell* was developing cracks in the seams and the ship seemed sail-heavy. Many mariners had criticized the placing of large masts on the ship when it was being refitted at Delft Haven. It was too late now—the *Speedwell* could not survive the pounding it would take on an Atlantic crossing!

The Allertons were below deck and they were discussing the condition of the ship. Bartholomew said, "Father do you think we are in danger with the ship leaking?"

Little Mary asked, "Are we going to sail on this ship? It is leaking and I'm scared!"

Isaac replied, "Everything will be all right. They can fix the leaks and we'll be safe, you can ask your mother, she knows that they can repair the ship."

"You children shouldn't worry too much, the ship is good and strong...like your father said, we'll be all right."

Little Mary was nervous but she felt assured when her father and mother spoke. She said, "Where are we going to sleep? " She held on to her mother s skirt for security.

They put into the port at Dartmouth to check out the *Speedwell* from stem to stern to find out if it could endure the rigors of the trip. The workmen found a few leaks, repaired them and said, "The ship is in fine shape."

Cushman spoke to Allerton about the ship, he said,

"Isaac, what do you think of the situation?"

"Well, Robert, I hope that Captain Reynolds is right when he says the *Speedwell* is now shipshape. It seems odd that the ship would need repair after undergoing an overhaul in Delft Haven."

Cushman said, "I know, Isaac. It does seem strange that we should be experiencing such trouble. We have only gone a couple of hundred miles and it certainly seems that the *Speedwell* is jinxed. I know you must have noticed the way it tips when we are underway. I don't know much about ships, but I fear that we will never make it across."

Isaac nodded and replied, "We lost valuable time when we put into port. Every day we spend here we are consuming provisions that we will need later."

While they were in port at Dartmouth, the Saints were getting angry at Christopher Martin on the *Mayflower*.

They were mistreated by Martin and he gave them the impression that he was totally superior to "riffraff". He was arrogant, surly and unworthy of the position as Governor of the *Mayflower*. He looked after the welfare of the Pilgrims and allocated provisions. They were not the only ones that were complaining. The sailors said, "He is interfering with our work and tries to tell us how we should do our details. He has never been on a ship before and suddenly he has become an expert seaman. If he keeps this up there will be some physical harm done to him. We won't take this abuse from him anymore."

Cushman thought he would visit the *Mayflower* when the *Speedwell* was being checked out. He listened to the complaints of the sailors and his friends from the *Mayflower*, who said, "He treats us as though we were not fit to wipe his shoes."

Unfortunately, Cushman couldn't help them. He mentioned Martin's brutal treatment to Bradford and Allerton,

"It would break your hearts to see the way they're treated and their sorrow. When I question him about the problem, he flies at me and says, 'You're becoming mutinous and I will hear none of their complaints from you. If the passengers want to complain they will see me personally, besides they are forward and waspish and very discontented'."

The passengers who were effected by Martin's behavior, and there were many, spoke to Robert Cushman again, while they were at Dartmouth. "He's continually finding fault with everything we do," Edward Tilley said. "Yes", said the group, "he tries to run our lives. He has a sour look on his face all the time and what peeves us most is the way he abuses our children. He'd walk right over them, if they didn't scurry out of the way."

"Mr. Cushman", asked Richard Warren, "Do you think that you or somebody else can replace him?"

"I don't know," Cushman replied, "I've spoken to several people before. I can try again, but you know he was selected by the Merchant Adventurers and it will be difficult. Maybe all the leaders can speak to him and show him the errors of his ways."

"You know what, Mr. Cushman," William Mullins said, "several of us are quite tired of Mr. Martin's attitude and we are ready to call the whole thing off and go home."

"William, before you make up your mind to take this drastic step, please wait until I can see what I can do to remedy this situation."

When Martin heard rumors of the passengers going to see Cushman, he made sure they wouldn't leave the ship by confining them to quarters. To avoid a complete rebellion he gave some excuse why they had to remain below.

In spite of this harassment, the Pilgrims seemed to resign themselves to the situation and when the *Speedwell* was repaired, they once again weighed anchor and set off.

They were making good time on the Atlantic, having gone about three hundred miles from Lands End at the South Western corner of England. Once again, "She's leaking like a sieve," Cushman said. With no hope for further progress they turned back to the port of Plymouth.

Manning the pumps, they could barely match the volume of seawater coming in. Fearing they would sink at sea, the passengers were understandably frightened and finally the *Speedwell* limped back to port.

Although they couldn't find any one special leak, they all agreed that it was impractical, if not impossible, to attempt the trip with such an undependable ship. With much reluctance they finally decided to put as much provision from the *Speedwell* onto the *Mayflower* as it would hold and it was packed to the gunwales. This done, they had to decide who would stay behind. It was found the *Mayflower* could carry no more than one hundred two passengers, tightly packed in, plus the crew. The other twenty passengers, who would remain behind, were composed of those that really didn't have their hearts in the mission and the discouraged.

Among those that felt discouraged, with good reason, was Robert Cushman, so he stayed with his wife and son, Thomas. In the meantime, he would continue to help the prospective company in any way that he could in England. Among the Saints remaining behind was Thomas Blossom and his wife and two sons; also, Cushman's friend, William King. He decided his future didn't include being "food for the fishes."

The mold was now cast...the *Mayflower* was ready to go to the New World, with the uneasy passengers. The others would return to Amsterdam and Leyden, except the Cushmans, who would remain in England.

The Cushmans stared at the *Mayflower* as the wind caught the main sail and it billowed out with a loud snap and caught the main sail and it billowed out with a loud snap and the ship behaved like a Great Dane on a leash, straining to go.

The passengers lined the railing, waving, and the ship seemed to list to port, but it really didn't, because it was a hardy ship and nothing could change its level course, it seemed. With the scene of the friends waving and many weeping... perhaps some of them were weeping because of the relief from anxiety caused by the knowledge that, luckily, they weren't aboard. They faded from the view of the passengers without knowing that neither would see the other ever again.

CHAPTER 6

On the Atlantic

1620

The passengers were composed of an odd lot. They were not all religious Pilgrims out of Scooby by way of Leyden. Only the Brewsters and William Bradford were from Scooby, England. The other forty-one Saints were from Leyden, who had originated from various parts of England. The Strangers were from London and Southwestern England, having been born and baptized in the faith of the Church of England. The Saints, although a minority, were in charge; they had organized the whole expedition.

The Pilgrims' common bond was their status as lower and middle class, they had no coat-of-arms in their background. On the most part, they were good people, they just wanted more opportunity and a life where each man was responsible for his own future and he could become "King" in his own home.

The leaders had finally come to the same conclusion as Cushman, Martin had to be replaced. They chose John Carver as Governor of the *Mayflower*. With high optimism, fear and some anxiety, looking toward an unknown future, the Pilgrims left Plymouth, England on the *Mayflower*, the sixth day of September, 1620. The absence of any Merchant Adventurers and Weston to see them off certainly did not go unnoticed by the Pilgrims. Although they felt slighted, this wasn't going to upset them in the slightest way, they had more important things to look forward to.

The repeated misfortunes of the *Speedwell* made most of the Pilgrims think of this as an ill omen for the future. They remembered the ill-fated voyage of another expedition that took place in 1618, that ended in disaster, the story goes:

An Amsterdam congregation of Separatists called the Franciscans and led by Elder Francis Blackwell, who was held in some ill repute by members of the Green Gate, who had known them in Amsterdam. They left for England and their final destination was to be Jamestown, Virginia. The group was always in trouble and one night at a meeting in England they were raided by agents of the crown. To save his own neck, Blackwell informed on Richard Masterson of Leyden and Sabin Staresmore, a friend of Cushman's who happened to be in London. The crown authorities were then looking for these men because of religious beliefs.

The Franciscans left England by crowding their group of two hundred onto a small ship and sailed for the New World in 1618. They ran into severe weather and were far off course. They were running out of water and disease broke out among the passengers and crew. The Captain and several officers that knew navigation, died. Six months after leaving Graves End, England and after a savage beating by the weather and being tossed about by an angry sea, they dropped anchor off Jamestown, Virginia. Of the original group, only fifty survived the voyage. They quickly dispersed on coming ashore. The leader of the group, Elder Blackwell, and his second in command, John Bowman died and had been buried at sea.

The passengers aboard the ill-fated ship had all the courage, anticipation of the future and background of those on the *Mayflower*, but the Pilgrims hoped that their misfortune would not happen to them. They figured that they had thought out most of the problems that would arise and they could cope with them. They only had half as many passengers and this alone was an advantage.

The sails were up and when the wind bellowed them out, snapping the *Mayflower* into action...they were on there way, at last. The passengers aboard the ship had a terrible time adjusting to their life at sea. The steady roll of the ship and the chill wind of the Atlantic in late October claimed its toll. There was no relief in sight; without exception they were all at their limit of endurance. Chilled to the bone, they huddled under the blankets while the stench of vomit permeated the ship. The ship's doctor was Giles Heale but Deacon Samuel Fuller was accepted by the Pilgrims and he tried to administer aid to all of them.

The Allertons were not immune to the seasickness and misery of the trip. Little Mary, like all the others, felt weak and she was pale and her hair was disheveled. She said, "Mother, when are we going to get to where we're going? I'm sick of being sick."

Bartholomew spoke up, "I wish the ship didn't smell so bad and roll back and forth so much."

Remember, who was usually quiet, said, "The cold...I wished it wasn't so cold. I keep shivering even with all my clothes on and the blankets over me!"

Mary Allerton said, "I know how you children feel, it hasn't been too pleasant for you. I only hope the little one (patting her stomach) is warm and comfortable. When she or he is born, we'll be in our new home."

Even some of the crew were sick. They were more

hardy and were able to bear up better than the passengers. Most of the crew were gleaned from the tough waterfront in London. However, on the most part, they were not very sympathetic to the passengers. They harassed, they harangued, they implied that the Pilgrims "would soon be food for the fishes when you fall overboard" or "pretty soon we'll run out of food and you can start eating the vermin."

Week after week, there were fair skies and a smooth sea, the ships company became bored with the monotony of the voyage. The Saints and the Strangers argued, the crew and the servants fought, all in all, it was a very disagreeable time. The crew didn't like the Saints, they thought they were too pious. The Strangers didn't like the servants because they thought they were above them. The servants didn't like the Strangers because they knew the Strangers were beneath them. The funny thing, if one could find humor in the whole affair, was that they were all in same boat, figuratively.

One of sailors who had verbally abused the passengers and who was the worst offender, became sick in the morning and by afternoon he was dead. So he became first, "in food for the fishes". Many Pilgrims assumed this was the work of the hand of God.

There were at least thirty seaman in the crew; they were coarse, vulgar and their curses and language made the passengers wince. The sailors were efficient however, scrambling up the riggings like monkeys, handling the heavy sails which was strenuous work but they made it seem like child's play. As time went on, the crew was gaining respect toward the Pilgrims and appeared sympathetic to their plight. Maybe this was a result of the fate of their fellow crew member who died, and they underestimated the religious strength of the Pilgrims.

The passengers had eaten monotonous meals of hard

tack, "Salt horse", dried fish, beer and cheese, with only an occasional hot meal. The Pilgrims were growing weary, it was a hum-drum existence, each day an exact copy of the day before. The children had run out of ideas trying to find things to occupy their idle moments. When the weather was clear and the sea calm, the Pilgrims ventured on deck to watch the endless sea. They might see a cloud or two, no birds, occasionally a school of Dolphins would leap out of the water. At night, the adults would pace the deck looking for the colorful sparkling, luminescent glow of algae which was visible.

Isaac and Mary were on deck with the other Pilgrims in the chilly night air getting a little relief from the confinement below.

Mary said, "Isaac, I feel sorry for the children, they are spending days on end trying to find something to do, they're very bored. I hope that we get there soon."

"I know they're bored...we're all bored. I didn't realize it would take so long to get there. I know once we get there we will have a lot to keep us busy. At least we can hope for something different to eat."

They gazed out into the darkness, then Isaac said, "How are you feeling Mary?"

"Do you mean now, or generally?"

"Both."

"Well, generally I feel fine. I just hope our young one is getting enough food. Right now, I'm starting to feel chilly, the wind is starting to act up."

"Yes," Isaac said, "I noticed it too. I guess it's about time we went below, it seems to be getting worse."

Suddenly, the wind increased in velocity, it was driving fiercely from the west. It was impossible to put up the sails for days. The *Mayflower* drifted aimlessly as the helmsman attempted to sail into the wind. Huge waves pounded her relentlessly and the heavy seas opened up large seams in the decks and superstructure, allowing the icy water to enter the ship. The frightened passengers huddled in their bunks below, they were saturated with sea water. Tables and chairs were flung across the floor, narrowly missing them.

The Pilgrims were in poor condition, the strain was beginning to show on their faces. The were losing weight, their eyes had a wild expression and their faces were gaunt and white, they were quite listless.

Suddenly, there was a loud cracking sound. Everyone held their breath...what was happening? The sound was heard all over the ship and everyone froze in their tracks.

A large beam at the structural center of the ship had given way under the strain. The sailors sprang into action.

They ran to the source of the sound and from their experienced viewpoint it seemed the ship would tear apart and sink. They tried to remain composed but this was the worst threat that had arisen during the entire voyage. The crew tried to prevent panic among the usual calm passengers. The Allertons gathered, holding each other. Like all the other families, they were extremely worried. Little Mary was crying and said, "Daddy, what is going to happen to us? Will the ship sink?"

Remember, who was also crying, said, "What will we do?"

Isaac said, "The crew will figure out what has to done. I think we should all have faith...we'll survive!"

Shouted suggestions were flying around the crowded hold as the *Mayflower* pitched around in the raging sea.

"I know how we can fix it...listen to me...I know how we can fix it." The passengers and crew fell silent as Edward Winslow continued speaking. "I have a printing press stored below and it has a large screw we can use to raise the beam. When we get the beam into place we can put other beams under it to hold it up."

The crowd roared their approval and Bradford said, "Let's give it a try...come on, we'll get the press up here."

Several men raced below and threw furniture around getting to the press. Desperately, they hauled the heavy press up. They grunted, pushed and shoved and finally put the press under the broken beam. They tightened the screw and gradually the beam was raised until it was level—it worked!

They repaired the beam by placing large studs under it and when they removed the press they breathed a sigh of relief, realizing that the danger had passed and the lives of those aboard were saved. Unfortunately, the press when placed under such a severe strain, was damaged in the process. It was useless now, but it had done its job.

A cheer had gone up for the men who had fixed the beam and little Mary was all smiles as she joined the cheering, along with the rest of the Allertons and ship's company.

Little did they realize when Winslow brought the press aboard that it would serve such a noble cause.

Although the wind had slackened a little, enough for the crew to put up the sails, it was still blowing hard. The sails were straining and the waves pounded the ship all during the day and night.

An incident happened which could have changed the fate of descendants of one of the passengers...if indeed there were to be any descendants. One morning, John Howland was below deck speaking with Isaac Allerton and William Bradford about England and tyranny. With cold, icy water coming through cracks, the foul and stuffy quarters were unbearable to the passengers. Each of the three men had a tankard of beer and after spending about a half hour shivering and finally almost sick from the vile odor, John said, "I think I'll go up on deck and get some fresh air."

Bradford replied, "You better mind the sea, it's pretty rough and windy out, maybe you should stay below till it gets calmer."

"No, I'll be all right." With that, Howland turned and made his way up to the pitching deck. It was indeed rough, the wind howling and with the sails bellowed out and straining. The ship was tipped and the deck was awash. Howland said to himself, "This is more than I expected." With that, he was suddenly propelled across the deck by a violent gust of wind. He grasped the wet, slippery railing and then lost his grip. He slipped and he tried to grasp the railing but his outstretched fingers missed the mark. Resigned to his fate, he said, "May God help me, I'm a goner!" In an instant, he was plunged into the raging, wild water below. His arms flared out and he grabbed a trailing topside halyard. He repeatedly went below the surface, his lungs straining for air. Water was entering his nostrils and he gulped as the salty water filled his mouth. He coughed some up.

With the freezing water numbing his hands, his mind racing, "Can I hold on? My arms are giving out!" The wind muffled most of the sound, but then, he suddenly heard shouts from the ship.

"Hold on...we'll pull you out!"

"Thank God," exclaimed Howland. "I've just about had it. I don't think I could have held on much longer."

Almost unconscious from the cold, he managed to hold on as rescue became possible. Gradually, he felt the halyard being pulled. If he could just hold on! His fingers were like claws, they had lost all sensations from the icy water. He had been under water too long...the racing speed of the ship pulling him along, bobbing him up and down. His mind wandered back to his childhood and the times he went fishing in the pond behind his house. The float he used did the same thing...bobbing and sometimes sinking...but now he was the float!

The sailors used a boat hook to grab him and then he felt their strong arms grabbing his coat...he had been saved from certain death. He was safe on deck and anxious deck hands wrapped him in blankets and his shivering finally subsided. He had not been a very religious person before this rescue, but the situation really set him to thinking. Why was the halyard trailing in the water? Why did I have the strength to hang on when my arms were numb from cold and I was at the point of total exhaustion? Why was I saved? What role will I have in life?

He was greeted by Bradford, who chided, "I'll wager you'll wait for a calmer day before you next venture forth on deck!"

In spite of his horrendous ordeal, Howland said, "I'll also wait for a warmer day to take a bath." Howland became ill because of this misfortune and he was advised to spend several days in his bunk.

A few days passed and one of the few good things happened aboard ship. Stephen Hopkins wife, Elizabeth delivered a baby boy named "Oceanus", this was their fourth child. Their other children were Giles and Constance whose mother was Stephen's first wife. Elizabeth was also the mother of Damaris, their other son.

The Pilgrims had become quite adept at the role as "sailors". They were now familiar with the roll of the ship and many were aware that they had developed "sea legs". They were able to spend some time away from the hold on the sunny deck of the ship. Although it was cold, it made life more tolerable.

On November sixth, tragedy came to one of the passengers, this was the first death among the Strangers. The unfortunate passing of William Butten, a twenty-two-year old, who had been Deacon Fuller's servant. He was well-liked by all aboard and had looked forward to going to the New World. He had developed a cold and a hacking cough, which never seemed to stop. One day he had a chill and then a fever, then came the inevitable deadly pneumonia. There was no relief available, few escaped from its clutches. He was one of the unlucky ones. He was buried at sea after a brief ceremony—just a few days short of sighting land. It was amazing there was only one death among the passengers on this difficult voyage across the Atlantic with their crude living arrangements and unbearable cold and damp weather.

CHAPTER 7

Provincetown, Cape Cod

1620

O ne day there was an expected shout from the look-out in the crows-nest. "Land-ho!" "Land!" "Land!"...the call was repeated throughout the ship. The passengers scrambled up on the deck to see what they hoped would be their new homeland. They had been seeing land birds for a couple of days and knew they would be experiencing a great thrill on arriving in the New World. A sliver of land appeared in the distance and gradually it grew until they could see trees and the sandy shore.

When they saw the shore a mighty roar went up and the excited passengers acted as one. There were many questions, they asked;

"What is the land like?"

"Are there many trees?"

"Can you see if there is any vegetation?"

"When can we go ashore?"

They gradually eased into a bay which was later known as Provincetown. They were now at the tip of Cape Cod in

New England. It was November 11, 1620 and the sun was now shining on a new day. The Pilgrims knelt and Brewster led them in a simple prayer:

"Thank God we have survived this ordeal
with little loss of life. May God help us
in our quest for a home in which we can
live and thrive. May we all have long life
and prosperity."   *Amen*

John Carver was amazed at the size of the harbor. "What a magnificent harbor, it could hold a thousand ships!"

Bradford said, "Yes John, it's a glorious sight to behold. I'm glad the trip is over, now we'll have to find a place where we can settle. The land looks a little desolate but of course it's almost winter and we can expect it. The coastline looks fine with its white sandy beach, but I wonder what lies behind it?"

The wind was bitterly cold but still the passengers wanted to go ashore and stretch and finally put their feet on land. Some, including the Saints who departed from Delft Haven, had been aboard the *Speedwell* and then the *Mayflower* for almost four long months. The *Mayflower* had departed from Plymouth, England sixty-five days before, which was a tribute to the human spirit and their endurance. That is why they selected the young and the fit, for only they could have survived this ordeal.

There were many aboard who were skeptical about the passengers going ashore without reconnoitering to see if it was safe. The most vocal opponent being Myles Standish, who had been selected to command the future militia in the colony. Myles Standish, who was to become an important figure in the governing of the new settlement and who became a legend in the history of America.

He was born in Chorley, Lancashire about 1584. He

was an experienced, hard soldier about thirty-six years old. An orphan, he was a soldier before he was twenty; fighting the Spanish. He also aided the Dutch when he was sent to the Netherlands by Queen Elizabeth I. He was unceremoniously nick-named "Captaine Shrimpe" by the enemy because he was short, had flaming red hair and his face turned crimson when he was in a rage, which was often. He was somewhat of an enigma. Very little was known about his background up to the time that he came aboard the *Mayflower* with his wife, Rose, although many said he was from a prosperous family and had outstanding ancestry. However, he was the right man at the right place and at the right time. His presence was over-bearing and demanded respect from his friends and enemies.

The passengers had been prone to listen to idle talk on the long monotonous voyage. Several of the passengers spread rumors and there had been a constant barrage of muttering by malcontents. This began to influence the Strangers into mutinous action. There had been rumblings among the passengers that they would do exactly what they wanted once they were ashore. They felt that nobody should tell them what to do; they didn't have to take orders. The Strangers complained that they didn't land at Virginia, they were in New England and they didn't ask to be brought here so the agreement was not valid.

"Why are we here?" Asked John Billington. "We're supposed to land at Jamestown in Virginia."

Bradford knowing that Billington had been nothing but trouble since he joined them in London said, "John, as you well know, we landed here for convenience. We had about reached the limits of our endurance and we were running low on drinking water. It is unfortunate we didn't land at Jamestown, but here we are. At least we are safe now and we should count our blessings that we had such a small loss of life during the hazardous trip we have just gone through. There are certain advantages to our being here; we are on our own, we can form our own government, we do not have to accept a government influenced by the British Crown. We can choose our religion and we're not a threat to any foreign government. We'll be left alone, we won't be entangled in any foreign war."

Billington said, "I guess you're right, our families will be safe, that's all that matters." He then left to go below deck.

Allerton, who was standing next to Bradford during this encounter said, "I wonder how long it will be before he speaks to another of his cohorts and completely distorts what you have said."

Although conditions aboard were the best that could be had under the circumstances, they were miserable, mostly due to the weather and overcrowding.

Bradford, Allerton and Brewster, joined with the others who were concerned about the fate of the colony and worried if this potential rebellion were to grow. "It could destroy any attempt at colonization and security." Bradford said. "We'll have to take steps to assure that this is stopped as soon as possible."

Bradford said, "Have you heard the story going around about Stephen Hopkins and his suspected involvement as a leader in a mutiny?"

"What do you base this story on? Do you have any evidence that he was really involved, William?" Allerton asked.

"Well, you know he's been to Virginia a couple of times in the past and trouble seems to follow him. He was shipwrecked once off Bermuda and he settled there and became a clerk. A mutiny broke out and he seemed to behind it. He was caught, brought to trial, found guilty and sentenced to death."

"What happened to him?" asked Brewster. "It's obvious the sentence wasn't carried out."

"He appealed for clemency by saying he was a married man with two children and he didn't think it was right to leave his wife alone in the world and the children fatherless. The court said that they would spare his life, if he would get out of Bermuda and return to England. Naturally he agreed and left. The other two participants were executed. That's not all, Hopkins now has two man-servants, as you know, Edward Doty and Edward Leister. They're ambitious, spirited and extremely violent. I believe they're also involved in mutinous conduct aboard the *Mayflower* along with John Billington."

Bradford said. "That's why I say that we have to counter any move they may make and eliminate this threat once and for all."

Allerton said, "By coincidence, Hopkins said he was in Bermuda and returned to England but he didn't say he was involved in a mutiny."

Brewster asked, "You mention his man-servants, Doty and Leister, but why would Hopkins work with them to make them independent if they were already indentured to him.?"

Bradford said, "I was wondering about that myself, it would seem to contradict his being involved. Perhaps he did a lot of talking of the mutiny in Bermuda on our long trip across the Atlantic and the others picked up the stories and put them into action. You know it's more than just coincidence that several rallying calls and slogans which were used in the Bermuda mutiny, had mysteriously appeared on the *Mayflower*."

Soon after hearing about the potential mutiny, there were those aboard that realized they would have to be responsible for the action of others. The more dependable among them realized they would be compelled to have some type of document establishing a standard for law and order. They set about writing an instrument and many saw the fine hand of Brewster in its composition. When it was finished, they called it the *Mayflower Compact*, it read:

MAYFLOWER COMPACT
In the name of God. Amen
We whose names are underwritten, the loyal
subjects of our dread Sovereign Lord King James,
by the Grace of God, of Great Britain, France
and the Ireland King, Defender of the Faith, etc.
Having undertaken, for the glory of god and the
advancement of the Christian Faith and the
Honour of our King and Country, a voyage
to plant the First Colony in the Northern Parts of Virginia,
do by these presents, solemnly and mutually
in the presence of god, and one another,
covenant combine ourselves together into a
civil body politic, for better ordering and preservation
and furtherance of the ends aforesaid: and by virtue
hereof to enact, constitute and frame such just and
equal laws, ordinances, acts, Constitution and officers,
from time to time, as shall be thought most meet the
needs and convenient for the general good of the Colony,
unto which we promise all due submission and obedience.
In witness we have hereunder subscribed our names
at Cape Cod, the 11th of November,
in the year of the reign of our Sovereign, Lord King James,
of England, France, and Ireland the eighteen,
and of Scotland the fifty fourth Anno Domini 1620.

The signers were in the order named:
John Carver, William Bradford, Edward Winslow, William Brewster, Isaac Allerton, Myles Standish, Deacon Samuel Fuller, Christopher Martin, William Mullins, William White, Richard Warren, Stephen

Hopkins, John Alden, John Howland, Edward Tilley, Francis Cooke, Thomas Rogers, Thomas Tinker, John Rigdale, Edward Fuller, John Turner, Francis Eaton, James Chilton, John Crackston, John Billington, Moses Fletcher, John Goodman, Degory Priest, Thomas Williams, Gilbert Winslow, Edmund Margeson, Peter Brown, Richard Bitterridge, George Soule, Richard Clarke, Richard Gardiner, John Allerton, Thomas English, Edward Doty, Edward Leister.

The leaders had been especially interested in having Hopkins servants sign. They figured this compact would terminate any further mutinous behavior.

The *Mayflower Compact* was an unusual instrument of government when you consider the backgrounds of the signers and the royal government from which they evolved, where they were among the lower strata. The *Mayflower Compact* was read from the upper deck to all the passengers, with Saints and Strangers in a very solemn mood. The leaders announced that John Carver was to be the first governor of the colony which they would form.

After the ceremony they gathered in little groups discussing the compact and congratulating Carver. The Saints were pleased to see Carver so honored after his devotion to their cause for so many years. Then the leaders organized a party of men armed with the latest military weapons. The weapons at the time were matchlock and flintlock muskets and long swords. They wore corselets and metal helmets. The matchlock muskets were about five feet long, with a smooth bore about .75 caliber. The gun powder which was carried in a leather pouch on their belts, was poured into the muskets and wadded, then a lead ball shot was dropped down into the barrel followed by a thick pad which was rammed in. The firing mechanism was also a time-consuming nightmare. First, a fine grain gun powder was put into a flash pan, then ignited by the glowing end of a slow match pressed down with a hammer-like action. This done, it was ready to fire by using a trigger. The matchlock weight was supported while being fired by a long metal rod with a bracket. The flintlock was a much lighter gun and could be rapidly readied to fire. They were used to defend themselves while the matchlocks were being prepared to fire.

The corselet or breastplate was a heavy, cumbersome steel plate that afforded some protection against arrows or lead shot, especially if hit at an angle, then the projectiles would be deflected.

Captain Myles Standish would lead the men and they would go ashore in a small boat to see if it was safe for the passengers to follow. There was now a document to exert the necessary authority once they were all ashore. The mutiny, at least for the time being, was put at rest. Although many deny the fact, there are those that will argue that the *Mayflower Compact* was the forerunner of the more sophisticated *Declaration of Independence* and the *Constitution* with its cry for freedom and equality.

After the party walked a few miles, they realized they were on a narrow strip of land with the Atlantic on either side. It had a very good, black, fertile topsoil and there were ample wooded and clear areas. Best of all, there was no sign of Indians or any sign of habitation, but they did find the most needed prize—fresh water. They found Juniper bushes which provided branches when burnt gave off a fragrant odor, which would do wonders for the passengers who had become accustomed to the stench of the hold, having lived there for months. A couple of days after the men returned from their fruitful trip along the coast it was about time for the women to go ashore.

"Come on Elizabeth," Anne Tilley said, "Let's get our bedding and other things we have to wash and go out to the beach. All the other women are getting their wash together."

Elizabeth Tilley, sister-in-law of Anne said, "Have you ever seen bedding in such a state! They haven't been washed for months! We'll have to keep them at arm's length, they reek of a stagnant odor. It's pretty hard to hold your nose with one hand and hold the blankets with the other!"

It was almost a carnival atmosphere; the children were all excited about finally getting off the ship and exploring the shore. The women and children were loaded into the small boats which the *Mayflower* carried and made the short trip to shore. They unloaded the boats with the children laughing and yelling while running up and down the beach under the watchful eyes of the armed guard and the women. It was indeed a treat to once again set foot on land.

But, for the women it was a different story. They had the unwelcome tedious task of washing all the bedding and clothes. They found a small, oval, fresh water pond near the beach, without ice. They heaped their wash beside them and started on their thankless job. The guards built bonfires to keep the women warm and heat the large kettles of water. They made frequent trips to the fire to warm themselves. Their hands were constantly in the water washing and rinsing the clothes and blankets of the accumulated dirt by pounding it with rocks. It certainly wasn't a holiday for the women; it was cold and the frequent clouds passing obscured the sun which had provided a little relief. While washing, they kept their spirits up by singing religious ditties and gossiping. The women, like the men, had hacking coughs which were aggravated by the chill in the air and their general weakness caused by the long and stressful voyage. These women who were doing their "domestic chores", were no less heroic than the well-acclaimed founding fathers. Nobody could doubt the silent courage that each had, while the men played soldiers.

The men removed the long boat or shallop from between the decks which had been battered by the heavy storms which they had endured. Her seams were opened up due to several of the passengers lying in her, space being so limited.

Carver was talking to Francis Eaton and he said, "Francis, you've got skills we really need to get the shallop back in shape. You've seen it, it's a mess and will require a great deal of work. I have a lot of confidence in you, I know that you can make it shipshape again. You'll need several men to help you. Pick out whoever you think can help you the most, I'm sure they will cooperate."

Eaton replied, "All right Governor, I'm sure we can fix it up and do a good job, I understand the shallop is going to be used for exploring the coast and for short trips. It's in pretty bad shape. You know that we had to cut it in half to fit below deck. I will need about five men to help and we can start today."

Others not involved in the repairs went along the shore and found tidal flats which contained shellfish and other seafood. They ate greedily on the succulent soft-shelled clams and mussels, becoming deathly sick from eating the large mussels, causing the Pilgrims to become pale, sweaty and nauseous.

Carver gathered the leaders and said, "I was talking to Francis Eaton this morning about the shallop and I agree that it will take several days of work to get it in shape. Time is running out and it's very important we find a place to settle. We have to build shelters for ourselves and for the provisions and supplies. I understand the winters here at Cape Cod can be very severe. Captain Jones will be patient with us, I hope, but I'm sure he understands our problems."

Bradford replied, "I agree with you, John, we'll have

to come to a decision pretty soon. When the shallop is ready we can explore the coast. In the meantime we can make short excursions on foot."

The Pilgrims were not the first white men who would explore the coastline of the Cape. There had been Dutch, French and English explorers and finally British fishermen. Long before them came the Norsemen. History tells us that Leif Erikisson, the son of Eric the Red, around 1002 A.D. set out from Greenland and ended up at Cape Cod, which he called "Land of the Grapes". This was probably attributed to the large, luscious grapes found at Martha's Vineyard. He returned to Greenland in 1003 with a load of timber. The next year another Viking called Thorfinn Karlsefore from Iceland, followed Leif Eirikssons's path and also expressed delight in the abundance of the delicious, large grapes that were found on the Cape.

*   *   *

One evening some of the crew gathered in the crew's quarters drinking beer and discussing the passengers. The boats-mate said, "What are these Pilgrims up to? They're certainly taking their own sweet time in leaving the ship. When are they going to find a place to settle?" The gunners-mate spoke up, "I guess they want to be sure conditions are right before they make up their minds. I don't blame them."

"They've been here for weeks," said the boats-mate. "They still haven't made a move yet. Besides we have to return to London while we still have some food left."

Another crew-member chimed in, "We should dump all of their things on the beach, get them off the ship and leave."

"You sure have some heart, John." said the gunners-mate. "They're not a bunch of animals. They deserve to be treated fairly. How would you like it if you were forced to leave under the same conditions? No shelter, out in the open in the wilderness, and you don't know if there's savages lurking around ready to kill you. If you think nothing of the men consider the women and children. One of the children—a baby—is only a month old! Some of the women are tired and pregnant!"

Just then Captain Jones came to the quarters and overheard the conversation. "What's the matter with you men? The Pilgrims will go when they're ready. They have more guts in one finger than most of you have in your whole bodies. I dare one of you men, that's complaining so much, to spend one or two days and nights out there in this cold and dampness and don't forget to look over your shoulder for the Indians sneaking around. I'll hear none of this talk, the Pilgrims will leave soon, they know they're holding us up, but they'll leave in their own good time." Having given them a piece of his mind, he left. The crew looked at each other, a few murmured, the rest shrugged their shoulders and said nothing. The gunners-mate smiled to himself and reached for another beer.

When they reached Provincetown Harbor, the first day, they noticed a river about five miles down the coast. The Pilgrims thought this would be a good place to settle. Sixteen men armed with muskets, swords, metal breastplates and helmets were led by Captain Myles Standish. He was assisted by William Bradford, Edward Tilley and Stephen Hopkins who offered Standish counsel and helped guide the others. About a mile down the white sandy beach they came across six Indians approaching with a dog. The Indians whistled to the dog and darted into the nearby woods.

The Pilgrims recklessly followed them, neglecting to realize there could be several more lying in ambush. They followed the tracks of the Indians all day, without sighting them once. Returning to the beach, Captain Myles Standish said, "Men, we'll have to spend the night here, we can build a couple of bonfires to try to keep warm. We can pick up the trail tomorrow." They gathered some brush and driftwood and soon they had the fires roaring. Warming their hands and feet they soon felt a little more comfortable. There was still the matter about security—here they were on a beach, with little or no combat experience warming their hands. The Indians, with their natural "know-how" of stalking wild animals were hidden in the woods. Their curiosity about the "invaders" was no doubt the topic of conversation and caused a certain amount of anxiety among the Indians. Who were these people in strange costumes? Are they going to stay or like other visitors go on to other places?

Ignoring the Indians, Bradford said, "The heat from the fire is certainly welcome. I think we'd better eat something before it gets dark. Who knows what the night might bring?" They opened their bags which contained some hard-tack, dried herring, cheese and bottles of beer. They soon finished their meal—this was the same menu which they had for the last few months.

Captain Standish, adjusting his breastplate said, "You better make sure your muskets and swords are within arms reach, we don't know what will happen next." They talked for awhile gradually drifting off to sleep, struggling to keep their blankets over them to provide a little needed warmth. Some of the men volunteered to do sentry duty through the night.

The next day they resumed the search for the Indians and wandered into the thickets which soon ripped their clothes and bodies and the net result was to make them look foolish. They admitted later that they had been strong in courage but weak in common sense.

They had no fresh water at this time but they were able to survive on beer and a small bottle of gin. When they found another small stream of fresh water, they were amazed at the pleasant taste. They brought some along to the ship which was out of sight up the coast. They were returning to the *Mayflower*, hugging the shoreline when they spied a sandy rise near the beach. In a large meadow nearby they discovered mounds of sand. Stephen Hopkins saw the mounds and exclaimed, "I wonder what's under them? It certainly looks like the Indians buried something."

Bradford said, "Maybe it's an Indian burial ground and we don't want to desecrate it, they no doubt consider it a holy place."

"Maybe they're not graves. I think that they would be in regular rows, in some order, if they were." Hopkins said.

Tilley said, "The only way we'll know is by digging them up. If they're graves we'll know soon enough and we'll stop digging."

The men agreed and soon they were eagerly digging away with their knives and swords trying to see what had been buried. After digging for a few minutes they came across corn buried in a large basket. The corn was multicolored and very interesting to the group as they had never seen it before. They filled their pockets and an old kettle which they had found with the corn and made their way to the ship. Upon arrival they put the corn into the common store and said they would save it for future planting.

Many suggested that maybe they could settle at "Corn Hill" where the ground was fertile and fresh water was available. Others thought the fresh water might dry up in the creeks and ponds during the summer, besides there wasn't a good harbor nearby to enable them to bring the *Mayflower* into a safe haven.

Then fate was again changed by a casual remark by one of the mates, Robert Coffin. He said, "I've been in these parts before on an expedition and I know a place called "Thievish Harbor" or Plymouth just across the bay. They called it "Thievish Harbor" because we had trouble with a "wild man" who stole a harpoon from us. Captain John Smith of Jamestown, Virginia fame, named it Plymouth when he also was on the expedition a few years ago."

After the "First Discovery" at corn hill, there was a welcome addition to the passenger list. There was the birth of Peregrine White, a son born to William and Susanna (Fuller) White. He was the first English boy born in New England and by coincidence his name translated means "Pilgrim" or "Trader".

Ten days passed and there was still no decision about where they would finally settle and establish their colony. They stayed close by the *Mayflower* as the weather was usually unsettled and storms of sleet and snow with cold winds became commonplace.

Eaton was still working on the shallop whenever the clear weather permitted. There was still more to be done and the Pilgrims decided they would use the shallop for small voyages along the coast, whenever the weather conditions changed for the better.

Once assembled the shallop was of impressive size. It was thirty-three feet long, nine feet two inches wide and three feet three inches deep. It had one mast and a jib sail. It would prove invaluable to them as land travel was slow and laborious.

The men who helped Eaton fix the shallop worked diligently, every hour that there was light. Many had never worked as carpenters before but they gained ability quickly. They took pride in their effort. They knew that every hour they worked was important to their survival.

The men were tired but they still had not lost their sense of humor. John Alden, who was one of the few who knew carpentry, had been carrying a board to the shallop when a tired co-worker straightened up from his stooped position and stretched the muscles in his back. Alden, grinning, said, "Come on, Allerton, quit your loafing. . . we have work to do!" Allerton grinned back and looked around supposedly to find something to throw at Alden.

The next day they were to board the shallop for a short trip to see if it was seaworthy. The men were anxious to test it and many of them rushed to find a place in the boat. When all the would-be "sailors" were aboard, they had trouble getting it off the shore, because of the accumulated weight. After much effort involving grunting and shoving, the shallop was free and they were now on their way. They put up the sail and when it caught the wind, it slipped through the water like a dolphin. Maybe not as graceful as a fish, but it was indeed seaworthy and ready for use by the Pilgrims.

CHAPTER 8

Provincetown, Cape Cod

1620

They organized an expeditionary force of twenty-four Pilgrims and nine of the crew members from the *Mayflower*. They were a foolhardy group, there were no such things as life jackets and they were weighed down with heavy breast-plates, helmets, swords and muskets. Captain Standish would be responsible for the military needs and the "indomitable" Captain Christopher Jones commanded the shallop and was designated "Chief of Party". They crowded into the shallop as the shadows of night disappeared, the sky was overcast and forebode a warning that the weather would create a problem for them. The situation was that valuable time was being lost by inaction and events demanded that the Pilgrims must search for a new home as soon as possible. They put up the sail and the wind blowing from the north-west bellowed the canvas and gradually the shallop picked up speed. The men settled down and spoke very little as the boat knifed through the water bound for their destination. Then came the inevitable; an increase in the strength of the wind and snow flurries appeared from a sullen, grey sky. Finally the stormy weather forced them to make a decision, some of the men would return to the *Mayflower* while most of the Pilgrims would go ashore to explore. Wading in the icy water up to their hips they finally made their way to shore. It snowed all day and night and accumulated a depth of six inches, the chill winds worked havoc on the bodies of the Pilgrims. They were extremely cold and miserable. They laid the blame on some of the deaths that first winter on this fool-hardy trip.

The ones in the shallop which had gone back to the *Mayflower* returned the next morning to pick up the Pilgrims. The Pilgrims, red-faced from the cold and embarrassment, admitted they hadn't accomplished very much, other than learn how to cope with the cold and they weren't too successful doing that. The good news was that the sun was shining brightly again and its rays provided a little heat and beauty reflecting off the snow-laden branches and crystal white covering of the landscape.

The group decided to continue the exploration by again loading up the shallop with its human cargo and setting sail for the nearby river. They found it too shallow for ships like the *Mayflower* but fine for boats. They didn't venture very far up the river, as they didn't find anything of interest and they knew they would have to have a harbor nearby to their settlement if they were to grow.

Meanwhile, when the men were returning to the ship and others were trying to get supplies for the passengers, there occurred on the *Mayflower* an unsettling incident that could have terminated the whole *Mayflower* venture. On December fifth, eight-year-old Francis Billington crept into a cabin that was being used as a storage area for guns, gun powder and other explosives. Looking at all the "off-limits" material was quite an adventure to this mischievous youth. He was toying with a musket when he pulled the trigger.

There was a loud explosion and the shot narrowly missed a keg of black powder, which, with the other explosives, could have blown the *Mayflower* to bits. When the crew ran to investigate the roaring sound of the musket, they were encountered by the terrified boy who dropped the musket and was about to exit the cabin. Upon seeing the close call to the ship and those aboard, the crew severely reprimanded him and made sure nobody duplicated his act by hastily putting a lock on the door and keeping a more vigilant eye open.

After the Billington episode the Pilgrims thought that maybe the Plymouth area might be worth investigating. They formed an expeditionary force of eighteen men including Coffin at the tiller. The group consisted of the intrepid Saints from Leyden; Bradford, Winslow, John and Edward Tilley, Carver and his man-servant John Howland. The Strangers were Captain Standish, Richard Warren and Stephen Hopkins with his servant Edward Doty and some of the crew. The group assembled to continue the exploration on December sixth. It was sunny when they started out and extremely cold. The men were bundled up and their frosty breath emphasized the chill in the air. Again the shallop was put into service and they made their way along the coast. By this time the wind was blowing hard and the frothy waves whipped across the bow cutting through their clothing and chilling them to the bone. Their clothes were frozen stiff; Edward Tilley and the Master Gunner passed out from the cold. Captain Jones said, "We'd better put ashore here and build a fire to get warm...we can't take too much of this."

They put into a sandy point beyond "Corn Hill" now called Wellfleet Bay. After disembarking from the shallop they gathered wood and began to build a fire. One of the Pilgrims said, "What's that down the beach?" He pointed out what seemed to be about a dozen Indians crowded around a black object. The Indians ran off, jumping and hooting into the nearby woods.

The party built a defensive position and shelter and in the middle was their huge bonfire. The next morning the party investigated the area where the Indians had been and were surprised to find a large black fish about fifteen feet long, which was actually a grampus or Howling Whale. The Indians had been cutting up the whale which had about a two-inch thick blubbery skin and would supply a lot of oil. The men climbed back into the shallop, set sail and moved down the coast. It was now calm, clear and a light breeze was blowing. Captain Standish said, "This area looks good. How does it look to you, William?"

"Yes, I think we should put in here," Bradford said. "We can stay overnight."

The men went to the back of the boat to weigh the end down so the bow would go far up on the beach when it landed. They exited the boat onto dry land. They immediately started to build a defensive shield which consisted of logs, branches and other nearby material. Captain Standish took charge and told them how to build the barricade and how to reinforce it, in case there was an onslaught by the Indians. A group of men were assigned to get fire wood and they built a large bonfire in the center of the gathering.

One of the crew members mentioned that he had been in this area several times but they didn't stay long. He said, "I was commanded by Captain John Smith and they traveled up the coast to a point in New England called Maine. Maine has a rocky coast but it was scenic as was the whole coastline of New England. Occasionally we caught sight of Indians but generally they seemed to stay out of sight. The Indians around Cape Cod acted a lot friendlier, some even came aboard our boat to trade, but there were others you had to watch out for, they were treacherous and I think they would kill you without a moment's hesitation."

They posted sentries and the rest of the men wrapped themselves in blankets and tried to get some sleep. They were awakened around midnight by a loud howling sound.

"What's that weird sound?", asked Winslow. "It has an uncanny sound...wait, there it goes again!"

The Pilgrims shot their muskets off in the direction of the sound but Standish told them to put a stop to this. "It's a waste of time and shot, if you can't see them, you can't hit them." He said. One of the crew spoke up. "It's not Indians you heard, it was wolves. I've been in this area before and there are a lot of them around here."

They heard nothing further that night.

The next morning at breakfast, after some of the Pilgrims had placed their muskets in the shallop, against the advice of Standish, there suddenly came the sound of howling and cries that they had heard the night before. A sentry cried out an alarm, ran to the others, followed by a shower of arrows. The Pilgrims retrieved their weapons from the shallop and fought off the attack. It was sudden but fortunately not deadly, nobody received a scratch. Their coats, hanging on the barricade were filled with arrows. Standish had fired a shot that chipped the bark of a tree near the face of an Indian and with a wild whoop it ended the brief fire fight when the Indians ran off. The Pilgrims chased after them, shouting, "Come back here and fight, you bunch of heathens!" They fired their muskets until the Indians were out of sight. "You bunch of cowards!" they yelled. Little did they realize the Indians could muster a force of a couple of thousand warriors at will.

The Indians were impressed by the sight and sound of the muskets when fired. However their own bow and arrows, when used effectively, were much superior. They were soundless and could penetrate a sand bag without effort. A lead shot fired by the musket would flatten once it met resistance, although it could put a terrific hole in an unfortunate Indian.

The little skirmish with the Indians happened at Eastham, where there now exists a street leading to the shore called "First Encounter Street".

The expeditionary force left "First Encounter Beach" and headed for Plimoth. The sea was calm and the weather fair but it soon changed...it started to rain and snow, the wind became a gale and the sea was rough and treacherous. Bradford, who was in the rear of the shallop, yelled to the other men, "The rudder just broke, you'll have to steer with your oars."

The men strained and struggled with their clumsy oars in the churning sea. The wind's steady roar made normal conversation impossible. Coffin yelled, "I think that I see the harbor of Plimoth ahead. It's hard to make out in the storm and the rough sea." The men were at the point of exhaustion but they kept going—they had no other choice.

They attempted to add more sail to the shallop to make better time and, unfortunately, the mast broke in three pieces going into the raging sea with the sail. They cut the mast away, which almost turned the boat over in the turbulent sea. But through sheer willpower and dwindling strength they were able to hang on.

The crew followed the direction of Coffin who recognized certain landmarks. He was dumb-founded when the shallop speeded up at a reckless pace on the crest of breakers pushing them toward a cove of which he was unfamiliar. They feverishly manned the oars and soon they were able to get to a more tranquil spot on the wooded shore. It was dark when they struggled to shore and luckily found some damp firewood which they would use to start a fire and warm them. They had found a spot where they could find some shelter from the storm; then with some difficulty they finally got the fire started. They erected a couple of lean-to's. The men spent a very restless night trying to get warm in their wet clothes. The Pilgrims hadn't given much thought to Indians in the area because they figured the Indians wouldn't be wandering around in that weather.

The next morning they found to their surprise they were not at Plimoth but on an island. They were to name it Clarke's Island, in honor of the chief mate who was the first to step ashore. The name exists to this day.

Exhausted by the previous night's effort against the wild sea and the elements, they made an effort to dry their clothes, clean their muskets and in general relax their tired muscles.

The next day was spent in keeping the Sabbath and resting. On Monday, the Pilgrims went on to Plimoth which was nearby. On their way, they tested the depth of the harbor and found it could accommodate large ships, then they went ashore into what would become their new home. Fresh water was found in large amounts as well as cornfields, wild berries and trees that were valued in England for their healing powers. They soon decided that it was the best spot available to them.

They returned to the *Mayflower* the following day to report the good news to the others. The Pilgrims were silent and stood looking at the returning men. There was bad news for William Bradford; his young wife, Dorothy, had fallen overboard while the ship was anchored and the sea was calm. There had been no outcry, no struggle for survival. No doubt she had reached the end of her endurance and could no longer stand the hardship. She had drowned the night after Bradford had left on his trip to Plimoth. History shouldn't take too dismal a view of Dorothy's fate. Many that were to follow the Pilgrims were speechless at the wild and barren land, with savages, which was quite a let-down after living in cities and villages with green fields and gardens in a civilized country.

Mary Allerton, upon hearing of Dorothy Bradford's death became very depressed. Dorothy was a friend whom she knew in Leyden for about seven years. They had become very close. She never realized what Dorothy had in mind. Dorothy had seemed discouraged with the conditions they had to endure and her separation from her son she left behind in Leyden. Mary eventually came to the conclusion, which was shared by others, that Dorothy had taken her own life.

William Bradford remained silent about her death for his entire life.

It required a unique character and immense stamina to be comfortable in such a savage environment. Dorothy probably would have survived in Leyden but this wasn't civilization with which she was familiar; it was a raw, brutal existence.

Mary had been having trouble with her pregnancy. She had problems with her diet and having the same monotonous meals week after week. Her children had been a problem on the trip across. They had no trouble for the first few weeks then time was against them, they got very bored. They had played the same games over and over, they were beginning to argue and pick on each other. The other women with children had the same complaint. The children weren't allowed on deck without an adult and some of the crew never had a good word for them. Now that they were anchored here at Cape Cod maybe there would be some relief. Little Mary teased her brother and when he chased her, she found refuge from him behind her mother's skirt. She peeked around her mother and made faces at her brother. Bartholomew asked his mother to tell her to stop acting like a brat.

Mary Allerton, finding herself almost at the point of desperation, said to the children, "Please, I know you are bored but try to find something to do. Mary, stop teasing your brother and sister!"

"Mommie, what can we do to have fun?"

"Why don't you play with your dollie?"

"She's asleep."

"Why don't you wake her up?"

"She's tired."

"So am I! I'm going to lie down and try to get some rest now. Please! Please try and amuse yourselves and don't tease your brother."

"Can I tease Remember?"

"Don't tease your sister either!"

"Oh, mother?"

"Yes dear, what is it now?"

"Have a good rest...I'll be good!

When Mary Allerton left to go to her bunk, Bartholomew began to scold his younger sister. "Why did you bother Mother when she is very tired and doesn't feel too well, either?"

"I didn't know she didn't feel well."

"Yes, she is tired, too. Didn't you notice that she falls asleep too much?"

Remember spoke up. "I know that you're my 'baby sister', but why did you say to Mommie that you wanted to tease me?"

"Well, I was just talking."

Remember said, "Can I play with your dollie for a few minutes?"

"She's asleep."

"Then wake her up. Besides, dolls don't really sleep

like people."

"Dorothy does!... well, you can play with Dorothy. I'll wake her up. You'd better take good care of her!"

Remember replied, "Maybe I don't want to play with your doll, anyway."

"Well, maybe I changed my mind, too."

"Keep your old doll. She has a stupid look on her face. Who would want to play with it, anyway?"

"You would."

Bartholomew looked at them both, shook his head in disbelief and walked away to join his friends. They were doing important things... they had a rat cornered.

CHAPTER 9

Plymouth, Cape Cod

1620-1621

The Pilgrims were on deck, bundled up against the cold and they seemed unusually quiet, staring at the silent; hostile shore. It was a beautiful winter evening and the brilliant full moon cast eerie shadows with the leafless trees and their grotesque branches, adding to the mysteries of the still night. They looked solemnly at the land before them. This was to be their new home. For better or for worse they had made their decision. They could return on the *Mayflower* but that would mean defeat. They had already sacrificed a lot, they would see it through to the end. They didn't know exactly where they would settle—should they stay here at Provincetown or move to Plimoth? Whatever their choice, it was to be a final act...once the die had been cast they would have to live with another decision—first the decision to stay and then the final spot where they would settle down.

After two or three days of haggling the merits of going to Plimoth, the *Mayflower* weighed anchor to go to their new home. This was after the insistence of Captain Jones that they would have to make up their minds soon, it was late in the season and they had only a limited supply of food aboard. It had already been six weeks since they landed at Provincetown, now they set sail for Plimoth. After several attempts to get into the harbor at Plimoth they finally made a successful run for it. The tired and weary Pilgrims were very happy and encouraged by the sheltered harbor. Although it was shallow, it made a pretty picture framed with pleasant woods and waterfowl overhead.

Bradford, along with other men, went ashore. He said, "I'll show you the cornfields that we found and the stream with fresh water and the other things you might be interested in seeing."

After walking in an area they hadn't yet explored, Winslow said, 'Did you notice we haven't seen any habitation of any sort except the cornfields? I wonder where the people went that planted the corn here?"

They hiked for several miles, always on the alert; in case of a surprise attack from the Indians. They climbed a hill and looked down on the harbor where the *Mayflower* was anchored. Hopkins remarked, "The ship looks like a toy floating in the harbor but it certainly looks impressive. It's hard to realize what it's gone through." The rest of the group looking at the *Mayflower* agreed.

They made the long trip back to the ship burdened down with armament. Usually, the women and children would line the decks of the ship and with anxious eyes would be on the lookout for their husbands or fathers to see if they made it back safely without running into danger. When they could see them, they had many questions...

"How many are there?...There's three missing!...No! There they are, they're all there. Is one limping? Maybe he twisted his ankle...I wonder if they ran into trouble with the Indians?"

That was the usual routine when the men went ashore until they were assured they all returned safely. Then they would breathe a collective sigh of relief when they all came aboard.

They set sail the next day in the shallop to a nearby river and explored as far as what is now known as Kingston. It was a nice spot but heavily wooded and they assumed it would be a severe handicap in trying to clear it for defense purposes and farming. The men went back to the ship weary after walking all day and slept soundly; tomorrow would bring a new expedition to Clarke's Island.

Having an early breakfast, the men prepared for their short trip to the island. They placed food in the shallop along with their muskets and swords and they wore their breastplates. Although they didn't expect trouble, they had to be prepared for it at all times. They went ashore on Clarke's Island near the spot where they had landed the first night. They explored the island and saw evidence the Indians also had been there recently and had built small fires.

Bradford approached Standish and said, "What do you think, Captain, could we use the island for defensive purposes?"

"It would prove effective all right, the savages would need a lot of canoes to get any kind of force ashore to attack us. I can see several problems with the island however. I think we would be very limited, if we wanted to expand our colony. I know we'll grow into a larger town and it wouldn't take very long with space for farming and other activities to take up the whole island."

"I feel the same way," Bradford said. "I just wanted to confirm it with you. I guess that the others also feel the same way." When the men on the expedition heard Bradford's and Standish's thoughts on Clarke's Island, they all agreed that it didn't quite fill the bill for settlement.

However, the men were in a happy mood. They knew that soon they would make the final determination as to where they would live. It had been a long time since they had left their uneventful lives in London and Leyden. Now they were in a position of self-governing. John Carver was their Governor and they had picked him. He would be their leader, but he could be voted out if he wasn't fulfilling his obligation. They felt proud of their new role and didn't truly realize they had been granted freedom. The people themselves would decide what would happen in the future.

They returned to the *Mayflower* and gathered the entire group of passengers to discuss the situation with them. They outlined the features of the various areas they had explored and stressed the fact that the best spot they had found was right in front of them. It had good soil, fresh water, woods, fruit and pleasant surroundings. Overall, it was the best area they could find without spending days or weeks exploring the coast and ending up with the same selection.

They finally agreed Plimoth would be their new home.

The next day all the male passengers and a few young ladies readied themselves to leave the *Mayflower* to see the land they would in all likelihood live on for the rest of their lives. They bundled up for the cold and excitedly climbed down a rope ladder to get into the shallop. On the way to shore the young people were in the bow of the shallop laughing and jabbering away. When they were ready to debark from the shallop, one of them, a sprightly lass of fifteen, declared, "I'll be the first one to land because I'm in the front of the boat." They finally bumped to a halt against a large rock. So, Mary Chilton scrambled to be first and she made it. In her small way she was to make history by being first to land on Plymouth Rock.

The Pilgrims explored the land for several miles in all

directions and made a decision to establish their new colony on high ground beside a brook filled with fish and was near the harbor. It was behind the large rock on which the Pilgrims used on their departure from the *Mayflower*.

Bradford said to Governor Carver, "John don't you think we should use these old cornfields? I think they've been abandoned for some time."

"Oh, of course William, it would seem such a waste not to; the soil looks like it is rich and in good shape."

"I can't imagine our people becoming farmers again this spring. Most of them had some farming experience in England, but their lives in Holland were altered and changed. We became a group of Woolcombers, Fusian makers and various other industrial workers. We lost our independence. We were risk-takers being farmers, where we had weather and droughts that guided our paths." Bradford said.

"We planted flowers," Carver said. "I think every family had flower boxes and gardens in Holland."

"Yes," Bradford replied. "It seems to be an English trait, growing flowers. I know the settlers will have to be very serious about putting their hearts into farming if we are to survive."

Winslow asked, "I wonder what could have happened to all the shelters for the Indian tribe that must have lived here...where did the Indians go?"

Most of the women stayed on the *Mayflower*; among them, naturally, was Mary Allerton, now about ready to deliver her fourth child. She said to Isaac, "I fear for the life of our baby, I haven't felt any movement lately."

Isaac replied, "I'm sure our baby will be fine. Mary Brewster will help you when you're ready and you will have help from the other women too."

Little Mary worried about her mother's welfare and

when her mother was asleep she asked Isaac, "Father, do you really think mother will be all right? She seems very weak."

"Don't worry little one. Your mother is healthy and soon you'll have a little brother or sister."

Isaac tried to appear cheerful and optimistic in front of his family, but he hid his true feelings very well. He was worried about his wife's announcing that there was no movement of her child and her very appearance...pale and drawn...as little Mary had observed, disturbed him.

Meanwhile, life was still going on around them. Twenty men volunteered to build temporary shelters and they left the ship with saws, axes and shovels. They picked an area which they felt would be a natural shelter from the wind. Soon there was the sound of chopping and sawing filling the air while a few armed men with muskets kept an eye out for Indians.

They intended to stay overnight, figuring the rest of the men would come ashore in the morning to help. Suddenly, a fierce storm arose, thoroughly soaking the Pilgrims; they hadn't a chance of finishing any of the shelters, which consisted of branches and turf. The rain turned to sleet, mixed with snow. They spent the cold winter night huddled together and trying to catch the body heat of each other.

Meanwhile, at the height of the gale, while the ship tossed about and tugged at its anchor. Mary Allerton delivered a stillborn baby. Mary was weak and drawn, she seemed to be at the end of her rope. She wanted to live for her husband and family and despite her condition she resolved to hang on.

Some of the men who were on the *Mayflower* tried to get the shallop ashore with some food for the volunteers, but conditions were so miserable and unsafe that it was impossible to maneuver the small vessel. They were unable to beach the shallop until noon of the next day. They divided the food among them and it was wolfed down by the hungry men who were still shivering from the cold.

They were unable to get the shallop off the beach for the next two days because of the weather. Hungry and weary, they had gone without real rest for several days. To add to their misery they were still chilled to the bone and unable to make a fire with the wet wood. The situation was not helped when an alarm was given that there were Indians in the area but the danger did not materialize.

They survived the night and the next morning they set off in the shallop to return to the *Mayflower*. The Pilgrims were warmly greeted by the other passengers who feared that some of them had been lost.

On December 25th all the able-bodied men went ashore to chop trees, saw timber, cut planks...no one rested that day. They laid the foundation of a Common House which was about twenty by twenty feet, this was to be their meeting house.

Nearby they erected small huts, mere windbreakers; however, they would provide a little protection from the elements and they could build a small fire inside each of them.

A small group stayed behind while the rest went back to the *Mayflower*, which was safely anchored about a mile and a half offshore. The returning Pilgrims, after having eaten, were given beer by Captain Jones who, unlike the Pilgrims, celebrated Christmas.

On shore, the "honor guard" had undergone a night of extreme discomfort with the high winds and heavy snow but at least this time they had the small shelters that provided some relief from the unbearable weather. The Pilgrims had a good supply of firewood and that helped to ease some of their problems. The weather seemed to be of the norm, week after week at noon it rained, changing to sleet and then snow during the afternoon and night.

The weather was a severe setback to the Pilgrims but undaunted they continued to lay out the town with ropes and stakes allocating house lots. Each lot was proportioned to the size of the household. The title for the home was only of a temporary nature, it didn't convey permanent possession. When the plots were divided, the Pilgrims drew lots to see who would occupy them. There was no favoritism here, or greed. When they were laying out the house lots, Standish said, "I think I should have my house lot next to Fort Hill. I'll be next to the platform where we will position the cannons. I can get to them in a hurry if necessary."

During all this activity of building, two of the Pilgrims, Peter Brown and John Goodman, decided they would go into the woods to find thatch for the roof of the Common House. They went in, despite the repeated sightings of Indian fires in the distance. Armed with sickles and a couple of dogs they set off. Some say they were more interested in bagging a deer. They wandered around all afternoon in a drizzle that soaked them to the skin. Feeling hunger pangs and totally exhausted, they laid down under some pine trees on the frozen ground to rest.Dozing off, they were suddenly awakened by a noise they heard off in the distance. Listening carefully...waiting...they heard the sound again, louder this time, it was definitely "Lyons" roaring.

The men at first, were paralyzed with fear. They summoned courage and leaped to their feet and madly dashed to a large nearby tree. They intended to climb it if the sound came closer. The dogs wanted to go after the "Lyons" but they were held at bay by their owners. In a short time the howling stopped. The next day after wandering aimlessly in the snow, they finally got their bearings and just before dark, stumbled into the area where anxious Pilgrims were waiting for them. The men were a sorry sight to behold; tired to the point of exhaustion, wet and having frostbitten feet, they were ravenously hungry.

The Pilgrims had feared the two men had been lost to the Indians, because Governor Carver had organized a search party and had spent hours looking for them. They found no trace of the two men other than their footprints crisscrossed in the snow, which were no help to the searchers.

A few days later, Goodman once again set off to test his lame feet, with his spaniel in tow. They had gone a short distance, at a slow pace, when suddenly his "Lyons" were in front of him in the shape of wolves. They tried to attack the spaniel but Goodman picked up a stick and tossed it at them, hitting one of the wolves. They ran off but later came back and circled him, much closer this time and "grinned" at Goodman. Again he picked up a club-like stick and held it at ready in case the wolves were to attack. Still "grinning" the wolves sat on their haunches, until tiring of their arrogant harassing, they finally loped away, deep into the woods. Unfortunately, John Goodman passed away soon after this episode, as a result of his prior exposure to the severe weather. He joined the ranks of the increasing death toll that was growing out of proportion.

The fatality list during the first year was growing daily, it had been a little more than two months since the passing of William Butten—Deacon Fuller's servant. He was joined in death by Dorothy Bradford, James Chilton, Richard Bitterridge, Jasper More—Carver's servant, John Langemore—Martin's servant, Edward Thompson, Ellen More and Elias Story—both Winslow's servants and now John Goodman and Solomon Martin.

The epidemic was now full blown among the Pilgrims and *Mayflower*.crew. They were afflicted with scurvy, pneumonia, tuberculosis and other diseases running rampant.

The Common House had been completed and was being used for the treatment of the more seriously ill, but the majority of the sick were still on the *Mayflower*. There were only seven Pilgrims well enough to care for the stricken. Among these were Elder Brewster and Captain Myles Standish, who weren't effected by any disease. The illness was brought on by adverse conditions on the *Mayflower* along with the severe weather they were now enduring.

The seven sacrificed their health getting the patients wood, building fires, preparing food, taking care of their beds, washing filthy clothes, dressing and undressing them. In addition some of the Pilgrims also administered to the crew; there were the boatswain, gunner, three quartermasters, the cook and others in the crew that soon died. Among the crew which they helped was one who possessed a vile tongue and had verbally abused the Pilgrims. He had trouble understanding the concern for his health by the Pilgrims.

He said, "The fellow crewmen who we associated and drank with, deserted us because they were thinking of their own well-being. They figured, if we die, we die. They wouldn't come to our quarters to aid us because they didn't want to become contaminated. You are truly unselfish Christians. I hope you will forgive me for the past abuse...I was a fool!" It was not long after this that he too died.

The Pilgrims feared the Indians would realize that many of the Pilgrims were dying and if the truth was known they wouldn't hesitate to launch an attack against them. The dead were buried secretly in the middle of the night on Cole's Hill and all traces of burial were removed. In January, Rose the wife of Myles Standish died along with five others.

A freak accident added to their concern and misery. A spark ignited the thatched roof of the Common House and the flames grew and spread until the whole roof was ablaze. Seeing the flames from the *Mayflower*, a large group sailed in the shallop toward the shore to investigate. They all suspected an Indian attack was responsible for the fire and the Pilgrims must surely be at risk.

Upon reaching shore they were relieved to find there were no Indians around. In the Common House, beneath this flaming inferno, the weak, sick men who were lying in bunks, side by side, jumped up to remove barrels of gun powder and their muskets to safety, away from the building. Although they were deathly ill, the swift action of William Bradford and Governor John Carver saved the building and lives. However, they lost almost all their clothes.

They had covered their heads with blankets to prevent the falling debris from burning them. They continued to battle the blaze with buckets of water. The heavy timber they had used in making rafters held up and prevented the building from collapsing.

The sick who had helped the others fight the fires were falling from exhaustion. The firefighters were tired but they helped the ill get away from the fire. Many of the sick had passed out and were carried away from the danger.

The wind was increasing in velocity and was blowing burning embers from the fire and starting smaller fires nearby. This kept some of the men busy extinguishing the smaller fires so they wouldn't get out of control.

The main source of the trouble was the Common House. The heat from the fire kept the men a great distance from the burning structure and the "bucket brigade" were tossing only a bucket of water each time. They had foresight in bringing the buckets from the *Mayflower* but even the so called "well people" had suffered bouts of high fever and were not fully recovered when they were called upon to exert such a demand on their limited energy.

Later, when the fire in the Common House and other small fires were extinguished, the Pilgrims rigged up a temporary roof to protect the sick from the elements. The sick that were originally in the structure were gathered and were able to return. The area in the Common House where the men had slept was cleared of debris and soon bunks were impoverished so the men could rest. In spite of the recent smoldering beams and the strong smell of burnt wood the men felt a sense of relief that they had saved the building.

Had they lost the Common House it is doubtful if they could have gone on with their plans for their new home.

CHAPTER 10

The beginning.......

10,000 B.C.

By way of background, just what was Cape Cod like when the Pilgrims decided to build their homes and spend their lives in the development of the land?

It was an idyllic setting, a painter's or poet's paradise, long white sandy beaches, rolling breakers sweeping into a picturesque shore. Mile after mile of virgin forests growing down to the shore. The forests consisted of oak, pine, juniper, sassafras and other trees. There were also walnut bearing trees, colorful birch trees, the swamps pushed large, hardy cedar trees toward the heavens. The nearby hills had red maples growing in abundance.

They would be blessed with food, too. There were countless deer and other game in the forests including wild turkey. The sea would help supply their needs too.

How had nature prepared this setting for the Pilgrims?

Going back only ten thousand years, which is quite

recent in terms of continued formation, we find that Cape Cod is a relic of the great glacial epoch which ended at that time. The Ice Age ended one million years ago and in its wake it spread sand, gravel, clay, boulders and stones. Large islands were formed; among these were Martha's Vineyard and Nantucket. They were made by thick glaciers which when melted dropped a huge load of debris. When the ice retreated it was replaced by more glaciers which thousands of years later slowly melted leaving more debris behind, mostly clay and boulders. It formed the numerous circular ponds which occurred when the soil cover melted.

The debris, consisting of large boulders and rocks, were carried south from as far away as Maine and beyond.

Geologists claim that the Plymouth Rock once found in the highlands of Labrador, traveled through Canada and Maine to its final resting place at Plymouth. When the glacier melted in the northern hemisphere, the water level in the Cape Cod area rose and left a ridge of deposits in a rugged outline. Gradual erosion of the sandy shores by the water's action, gradually formed the graceful arm of the Cape. The shore's drifting sand was carried by the wind and the ocean's current made the thin curved hook to form the harbor for Plymouth.

CHAPTER 11

Plymouth, Cape Cod

1621

The Indians had done nothing threatening; nevertheless, the Pilgrims were a little leery about their antics. They sulked about and behaved in a most suspicious manner. When the Pilgrims approached, the Indians then ran off. It gave them an eerie feeling of impending danger. Were the Indians aware of the declining ranks of the Pilgrims? Many were dying almost daily now and the rest could not put up much of a fight if they were attacked. It was a time for prayer and vigilance and the Pilgrims had nothing but bluff to influence the savages who could at any time overwhelm them.

During this time, tragedy overtook the Allertons. One day Isaac and his children were trying to care for Mary Allerton, who was still on the *Mayflower* and by this time failing miserably. She had a high fever and was stricken by a disease which was sapping her last bit of strength. She had never recovered from the debilitating reaction of her failed pregnancy, this disease added to her problems.

She spoke to Isaac in an almost inaudible whisper, "Isaac, I don't think I'll make it this time. I have always loved you and the children and I know you'll always look after them. Please find a caring woman and marry her. The children will have a woman to care for them. I want you and the children to be happy and fulfill your dreams."

Isaac said, "Mary you know we all love you. You have an inner strength that you can rely on. You will get over it, you'll see."

Mary looked at Isaac fondly and said, "Please promise me you will marry again and love somebody that will take care of our children."

"Yes Mary, I'll do that, but you'll recover from this."

Mary replied, "Good...will you get the children so that I can see them?"

Isaac gathered the children around their mother and she held the hand of each in turn. "I'm going to join the Lord soon and I won't suffer anymore. Please help your father and ...the rest was inaudible...and then silence, she had turned her head, her eyes staring straight ahead.

"Mother...Mother", Little Mary urgently wanted her to continue. "Father, why doesn't mother speak?"

Isaac said, "Children, your mother has left us. You children will have to be strong, like your mother was. I'll be here to look after you." He covered Mary's face with a blanket and led the children away. She would join the others at Cole's Hill when it got dark. It was February 25, 1621.

The deaths of the Pilgrims from disease; the frequent appearance and the sudden disappearance of the Indians, went on for weeks on end. They were wearing the Pilgrim's nerves to a frazzle. The Pilgrims went on in their daily work in spite of the problems; building homes on the days it did not rain or snow, trying to fish and catch game so they wouldn't starve to death.

However, there were some lighter moments. The curious, and highly inquisitive eight-year-old youngster, Francis Billington, who almost blew up the *Mayflower*, had climbed to the top of a large tree and sighted what he thought was another great sea. He yelled at the top of his voice, then he scurried down the tree and ran, shouting, "I found a sea... I found a sea...it's over there!"

The Pilgrims soon gathered around him questioning him about what he had seen.

He explained, "There is a big sea. There!" He pointed out the direction to them.

After investigating, they found a body of water, it was in reality a large lake, which they named "Billington's Sea" in his honor...it still goes by that name.

One day, Indians had ventured near the plantation. There were twelve painted savages sneaking up and an alarm was given. The Pilgrims were working in the woods clearing trees and shrubs, they dropped their tools, grabbed their muskets and assembled at the unfinished plantation. After a period of time elapsed and there was no sign of an attack, Captain Myles Standish and Francis Cooke set off to reconnoiter to see if the savages were still around. They didn't find any but were astonished to find their tools missing.

The Pilgrims now sensed an urgent need to become more organized as a fighting unit. They named Standish "Captain General or Commander in Chief." His was the ultimate word on defense of the plantation. Each man would have a musket, helmet, breast plate and sword at his home and be ready to assemble at an assigned position in case of an alarm.

They had close order drill which at first embarrassed their Commander in Chief with their awkwardness, but they gradually improved...this was not their strong point.

From the *Mayflower*, the Pilgrims brought a large cannon which was in three pieces and when it was put together it weighed 1,200 pounds. The men using ropes and pulleys struggled to get the cannon up to Fort Hill and finally placed it between two smaller cannon on a platform. The larger cannon had a limited range of 360 yards, far less than a quarter of a mile. The smaller cannon were deadly up to range of fifty paces. They were also deadly to the Pilgrims who risked their lives from an explosion when fired.

Due to illness, the Pilgrims wasted a month in building up their defenses. They were holding a meeting one day to get it back on track, when suddenly Governor Carver jumped up and shouted, "Who is this coming? It looks like an Indian!" It was indeed an Indian. Tall, powerfully built and armed with a bow and arrows, he strolled from the woods, crossed the clearing and headed straight toward the Common House where they were discussing the training of the militia.

"Stop him...see what he wants," yelled Carver.

The Indian was halted at the door. Undaunted, he shrugged off the Pilgrims who stopped him and said in perfect English, "Welcome, Englishmen!"

The Pilgrims looked at him in amazement and blank silence. He asked for beer. Having none at the time, they offered him "strong water" or gin, a biscuit, cheese, pudding and duck. He ate and drank the offering saying, "It's very good!"

They covered him with a bright red coat to cover his nakedness, he wore only a leather loin cloth, much to the embarrassment of the Pilgrims. He said, "My name is Samoset and I came from Pemaquid which is far north in Maine. I came to this area a few months ago to visit."

The Pilgrims were dumbfounded and impressed with the vocabulary of Samoset. He had picked up English from the visiting fishermen from England, when he helped them on their ships. He said, "The land you are now on, which you call Plimoth, is really known as Patuxet, which means Little Bay."

The Pilgrims told Samoset how they had taken the corn that was buried at Corn Hill and they would pay him and were sorry if he became upset at their admission. He said he would take a small payment to ease their conscience but he was happy if it helped them survive.

"Why don't you ask him about the cornfields?" asked Bradford, who had attended the meeting although feeling the effects of his illness.

Carver laughed and said, "Why don't you speak to him yourself, William. I'm sure that your English is up to it."

Bradford said to Samoset, "I guess you know what I'm going to ask."

Samoset said, "Yes, it was a great tragedy that fell the tribe at Patuxet in 1617. Once they were as numerous as the trees in the forest, then a plague hit them and just about wiped them out."

Many other tribes in the area were decimated by the plague which was probably smallpox. The Pilgrims wouldn't have had a chance to survive if the sickness hadn't reduced the tribes to a manageable size.

Samoset said, "I have a friend of mine who is the strongest chief in the area, he is known as "Yellow Feather" or Massasoit and another friend called Squanto who has been in England and speaks English better than me."

Massasoit was the sachem (chief) of the largest tribe in an area later to be known as Rhode Island and his power extended into Cape Cod and as far north as the Merrimack River. He was also the Big Chief of the tribe which attacked the Pilgrims at "First Encounter Beach".

Samoset finally left that night, after much persuasion to stay by the Pilgrims. He promised he would return soon with things to trade. Good as his word, he returned the next day with five braves dressed in deerskin and bearing beaver skins. The Pilgrims were pleased with the furs but they couldn't touch them or barter with the Indians because it was the Sabbath. "We can't trade now but come back later and bring your beaver skins and other things you want to trade," they said.

However, the Indians stayed overnight; the Pilgrims gave them gin and tried to make them welcome. They danced around in a frivolous manner much to the dismay of the Pilgrims who frowned on dancing, especially on the Sabbath.

They were amazed when the Indians brought back the tools which were stolen from the Pilgrims.

Samoset spoke to his friend Squanto (Tisquantrum) and convinced him to visit Plimoth Plantation. He came with him one day and Samoset introduced Squanto to the leaders of the colony. He was very impressive and well liked by Governnor Carver, Bradford and the others. He volunteered to help them raise crops, hunt and fish. Squanto told the Pilgrims an interesting story which involved his experiences with the English. It seems that Captain George Weymouth exploring in 1605 for the English Plymouth Company took Squanto to England. Squanto returned in 1614 to become an interpreter to Captain John Smith. Eventually, Captain Smith returned to England, leaving Squanto behind.

Along came a fishing boat, commanded by Captain John Hunt who filled his ship with cod and before he departed for England, lured twenty healthy Indian braves, including Squanto, aboard. Overpowering the Indians, he took them to Spain and sold them on the slave market for 20 pounds each. Some escaped and made their way to North Africa. Squanto, with several others, were taken by an order of friars and were converted to Christianity. Squanto made his way to England and went to work for an English gentleman. He became homesick for New England and he met Captain Dermer who said he would take him to Cape Cod after he delivered some cargo to Newfoundland.

Squanto returned to Pauxet (Plymouth) in 1619 to find it deserted. His relatives were all dead, their skeletal remains lay throughout the area, bleached white by the sun and the elements. They all died horribly of a plague which was no respecter of age or sex. Their cornfields remained, but now he was the last of his tribe. Captain Dermer was unfortunately killed by arrows while he was at Martha's Vineyard (Capawack), so Squanto lost his only friend.

Squanto, being well received by the Pilgrims, visited Massasoit and told him about the nature of the people and the friendly reception they gave him. He said they were very friendly and honest and he would try to help them any way he could. He suggested that Massasoit should visit the Pilgrims because he knew they wanted to be friends with all the Indians.

One day there was turmoil at the Plimoth Plantation; Mary Allerton came out of her house and saw men running around and getting into their battle gear. "What's happening?" She said. The men ignored her and went on assembling the troops.

Bartholomew came out of the house and said, "Why are the men getting their muskets ready, do you know why they're doing this Mary? ...I think we better get into the house... quick...look up there!" They ran into the house and Bartholomew barricaded the door, piling up furniture and pushed a barrel against it.

On a hill overlooking the Plantation was the awesome sight of the huge Massasoit and sixty braves in full war paint lined up. They stood motionless staring at the Pilgrims, who in turn stared back. This went on for several minutes. Then, out of the ranks, spoke Edward Winslow, "I'd like your permission to talk to them to see what they have in mind." Captain Myles Standish replied, "I don't think it will do any harm, but you better go unarmed. They outnumber us three to one."

Winslow removed his breastplate and helmet, tossed them aside along with his sword and placed his musket on the ground in full view of Massasoit. He started walking up the hill, saying to himself, "This could be my last time on earth, maybe they will understand that we have no ill will against them. We want to live with them as neighbors and have peace." When he reached Massasoit he gave the Indians a sign of peace and showed them he was unarmed. He said the Pilgrims wanted peace but they would fight if the Indians attacked them. He pointed at the cannons and said, "They have a mighty roar but a stronger bite...we do not want to use them, we came to this land in friendship and peace."

Massasoit, in sign language and broken English said, "We also come in peace. My friends Samoset and Squanto told me about you Pilgrims and said that I should meet you."

Winslow breathed a sigh of relief and said, "Welcome to Plimoth Plantation." He motioned to Massasoit that he would explain the situation with Governor Carver and the Commander in Chief and would return. He retreated down the hill and told Carver and Standish about his friendly conversation with Massasoit. They agreed that they would welcome him and his men if they really came in peace. "We have to take a chance, they have us outnumbered and who knows how many might be behind them over the hill." Standish said. "Before you go back, here are some gifts which might help to show that we want to be friends."

Winslow went back up the hill and smiled at Massasoit, he motioned that the Commander in Chief and the Governor and the people wanted to meet him and his braves.

Samoset was with Massasoit when he invited the leaders of the Plantation to come up the hill to have a pow-wow and talk peace. Winslow said, "I have gifts for you from the great Governor and the Commander in Chief, they want to welcome you to our home."

He gave the gifts to Massasoit and his warrior brother, Quadequina, and to some of the braves. He said, "King James and Governor Carver honor you as a friend and the King used words of peace and love for you, as did Governor Carver."

Winslow volunteered to act as a hostage of Quadequina while Massasoit went to the Plantation to visit and hold their pow-wow. Massasoit and Samoset nodded approval and walked down the hill followed by twenty braves who had left their bow and arrows behind.

One of the first things that Massasoit said, after he convinced the leaders that he sought peace with the Pilgrims, was to tell Captain Standish that Winslow was a brave man to come up the hill unarmed and he wondered if all the white men were that brave. Never one to miss an opportunity, Standish pondered a minute, sensing that he couldn't underestimate their strength, assured Massasoit that all the white men were indeed brave and showed superhuman courage in battle.

The Pilgrims had known from Samoset's first visit that the information he provided about the location, size and morale of the various tribes would prove invaluable to them. They knew their salvation would hinge on having Massasoit as a friend because he could be a deadly enemy.

The last of the passengers had left the *Mayflower* on March 21st, 1621. All the forces they could muster were now at Plimoth Plantation and they were a sorry sight to behold especially by the Indians.

In contrast, the Indians made an impressive sight when they entered the colony; powerfully built, they were much taller than the Pilgrims. Massasoit was almost two feet taller than Myles Standish, who tried not to look intimidated by the sachem, (chief) who marched through the plantation to his left. The braves followed their leader looking straight ahead and painted in gaudy colors. They were followed by the Pilgrims who were decked out in their armament.

The procession walked down the main street of the town which was now lined with the curious women and children who had left the safety of their homes to witness the arrival of the Indians.

Mary, holding her brother's hand for security said, "Bartholomew, do you think they'll hurt us?"

He replied, "They better not, we have muskets and stuff and Captain Standish wouldn't let them."

Mary said, "But they look like bad men, why do they wear paint on them?"

Bartholomew said, 'They want to look evil so we'll be afraid of them. But we're not afraid ..are we?"

Mary looked at her brother and said, "Yes!"

The Indians and the Pilgrims leaders went to a house that was almost completed and made arrangements to treat the sachem royally. A loud ruffle of drums was heard accompanied by brass horns. Governor Carver came to the house with a squad of soldiers to greet Massasoit. They kissed each others hands and then Carver toasted Massasoit with a glass of gin; whereby Massasoit grabbed a large pot containing the liquor and attempted to drain it He broke into a sweat and attempted to appear nonplused. The main purpose of the meeting was to make sure that the sachem liked the Pilgrims and realized that although the Pilgrims were brave and would fight, they wanted to be friends and they would make peace that would last forever between them.

They came to an agreement that if one Indian wronged a Pilgrim, the Indian would be held responsible to the white man and would have to report to Plimoth authorities for trial. It worked the same way with the Pilgrims. If they were guilty of a crime against an Indian they would go to Sowans (Sowans was the tribal headquarters for Massasoit, some say it was in Warren, others say Barrington, Rhode Island.)

Muskets and bow and arrows were to be left outside their respective towns when they visited. They also initiated a mutual defense pact stating if they were attacked by an unfriendly force the other party would come to their aid.

Massasoit and Carver signed the document and when the sachem departed, they kissed hands again.

For several days the Indians pushed their friendliness to the limit. It seemed that every time the Pilgrims turned around they found Indians that wanted food, drink and entertainment. In spite of the friendly feeling with the Indians, the Pilgrims were still skeptical and hoped that being sincerely interested in peace, the Indians would not take up arms against the Pilgrims. They were worried that the Indians would see fewer Pilgrims around due to the deaths.

During the month of February there were other deaths beside Mary Allerton. William White, William Mullins and fourteen others died. On March 24th, Elizabeth Winslow also died. She was the wife of Edward, the diplomat, who so heroically encountered Massasoit.

Each death was a blow to the remaining Pilgrims. The loss of so many left a void in the lives of relatives and friends in the colony. Unfortunately, there were many others that were sick from diseases and close to death. Many Pilgrims wondered if they would all eventually die from the diseases and the general harshness of the environment.

They also thought of the friendship with the Indians.

Would it work out? Would it be that they would wake up to see hundreds of painted savages surrounding them, shooting flaming arrows into their midst?

The optomists felt that everything would work out satisfactorily for them. Some were so ill the future really didn't matter.

Every day there were more deaths... every night there was the silent funeral procession to Cole's Hill to bring the dead to their final resting places. They hoped the Indians weren't watching too closely and keeping tally of those Pilgrims now absent.

CHAPTER 12

Plymouth, Cape Cod

1621

The new year (March 25th by the calendar used by England) brought another election which unanimously re-elected Carver as Governor. Meanwhile, the Indians were dropping in on the Pilgrims at all hours during the day and night trying to get food and drink and bringing their wives and children. This got to be a good thing for the Indians but the Pilgrims were a little distressed because their food supply was being depleted. They felt they would have to put a halt to this soon. The Pilgrims selected two envoys who would travel to Sowans; Stephen Hopkins and Edward Winslow, who had established himself as a budding diplomat for the colony.

Their mission was to convince Massasoit that the Indians were coming to the plantation in droves, cutting into their food supply. Although they treated the Indians as friends, they were abusing the privilege. They were also concerned about finding a shortcut to Sowans in case of emergency; it was about fifty miles away, in Rhode Island.

They had an Indian guide and traveled by day and night overland through swamps and dense woods. To supplement their food from the plantation, they ate small game and various shrubs, which proved to be tasty and hearty. The guide was friendly and could speak only a few words of English but he communicated by hand signs which the Pilgrims understood.

After they had traveled many miles their guide said that they were almost there. They rounded a bend near a river and they saw a small village with round, neat huts, smoke filled the air. The squaws were cooking meals over small fires in front of the huts. They seemed happy and were joking with their neighbors. They turned away from their work to look at the Englishmen and the Indian who was walking with them. The guide greeted the Indians and in turn they smiled at the Englishmen. The women motioned to the food and said they could have some. The Englishmen were a little reluctant to eat, because they didn't know what was in the pot. They heard wild stories about the Indians and their choice of food; this was one time they didn't want to try "pot luck".

They soon found that Massasoit was away from the village but would return the following day. They would spend the day, resting and eating their meager supply of food which they had brought from the plantation. The Indians tried to amuse them by having running races, and other games in which they were very proficient. They showed them their archery and other skills which they had developed in the wild. Hopkins and Winslow took note of their skill with their bow and arrows and hoped that someday they would not have to face them in battle.

The next day about noon, Massasoit came into the village with several of his braves. He was welcomed by Hopkins and Winslow who fired off their muskets in salute. Massasoit seemed to ignore the bargain with the Pilgrims to leave all muskets outside the village when arriving. But Massasoit was impressed with the white man's thunder stick. Squanto came about an hour later and greeted Massasoit and Hopkins and Winslow. Now they had an excellent interpreter who could speak to Massasoit without hand signs.

They had a gift for Massasoit...a red coach coat, similar to the one they had covered Samoset with when he first arrived at Plimoth Plantation. They improved the design of the coat for Massasoit by adding a piece of lace to dress it up. He accepted the coat and paraded up and down in his new finery. Winslow glibly told him, "It's a small token of our love for you."

Then Winslow explained diplomatically about the Indians visiting Plymouth and eating the food. He said, "We don't know how our crops will be this year and we could be in peril unless we are very careful about how we distribute our food."

The chief agreed with Winslow saying, "My braves will not bother you again. You Pilgrims have been very friendly with us and we do not want to lose you as friends."

The Pilgrims hadn't eaten much that day and they hoped the sachem would feed them but they went to bed without food. They shared the bed with Massasoit and his squaw, joined in the middle of the night by two braves who laid on top of them, in effect they were using them as a mattress.

The next day Massasoit caught a couple of bass which were put into a pot, cooked and shared with forty hungry braves. Winslow and Hopkins who shared the "feast" were hungrier than before. With the restless night spent with lack of sleep, they were eager to go home, get some food and much needed rest.

Although the sachem tried to get them to stay, they convinced him that they must return to the plantation. They felt that in spite of the lack of food and rest, they couldn't stand another night with the braves singing themselves to sleep; it was the worst singing they ever heard.

Before they left for Plimoth, Winslow asked Massasoit if he knew a shortcut for their trip. Massasoit drew a map and it seemed that it would shorten their trip. Massasoit said, "If you leave Squanto behind, I will round up beaver skins, corn and other things that you Pilgrims need and this will make up for my braves rude behavior at the plantation."

Winslow figured that this was a gift from heaven, maybe they could solve some of the problems with the Merchant Adventurers by trading with Massasoit. He could supply much needed food and other items at a fraction of the cost.

Winslow and Hopkins with their original guide, used the map drawn by Massasoit and made their way back to Plimoth.

The Pilgrims turned out and gave the men a warm welcome. The returning men were only interested in eating and getting some needed rest, they were ravenously hungry and exhausted.

In the meantime, the *Mayflower* finally left Plimoth on April 5th to return to England. Captain Jones had stayed well beyond his expected time for departure. Partially because his crew had suffered severely with illness and many had died a sudden death. The Pilgrims had pleaded that he should stay until they could regain some of their strength after suffering many diseases.

Captain Jones heeded their desperate call for help and remained, proving he was compassionate and caring. Most of the crew felt that they had been away from home too long.

It was now time to plant, "The leaves of the white oak were as large as a mouse's ear." This was their yardstick for developing a New England green thumb.

Squanto explained about the use of herring as a fertilizer. He said three herring were to be placed under the soil in spokewise fashion under each hillock.

They would prepare twenty acres of land, by hand, to plant their corn crop. They toiled day in and day out from dawn to dusk. They prepared 9,600 hillocks, and placed the fertilizer in each. This involved collecting 28,800 or roughly 40 tons of herring by using baskets and carrying them to the fields.

Squanto showed them how to make a weir in the stream to catch herring. When it was finished they were able to trap up to 10,000 herring in a single tide.

When the corn seeds were planted they required watchful eyes twenty-four hours a day to protect the crop. The crows would come by day to get the seeds and the wolves came at night to dig up the herring. When the corn plants started to develop, each hillock was "earthed up" and they removed the smallest stalks so the largest could survive.

Squanto was a godsend to the Pilgrims. Without him they surely would have starved. He acted as adviser telling them where they could find supplies and the price they should pay for them. He acted as an interpreter to the Indians and guide for the many trading expeditions. He lived closely with the Pilgrims and they honored him for his service.

The Pilgrims were on their own now and about a week later tragedy struck again in the death of Governor Carver. While working in the fields on an exceptionally hot day in April, he complained of head pains and suddenly he went into a coma. Two days later he was dead, at age fifty-five. He was mourned by all and remembered for his fair and equal treatment with all the Pilgrims. They also remembered his service to them while he was in London with Robert Cushman. Together they had labored for years to organize and finance the trip to the New World. Now he was gone. He was survived by the elders who still commanded great respect for their wisdom and dedication to their cause. They were giants in their era, they were; Brewster who was in Plymouth, Cushman still handling the Pilgrims business in England and Reverend Robinson who was still living in Leyden. He had planned to be with the Pilgrims and hopefully could make the trip soon.

By this time the original contingent of one hundred and two passengers had dwindled considerably to about half of their original group.

Many of the survivors were recovering from the plague. Allerton was speaking with William Brewster one day and he said, "I've made a list of those who died since we came to the New World. It's very depressing. You knew them all, but when you see them listed, it really hits home. Here is the list:

Mary Allerton
Dorothy Bradford
John Carver
John Crackston

Moses Fletcher
John Goodman
Degory Priest
Thomas Rogers
Edward Tilley
Anne Tilley
Mrs. John (Eliz.) Tilley
Thomas Tinker/wife son
John Turner/two sons
William White
Elizabeth (Barker) Winslow
Richard Bitteridge

Edmund Margeson
Christopher Martin
Mrs. Christopher Martin
Solomon Prower
  (Martin's servant)
William Mullins
Alice Mullins
Joseph Mullins
John Rigdale
Alice Rigdale
Rose Standish
Thomas Williams
John Allerton
Thomas English
John Hook (My servant)
Roger Wilder
Jasper Mores
  (Carver's servant)

James Chilton   William Butten (Fuller's servant)
Mary Chilton   Richard Mores, brother
       (Brewster s servant)
Richard Clarke   John Langemore
       (Martin's servant)
Sarah Eaton   Robert Carter (Mullins servant)
Edward Fuller   Edward Holbeck (White's servant)
Richard Gardiner   Edward Thompson
       (White's servant)
Ellen More (Winslow's servant)

Brewster said, "It seems unbelievable that they are all gone—they had such devotion—such dreams."

*   *   *

William Bradford, who was one of those still recovering was given an unusual honor. He was elected Governor to replace John Carver. Bradford was only thirty-three years old but he was acclaimed for his leadership qualities. He was joined by Isaac Allerton who had been elected Assistant Governor at thirty-four, being recognized as a shrewd, sharp trader.

Five or six weeks after Governor Carver's sudden death, another tragedy followed. Mrs. Catherine Carver, the constant companion of John, who was mourned by all by his death joined him. The Pilgrims thought that she had died of a broken heart.

One day Mary Allerton came into her house, breathless, and excitedly said, "What do you think happened? I know something you don't!"

Remember and Bartholomew said in unison, "What happened now?"

Mary said, "Young John Billington is missing! They don't know where he is!"

Remember said, "Maybe he's hiding someplace...he's always up to something."

"No, I don't think he's hiding. His whole family is looking for him, he's been gone a long time. They don't know why he left."

Bartholomew, taking it all in, said, "Maybe he ran away from home. He said he'd like to explore someday. Let's go out and see what's doing."

There was a great deal of anxiety in the plantation when the Pilgrims discovered that seven-year-old John Billington, Junior, was missing. The whole populace turned out to find him, yelling his name and looking under and around the structures. He was nowhere in sight. This latest episode was typical of the Billingtons. They were an independent lot, having no respect for authority, they seemed to thrive on strife. However, John was young and lost and really couldn't be blamed for his upbringing.

A large force was sent out in all directions to find him. Was he kidnapped by the Indians...attacked by wolves? Had he just wandered off into the woods? Day after day the Pilgrims searched for him in all areas with no success. After a week or more they heard from Massasoit, who had good news for the colony. Young John had been found unharmed. He was twenty miles away at the Cape, safely being take care of by a friendly tribe. He had survived in the wilderness by eating berries and he was none the worse for his experience.

Young Billington s father and a group of other men went to the Cape to get him in the shallop. Stopping at Cummaquid they were told that he was further south but while there they were invited to eat by the friendly sachem, Iyanough.

After they had a quick meal they set off in their shallop accompanied by the sachem and two of his braves. They rode for awhile, the lone sail flapping lazily in the mild wind, taking them slowly to Indian territory.

When they reached the area where young Billington was staying, Squanto was sent ashore to get the chief of the tribe, Aspinet.

The Pilgrims were impressed when they saw Aspinet and his train of warriors following behind. His colorful headdress and deerskin robe set him apart. They came to the water's edge and a huge brave had John on his shoulders as he strolled into the bay toward the shallop. Young John had several strands of beads around his neck and a big grin on his face, unaware of the turmoil that he caused. He got into the boat and hugged his father who was smiling.

The Pilgrims had been overwhelmed at the friendly and peaceful manner of the Indians and the courtesy shown by the sachems. They hoped they could build on this incident and really have a peaceful future.

An Indian chief named Hobomok, who was an underling to Massasoit, came to Plimoth Plantation to live. Hobomok was a unique individual who had been trained since youth to be courageous and strong. He was given the title of "Pinese." To earn this title Hobomok was required to excel in many things; he had to be a chief, warrior, priest, statesman, and above all, an individual with profound wisdom. As one of Massasoit's top chiefs, he reported to Massasoit all of the happenings at the plantation so there soon became a rivalry with Squanto. Although this continued dispute was discouraged by the Pilgrims, it almost proved to be their undoing by almost losing Massasoit s friendship and a close call to the lopping off of Squanto's head.

Things were becoming routine, they had completed most of the houses and they were working on a huge wall, made of timber, surrounding the colony. They assumed it would be a strong defense against an Indian attack.

While this was going on, Squanto and Hobomok went

to an Indian village called Nemasket (later known as Middleborough Village) about fifteen miles westward, to spend a few days. Hobomok came back after one day, excited and related that Squanto had been stabbed and killed by a tribal chief called Corbitant. Hobomok said that he also would have been killed by Corbitant but he escaped and ran back to the colony. A false rumor soon spread through the plantation that the powerful Narragansett tribe had attacked Massasoit, captured him and Corbitant was a party to this treachery. The Pilgrims were upset by this news because they thought they would soon have to fight the Narragansetts.

In accordance with the peace pact that the Pilgrims had with Massasoit, it demanded action right away. A council was called and they agreed that Myles Standish along with a force of fourteen heavily armed men, would go to the village of Nemasket and raid the village at night and try to capture Corbitant and make him account for his actions.

They set out and finally reached Nemasket. Creeping into the village while the Indians slept, they surrounded Corbitant s hut. Using a prearranged signal, they fired their muskets and charged forward. Grabbing one of the braves, Hobomok demanded to see Corbitant.

The Indians were terror-stricken at the Pilgrims' sudden appearance in the hut and they were ordered to stand still. Trying to escape out a side door, three braves were wounded by the Pilgrims firing their muskets in the dark at them.

Standish assured the Indians they wouldn't harm the women and children nor the braves if they obeyed the command of the militia. They came to seek justice and avenge Squanto and to punish some of the Indians who had used defamatory insults against the Pilgrims.

They wanted to have Corbitant brought in front of them to explain his actions. The braves looked at each other and acted as though they didn't understand. Standish was told the sachem was not there but would return the following day.

Hobomok suspecting Squanto might still be alive, climbed up on the hut's roof and called for him. Soon Squanto came walking along followed by several braves carrying their favorite provisions as a peace offering to the Pilgrims. The Pilgrims were angry at Squanto and couldn't understand how Hobomok could have been so mistaken.

They were beginning to suspect that maybe this rivalry between the two belligerent Indians was getting out of hand. They would have been very angry with Corbitant if he had been in the village when they arrived. They rounded up all the Pilgrims along with Squanto and returned to Plimoth plantation. In no way were the Narragansetts involved with this situation.

They brought the wounded braves back to the plantation to nurse them back to health. Once treated, they returned to their village, none the worse for wear. Soon the word got around about the raid the Pilgrims made on Nemasket. As usual, after the event was over, the details were greatly exaggerated. The reaction to the raid was stunning, all of the nine sachems of the tribes on the Cape came to the plantation to make peace and say they were loyal subjects of King James. Corbitant also made peace, using Massasoit to influence the Pilgrims. No one ever said anything about the reaction the Narragansetts had, they only understood the Pilgrims were ready to fight them.

Now that events were starting to normalize and the planting had been completed, there was an occasion to celebrate the first wedding in Plimoth plantation. The widow of William White, Susana, who was the sister of Deacon Fuller, married Edward Winslow, a widower of just two months. They were married by Governor Bradford at a civil ceremony.

Hasty weddings became quite common because those that were left after the great sickness had fully recovered and were anxious to care for others. So it was with Myles Standish. After his wife Rose had died and a reasonable length of time had passed, he saw no reason not to marry again. He thought, "Why should I live alone?" He looked around the colony and Priscilla Mullins caught his eye. He had always admired Priscilla—but at a distance. He had always thought...mostly to himself...she's young, pretty and would make a wonderful wife!

Captain Myles Standish, by all standards, was tough, with a wrinkled brow, crows-feet at the corner of his eyes, a weather-beaten exterior and flaming red hair which now held streaks of grey. Contrast this with Priscilla's youth with fair skin and shiny brown hair—perhaps she wouldn't want to marry me, he mused.

He'd ask young, bashful John Alden to approach her for him, besides John owed him a favor.

John Alden met with Priscilla and extolled the virtues of Myles Standish. "Why don't you speak for yourself, John?"

John did!

In a civil ceremony they were the second couple married by Governor Bradford in 1622. (They had a long married life with nine children.)

Priscilla was the lone survivor in the Mullins family, after her father, William, her mother, Alice, and brother, Joseph, all died in early 1621 of various diseases. She had been taken in by Mary Brewster who comforted her as a daughter after she became an orphan.

*   *   *

Seeing that life would be more secure for them, the Pilgrims decided to explore further north to Shawmut (later

called Boston) in their shallop. On the way they passed islands which they named after Brewster and they discovered a
long peninsula near the southern part of a large harbor
which was named for Isaac Allerton called Point Allerton,
another spot was called Squantum.

On viewing the harbor, they were disappointed that
they had not explored further north before they selected
Plimoth to be their new home. It had many advantages not
found in Plimoth but Bradford philosophically noted God
had chosen Plimoth for them and probably this harbor would
be chosen for another purpose in the future.

When they were leaving the shores of the harbor, a
group of Massachusetts Indian women wearing beaver coats
followed them to the shallop. The Pilgrims showed them
some colorful trinkets they would swap the women for their
coats.

They eagerly stripped them off, grabbed for the trinkets, then tied branches around their naked bodies. The
Pilgrims then returned to Plimoth and told the others about
their adventures and the humorous barter for the beaver
coats that proved so profitable.

Now it was time to bring in the crops, the weather was
warm and the Pilgrims all gathered for the event. The corn
was unexpectedly abundant due to Squanto's help. The seeds
had been brought from England; wheat, barley and peas
which they had also planted. The results were a disappointment to the Pilgrims who had depended on a good crop.
Bradford said, "We either planted them too late or the seeds
weren't very good to begin with."

The Pilgrim's crop was welcome, they had depended
on a meager amount of food from the *Mayflower*, when it was
anchored offshore. Now they could completely satisfy their
hunger. The Pilgrims were elated at their harvest and they
wanted to celebrate in a day of giving thanks for their good

tidings. They now had sufficient corn and were at peace with all the Indians, they could roam the woods and hunt at will.

Their homes were being built and everything seemed to be going their way. They gathered waterfowl, turkey, lobster, partridge, clams, shellfish, leeks, watercress and other greens, pumpkin for pies, wild plums and dried berries.

Look who else came to dinner! Massasoit came to the plantation accompanied by ninety hungry braves. The Pilgrims were wondering how they could feed then all when Massasoit said that he would send some of his braves out to hunt. They came back with five deer they had bagged with their bow and arrows and added them to the food supply and the Pilgrims now knew they had enough to feed them all. It was a wonderful occasion and they thoroughly enjoyed themselves. There was a review of troops led by the Commander-in-Chief Standish, games of chance and skill and lots of food washed down with red and white grape wine, which was strong and sweet. They had "popcorn" which was new to the Pilgrims, but long enjoyed by the Indians.

The "Thanksgiving Day" extended into three days of festive and soul fulfillment happiness. From the first day, the Allertons, like their neighbors, enjoyed themselves immensely; they had never eaten so much.

Bartholomew met with several of his friends about his age and they wandered around the plantation. They stared in awe at the Indians with their bronzed, strong bodies and black hair tied with leather thongs. The braves proved their athletic prowess and skill in many of the games that were new to the Pilgrims but centuries old to the Indians, such as Lacrosse.

Mary and Remember were playing with children under the watchful eye of Mary Brewster, who had become a second mother to them since their own mother passed away on the *Mayflower*. The women were friendly to the Allerton children because they appreciated the position of growing up without a woman's touch and they really liked them, they thought they were obedient and well behaved.

Each day of their festivity was a wonder to the children and also to the adults. They were enjoying themselves. The Thanksgiving event was like an elixir to the Pilgrims after the devastating effect the plague had on their families and the hardship they endured. It was good to smile again.

(Thanksgiving became an annual feast in New England but only celebrated nationally when President Abraham Lincoln declared it a national holiday about two hundred and fifty years later.)

Finally the celebration was over, the Indians departed for their village and the Pilgrims were settling down to their daily routine. They went to the Common House where the corn and other supplies were stored and they reassessed the inventory. They were taken back when they found they had grossly overestimated the size of the harvest and they found, much to their chagrin, they only had half the amount that they would need. The ration was again reduced in half, they figured they would have to survive on this until the next year's harvest. They assumed there was nothing they could do to remedy the situation and they had to live with the problem. They prepared to get ready to withstand the expected onslaught of the coming winter months.

*   *   *

An Indian messenger came to the plantation one day and announced that a large ship was seen off Cape Cod heading for Plimoth. Thinking that it was a French ship from Canada that could do them great harm, Bradford's council was assembled and they were very concerned. Standish mustered every man and boy that could handle a musket and ordered them to report to Fort Hill. When the vessel sailed into sight, Standish fired off a warning shot that reverberated through the town. The populace came into the streets to look out into the bay to watch the approaching ship. They wondered if the ship would answer in kind or send a murderous volley of cannon shot into their midst...there was no response.

The people in town held their breaths, when they spoke they spoke only in whispers...the children were hushed.

CHAPTER 13

Plymouth, Cape Cod

1621-1622

The ship sailed straight for Plimoth and the crew seemed to ignore the ominous attempt of the Pilgrims to intimidate them. Then they ran up their colors, it was the Cross of St. George, at last a merchantman from England, it was November 11, 1621. The ship was named the *Fortune* and its home port was London. The ship's master or Captain was Thomas Barton. It landed in Plymouth exactly one year after the *Mayflower* landed in Provincetown.

The *Fortune* was much smaller than either the *Speedwell* or the *Mayflower*, it carried only thirty-five passengers, and fortunately they were all in good shape. The *Fortune* had put into Provincetown also and had stayed there for three weeks before heading for Plimoth. There was no reason given but there were rumors that many of the passengers, mostly Strangers, were becoming mutinous because they wanted to go on to Virginia.

The Pilgrims were rejoicing on shore and they were anxious to see who the settlers were. One of the first to land was Deacon Robert Cushman and his son, Thomas, now fourteen years old. They were followed by Jonathan Brewster, now about thirty, who was a widower and the son of William and Mary Brewster. Other passengers included master mason Thomas Morton and two French speaking wallons, Philippe de la Noye later called Delano and Moses Symonson known as Simmons, who were Saints from Leyden.

The Merchant Adventurers had recruited the rest of the passengers who were Strangers and were from London. Among the new arrivals were John Winslow, who was Edward's brother and Thomas Prence; also, John Adams and a few women, one of whom was Martha Ford, who had delivered a son on the voyage. The rest of the Strangers were young men who left England with very little food or pots to cook in and no bedding or clothes. The whole group welcomed them in spite of the lack of provisions and the depleted food supply in the colony.

Cushman, whose wife remained in London, delivered letters to Governor Bradford from Reverend Robinson and Thomas Weston. Reverend Robinson having heard from Captain Jones about the fate and untimely deaths of so many in Plimoth Plantation and their hardship aboard the *Mayflower*, evoked much sympathy for them. He mourned the deaths of so many of his close friends. In his letter, he also wrote that he would come to the New World with others to join him, as soon as possible.

True to form, the letters from Weston were sarcastic and heaped abuse upon the Pilgrims. He didn't mention the hardships that the Pilgrims endured; the deaths, the weather, the time spent on building shelters, their lack of food...nothing but complaints. He wanted to know why they didn't sign the amended Articles of Agreement. He wondered why they kept the *Mayflower* so long and sent it back empty. He must have known what the Pilgrims had gone through but he finished the letter saying the Merchant Adventurers should have nothing more to do with them, although if they would change their ways he would stick with them. It was signed, "Your very loving friend."

Governor Bradford, Allerton, Standish and Brewster were speaking to Cushman about the letter they received from Weston and they were a little upset, to say the least.

Allerton said, "What kind of a man is Weston, he just ignores the problems that we had, forgets the deaths...does not even mention them or offer any sympathy."

Brewster replied, "I know it, Isaac, he is hard, callous and cares only for himself, not for others. We certainly overestimated him when we were in Leyden."

"The terms of the patent we have here, gives us very little for all our effort," said Bradford. "The Merchant Adventurers, without any risk to speak of, make a bonus when we pay them a profit for seven years. They will get a bonus, fifteen times what we will get. They go on to say that after seven years we will be "free"...are we now slaves?"

Cushman then said, "I know you are all correct in your criticism of the patent and of Weston. I know him better than most of you. I tried to work with him in London and as you know, many times I ran into a stonewall when I attempted to give an opinion. I guess you all realize now what a problem Carver and I had in London trying to organize getting supplies and arranging to hire the *Mayflower*. Regardless of what we think or feel we still have to depend on the Merchant Adventurers. We need supplies and I don't know where we can get them, other than through them. I hate to admit it, but they hold our fate in their hands. Unless you have an alternative plan, I think we are forced to sign the agreement. Do you know anyway we can avoid signing?"

Bradford asked Standish, "Can you think of anything else we can do, Captain?"

"No, I can't William. I think we'll have to go along and pay them off as soon as possible."

"How about you Isaac? Do you have a plan?"

"No, William—I agree with Myles—pay it off as soon as we can."

"I agree," said Brewster. "I dread going along with this agreement, but as far as I can see, it s the only way."

Cushman remarked, "Then I guess we all agree on this."

"We will have to sign and you can take it back with you to the Merchant Adventurers." Bradford said.

Cushman's trip had been made in haste from London so he could warn the Pilgrims of the imminent cutback of supplies by the Merchant Adventurers. He had to convince the Pilgrims of the serious nature that the Adventurers viewed this problem. The original agreement was to give each colonist, after seven years when the agreement was over, 100 acres of uninhabited land and the liberty to fish and make a living unmolested. The Merchant Adventurers were to get 1500 acres each. This was known as the *Pierce Patent* and confirmed the *Mayflower Compact*'s guarantee of self-government.

The farmers were starting to act up, especially the Strangers. They wanted to divide the land up into plots that would be given to each one that tilled the soil. This was contrary to the articles of Agreement and Cushman knew that the Merchant Adventurers would find fault if this was done.

Therefore, Cushman gathered the people from Plimoth Plantation one day at the Common House and delivered a speech called, "The Danger of Self Love." He expressed himself, quoting the bible, by saying, "Let no man seek his own, but every man's wealth!" It was an answer to those that wanted to divide the land up into individual lots. He went on to say, "you want to live better than your neighbor although you do the same work." This lecture seemed to silence the farmers who were so intent on being on their own.

Cushman was thinking of the welfare of the settlers who he felt would be at great risk if they acted contrary to the wishes of the Merchant Adventurers. Once the settlers paid them back they could do anything they wanted. In the meantime, they would build on their successes and they would have many. This was a new experiment and the Merchant Adventurers themselves felt that working together they would produce more.

To compensate for the anger of the Merchants over the return of the empty *Mayflower*, they set about loading the *Fortune* with hardwood, wainscoting, clapboard and several hogs-heads with beaver and otter pelts obtained from the Massachusetts squaws and Massasoit. This load was about half of what the Pilgrims owed to the Merchant Adventurers. They knew this would make them happy and show good faith and end any hostile feeling. They hoped this gesture would convince them to make another advance. Cushman was to return to England on December 13th. As he said, this was a quick trip to Plimoth to calm the rage of the Merchant Adventurers.

Cushman asked Bradford if he could look after his son, Thomas, while he was in London. He hoped the business with the Merchant Adventurers would be over soon and then he would return to Plimoth to live.

Bradford gladly agreed to the arrangement saying that he always liked Thomas and he would see that he was well taken of while he was in his care.

Cushman appreciated his acceptance of his son and said that Thomas always looked forward to coming to Plimoth and he regarded this to be quite an adventure.

"I'm happy that Thomas will be with us, you can rest assured he will be treated like a member of the family and I'll be totally responsible in continuing his education."

"I know you will have his interest at heart, William. That's why I feel confident in leaving him with you."

Robert Cushman said to his son, "Governor Bradford will be watching over you until I get back. He will take good care of you. I know you will behave and be a credit to our family."

Thomas said, "Well, I'm sorry that you have to go back. Maybe you'll be able to return soon. I certainly won't be a burden to Governor Bradford, I've always like him and he is a fair and reasonable man. I'll be glad when mother and you return and we'll be able to start life here as a family again."

Cushman hugged him and Thomas said, "Do you want to go on a walk around the plantation and see all the people you know?"

"I'd like that! It's pretty chilly outside so we'd better bundle up." They left the Bradford house and wandered about, watching with interest the men cutting logs and making planks out of them. Others were making bricks, they had learned this craft through necessity. Some were putting the finishing touches on the homes that resembled English fishing huts. Before their coming to the New World, most had never done this type of work, nor worked as hard.

Everywhere the Cushmans went on their walk, they saw activity. Pilgrims that were once busy in the textile trade, as was Robert as a woolcomber, were now enjoying a new life.

These men, who had been seasick on the *Mayflower*, were now busy as fishermen, farmers, builders or whatever the job called for at the moment.

They stopped at the Allerton home and Isaac was there with his children. Robert always thought of Isaac as a good friend. Isaac welcomed them and they had a long chat trying to catch up to date on all the things that happened.

Isaac related the trip across the Atlantic and the death of his wife, Mary, on the *Mayflower*. Cushman expressed his sympathy to him and his family and said he had received a letter from Reverend Robinson telling him about Allerton's loss.

Beer was still available but the supply was running low and Allerton supplied Cushman sparingly. The children were running around playing and they were trying to keep quiet but it was almost impossible in such a small area. The main attraction for young Mary was Thomas, she couldn't seem to take her eyes off him. When he spoke, she gave him her undivided attention. Later, when the Cushman's were leaving, Mary worked her way up to the front of the line so she could say goodbye.

Several days later, it was time for Cushman to leave the plantation and go back to London. He went with his son and spoke to all his old friends, he told them he regretted leaving but he would be back soon and join them. He was well liked by the Pilgrims and when they bid farewell, there seemed to be a sense of finality to his departure.

He boarded the *Fortune* just before departure and after the ship had been loaded down with goods destined for the Merchant Adventurers in London. He was at the rail waving at his son and friends. The crew was very busy and orders were being shouted, as the ship made its way out of the bay at Plimoth. Slowly the ship faded from view and the crowd had now dwindled to a small group.

Bradford said, "Well, let's go, Thomas, we will see your mother and father soon. It's about time we had something to eat, let's go see what we have in the cupboard."

When the *Fortune* sailed, the Pilgrims were very optimistic. They had sent the Merchant Adventurers more stock than they had hoped for, surely this would prove they had made a good investment in the honesty and steadfastness of the Pilgrims and Plimoth would be successful.

Behind the scenes there was much intrigue going on.

Cushman had the signed letters of agreement from the Pilgrims carefully tucked away in safe place. He also had a letter from Bradford to Weston. Bradford was incensed Weston and the insensitive manner in which he treated the Pilgrims. Cushman also had a manuscript from Bradford that he wanted published in England.

Bradford found out that the Strangers in the colony had secretly sent a letter back on the *Mayflower* complaining about the leaders and saying they spent all their time tending meetings and they were accomplishing nothing. The full load of articles on which the Pilgrims had long labored and put aboard the *Fortune*, would prove that the Strangers weren't telling the truth and Weston spoke out of turn by saying the Pilgrims were lazy. Bradford was particularly angry at Weston for criticizing John Carver who had spent his life helping others. In all probability his life was shortened by his worry over the Pilgrims. The writers of the letters were Strangers and were from a bunch of malcontents that hadn't done any good for the welfare of the colony and the Pilgrims didn't think they would. They were saddled with them and they could lay the blame at the doorstep of the Merchant Adventurers because they had recruited the Strangers in the first place to get passengers on the *Mayflower*.

The *Fortune* was enroute to England with hardly a care, making good time on the high seas, sails billowing out and straining under a sharp head wind. Suddenly a ship loomed in the distance and then it overtook the *Fortune*. It was a bigger ship and obviously much faster, its full complement of cannon intimidated the smaller ship and finally the *Fortune* was taken over by the French privateer. They were boarded by the sailors from the privateer and disarmed. The crew and passengers of the *Fortune* were all assembled on deck and the belligerents assumed control of the ship. Cushman, along with the others, was herded below deck and was guarded by several, sneering, swarthy, sailors who brandished cutlasses.

They taunted the prisoners and belittled them by pretending to strike at them with the swords, and laughed when the prisoners cringed at their antics.

Cushman tried to remain composed but it was difficult when he didn't know what would happen next. He bowed his head and prayed silently and wished this nightmare would go away.

The ships headed east with the pirates now in control of the *Fortune* and the British Merchant flag was taken down. They traveled for a full day and then saw a small island coming into view. They headed for the island and pulled into a shallow inlet.

Some of the sailors from the privateer rowed a small dingy toward the island and landed at a pier. They walked inland after speaking to some civilians on the beach, who had evidently given them directions. In a short while they returned with several civilians who were very friendly and joked with them. The sailors rowed back to their ship while the civilians waited for them on the beach, sitting on a cement bulkhead.

The intruders next deftly eased the *Fortune* to the pier and secured the ship with their huge hawsers. Then the prisoners had to evacuate the ship. They were forced to walk inland for a short distance, past the unkempt, laughing civilians and entered a run-down town with decaying garbage in the streets. The prisoners entered a dirty, grey building that had been converted into a dingy prison. The crew and passengers of the *Fortune* were crowded into a hall where they were separated from the group and forced to empty their pockets and turn them inside out. Then they were led to several empty cells where their hats and shoes were immediately confiscated by unshaven guards who laughed at them. They were forced to walk on dirty, insect-ridden floors in their stocking feet.

Later, they were given tepid, strong-smelling water to drink to wash down a meal of stale bread and non-descript meat. On occasion, they were given a half-cooked vegetable which graced their dented, metal dish. The prisoners tried to figure out a way to escape but Cushman said, "If we can survive this ordeal, I think that we'll come out of this all right. I don't think they want to kill us, no one has been hurt so far. Why feed us...when they could kill us and save the food."

One of the *Fortune*'s crew spoke up, "I don't know how long we can live on the meals we're getting!'

Cushman said, "I know we can get sick once and awhile from the food, but I don't think we will be held long. Unless we are held for ransom, my guess is we'll be set free."

Another sailor said, "Breaking out would be next to impossible, we have nothing to pick the locks with, no weapons and we're divided up in our cells. Even if we were able to get out of this jail or prison or whatever they call it, the civilians seem to be friendly with the ones in charge and they'd turn us in as a favor to our captors. I agree with Mr. Cushman, it's only a matter of time before we're released."

They were imprisoned in this hellhole for several weeks until one day some guards came in and stood outside their cells and waited.

One of the imprisoned, sidled up to Cushman and in a low voice said, "I wonder what they're up to now?"

"I don't know, but if they wanted to kill us I think they would have emptied out one cell at a time, in order to control us."

Soon, the sergeant of the guards, opened the door of Cushman's cell and said, "Allez" and pointed to the exit door. The prisoners came out in single file and walked through the door into the bright sunlight.

The haggard and weary men, with drawn faces and heavy, ragged beards, blinked in the unaccustomed, penetrating light, and stumbled down the cement steps. This led to a courtyard with abundant, wild grape vines partially covering a wall spattered with musket shot. They were told to stand against the wall and remain still.

Soon another group of prisoners came down the stairs accompanied by several guards. They were told to stand in front of the first group of prisoners and remain silent and still. Another group followed them and were given the same instructions. Then the last of the prisoners filed into the yard and joined the others. When they were all in the courtyard they were ordered to form three lines and walk through the now-open metal gates at the end of the yard.

They were a pathetic lot, gingerly picking their way through the rough, cobblestoned, debris littered street. They went down the hilly road, leading toward the beach. In a few minutes they were back at the *Fortune* and many changes had been made. The ship was now floating higher in the water and several pieces of the sails were missing.

When they got closer they also saw that the cannons were missing along with many items on deck that were made from brass. Once aboard, they found that all the goods and lumber items destined for the Merchant Adventurers had been looted.

"How could he explain this to Merchants, had who been so critical?" thought Cushman. "The Pilgrims had worked so hard and were proud of the fact that they could accomplish so much under such awful circumstances."

Cushman hurried below deck. He was concerned about his personal belongings. He had placed the documents under a loose plank to hid them from the crew who weren't exactly a bunch of altar boys. He looked around and being satisfied there was nobody in sight, he removed the plank. Growing accustomed to the dim light, to his relief, he saw the documents were intact.

The crew, anxious to get away from the island, made the ship ready to sail. The hawsers were removed and the ship started to move and then the crew turned the ship. The remaining sails caught a small gust of wind and gained a little speed. Soon they were free of captivity from the pirates of this unholy island. They noticed the French privateer was gone and nowhere in sight. They were probably bound to go out to sea to do the hellish work of the devil.

The navigator set a course for England and they limped their way back. They were good sailors, despite the handicap they were able to arrival safely.

Cushman, on returning home, discovered that once again turmoil had taken place among the Merchant Adventurers.

Arguing among themselves, unhappy with Bradford's letter to Weston and particularly the loss of supplies on the *Fortune* made them boiling mad. Seeing the contact between the Pilgrims and the Adventurers held by a thread, Cushman tried to convince them that the Pilgrims were in dire straits and with the additional passengers from the *Fortune* and the poor crops they would surely starve if they weren't given aid as soon as possible. He said they were sincere in sending such a large cargo back to England but unfortunately the French seized it. Cushman pleaded with them to remain a viable united company and the Pilgrims would prove worthy once they overcame this past misfortune. After much arguing and persuasion they finally agreed to continue to assist the Pilgrims. They would no doubt duplicate many times the astounding amount of material they had sent to the Merchant Adventurers to repay their debt.

Cushman had a pamphlet published, written by "G. Mourt", called *Mourt's Relations* that was attributed to William Bradford and Edward Winslow. It was a publicity agent's dream, giving the optimistic view of Plimoth Plantation in its quest for settlers, particularly men and women that would work and prove to be an asset to the colony. They mentioned the fact that one could find wild fowl at will, succulent clams and lobsters practically at their door, peace with the Indian tribes and the Indians were a great help to the settlers. The pamphlet also mentioned the advantage of making the sea trip to Plymouth and participating in making a new civilization with unlimited economic benefits. This should challenge any person with an ounce of ambition.

Cushman had added some thoughts to *Mourt's Relations* and contrasted Plimoth with the Old World where neighbor was fighting neighbor for food and advantage in trade and jobs. Unemployment was high in Europe and a lot of people were poor. The brochure was designed to get more people interested in coming to Plimoth and they would be screened to keep malcontents away, if possible.

Back in Plimoth the passengers of the *Fortune* had been absorbed into the homes in the plantation and with the severe shortage of food and the overcrowding, the Pilgrims were resigned to spend a miserable winter. To add to their misery they were faced with another Indian problem. A brave from the powerful Narragansett tribe came to Plimoth and delivered arrows wrapped in a rattlesnake skin. They had planned this message to be delivered to Squanto but being told he would be absent for a few days the brave left them and tried to depart in a hurry. Bradford turned the brave over to Myles Standish, Hopkins and Winslow who attempted to question the Indian and find out the purpose of the arrows. The brave convinced them he wanted to be a friend and then departed.

Upon Squanto's return they found out the arrows were meant to be a challenge to the colony. When Bradford's council knew the reason for the arrows, they immediately sent Canonicus, the chief of the Narragansetts, another snakeskin filled with shot and gunpowder. They heard nothing further from him and then a few days later he returned the snakeskin, unopened.

The Pilgrims continued to build the wall which was eleven feet high and a mile in circumference, it had gates for entrances which were locked and guarded at night.

Knowing that the Narragansett tribe could field several thousand braves to attack them, they were desperate to finish the wall as soon as possible. This was a superhuman effort to complete. They spent every working hour on their defenses.

The Strangers said they wanted Christmas as a holiday, so they wouldn't work. The Saints continued to work building the wall. When they returned for lunch, Governor Bradford saw the Strangers in the streets playing games, including cricket. The Governor sensing the unfairness of the situation took the implements away from the Strangers and told them to go home and pray if they were so devoted.

CHAPTER 14

Plymouth, Cape Cod

1622

S tandish divided his "army" into four companies as squadrons and each had a commander. They were headed by Bradford, Hopkins, Allerton and Edward Winslow. Each of the four walls would be guarded by a squadron. The new arrivals to the colony were made part of the militia and were assigned to the squadrons. One company was given special recognition. The group was composed of Saints which had the job of reporting a fire, surrounding the building and with their backs to the fire, muskets ready, they prevented any of the Strangers from doing more harm. There were many suspicious fires in Plimoth that only could have been started by someone inside the town, they suspected one or more of the Strangers. They couldn't understand why someone or some group would want to destroy the plantation.

When things became settled and they had finished the wall, the council was a little concerned about the depletion of furs and other items they procured by trading. They decided that it was about time to visit the Massachusetts women again for trade. Hobomok advised against it saying, "The Massachusetts tribe is allied with the Narragansetts and they have plans to cut off Plimoth and destroy it. Squanto is behind the plot."

After speaking with Standish and Allerton, Bradford decided they would have to go on the trading mission. They assumed that if the Indians knew they were staying close to home they would take this as a sign of cowardice. They also had to travel in the woods to hunt and to roam unafraid, or they would surely starve to death. So Standish with ten heavily armed men accompanied by Squanto and Hobomok, started their journey in the shallop to Boston. They had gone only a short distance near the Saquish Head, when suddenly they heard three booms from the cannon back at Plimoth. Startled, they turned about and hurried back to the plantation wondering what had caused the militia to sound the alarm.

Meanwhile, one of Squanto's Indian friends with a bloody face, giving furtive glances over his shoulder, as though he was being chased, motioned to the men working in the fields to hurry home because they would be soon attacked. He yelled, "I come from Nemasket. Massasoit and Corbitant along with many Narragansetts are coming here to kill all the people in the colony!"

The militia organized by Standish was ready to meet head-on any attempt to overpower them. It was during the assembly of troops, that they shot off the cannon to warn the Pilgrims and hopefully to frighten any lurking Indians.

Standish and his men hurriedly beached the shallop and in their heavy armor, scrambled up the hill to join the others. Panting from exhaustion, their hearts pounding from anxiety and excitement, they finally got to the fort at the summit of the hill. Standish yelled, "What's happening...are we under attack?"

Bradford said, "No, the whole thing was a hoax." He went on to explain the reason for giving the alarm.

Hobomok insisted, "Massasoit is a loyal friend and wouldn't be a party to such a deceitful trick!"

Bradford said, "I can't believe that Massasoit would have his hand in such a plot, he is like a brother to me. What do think happened? We will have to get to the bottom of this so-called trick."

Hobomok, impatient to talk, said, "I still think Squanto is behind a plot to cause trouble with the tribes. He wants the white man to fear the Indians and Squanto will solve the problem by having the tribes come to like the white man and then live in peace. Squanto will then be admired and become a hero to the white man."

Bradford looked at Allerton and neither spoke. Later, when Hobomok left, Bradford said, "Well, what do you think Isaac?"

"I think that there is a lot of rivalry between Squanto and Hobomok and they're both trying to impress us and be liked more."

"The trouble is, they're both likable and are valuable friends to us." Bradford then laughed and said, "They're both jealous of one another. Why don't you tell Hopkins and I'll tell Winslow about the situation with our Indian friends. We won't take sides but try to take a middle course in dealing with this. Who knows, maybe they'll become friends with one another. Squanto is always playing tricks on people but if he is responsible for this "trick" then he's going too far. He's a good friend to us, he's smart and cunning but Hobomok has all these traits, too."

Hobomok had sent his wife to Sowams letting the Indians think she was there on business. Everything was normal in the village so she told Massasoit about the alarm and the anxiety it caused at Plimoth and Bradford's complete faith in him. Upon hearing all the details, Massasoit broke into a rage, blaming Squanto, who he thought was at the root of the trouble. He told Hobomok's wife he was grateful for Governor Bradford's confidence in him and he vowed that he would keep all phases of the peace treaty that he signed at Plimoth.

When Hobomok's wife returned to Plimoth and told Governor Bradford about her visit to Sowams and Massasoit's faith and respect for Bradford, he was pleased. "I knew he wouldn't have anything to do with a conspiracy. Thank you for going on the trip to Sowams, it was a great sacrifice to you and it was a great service to our people in Plimoth."

After she was gone, Bradford said to Allerton, "Do you really think the culprit might be Squanto?"

"Everything seems to point to him as the villain...but why? What would he gain by this scheme...unless we accept Hobomok's theory as correct."

"Well, you know that Squanto can be quite devious. I hope that it blows over. I'll take Squanto to task for his actions and see how he reacts to it...I guess it will be safe to go to Boston now. It appears to have been a false alarm. I'll tell Standish he can go, whenever he and the men are ready."

The next day Standish set off again with his original group to visit the Massachusetts tribe to get beaver pelts. The men in the shallop had a brisk wind at their back and they made good time. They joked about the last time they went to Boston and met the women from the Massachusetts tribe, they wondered if they wanted to trade again. They rounded the corner near Allerton's Point and were soon in the Massachusetts Indian area. Bradford, who had accompanied the men, said to Standish, "Don't forget to notice any change in attitude in the members of the tribe...but I know you will—it's a natural instinct."

The Indians came up to the boat when the Pilgrims

pulled ashore and greeted the men. There were few women this time but the group was very friendly. The squaws who had received beads for pelts wanted to trade again. This time they were holding the pelts up for the Pilgrims. They had food and fresh water for the Pilgrims and acted as though they had no fear of the weapons. The Pilgrims were treated as friends.

After a successful trading expedition, where they encountered no trouble at all, Bradford, Standish and the others returned on the twenty five mile trip to Plimoth.

When they approached the pier, a large group of Pilgrims were there to welcome them and see how they made out on their trip. Bradford, on exiting the boat, was surprised to see Massasoit in the group. Massasoit bore an angry, troubled face. Bradford wondered why he was acting this way. He went to the Common House with Massasoit and his braves and Standish had an equal number of militia with him.

Allerton, Hopkins and Winslow who made up the council were also in attendance. After they had served refreshments to all, Bradford looked Massasoit straight in the eye and said, "You have a troubled look, my friend. What can I do to change this?"

Hobomok was with him to interpret and he said, "I demand justice against Squanto! He is the cause of great trouble and is trying to spoil the friendship between my tribes and you Pilgrims. Under the terms of the peace treaty I am in my right to demand his death."

Bradford said, "Squanto has been severely censured and he admitted that he had committed some mischief, but he is very sorry for that. He said it wouldn't happen again."

Massasoit looked at Bradford steadily for a few seconds and said, "You are a fair man and I will accept your story."

When Massasoit accepted Bradford's explanation, he

immediately left to return to Sowams and tactfully refused Bradford's offer to stay overnight as a guest in Bradford's home.

When Massasoit was half way to Sowams he was thinking over the situation with Squanto and suddenly he again burst into a rage.

Massasoit said to one of his chiefs who had accompanied him, "Go back to Governor Bradford and say that I demand the head and hands of Squanto immediately. I am using the terms of our treaty and this is a test of our friendship."

The chief went back to Bradford and relayed the message from Massasoit. Bradford was shocked at his change of heart and said, "Tell Massasoit that he is taking a valuable part of our existence because Squanto is of great value as our interpreter and guide."

Bradford realized the predicament that he now found himself in and for which he was not responsible. If he was to protect Squanto further, he could lose the friendship of Massasoit and the cancellation of the treaty. He had heard rumors that Squanto had a new "trick." He told the Indians that he knew where the Pilgrims had hidden the plague. They could use it at any time on the Indians and they would infect them resulting in their death. Bradford also heard that Squanto was taking bribes from the Indians to convince the Pilgrims not to use the plague's curse on the ones that were paying the bribes.

Squanto was summoned by Governor Bradford to appear before him to answer the charges against him but they were interrupted by an alarm given by a lookout.

CHAPTER 15

Plymouth, Cape Cod

1622

A boat had been sighted nearby and it passed beyond the colony to return to the Plimoth harbor. The Pilgrims had an inherent fear that the French would come to Plimoth from Canada and intrude on their lives. The Pilgrims had no real force to back them up, they were on their own.

It was only a shallop from the ship *Sparrow* owned by Thomas Weston who had gone to Maine from England. The Pilgrims disliked Weston for his disregard fur their feeling in their fight for life when they reached America and before they left on their long voyage across the Atlantic. The shallop had sailed from Maine directly to Plimoth. There were seven passengers on board and a letter from Weston Gradford stating the passengers were not interested in becoming colonists. Weston expected the Pilgrims would take these new arrivals into their homes, feed them, give them corn seed and anything else they might need for their survival. The "New Comers" would eventually open a salt mill on an island in front of Plimoth and the profit would go to Weston and his partner. Weston said this was in partial payment for what he had done for the colony. He signed the letter "Your loving friend". Bradford wondered just what Weston had contributed to the colony to merit such consideration from the Pilgrims. Bradford couldn't figure out the brazenness of this individual after Bradford had sent such a blistering report about Weston to the Merchant Adventurers.

The Pilgrims were still facing starvation and they had four months to harvest time, but they felt sorry for the passengers so they accepted them into the plantation.

An accompanying letter from Weston spelled impending disaster for the Pilgrims. They were told the Merchant Adventurers had just about broken up by arguments and other discord. The letter was concealed from the Pilgrims because the Council thought they would tell them about it when the situation got a little better. The letter was shown only to trusted friends and the Council. They agreed Weston would attempt to seize control of the colony by virtue of having money to buy supplies and most of the Pilgrims, through necessity, would have to go along with him.

They suspected that many of the "Wild men" that arrived on the Fortune had been recruited by Weston to create mischief in the colony. This could give the reason for the sudden rash of unexplained fires.

With all the trouble that had arisen, Bradford had not solved the problem with Squanto...only delayed it. The problems that Plimoth had in that small colony were enough to try the souls of men governing large countries in similar conditions. However, there was a silver lining in that cloud that hung over the plantation.

A letter had been delivered to the Pilgrims from a stranger, a Captain John Huddleston who was the master of an English fishing vessel in Maine. The letter said that three hundred and forty-seven settlers in the Jamestown, Virginia colony had been massacred by the Indians and gave warning that this could happen to them and be sure to have strong defenses.

Seeing a hand extended in friendship by a person they had never met, they wanted to meet this skipper who was aboard a ship 150 miles north in Maine waters.

Setting sail in their shallop, this inexperienced crew went on uncharted waters to meet the friendly captain and see if it was possible to get provisions for the near-starving Pilgrims. Bradford and his crew finally reached the area in Maine where Captain Huddleston's ship was anchored. To confirm that he had the right ship he yelled, "Is there a Captain Huddleston aboard?"

"Ahoy, I'm Captain Huddleston...who are you?"

"Hello, I'm Governor Bradford of the Plimoth Colony ...can we come aboard?"

"Governor Bradford! Hello, glad to see you. You and your men are welcome to come aboard. Toss up a line from your boat and use the rope ladder to climb up."

Bradford and his crew came aboard the ship and were graciously received by Captain Huddleston, who shook hands with them all. He introduced his mate and several of the crew members that were available at the time. Huddleston explained that he made several trips a year to the fishing banks off Maine and the catch was unusually good. They salted the fish so that they would keep for a long time for the trip back to England. He asked if they were hungry...they were! Huddleston told the cook to prepare a big meal for them. They ate every scrap of food that was placed in front of them.

Bradford and his crew really enjoyed the food and beer that seemed to be in abundance on the ship. It had been some time since they had eaten so well.

Huddleston said, "I assume that you received my letter or you wouldn't be here. Tell me, Governor, is there any-thing we can do to help you?"

"Well Captain there is something that we hope you can do. We'd like to trade some items for food. Our people are starving and are in desperate need of assistance. They are tending the fields to produce crops and we try to harvest clams, lobsters and herring but they seem to be in short sup-ply. I wish that you could meet them, they are good people, determined to succeed against all odds. Before the *Mayflower* returned to England, Captain Jones had asked if there was anybody who would like to return home. Nobody accepted his invitation in spite of hardship and deaths of about half of our company. They have endured a lot and the women and children have also shown great courage. So I speak for them...we need food!"

Captain Huddleston was moved by Bradford's account of things that were happening at Plimoth Plantation. He inquired about the Indians and wondered if they were a threat.

Bradford and some of the Pilgrims spoke up, "So far we haven't had any problem with them, we won't be the ones that start any trouble. But if trouble comes, I think we can give a good accounting of ourselves. We want peaceful rela-tions with them; we'll go out of our way to be fair but we will not be taken advantage of by the Indians.

Huddleston replied, "I guess the Indians at Cape Cod are friendlier than the ones at Jamestown. You know from my letter what happened there. Well, back to your situation. We had an unexpectedly good catch and we're heading back to England in a few days so our food supply is ample. What were you going to trade?"

"We have some muskrat pelts and I guess you're not interested in trinkets..." Bradford laughed when he men-tioned "trinkets".

Huddleston said, "Well, Governor, I don't think we can use the muskrat pelts or your trinkets, but we'll give you what we can spare and the next time we are in these waters we might come to Plimoth and you can give us a good meal in return. There are other fishing ships in this area and I'll see how much food they can spare...we don't want them to get fat on the job. I think most of them had a good catch so they too will be going back to England soon."

Huddleston, towing the Pilgrim's shallop, went to the other English ships and introduced Governor Bradford and he told the captains the story of the Plimoth Plantation and they responded very generously. They loaded the shallop up with supplies from each ship until they had reached a limit on the amount they could safely carry.

Once they were ready to return to the colony, the Pilgrims who had thanked the ships' captains now were left with their principal benefactor, Captain Huddleston.

The Pilgrims were finally ready to leave the ship and board their loaded shallop. They shook hands with the crew and Captain Huddleston and bid him farewell. Governor Bradford took his hand and said, "You're a good man Captain Huddleston and the people of Plimoth will appreciate what you have done for them, they will never forget you. We look forward to you and your crew coming to Plimoth someday. I'm sure you will all be given a rousing welcome by our people. Thank you again from our hearts, we appreciate your effort."

With that, he climbed down the ladder, and joined the waiting Pilgrims in the shallop. They put up the sail and headed for Plimoth...waving to the captain and crew. The shallop was loaded to the gunwales with much-needed supplies and the men were jubilant and talked about the success of their trip. It was fortunate they had calm seas on their way back or they would surely have swamped the boat.

Eventually, they neared home and as humble as it was, it was a welcome sight. They unloaded the shallop and placed the supplies in the Common House. The men were a welcome sight.

However, they were shocked to see the Pilgrims working in the fields and they were skin and bones. They staggered from weakness and some were swollen with hunger.

The supplies were happily received but they didn't go very far in feeding all the inhabitants of the plantation.

It was then that Winslow took a lot of criticism about his writing *Mourt's Relations* and his idea of getting more settlers to Plimoth. The Pilgrims cited their lack of food and their attempts to replenish their meager supply. Waterfowl was out of season, they couldn't fish, although there were plenty—they had the wrong hooks and lines. They were down to a quarter loaf of bread a day; this was doled out by Governor Bradford who feared they would eat all the bread if it wasn't rationed and they would starve much sooner.

The Squanto affair still was not resolved. Massasoit was luke warm to their relationship and the Narragansett and other tribes ridiculed the Pilgrims' lack of strength.

The Pilgrims decided they had not choice but to reinforce the defenses of the plantation. Leaving the fields, they proceeded to strengthen Fort Hill by building a large log house of solid oak. They utilized the platform on which they placed the cannon and built on that. The fort now had cannon muzzles poked out of openings. The new fortress had a guard day and night and it served in other functions in turn as the town house, meeting hall and a court of justice.

The Pilgrims, in solemn ceremony, attended services in the fort on the Sabbath with a flintlock in one hand, and a Bible in the other. They were an impressive sight when the assembly, called by drum beats, went to Captain Standish's door with their firearms. They marched three abreast led by a sergeant. Behind them came the Governor with his long robe of office. The preacher, William Brewster, was on his right and on his left was Captain Standish, holding a small cane. The townspeople, dressed in their finest, made up the rear.

The Pilgrims were very sincere in their faith...in fact there was a fine for not attending service on the Sabbath. Very few paid this fine, most wanted to go to the service.

The Pilgrims struggled along and in the summer they were happy to see two ships in the harbor...maybe they would have much needed supplies. The ships were the *Charity*, a hundred-ton ship, with the *Swan*, a vessel of thirty tons. Together, they were crowded with sixty passengers. With the ships came another sarcastic letter from "your loving friend" which stated that Weston was no longer one of the Merchant Adventurers and there would be no further contract with them. He had obtained a patent to form a colony at the Southern part of Boston Harbor and as an afterthought he asked the Pilgrims to care for some of the passengers while the ships went to Virginia to drop off supplies and other freight and some passengers. They would pick up the passengers on the way back and only stay temporarily at Plimoth. Although he said the master of the *Charity* was to give the Pilgrims 2,000 pounds of bread and many fish, the Pilgrims didn't trust him.

Robert Cushman sent a letter to the Pilgrims through a trusted friend. It stated that the Pilgrims would do well not to trust the men that Weston sent. He also mentioned that Squanto should notify all the tribes that the men who recently arrived were not part of the colony and they were not responsible for their actions.

Another letter that was retrieved by Winslow was hidden in the sole of a shoe of another trusted passenger which also strengthened their suspicion of Weston's motives. It said that Weston had quit the Merchant Adventurers and they were well rid of him. It was signed by two Adventurers, one of them being Edward Pickering who had been a member of the Green Gate congregation. They also warned of Weston's sneaky motives and especially to be aware of his brother, Andrew, who was in charge of one of the ships...they were about to do great mischief to the Pilgrims.

As good Christians, the Pilgrims turned the other cheek and invited the new passengers to join them in their already crowded homes. The new arrivals later went into the fields supposedly to work but they did nothing, their only concern was to steal the corn. There were continual complaints and back-biting by Weston's men.

Not being skilled farmers, the Pilgrims once again looked ahead to a poor harvest. They spent valuable time away from the fields in making the plantation more secure. They feared for the future and the knowledge that they could not depend on the Merchant Adventurers if what Weston had written in his letter was true. They could not trade with the Indians because the trinkets and other articles which they used in their bartering were now gone.

Morale reached a low point, one had not far to look and see despair written on the faces of the Pilgrims. Hollow-eyed, pale, thin, they seemed to be a dismal lot, their clothes in dire need of replacement hung on them. However, they never lost their will to succeed or determination to live.

One day as they made an effort to continue work, one of the Pilgrims, shielding his eyes from the sun, said, "What's that in the distance...I think I see a sail."

Others joined in, "Yes, it's a ship! There's a ship coming! I hope they have food!" When the ship came into the harbor they found that it was the *Discovery*, en route to England from Virginia, having a big supply of items needed by the Pilgrims to trade with the Indians. The skipper, sensing their desperation and sorry plight, tried to take advantage of them by saying, he would only sell them in bulk quantities. The Pilgrims had nothing to trade but the beaver skins and the skipper said that he would give them three shillings per pound, when they were actually worth about twenty shilling per pound. They were forced to take this paltry sum or starve. Where the skipper didn't steal like a pirate would, he did the next best thing. Ironically, the skipper had been a pirate. His name was Captain Thomas Jones, not related by any means to Captain Christopher Jones who had befriended the Pilgrims after the *Mayflower* trip.

Captain Christopher Jones died in England on March 5, 1622, himself a victim of the plague.

In spite of the low, almost ridiculous price that the Pilgrims had to accept for the beaver pelts, they now had items that they could trade with the Indians for foodstuff.

Weston would start a colony at Wessagusset (later called Weymouth) and when the *Charity* set off for Virginia, the *Swan* remained behind in Plimoth. Always one to seize an opportunity, Weston suggested to the Pilgrims that they join in an expedition to trade with the Indians around the Cape.

Towing the Pilgrim's shallop, the *Swan* went beyond the Cape's tip at Provincetown into the rough shoals and turbulent coastal waters on the southern side of Cape Cod. The Pilgrims had entered these waters on the way to Provincetown when they first arrived in America. They had experienced the wild and treacherous sea and were very happy when they were able to leave the area.

Squanto convinced the captain of the ship that he knew the waters and would be able to cope with it, having sailed there a couple of times. Encountering many close calls and many other problems, they finally entered a harbor that had been the scene of a French encounter with the Indians several years before.

The Indians remembered the brutal treatment they suffered at the hands of the French sailors and when the "White men" came ashore, thinking it might be the French again, they hid. Squanto was finally able to find some Indians and he convinced them that the English were friends and only wanted to trade for food. The Indians came out to welcome them and gave them venison and other food to eat. They agreed to trade with them and the party ended with the Pilgrims getting eight hogsheads of corn and beans.

While at the Indian village, Squanto was stricken with a fever and a nose bleed and in spite of help from the crew and the Indians, he died two days later. Before he died, Squanto bequeathed his worldly goods to Governor Bradford and he hoped he would go to the white man's heaven because he didn't want to meet Massasoit in the Indian's "Happy hunting grounds."

The *Swan*, with its crew, went to the Massachusetts tribe near Boston to trade. Finding the Indians sick from the plague, they returned and passed Plimoth and went to the bottom of Cape Cod to the Indian village, Cummaquid. They used their shallop to go ashore because the water was very shallow. The local sachem, a young man in his twenties, was the one that the Pilgrims had met a year before and were very much impressed by his manner. He agreed to supply as much food to the Pilgrims as his town could spare.

The *Swan* then proceeded along the Cape to the country of Nauset where the Pilgrims were friendly with the natives. They filled ten hogsheads with beans and maize, then a sudden gale stuck and almost wrecked the shallop. The towline of the shallop snapped and the boat was smashed on the beach.

It was impossible to load the *Swan* without the shallop.

The Pilgrims told the Indians they would return for the shallop and the food, which had been covered with Indian mats. They cautioned them not to touch the hogsheads or they would have to account to Captain Standish, who happened to be sick in Plimoth at the time. He would treat them harshly if they were disturbed but if the shallop and the supplies were untouched it would be a sign of their friendship and honesty to the Pilgrims.

Weston's men sailed back to Wessagusset from Nauset, and Bradford and the Pilgrims set out on foot for Plimoth forty miles away. They had to stop at Cummaquid and the size of the *Swan* made it impossible to get ashore to land the men.

They reached Cummaquid and asked the chief if he could send braves to protect their supplies until they could pick them up after they had repaired the wrecked shallop.

The *Swan* put into Plimoth on their way to Wessagusset and they unloaded four of the eight hogsheads, which was the total supply available after their mission which was finally completed after weeks of work.

They still had ten hogsheads back at Nauset and at Cummaquid which were needed desperately by each colony. They had endured wild and harsh winter weather and heavy seas but in spite of the hardship they had undergone, now the shallop would have to be repaired before they could retrieve the hogsheads.

Bradford returned to Plimoth, rested, and then set off the next day to nearby Indian villages. They finally got to Corbitant's village and after a good reception and welcome they received corn from the Indians and after promising money to the Squaws they were assured delivery of the corn.

Bradford and his party next went overland to Manomet (now Bourne) and was impressed when they met the sachem of the tribe. Once again the Pilgrims were well treated by the Indians. They obtained corn and beans, but not having any way to transport it, they left it there until the shallop was repaired and the *Swan* could pick it up. Weston's men on the *Swan* had already promised they would pick up the supplies that were being accumulated by Bradford, but things were in a turmoil in their colony. Things were fast approaching the condition at Plimoth, but this was due to their mismanagement of their food supply.

In spite of the generosity of the Indians there still wasn't enough food to feed the Pilgrims. Failing more every day the Pilgrims wondered if they would ever break the chain of doom that was slowly strangling them.

The morale and conditions at Wessagusett were such that the Pilgrims were convinced that the *Swan* would never go to the Cape to pick up the supplies. The Pilgrims couldn't understand why the men at Wessagusett wouldn't make the effort to get their share when they needed the supplies so desperately.

CHAPTER 16

Plimoth, Cape Cod

1622

Weston's colony was gradually falling apart. The men were selling their blankets and the clothes off their backs for food. They labored for the Indians, cutting their wood and getting their water, all this for a cupful of corn. Some stole the Indians' corn, much the same as the Pilgrim's had but then there was a difference. The Pilgrims didn't know whose corn they took when they first landed and they also later paid for it. On another occasion at Wessagusett, a strong, able-bodied man, accused of stealing corn several times, was sentenced to death for his crime but an old, feeble man was substituted and went to the gallows.

Governor Sanders of Wessagusett sent a note with a brave from the Massachusetts tribe and wrote that they wanted to go to Maine and contact the fishing boat captain and try to get supplies like the Pilgrims had done. They were afraid they couldn't make the trip to Maine and back before most of the people in the colony would die of starvation, so they had an alternate plan. They would attack the Indians and take their corn. The Massachusetts tribe told the Weston colony that they had given them all the corn they could spare, but they were convinced the Indians were lying.

Bradford was dumbfounded when he read the note sent by the Governor and he realized the serious implication it held if the plan was carried out. Bradford asked the messenger if the Massachusetts tribe had any corn to sell. The brave said, "We have very little and we hope that we can survive until we have another harvest."

Bradford called the council together; it consisted of Allerton, Standish, Winslow and others that had now been included. When Bradford told the group about the Massachusetts tribe's lack of corn and the measures that Weston's men were thinking of taking, they fired back a firm note to Governor Sanders. Condemning the proposed action in no uncertain terms, they urgently stated this harebrained scheme could endanger both colonies by an attack of hundreds if not thousands of enraged Indians. They said the colony of Wessagusset could not count on the Pilgrims for support, in fact, they wanted nothing to do with it. The Pilgrims hoped that it wouldn't reflect on them and cause trouble among the numerous Indian tribes that inhabited most of the land around them.

They suggested that they should do what the Pilgrims did under the same situation. They should gather groundnuts, clams, mussels and other natural food items so they could survive. Doing this, they remained friends with the Indians and were able to roam in the woods looking for game and turkey eggs.

Unfortunately, in a short time the plan of Sanders and the Weston colony was known to the Massachusetts tribe and although it hadn't been carried through, there was always that threat.

Standish had recovered from his fever and he immediately set off for the Cape to retrieve the supplies that Bradford had left behind and to repair the shallop. Aspinet had kept guard over the supplies in his care, as he had promised. Some of the items were missing, Standish seeing this, face red with rage, he called on the sachem to explain their whereabouts or he would take revenge. The sachem was used to the friendly manner of Governor Bradford and Winslow and he was shocked at Standish's behavior.

The next morning the honorable Aspinet came to Standish with the missing trinkets, scissors and a few other things that were missing and apologized for the theft, saying the thief had been severely beaten for the crime.

He gave Standish some corn bread that had been baked the evening before by his squaws. Standish seemed appeased after he had the bread, but he still warned Aspinet that the Pilgrims respected honesty and that is what they expected. The group from the colony soon repaired the shallop with wood they had carried from the plantation. The work was supervised by Francis Eaton, who had worked on the shallop before and was quite proficient in carpentry.

The shallop was loaded with the supplies that Bradford had left behind. Standish reluctantly waved to Aspinet as they were leaving and the sachem beamed. Maybe the stories the chief heard about Standish were untrue, Aspinet thought. The shallop was heading for Plimoth and Standish was still complaining about the theft of the items. The Pilgrims reminded Standish that the Indian braves had guarded the boat for several days and received no reward for this. He merely shrugged. The Pilgrims looked at him and then at each other and shook their heads, grinning.

After dropping off the supplies at Plimoth, eating and resting for a while, they once again boarded the shallop and headed for Cummaquid. The sky was overcast and the weather seemed to be getting chillier by the hour. They hoped that they were dressed warm enough to overcome the expected cold trip.

They were going along at a good clip with a strong wind behind them. The sky was getting darker in the north and suddenly it started to snow. The men were undecided as to call off the trip and thought it wise to return to Plimoth, but they were close to the Indian village of Cummaquid and they decided to go on and seek haven there.

The light snow was increasing in intensity and their visibility was becoming limited and so they headed closer to shore. The snow storm had increased to blizzard conditions and they took down the sail and hunkered down to wait out the storm. They had no idea where land was and just drifted, pushed by the wind. They were resigned to the idea that they would have to spend the night in the open boat. They knew they were in the harbor near Cummaquid and sheltered a bit from the cold wind, the advance of the boat stopped but they were engulfed by the snow.

Ice blocks were floating by the boat and they had dropped the anchor to prevent drifting. They didn't know where they would end up if they went forward; the Pilgrims were shivering through the night and there was very little talk.

The next morning the sun's light was just beginning to break in the east and the boat was covered with snow and so were the men. Their stilled voices suddenly came to life and the men complained about the cold and their lack of sleep.

Their boat was now frozen in place and could neither move forward and backward. They tried to use an oar to crack the ice and they were banging away trying to get free.

Allerton said, "There are some Indians coming in canoes and they're chopping the ice ahead of them. Maybe they can help us get out of here. The Indians smiled at the Pilgrims and motioned they would get them out. They came up to the boat and with their tomahawks and clubs they soon had a path that the Pilgrims could follow to the beach.

The men were chilled to the bone and when they were safely on shore, Iyanough, the sachem, brought them into his hut to get warm and to get something to eat.

The Indians had seen the boat early in the morning and had quickly come to the aid of the men. The Pilgrims told them that they were there to pick up the supplies that were left behind by Bradford.

The Indians were still guarding their supplies and they also offered to sell them more corn. They also would help the Pilgrims load the Shallop whenever they were ready to leave, but they were welcome to stay until they recuperated. They were warmed and had food but then Captain Standish came upon the group that was relaxing.

Captain Standish was livid with rage. He had gone to the boat and noticed some items missing. He told the men to get their muskets, form up in ranks, and surround the hut that belonged to the sachem. He demanded that the missing beads be returned. Iyanough being a gentle person, suggested that maybe they had missed them when they first looked in the boat and why not look again. Sure enough, there they were, under a seat. Standish surmised that the thief had somehow returned them to the boat unseen. In spite of their kindness, Standish concluded that they didn't want to be friends.

Aspinet and Iyanough had proven their friendship by guarding the Pilgrims' supplies and if they wanted to do harm they could have stolen the beans and maize and the Pilgrims would surely have starved to death.

Standish was getting a poor reputation among many of the tribes on the Cape, but they still feared him and the potential power of the Pilgrims. The Pilgrims had gone to Manomet where Governor Bradford had been impressed with the tribe and the sachem, Canacum. However, when Standish visited the village he was disappointed at the reception he received and thought that he was treated coolly but he still got the supplies. No doubt the sachem had heard about Standish's antics at his previous stops.

While at Manomet, an arrogant brave called Wituamet from the Massachusetts tribe came into the chief's house with another brave and started to ridicule the Pilgrims in general and Standish in particular, calling them babies.

Wituamet said to Standish, "You Pilgrims helped to plan the death of our tribe by joining with the devil, Weston. You are in cahoots with him and his men. I know all about your plans. Weston will attack with his men and when we are engaged in battle you will then sneak in and attack us when our backs are to you. But you will not defeat us, all our lives we have been warriors and we do not fear the white man or his thunder stick. We will destroy both your villages, Wessagusett and Plimoth and no living thing will survive."

Standish was dumbfounded by Wituamet's remarks and his anger was mounting as his face turned red with rage.

Wituamet turned to Canacum and passed him his huge hunting knife and said, "We should start the killing here. Kill the yellow dog Standish and his men and all out brothers will rise to finish off the white men."

Canacum passed the knife back to Wituamet and said, "I will have none of this We get along well with the Pilgrims and they will find us their strong friends."

Standish was indignant and shouted at Wituamet, "I will never forget the action you took today...you will pay for it! I would do it now, but I am in the house of a friend and it can wait until later."

Meanwhile, a brave from Sowam came to the plantation with disturbing news. They had picked their best runner and he had traveled the long distance to Plimoth. He was exhausted after the grueling run and delivered the message that their sachem, Massasoit, was gravely ill.

Hobomok translated this news to Massasoit's new found friend, Edward Winslow. Winslow was deeply grieved by this turn of events and he asked Hobomok to join him on a trip to see Massasoit.

Not knowing what Massasoit's illness was, Winslow prepared several packets of medicine to carry to Sowam and he and Hobomok would leave at once. Before they left, Bradford said, "Tell Massasoit that all the people of Plimoth feel sorry for him in this trying period and they will offer a prayer for his quick recovery."

On the way, when they were in Chief Corbitant's territory, they heard from some Indians that Massasoit was already dead and Corbitant would take over as the great Chief of the tribes that Massasoit led.

Winslow and Hobomok stopped off at Corbitant's village to offer their congratulations, being ever the diplomat, Winslow thought this would be proper thing to do. They found that Corbitant was already in Sowam and to their great surprise they were informed that Massasoit was not dead.

After a quick meal, Winslow and Hobomok once again continued on their way to Sowam. It was night by this time but they followed a well-worn path through the dense woods.

The going was very difficult, they were continually getting slapped by low hanging branches and were tripped by exposed roots of large trees. In spite of Winslow's youthful stamina and Hobomok's experience in traveling through forests under severe conditions, they both wore signs of their exhaustive fast pace.

When they neared Sowam, the first beams of sunlight pierced the foggy darkness and the birds were starting to chirp to greet the arrival of a new day. The men passed through a meadow on the outskirts of Massasoit's village, stirring the small creatures that noisily made way for the intruders, invading their space.

In the distance they could see Medicine Men dancing around Massasoit's house, ridding the place of evil spirits. Winslow and Hobomok reached the house and were surprised to find it crowded with Indians. The relatives and friends who were concerned about his health were standing around a cot upon which lie Massasoit looking very pale. The Indians fell silent as Winslow and Hobomok walked up to Massasoit's side. Massasoit looked death-like with his eyes shut until Winslow said he was here to help him, with his friend Hobomok.

Massasoit opened his eyes and said, "My friends, I hoped that you would come. I'm sorry that I can't see you...I have lost my vision!"

Winslow and Hobomok offered to help Massasoit and said they would do everything they could to make him well. Winslow unpacked one of his parcels and took out a white powder and with great care he administered it through Massasoit's clenched teeth with the tip of his knife. After Massasoit swallowed the white powder, Winslow washed out Massasoit's mouth and scraped his swollen tongue. In a few minutes he asked how Massasoit felt.

Massasoit said, "I haven't slept for two days and I'm also constipated!"

Winslow gave him more of the white powder and miraculously he recovered in half an hour. When Massasoit rested for a few minutes he tried to get up and clumsily struggled to get off the cot. Finally he stood and extended to his full height and said, "You have worked wonders for me. Can you also clean out the mouths of the rest of the tribe?"

Winslow agreed and despite the foul odor that he soon encountered he completed the task.

They both agreed to stay with Massasoit in the village

until he fully recovered. One day Winslow said, "Great Sachem, it seems that you are feeling well again and it's time we leave to return to the Plimoth Plantation."

Massasoit took Winslow's hand and said, "Winslow, you are a friend for life. I love you like a brother and I shall never forget what you have done for me and my people."

Winslow said, "I helped you because you are my friend. You are a friend to me and to the people of Plimoth."

They finally left the village and Winslow asked Hobomok, "Do you want to stop at Corbitant's village? I'd like to talk to him and find out how peaceful he really is!"

They retraced their steps and joked about how easy it was to find their way in daylight. They were making great time and stopped several times to drink cool water from brooks which meandered their way down crooked paths to the ocean. By mid-afternoon they took some food from the packs they were carrying and ate sparingly. They wanted to reach the village before dark so they increased their pace. Several hours later they had reached the village and a brave had relayed the message to Corbitant that two men were approaching, one Indian and a white man.

Corbitant and several of his braves were waiting for Winslow and Hobomok when they entered the village and were warmly welcomed. Corbitant had left Massasoit's village when the chief was recovering and he came directly to his own village. Winslow didn't have much time to speak to Corbitant at the time, so he thought he would take this opportunity when he had more time to spare.

Corbitant's attitude really surprised Winslow. The chief's friendly reception and hospitality amazed him. He was a witty and a gracious host, contrary to the impression that he made before. Corbitant lived in a large house set aside from the living quarters of the tribe. They occupied huts which were dome-shaped and were made from bent saplings and covered with woven reed mats. Sometimes these mats were replaced by huge slabs of tree bark which were heavy but when placed in a staggered pattern were watertight and warm in the winter, cool in the summer.

The huts in winter were snug when a fire was built inside and the design wouldn't allow snow to accumulate on the roofs.

The Indians in the village seemed to be happy and they danced around a large bonfire and chanted their songs that went back to antiquity. The braves were showing off their physical prowess and skill with their bows and arrows. They gave exhibitions of wrestling and occasionally they went too far and one of the contestants would limp off injured, physically and morally broken. Tomorrow he'd be well again and the contest would resume.

Edward Winslow and Hobomok laughed heartily at the Indians antics when they tried to amuse and entertain their guests. The guests were given food and a beverage made from berries. Eventually they were given cots to sleep on and it didn't take long to fall asleep—it had been a long day.

They were reluctant to leave the next morning because they were having such a good time. Corbitant wished them a good trip home and he said they were welcome to return any time. Winslow returned the offer, saying that Corbitant would be welcome anytime he cared to come to Plimoth. Before leaving, Corbitant had one of his squaws prepare a light meal that Winslow and Hobomok could eat on their way to Plimoth.

Once they were on their way, Hobomok had a startling story to tell Winslow.

"When Massasoit was feeling better, he had called me aside and said the Massachusetts tribe had convinced the tribes on Cape Cod they were going to destroy Plimoth and

Wessagusset. He also said the Indians should stick together and drive the white men out. Massasoit suggested that I should tell you at the appropriate time and advise you that the Pilgrims should attack the Massachusetts tribe first and kill the braves. Massasoit said he couldn't tell you directly because of his position as a sachem."

Hobomok also said, "I waited to tell you after we left Corbitant's village so he wouldn't suspect anything was wrong. I don't know if Corbitant is involved or not. I know it's hard to act natural when you know a hidden secret and you're involved in what could become a life and death act.

When they finally arrived at the plantation, they saw Bradford and his council and informed them about Massasoit's recovery and then told him the story that Hobomok had related to him about the Massachusetts tribe.

Standish tied the incident together with the happening with Wituamet but he didn't know the other tribes had been approached by the Massachusetts tribe.

Bradford said he too was informed by Standish and didn't know the extent that the Cape Cod tribes were also involved.

The rumblings from the nearby tribes around the Cape increased, they had heard of Weston's planned attack on the Indians. The Indians suspected that the Pilgrims were involved because many of Weston's men had been at Plimoth and the Pilgrims joined them in the food gathering expedition, so they must be friends.

Bradford, after hearing of Massasoit's suggestion that they attack first, confirmed his thought about the threat. Under the circumstances and for their survival, Standish and the others in the council agreed they would have to make a preemptive strike against the Massachusetts tribe and also get rid of Weston's colony. This would eliminate an uprising that could destroy Plimoth Plantation. They were united in a plan that would send Standish and only eight armed men, to avoid suspicion, to Wessagusset. They held a general meeting of the Pilgrims where they outlined the plan and they reluctantly agreed to it. Part of the plan was to inform Governor Sanders of Wessagusset about the reason for the trip, to act friendly to the Indians and to lay traps to ambush them. Standish was intent on cutting off Wituamet's head to revenge him for his actions at Manomet.

Standish and Hobomok with eight heavily armed men went to the pier to embark on the shallop. The populace of the town turned out to see them off and wish them well. Myles Standish was the only true soldier in the group. The others were militiamen who had not gained experience in Indian fighting but were well-versed in close order drill.

Their trip was uneventful and they soon found themselves at Wessagusset. They had passed the *Swan* which was anchored outside the village in the bay and found nobody aboard.

Hobomok said, "Where are all the men? Why don't they at least have one guard aboard the ship?"

Standish prepared his musket and fired it into the air. Soon Weston's men came straggling into view on the beach and walked up to the Pilgrims. the Pilgrims had interrupted their search for groundnuts in the woods and clams in a nearby inlet; this was their primary source for food. Sanders was also in the group and Standish explained why he was here and so heavily armed. The men in the colony were dirty and unkempt and didn't engage in conversation.

Governor Sanders and the men of Wessagusset were interested in what the Pilgrims were saying about the Indians and the plan of attack. They agreed that the plan would work and they were anxious to put it into action.

They found room in nearby shelters to bivouac the Pilgrims and Standish was provided with his own headquarters and living quarters in another building. The Pilgrims had their own food and noticed Weston's men eyeing their modest meals with envy.

The next day two Indians braves, Pecksoit and Wituamet, came into Standish's headquarters accompanied by another brave and Wituamet's eighteen year old brother. They wanted to know why Standish and his men had come to the colony and if they came to kill them. Then angrily showing contempt for Standish, Wituamet drew out a long knife and said, "I have another just like this at my house which I used to kill both French and English."

Standish, though outnumbered, listened to this berating for awhile and sensing that the group was determined to kill them decided that now would be a good time to start the attack. Standish seized a knife tied to a string around Pecksoit's neck and plunged it in the tall, powerful, brave's chest and he died instantly. Standish's men soon dispatched Wituamet and the other brave and hanged the brother. The village was shocked and taken by surprise but this was only the beginning. Standish and Weston's men proceeded to kill all the Indian braves they encountered. They were careful to see that the women and children were not harmed. Another group of Indians were driven back while shooting a shower of arrows, dodging behind trees in their retreat. Hobomok, losing his temper and proving he was a great pinese, deliberately tore off his coat and chased them, outdistancing the Pilgrims.

The Indians then took refuge in a swamp yelling at Standish and his men. Standish responded, "Come out and fight like men...you sound like a bunch of squaws!" Seeing that the Indians would neither come out of the swamp nor fight, Standish returned to Wessagusset and asked Weston's men what they planned to do? They couldn't stay here without means of defense. He suggested they could return to

Plimoth hoping that the Pilgrims would then have access to the *Swan*.

However, Weston's men and Governor Sanders thought they would take the *Swan* to Maine and see if Weston was there. They could probably work their way home to England with the English fishing fleet, after they had given Weston his ship back. It didn't take them long to abandon their colony and get out of New England.

Standish had accomplished three things in the brief but deadly encounter. He had eliminated Weston's colony, he had intimidated the Massachusetts Indians and he had the head of Wituamet. He brought nothing back to the plantation but the head on a spike, where he and his men were received triumphantly by the Pilgrims.

When the tribes on the Cape heard the story about the raid by Standish at Wessagusset they were terror-stricken and wondered if they might have said something in the past that might have displeased Standish. They hid out in deserted areas and swamps, fearful of the wrath that might befall them. Unfortunately, many of the sachems took sick and died of worry. Ironically, many of the Indian chiefs were friends of Bradford and the Pilgrims. The sachems that died were Canacum of Manomet, Aspinet of Nauset and Iyanough of Cummaquid. The Pilgrims would miss them. Actually, the Indians had no reason to fear Standish as long as they were peaceful.

When Reverend John Robinson heard the story from one of Weston's men that returned to Leyden, he sent a letter that complained about the killing of the Indians and the abuse of the Wessagusset colony.

CHAPTER 17

Cape Cod

1623

The adventure at Wessagusset did nothing to solve the Pilgrims' problems. They were still concerned about food. They would go to bed hungry and not have the slightest idea where they would find the next day's food supply. Their hunt for food in the woods was now threatened by the Indians, especially from the powerful Narragansett tribe.

The Pilgrims decided they couldn't go on barely surviving on the meager crops that they were now harvesting. They knew it would have to be an all-out effort, a drastic change and it would have to be done soon.

In the spring of 1623 there came a turning point in the economy of the Plimoth Plantation. The Pilgrims turned aside their communistic viewpoint of the Separatists with their ideas of communal participation in growing the corn crops. Like other communist policies, it was idealistic but impractical. The communists idea that humans can work like ants or bees in harmony overlooks two basic facts...people have brains...insects have instincts. Most of the Pilgrims didn't like the idea of working in a group. When Deacon Cushman gave his lecture on "Self-Love" he meant well and that was the thinking at that time. The Pilgrims never worked together as a group wholeheartedly, their total makeup was one of rugged individualism and ambition, or else they wouldn't have journeyed to the New World looking for an opportunity to better themselves.

Bradford and the other leaders agreed that each Pilgrim should have his own land and do with it what he may. They were hesitant to change because the *Articles of Agreement* specified that they should have one farm in common. The Merchant Adventurers had not disbanded, as Weston had said, so the Pilgrims wanted to live up to their end of the bargain. They thought that the change would benefit all, at least they would give it a try.

They finally came to an agreement that the land would be divided, but only on a temporary basis and no one would own the land he farmed. An acre was allotted to each person, the head of the household being responsible for planting corn and other crops in "his domain". Each planter had to allocate a small part of this crop to pay for the services of people that could not be involved in planting, such as fishermen, carpenters, public officials and others. This was their first taste of taxes.

Once again lots were chosen by the Pilgrims drawing numbers. The preferred land was all in one group near the brook and this was given to the "Old Timers", the ones that came over on the *Mayflower*. The next group to select their lots were the passengers from the *Fortune*, this was the land further north. Making these changes to allow Pilgrims to plant corn and other crops as they could manage would prove to be a Godsend.

The women and children now eagerly went into the fields to work, it wouldn't be a lazier person sharing equally with a hard worker. The Allerton children, Bartholomew, Remember and Mary were also involved in farming. Remember said to Mary, "I think that you're too little to be out here."

"I am not. I can help, too. I can dig the ground just like you."

Bartholomew then said, "I wish the both of you wouldn't argue so much. Mary can help us, she can dig until she gets tired, then she can rest."

Remember said, "Well, she can't do much, she's so small."

Mary answered, "I'm not much smaller than you and every bit helps, doesn't it Bartholomew?"

"Can we go to work now?" Bartholomew asked, as he used his hoe to dig some dirt.

This was the beginning of private enterprise in a small way. It was contrary to the teaching of Plato, which in essence was the theory of the Merchant Adventurers.

After they had planted the crops, the men were trained in groups of seven to man the shallop which had been crudely fitted out to be a fishing vessel. The shallop was kept at sea for days at a time, in all kinds of weather, each crew determined to bring in a supply of fish to feed the starving Pilgrims. When one crew arrived at Plimoth, the fish was removed and a fresh crew shoved off to spend up to a week fishing.

All the men in the plantation spent their days either hunting deer in the woods, shooting waterfowl or fishing, once the tilling of the soil, and planting were over. The women and children were busy finding groundnuts and turkey eggs in the woods and clams and shellfish on the beach They were surviving on their own, they didn't know when they could expect another ship from England.

*   *   *

The Pilgrims were surprised but not pleased when a visitor dressed as a blacksmith appeared at their plantation along with several other men. The last person in the world they expected to see was Thomas Weston, complete with an alias. He said he was attacked by Indians after he had been shipwrecked north of Plimoth. He claimed that he was lucky to escape with his life. The Indians had taken all of his clothes except his shirt. He was able to get some clothes when he stopped at New Hampshire. He said that he visited Plimoth to see how his old friends were making out. All smiles, he could barely hide the bitterness that he still felt about the abandonment of Wessagusset. He asked the Pilgrims if he could borrow a small quantity of beaver pelts. He promised that a ship would soon arrive and the Pilgrims could have anything they wanted on the ship, because he owned it

Not believing anything he said, the leaders refused him, saying that they didn't have any pelts to spare because they needed them to trade. They said, "If we were to give them to you, we surely would have a mutiny on our hands."

After much pleading and promises from Weston, the leaders felt sorry for him and said that he could borrow one hundred pelts which weighed about 170 pounds. They would give them to him only on the condition that he would keep it a secret, they said they would tell the Pilgrims later. He agreed saying that he wouldn't tell a soul. Once he got his hands on them he lost no time in telling the Strangers who weren't too friendly with the Saints, about the arrangement he had with the leaders and saying to keep it quiet. He thought, "Now I have them right where I want them!" When news of the transaction came to the attention of the Saints, there was a period of hard-feelings toward the leaders. Gradually the rift simmered down between the leaders and the Saints and in the meantime the Strangers gloated along with the diabolical Weston, whose ship didn't come in.

But, another ship did came into the Plymouth Harbor in June. It was the *Plantation* and the Captain was Thomas West who had been named Admiral of New England. He had been given authority to impose fees for fishing along the Cape. Ignoring the threat, the fishermen stubbornly refused to give in to his demands and he found it impossible to collect the fees, so he gave up the idea without a battle.

His next attempt to make money was when he presented the Pilgrims with two hogsheads of peas "Fresh from England" at the exorbitant price of £9 ($450) each. The Pilgrims proved to be as stubborn as the fishermen. They said, "The price is too high and besides we have gone so long without them, we no longer miss them and could do very well without them."

His days as a merchant were limited, every attempt by him to capitalize on his weird ideas fell far short.

They heard that a ship was coming and would soon be at their colony. The Pilgrims lined the pier anxiously looking to the bay for the arrival of the ship which might contain friends or relatives. They wondered why it was taking so long and worried about the fate of the passengers and crew. Many stayed on the pier and others left to do their work which they felt was very important to the welfare of the people.

Someone on shore, high in a tree, yelled, "I see it. There's a ship coming!"

Below, a youth asked, "Where is it?"

"It's off to the left...it's a big one!"

"I see it now! They're putting down a sail."

The people on the pier picked up a chant, "Here they come! Here they come! Now they're safe."

One child straddling his father's shoulders so he would have a better view, asked, "Who are the people on the ship? Is it somebody we know?"

"Your aunt and uncle and their children are coming to Plimoth...I hope they're on that ship!"

Now the ship loomed larger and the people on the ship could be seen on deck looking at the Pilgrims on the pier. The passengers were excited and laughing with joy.

Word had passed through the colony that the ship was sighted coming into the bay...almost all the people in the colony were now on the shore waiting.

The crew maneuvered the ship into the pier opposite the plantation. The ship was named the *Anne* and was a hundred and forty tons. On this trip it carried sixty passengers and best of all it carried much needed supplies.

When the *Anne* set sail from England she was accompanied by a smaller ship called *Little James*. The little ship was only forty tons and was built to order by the Merchant Adventurers for the purpose of leaving the ship at Plimoth for the Pilgrims use for fishing and trading. A severe storm arose on their way over and the two ships became separated. The *Anne* was a faster ship and soon outdistanced the *Little James* and during the night they were out of sight.

For several days and nights there had been severe and violent storms and there was still no sighting of the smaller craft. The passengers on the *Anne* felt that the *Little James* had met with an unfortunate end and all aboard lost.

Then, ten days later, a cry went up from Pilgrims standing on the pier, "Look...there..." from the excited watchers who were pointing out beyond the bay. "A sail! Maybe it's the *Little James!*"

It was the lost ship and it limped into the bay with a bitter Captain John Bridges. He cursed his inept crew that was hired by the Merchant Adventurers. When he docked at the pier he was fuming about the crew, saying, "They don't know which end of the ship goes forward!"

There were ninety-three passengers aboard the two ships, thirty-two Saints and sixty-one Strangers, that would add to the growing colony. Among the passengers were the two Brewster children, Patience and Fear, who had been left behind in Leyden with friends. Mrs. Hester (Mayheiu) Cooke, with her three children joined her husband Francis and her son, John. Mrs. Bridget (Lee) Fuller was reunited with Deacon Samuel Fuller. The last of Scooby congregation to reach Plimoth was George Morton with his wife Juliana (Carpenter) and four children, a nephew and his wife's sister, Mrs. Alice Southworth, who would soon marry Governor William Bradford. Isaac Allerton greeted his sister, Sarah, who was the widow of Degory Priest, who had died in Plimoth during the great plague. Sarah was married to Cuthbert Cuthbertson, her third husband, who accompanied her with their five children from previous marriages. John Jenny, a brewery worker, came with his wife, Sarah, and their five children.

The Pilgrims expected to see Reverend John Robinson on the ship but unfortunately he was not among the passengers. They clearly missed his wise counsel and gentle manner.

Suspicion was growing that the Merchant Adventurers were behind his absence, they suspected a conspiracy to prevent Robinson from joining the Pilgrims at Plimoth, but they didn't know why.

There was a handy addition to the colony, a shipwright named Edward Bangs and another barrel-maker that would join John Alden in his craft as a cooper, his name was Robert Bartlett. Another welcome sight was a carpenter, who could help in the much needed construction of homes, he was a twenty-four year old named Thomas Clarke, no relation to the sailor named Clarke who was first to set foot on Clarke's Island.

Roger Conant, a capable and pious man, who with his brother, Christopher, joined the others under an arrangement worked out with the Merchant Adventurers. Richard Warren, who had arrived on the *Mayflower*, enthusiastically welcomed his wife, Elizabeth, and five daughters. John Hilton, who came on the *Fortune* as a young wine maker, met his wife Virginia and his two small children, a boy and girl.

One Merchant Adventurer, Timothy Hatherly, decided he would try his hand at being a settler. Francis Sprague, who came to Plimoth to "Please the palates" of the Pilgrims would open the first tavern in New England.

Captain Myles Standish strolled through the crowd, unloading from the ship. He was looking for a particular person. He was concerned with finding his bride-to-be among the passengers, but he wasn't sure that she'd be there.

He had asked his deceased wife's sister, Barbara, to come to Plimoth to marry him. In spite of the problem of getting to England and the infrequent appearance of ships at Plimoth, Standish had been wooing Barbara by mail after his wife died in the great plague and after being rejected of marriage by Priscilla Alden.

At last he saw a familiar figure and with great military bearing and aplomb, approached her and gave her a peck on the cheek. He took charge of her luggage and they left the ship with Barbara excitingly telling him about her trip across the Atlantic and Myles looking straight ahead and nodding.

Barbara would be the guest of the Bradfords until she married Standish. In the meantime, there was the matter of the courtship of Barbara. Later, they were seen walking arm in arm around the plantation. Standish pointing out points of interest with his walking stick and his red beard and long mustache neatly groomed.

Later in the year, there was almost a calamity in the colony when the home of Timothy Hatherly caught fire. Before the flames spread, Hatherly tried to get his personal effects from his house and he made repeated attempts before the heat and the apparent danger involved stopped him.

Everyone that was able-bodied formed a bucket brigade and getting water from the brook, threw it on the blaze. They tore at flaming planks with hooks and tried to rip them off the building.

They also tried to wet the adjoining buildings in an attempt to prevent the flames from spreading. Several homes were targets of sparks being carried by the wind which was steadily increasing. Women swinging damp cloths fought off the sparks that landed on their homes. Everyone in the colony was busy with the fire and the terrible consequence which would occur if it were to spread.

The small children were crying and worried about their own homes and some of the adults tried to get them into a group away from danger. The weakened condition of the people played havoc in their exhaustive firefighting. Then, it was over, the last flames had gone out and Hatherly's house was a smoldering, blackened heap. The other homes were slightly damaged but could be fixed quickly with a little effort.

The townspeople slowly made their way to their homes. In the light of day they would check the damage, now they only wanted to sleep.

The arrangement that the Merchant Adventurers had with certain passengers on the *Anne* was starting to backfire. They would make no contribution to the common store, or have any stock rights, nor would they be able to trade with the Indians. They were subject to all the laws of the *Mayflower Compact* and would do duty with the militia. This was an idea whose time had not come and there was a lot of friction in the colony with this new plan. The Pilgrims wanted all the colonists to give and share equally in good times and bad.

The recent arrivals had read the optimistic writing of

Winslow and Bradford in *Mourt' s Relations* and from letters home, written by the Pilgrims, These were done when things were looking good for them. They were dismayed when they saw the Pilgrims in rags, pale and drawn, in stark contrast to their image of healthy people as depicted in the publicity they had read. Upon seeing them, they wished they had never left home. The disappointment over what they saw was not limited to the newcomers, the Pilgrims wept when they saw the new crop of passengers. There were some that would prove to be helpful and good citizens but the majority were soon judged to be lazy and shiftless and would be sent home the next year.

Robert Cushman had sent a letter to Plimoth saying that he was not responsible for the character of the company that was sent. He said that if he wasn't there, in London, it would have been much worse. "Send them back to England and tell the Merchant Adventurers to send honest men and you should send all undesirables back to London if they do not fill the bill," Cushman wrote.

The "Old Comers" consisting of members of the *Mayflower* and the *Fortune* were upset about the conditions that would develop in the colony and there was the present danger of starvation. They knew it would take about a year for the new arrivals to be self-sufficient as far as crops went and they didn't want them to be eating the Pilgrims food. The Pilgrims went to Bradford and stated their problem and they came to an agreement that the new arrivals would depend on their supplies which they carried on the ships until the first harvest and the Pilgrims would keep their own food.

Staying in Plimoth for six weeks, the *Anne* left for England loaded with cargo and Edward Winslow, the diplomat. Winslow would see the Merchant Adventurers and tell them about conditions at Plimoth and the strides that had been made and request more and frequent supplies. He also had publicity to be printed in London, "Good News from New England" or "A True Relation of Things very Remarkable at the Plantation of Plimoth in New England" which would be printed the following year.

There was soon to be another wedding in Plimoth. Governor William Bradford, a widower for almost three years, was going to marry Alice (Carpenter) Southworth. Alice was herself a widow having lost her husband in Leyden. He had also been a renowned Separatist. Alice came as a passenger on the *Anne* in August, strictly for the purpose of marriage.

They were married in the Meeting House by Elder William Brewster, a long time friend of Bradford. They had been friends since they first became acquainted in their church in Scooby, England. The friends of Bradford, and there were many, attended the wedding. Many couldn't fit in the Meeting House and they were gathered outside. It was a sunny, hot day on August 14, 1623. After the wedding ceremony, they had a feast at Bradford's house of roasted venison, plums, grapes, watercress, wine and beer.

Mary Allerton was with her brother and sister at the wedding and reception and they were thoroughly enjoying themselves, running from one group to another. The other children in the colony were having the time of their lives, joining in the celebration. Governor Bradford went among the people in the colony with Alice introducing his new wife. Alice was very personable and the Pilgrims immediately liked her.

*   *   *

There were other items that the Governor had to

attend to in his normal duties. He was concerned about the defense of the colony and so he asked for a meeting with Captain Miles Standish and other members of his council.

When they had their meeting, Bradford questioned Standish about the preparedness of the militia and he wondered about the role of the Indians in their life. Was the relationship with them still working with peaceful intentions? They had their sources of information directly from friendly Indians that were helpful in guiding them and relieving their tension.

On other issues, the council agreed that things seemed to be better than they were in the last couple of years.

CHAPTER 18

Plymouth, Cape Cod

1624

A ship put into Plymouth Bay that was soon to cause the Pilgrims much added grief. It had on board the son of Sir Ferdinando Gorges. He was the ship's Captain and was named Robert. The ship was loaded with immigrants and a patent to an area north of Plimoth and they had the authority to control that area as well as Plimoth. The letter of authority stated that Governor Bradford could stay on as an assistant but only on a temporary basis, then he would be relieved of his duties. While this was bad enough to take, along came Reverend William Morrell in his Anglican vestments with his letter of authority giving him jurisdiction over the churches in New England.

Captain Robert Gorges summoned Weston to answer charges against Wessagusset. Weston's arrogant manner and quick tongue caused him trouble but once again the Pilgrims came to his aid. He left Plimoth on the *Swan* to sail to Virginia but not before he ridiculed the Pilgrims. As to the debt he owed for the beaver pelts, he didn't pay one penny and laughed at his creditors, who were left holding an empty bag.

Captain Gorges sailed north and went to the deserted town of Wessagusset along with some discontented members of the plantation, mostly composed of those that were friends of John Oldham. There was Timothy Hatherly, whose house had been destroyed by fire and almost burned down Plimoth with it.

In a short while the group didn't like Wessagusset and the surrounding area, they thought that it was too wild. Despairing of this, once more Wessagusset was abandoned. Some went to Virginia, others returned to England including Reverend William Morrell with his long Latin poem about New England. He spent most of the time working on his poem while he was at Wessagusset. In spite of the blustering and threats from Captain Gorges, the problems of Plimoth had been solved...by doing nothing.

*   *   *

Another event was happening in the colony. Captain Myles Standish was decked out in full military gear, his red hair combed and his mustache and beard neatly trimmed. It was a big day for him, he was getting married to Barbara. Priscilla Mullins had married John Alden the year before, preferring John to Myles. So there he was, with his militia in full attendance and the townspeople waiting in respect for their captain to appear. They, like all the others before them, were getting married in the fort's Meeting Hall.

Governor Bradford was waiting in the fort to perform the ceremony—then Myles came in and stood before him. Barbara, on the arm of Elder William Brewster, gave shy glances and smiled at the friendly faces of the Pilgrims as she walked among them to Standish s side. After a brief ceremony, they were married and the crowd gathered to offer their congratulations.

Meanwhile, things were beginning to look up in their harvest of crops. Their new method of planting individually and not as a group was paying off. At last they had conquered the mystery of getting a good crop, but many attributed it to their prayers. Who would doubt the power of prayer. There seemed to be a positive side to the Pilgrim's prayers that was undeniable in results.

With everything going so well for them, some said it's going too well, something will happen soon. It did! A drought hit the plantation from the third week in May until the middle of July. The fish fertilizer helped a little with some of the moisture but soon the corn wilted and was in danger of crumbling to dust...without the crops they would be doomed. The Saints desperately turned to God and held a "Solemn Day of Humiliation". The day chosen was hot and sunny and there wasn't a cloud in the sky, when they gathered to pray for rain. The Pilgrims drifted into the fields, gaunt, depressed, but intent to sacrifice their day in a last ditch effort to save their crops When they were all present, Brewster led them off in a prayer to relieve them of this calamity which was slowly but surely, leading them down the road to misery. The bowed their heads and offered a prayer for rain. After praying for nine hours, they seemed to be resigned that maybe it wasn't really going to work. There were still no clouds and the sun was unbearably hot. They silently walked out of the cornfields and went back to their homes, wondering what the future held for them.

Shortly, there appeared some dark rain clouds in the distance—then more and more. During the night and then continuing for two weeks, gentle showers fell on the crops and nourished them. The crops soon regained their strength and thrived.

Hobomok was wondering why they met to pray when it was not the Sabbath. The Pilgrims told him they wanted to pray for rain. He said, "When the Indians pray for rain, it comes down in such volume and violent downpour it lays the corn flat and washes away the soil!"

The other Indians had also witnessed the Pilgrims assembling for the prayer and were amazed at the results; they had never seen anything like it. It continued to rain gently from time to time throughout the summer until harvest time. The harvest was beyond expectation; it could well cover their needs until the next harvest. They even had a surplus they could sell. Never again would they return to the days of the shortages which meant near starvation. After the harvest the Pilgrims readied the plantation for the coming of winter.

*　　*　　*

The birds were flying south for the winter. They would gather in the nearby trees, squawking, until it seemed that the branches would bend under their weight. Then, on what would appear to be a prearranged signal, they would suddenly fly away from the trees and leave behind ...silence. This would be followed by another flock of birds, probably another species, and the routine would be followed exactly. This exercise had been going on for thousands of years.

Not to left out of the equation were the wild ducks and geese. Long V-shaped lines of ducks also squawking and beating their large wings, made their way to their favorite spots in warmer climates, hundreds of miles away. On their way they would stop at large ponds and lakes and gather more of the same species to make their flight south, to land at the pond or marsh, just another mystery for mankind.

The trees were undergoing their ritual of changing their green leaves which had nourished them for months to their colorful fall foliage and then they would dry out and drop to the ground and rot supplying more nutrients to the soil during the winter.

It got colder and the wind blew from the northeast with nothing to stop it. To combat the cold, the Pilgrims had laid in a good supply of wood for the fireplaces, enough to last until spring. The squirrels and other animals were ready for winter—so were the Pilgrims—now let it come!

When the first snow fell, the children were all ready to enjoy themselves. The men made sleds out of barrel staves and boxes, for the children. Some children tied barrel staves to their feet to ski down Fort Hill. Thomas Cushman pulled Mary Allerton up the hill to the fort and with much soul-searching she finally agreed to slide down the hill with him in control. As they picked up speed, Mary screamed and held on to the sides of the box for dear life. Thomas mocked her fears and finally they came to a halt when the sled turned over and spilled them to the ground.

"That was fun." Mary said, "Let's go down the hill again!" They went up and down the hill several times until Thomas tired of pulling Mary up the hill, although he was the one that suggested her riding both ways. They, like all the other children, made use of the hill when it was snow-covered.

The morale was improving in the plantation, but for the Allerton children things were still upset, with Isaac being gone for months on his business trips to London and not having a mother to be with them in their growing years. Mary still had her brother and sister and doll to comfort her and Thomas Cushman was like a big brother to her.

The Brewsters and the Bradfords looked in on them and Fear Brewster stayed at their home often.

Fear Brewster, although young in years, acted as a big

sister to them. She tried to teach the children how to cook and tend to their household tasks. Mary was only seven years old and much too young to accept the responsibility.

She tried hard to please Fear, but her young years and physical strength proved too much of a problem for her to do a good job.

Remember was only a couple of years old, but the difference in age was enough to allow her to adapt to this work much easier.

Bartholomew was very helpful around the house, doing the "man's work". He chopped wood, got the water in huge buckets and helped in harvesting clams and other odd jobs.

All in all, they all helped each other. They were very cooperative.

CHAPTER 19

Plymouth, Cape Cod

1624

On March 25th, 1624 the Pilgrims celebrated New Year's day, it was also the day they would hold elections for a Governor and his assistant, but it was a foregone conclusion as to who would be elected. Bradford had a hectic time with all the problems he had to solve. Seeing that the colony was starting to stabilize and develop, he tried to convince the Pilgrims that he would like to step down as Governor. That was not to be.

The citizens of Plimoth got up early, as usual, and were in a holiday mood. They went to the polls and voted unanimously for Bradford to reelect him and said he should go on being Governor. He had done a good job representing all the people and he had a sympathetic ear for all complaints both from the Saints and the Strangers.

To share his problems, Bradford would have five assistants. Isaac Allerton would be chief among the assistants. He would be aided by Edward Winslow, Captain Myles Standish, Richard Warren and Stephen Hopkins. They would serve, as before, to be the voice of the people in executive, legislative and judicial matters. Bradford's appeal to give the position of governor to another seemed to fall on deaf ears, he was their favorite...he had the job whether he wanted or not.

*   *   *

The next ship to appear at Plimoth was the *Charity*, under the command of Captain William Pierce, "The Ferryman of the North Atlantic", who brought the bulk of the settlers to New England. On board, returning from England, was Edward Winslow bringing items that could be traded with the Indians and much needed hooks, nets and other fishing gear. They could not fish for other than striped bass, because they didn't have the proper hooks. Also on board the *Charity* was a ship's carpenter, a salt maker, the Reverend John Lyford, and other passengers. There also were three heifers and a bull, the first of its kind in the New World. An extra dividend, deeply appreciated by the people of the colony, was much needed clothes. Robert Cushman sent a letter along, saying that he had spent all the money on things that Plimoth would need to enter the fishing, ship building and salt making trades. He was sorry he couldn't have sent butter, sugar and "other comfortable things". He said, "Once you have these trades going efficiently you will be more independent of irregular and uncertain supplies. Giving the ship's carpenter complete authority over the other works would prove to be wise because the carpenter is very skilled. He can direct the others in making ketches for fishing, a lighter and several small shallops." He also said, "I have no evidence of the skill of the salt-maker although he assured me that he knew all about the craft. Perhaps some men in the colony can work with him and learn the trade, so that they will become skilled, too."

Cushman stressed the importance of using care in writing letters home. There were some that pictured Plimoth as a loving paradise, other letters from the Strangers and filled with lies, said that the Pilgrims were starved in body and soul and, like savages, they ate stray dogs and pigs that had died in the streets. It was sad that the impression of the colony was so distorted by a few discontented Strangers.

The Strangers were complaining to the Merchant Adventurers, as usual, about the lack of sacraments at Plimoth Plantation and the children had not been taught their catechism or how to read, They went on, saying the country was barren, there were wolves, foxes and mosquitoes, which were a nuisance. They also said that the water was bad, the Pilgrims were lazy, there were thieves among the towns-people...they went on and on...*ad nauseam.*

The treasurer of the Adventurers, James Sherley, who was a friend of the Pilgrims, wrote for an explanation, more tongue in cheek than strident. When Bradford received the letter he was furious with the Strangers and immediately sat down and wrote to Sherley. Never, he wrote, have we had complaints about religion. Although we haven't had our pastor, Reverend John Robinson, to guide us, we have the Lord's Supper on every Sabbath and we have baptism as often as we can. We have no school teachers as there are none available; parents try to teach their children at home. The settlers are not lazy, they all work—work hard, although some of the Strangers do not have their hearts in it. As for the thieves in the colony...we are bound to accept people of questionable character from London and if we have to take those with a background in thievery, we are not equipped to reform them. If you want a hardworking colony, send us men with good character, otherwise we may have to send them back to you.

Bradford sent the letter along with other letters that were sent to Brewster also the one he received from Reverend

Robinson. Although the situation was still grim, the changes in crop growing were beginning to pay dividends for the Pilgrims. It offered them the chance to use corn as money, it became more valuable than silver, with the "New Comers" as eager buyers.

The new pastor that arrived on the *Charity*, Reverend John Lyford, had graduated from Magdalen College in Oxford, England. When he came ashore with his wife and five children he bowed and scraped and practically groveled to the Pilgrims. He appeared to be the humblest person in the world.

The Pilgrims fed him and his family well and accepted them into their midst. He was in his late forties and had spent his years ministering in small churches in England and Ireland. He was given the best quarters in town with the largest allowance for food and to top it off, he had been given the services of a servant, to be at his beck and call.

Elder Brewster was available with his assistants to give Reverend Lyford counsel and to help him in any way they could in his "weightiest business". Lyford, after only a few weeks in the colony, said that he wanted to be part of the colony and would join the congregation and give up his duties as an Anglican clergyman. Soon he was to share Brewster's pulpit, teaching on the Sabbath. The Pilgrims felt that congratulations were in order because it had taken only two weeks to convert Lyford. A short time later the Saints noticed a profound change taking place. Most of the malcontents in town were gravitating toward Lyford and Oldham in a strange conspiracy. There were meetings and whispering going on in the group and it was done secretly.

When William Hilton's wife gave birth, she wanted her child baptized in the Anglican religion; both she and her husband didn't want to join the church at Plimoth. They appealed to Reverend Lydon, who by then had converted to the Pilgrim's religion, to baptize the child. So Reverend Lydon then arranged a private ceremony. The Saints were incensed at his going behind their backs, but they didn't want to take action then, they would bide their time and let the indiscretions mount.

The *Charity* returned to Plimoth after a brief fishing expedition to the north and it was getting ready to depart for England. There was a report that Reverend Lyford was busy writing letters that would be sent to England aboard the ship. It was also observed that he spent much of his time with the Strangers, whispering and dropping remarks causing them to laugh out loud and nodding their heads in agreement. He was no friend of the Saints!

Finally, the *Charity* weighed anchor and slowly left the bay. Unknown to Reverend Lyford and Oldham, the governor and several men had left earlier in the shallop, under the cover of night, ready to intercept the ship now far out, stopped in the bay. The group boarded the ship and with the complete cooperation of the Captain, searched the crew and passengers and came across twenty letters written by Lyford and several by Oldham. Patiently they made copies of the letters and kept several intact so they could have them in the writers own handwriting. They figured that it was a good night's work. They headed back to Plimoth with the evidence they needed against the conspirators.

Lyford and Oldham found out about Bradford's group's trip to the ship but they didn't know why they had gone. They assumed that they had gone to dispatch some important papers, which they had forgotten. Suspecting nothing after a few weeks went by without hearing any complaints, they felt secure that the Saints were unaware of their activities. They underestimated the guile of the Saints, who were biding their time in springing the trap against them.

When Standish called Oldham to stand watch, the roster indicating it was his turn, he refused and started to argue. Drawing his knife against Standish and starting to berate him, he ranted and raved against the colony. Bradford was a long distance away but he heard this outburst by Oldham, and hurried to the scene to restore order.

Not that Standish couldn't handle Oldham. Oldham continued like a wildman and used foul and obscene language within earshot of the whole colony. Under Bradford's orders they grabbed him and the militia then took him to the fort, put him in chains until he came to his senses. He continued to yell and shout obscenities until finally he was spent and quiet.

Lyford contacted all the malcontents and they had a public meeting on the Lord's day. The Saints now played their trump card. They had the evidence that Lyford and Oldham had plotted against the plantation and their church. They had continued, without hesitation, their deceit of underhandedness toward the colony. Called to stand trial for plotting against the colony and attempting to gain control, Lyford and Oldham were confident that the court had no evidence to prove their case. All the Pilgrims attended the trial which was held in the fort. Several of the militia companies, armed and in precise military marching order, headed by Captain Myles Standish with his sword in hand, went to the fort with Lyford and Oldham in tow.

They passed the grinning skull of Wituamet which was still affixed to the fort and a grim reminder to the prisoners of the justice that could be expected in the colony.

Inside the fort was a large room with light filtering in from the narrow slots, painting a gloomy picture of the scene at the trial. Seated at a long table with his assistants, Governor Bradford opened the trial against the two prisoners by reading the charges against them.

Lyford and Oldham complained that the Saints only wanted Separatists in their colony, forgetting the Strangers were now accepted as citizens of the plantation. They were angry that the settlers had stopped the Oldham group in their traffic of stolen goods. Lyford complained about the shortage of food and Bradford immediately set him straight by saying that he was given the most generous supply of food in the colony.

The prisoners seemed to think the trial proceedings were a joke and they smirked. Oldham said, "The charges that you made are false, I dare you to provide proof of our alleged guilt."

Bradford could not have planned it better and he seemed to relish his actions as he prepared to read the letters that were copied on the *Charity*. Bradford presented one of the letters that Lyford had written, it read: "Send a large group of non-separatists so they can overwhelm the Saints when they vote, then we will have the majority voice and we will win all elections and dominate the colony...we can have our own way." Part of the next letter by Lyford read: "You should make every effort to keep the Saints in Leyden from coming, especially their pastor John Robinson or all will be lost."

A letter that Oldham wrote read: "You said you have a captain that wants to come over, well you should make him a general and he can replace their Captain Standish who acts like a silly boy." He wrote in contempt.

Silence filled the room...not a soul stirred, then Oldham burst out in rage at Bradford and his assistants, "How dare you intercept our mail and read it!" He was playing to the court trying to get support from the Strangers. He urged them on to open revolt. "Where is your courage? You have complained to me about a lot of things...now stand up and defy their authority...I'll be with you!"

Still, there was silence! Nobody moved, no voice was

heard in opposition. Then crying profusely, Reverend Lyford burst out saying, "John Billington and others deceived me with their frequent complaints. I have written things that I now know were false and mischievous. I have maligned people who took me in and were kind and generous. I have failed them and I can never make amends...I am a reprobate," and he went on and on—then he was silent, sobbing and looking at the floor. Never once did he mention how he had failed his own family!

The council agreed they were guilty and they would have to leave the colony. Oldham was to leave at once although his wife and children could stay temporarily until he was settled. Gathering his belongings and supplies, Oldham left, going north about thirty-five miles to establish the colony of Nantasket, near Boston. He took many of the malcontents with him. Among those going was Roger Conant who later founded Salem, Massachusetts. He was welcome to stay in Plimoth because he was always considered an asset to the community, but he chose to leave.

William Hilton left with his wife and children and joined David Thompson, a Scottish trader who had established himself in an area that was later to become Portsmouth, New Hampshire. Hilton was later to move and founded the town of Dover, New Hampshire with his brother, Edward, a fishmonger from London.

Reverend Lyford was given six months to leave Plimoth, but the Pilgrims would forgive him if he would mend his ways and abide by the policies of the colony. He begged them to stay and would confess "His sins pubikly in ye church," with tears larger than before. Deacon Samuel Fuller and other tender-hearted Pilgrims fell to their knees and asked his forgiveness for the manner in which he was treated. He forgave them and resumed his teaching. This lasted about two months and once again he was back to letter-writing to the Adventurers. Among the many complaints was his criticism of the church in Plimoth. Again the letters were intercepted and this act was added to the complaint against him by his wife to Bradford concerning his antics with the maid. He also defamed the well-liked Elder Brewster in his letters.

The Lyfords were ordered out of the colony but they remained until the sudden appearance of John Oldham, who had been forbidden to set foot in the plantation. Immediately, trouble broke out between the Pilgrims and him. Standish again marched him to the fort to cool off. Once again, he ranted, raved, shouted profanities and threatened violence against the members of the colony. He was in a locked cell at the fort and Standish threatened to put him in chains and gag him if he didn't keep quiet. All the threats of punishment fell on deaf ears.

Oldham praised Reverend Lyford and said, "He has a lot of courage—he'll still defeat you. Even now he's plotting to take over your colony. Mark my word, he'll succeed!"

Standish contacted Bradford and related the outburst of Oldham and his actions. Oldham blurted out that Reverend Lyford was continuing to try and undercut the Pilgrims and tried to spread distrust and malicious deceit.

Bradford said, "We've been very suspicious of his activities since the trial and I believe this information given in the heat of anger by Oldham seems to clinch all the arguments. Tell both Lyford and Oldham that they'll be leaving Plimoth—never to return."

The next morning was the day of their departure having been notified the night before. Reverend Lyford, fighting back tears, wanted to know why they were doing this to him. Bradford reminded him of his shortcomings and he dropped the matter by walking away. Then Standish with his militia marched Oldham to the beach, where there was a company of militia ready to give Oldham a "bob upon the bumme" with the butt end of their muskets. He was then loaded in the shallop and was given a firm bit of advice, "goe and mende ye manners". Reverend Lyford left with Oldham. Oldham was standing in the shallop angrily shouting at the crowd while Lyford was silent looking down, crestfallen.

This incident and the fairness of the trial had a sobering effect on the Strangers; they now wanted to join the church and become more active in the community...they wanted to cooperate. Lyford and Oldham's destination was Nantasket but, unfortunately, the Pilgrims would see them again.

CHAPTER 20

Plymouth, Cape Cod

1625

When Winslow returned from England on the *Charity* he also brought a patent for some land on Cape Ann about sixty miles north of Plimoth. The patent had been issued to Edward Winslow and Robert Cushman and was signed by Lord Sheffield.

In the spring of 1624 the Pilgrims embarked on a voyage to use the patent and they decided to use the land fur base when they went fishing. Upon arrival, they built a wharf, it was rough but it would serve their needs. It was a poor season for fishing and added to their disappointment was the inaction of the captain of their vessel, who did nothing but eat and drink most of the time. Normally the fishing was good in this area. A little discouraged they packed their things and returned to Plimoth, they would try again next year.

Returning in 1625 they were surprised to see Lyford and Oldham and company using the wharf the Pilgrims built. They moved up from Nantasket at the invitation from a critic of the Saints, an Adventurer named Reverend John White. Along with Lyford and Oldham was Roger Conant, superintendent of the settlement. Lyford was their pastor and Oldham was the overseer of trade.

Captain Standish, upon seeing them acting so brazenly on the Pilgrim's wharf, demanded that they surrender the wharf immediately or there would be trouble.

Rolling up hogsheads to form a barricade, they laughed at Standish when he said that the Pilgrims had a patent from London for the land that they were standing on. "The patent is worthless," they claimed and Standish grew red with rage and was prevented from great violence by Roger Conant and Captain William Pierce. Finally subdued the Pilgrims gave up their wharf on condition that the Lyfor and Oldham group would assist them in building a new one The Pilgrims were intent on making their venture successful so they sent for the salt-maker that Winslow brought from London to do the fish curing. He had attempted to build a warehouse in the colony for the storage of fish and a year later he gave up. Now he was set to prove his knowledge of salt-making. He arrived at Cape Ann with his salt-making pans and attempted to build a warehouse. By summer the warehouse had burnt down destroying all the pans. Although he was a hard-worker, he didn't know the mystery of salt-making.

Conant and the others left Cape Ann the next year and moved about fifteen miles down the coast and founded a town called Naumkeag (later known as Salem). Lyford became the pastor at Naumkeag and was moderately successful. However, the Pilgrims never forgave him. Oldham became a trader who prospered and once again made friends with the Pilgrims. News of the dispute traveled to England and there were to be repercussions.

The Adventurers were greatly upset when they heard

of the Lyford-Oldham trouble with the Pilgrims. When Winslow went to London to explain the situation he met a stonewall of resistance. They were no longer interested in continuing support for the Pilgrims in no uncertain terms, calling them lazy, cruel and without pity. Cushman tried to appeal to them and to listen to their side of the story, he said you should not judge them too harshly. Finally the Merchant Adventurers said that they would go on under certain conditions. They insisted on a direct voice in governing the colony, which had been assured under the patent that was granted to Plimoth. The Pilgrims were also to use the French discipline and do away with the "Brownists" and other church differences.

Ultimately, Reverend Robinson could go to Plimoth if he became an Anglican! The Pilgrims said the proposal was "reasonable"...and ignored it...another problem had been solved. What galled the Pilgrims most was the sanctimonious lectures that were given by the Adventurers on how to raise their children and how the adults should behave. "Live together in love without telling stories about your neighbors and help the weak." No group of people on earth were less deserving of this undue criticism then the Pilgrims.

Through Robert Cushman's dogged determination, a small group of Adventurers agreed to continue under the same joint stock method. They were Sherley, Collier and Timothy Hatherly whose home was burnt down in Plimoth and who had returned to England. They said that the goods in the common store were not to be touched and they could remove only what they needed. The Pilgrims were to collect all the valuable goods they could find and send them to England to help settle their debts. The Pilgrims were on the spot, they had no recourse but to go on as usual. They had to buy their goods at exorbitant prices and they desperately needed the supplies carried on the *Charity*. The profit of the sale went to Sherley and his partners. Allerton and Winslow were appointed agents for the Adventurers to handle the sale.

Loading the *Charity* with fish and the *Little James* with Cod and beaver pelts, alone worth 277 pounds, the Pilgrims figured that they would be doing fine in paying off the debt. Captain Standish was aboard the *Charity*. He had decided at the last moment to go on the larger ship for comfort's sake. He had originally planned to go on the *Little James* where he could keep his eyes on the beaver pelts, but he thought they would arrive safely. The Merchant Adventurers came to the conclusion they would return the *Little James* to England and replace the men who had sailed her to Plimoth with an experienced crew and then return to New England.

The *Charity* towed the *Little James* to keep the ships from being separated. Crossing the Atlantic proved uneventful, they had calm seas and mild weather most of the way. They were on the home stretch and entering the English Channel when a wild storm suddenly struck and they had to cut the tow line with the *Little James*. In a short while the weather changed but the *Charity* was nowhere in sight.

A pirate ship loomed in the distance and with its greater speed soon came abreast of the *Little James* and with practically no resistance from the crew, seized control of the little vessel. The pirate ship from the Barbary Coast towed the captured ship and returned to Morocco. The pirates sold every item the Pilgrims owned and to make matters worse all those aboard were sold into slavery and never heard from again. This caused much sorrow in Plimoth and with the Merchant Adventurers.

Standish had gone to London to see the Merchant Adventurers because he was one of the last to be in disfavor with them. They just hoped that he would be more civil to them than when he severed the head of Wituamet and put it on a spike in Plimoth plantation. They didn't want to end up sharing the space next to him. Standish told the Adventurers that the Pilgrims would like to buy better quality supplies from them at a lower price.

He asked the Council for New England to bar further influence of people to disclaim a valid patent, such as the one they had obtained for Cape Ann. Oldham was the villain at Cape Ann when he ignored the patent claim, causing the trouble with the Pilgrims.

Robert Cushman invited Standish to his home while he was on his trip to London. Naturally, Cushman was very interested in hearing about his son, Thomas, and other things happening in Plimoth.

Standish gave Cushman a letter which Bradford had entrusted to his care. He wrote: "Beware of Oldham who is now in England and has threatened to get even with you." John Billington was also mentioned as a threat, but his whereabouts were unknown. "Billington is no good, never will be and will some day die as a scoundrel." He said that Thomas Cushman, who was living with his family, was in good health and if he continued with his good character, he would develop into a good man. He said, "Thomas is taking advantage of my library of three hundred volumes and seems eager to learn from them. Elder Brewster is also interested in Thomas's education and is helping him in his studies. He has been tutoring him in many subjects and he has access to his library, which consists of the writing of Roger Bacon, Socrates and other Greek and Latin authors. His library exceeds mine by a hundred volumes and they are varied in nature. Thomas will be well-educated if he continues to have such interest in our books and remains a student of Elder Brewster. I am going to open a school for politics and public administration for my sons, stepsons and my nephews and you can rest assured that Thomas will be included as a student."

Cushman gave Standish the letter to read and he said, "Things seem to be going well in Plimoth and I know that Bradford is doing a good job in taking care of Thomas. My wife and I will be going to live in the colony soon. I'll be happy to join my old friends."

Meanwhile, Standish remained in London to be with the Merchant Adventurers, to try to influence their opinion of the Pilgrims and their undeserved criticism. He was making headway and many of the Merchant Adventurers were starting to see that, indeed, there were two sides to the story.

There were many Londoners that were now affected by the plague. Those that could afford the trip were fleeing the city and going to the countryside to get out of the congested city. They thought that they could avoid the plague.

Standish was waiting for a boat that would take him to Plimoth. He had borrowed 150 pounds at fifty percent interest, proving once and for all, his skill was in military matters, not financial. He was buying a few things to take back to Plimoth and the rest went for expenses.

In a week or so he would be leaving England.

CHAPTER 21

London, England

1625

A few days after Standish visited Robert Cushman and his wife, Cushman was spending some time with the Merchant Adventurers when he suddenly felt faint. He started to sweat and he felt very weak. "I'm not feeling well, I think that I'm coming down with something. I'll go home and maybe if I rest for awhile I'll feel better," he said.

Sherley, who was concerned with Cushman's appearance, said, "Do you want somebody to go with you?"

"I would say no, normally but on second thought if somebody could accompany me, I would really appreciate it," Cushman said. With a clerk to aid him, Cushman slowly made his way home. When he arrived, his wife came to the door and was alarmed at his appearance. He was haggard and pale and needed assistance in getting to a chair.

"Robert what happened? You look awful! How are you feeling?" Mary asked.

"I feel weak. I think I'll lay down for awhile and rest."

The clerk that had helped Cushman to his home, left

when Mary said that she could manage and thanked him for his assistance. She helped Robert out of his clothes and into bed and said, "Do you think I should get a doctor to check you?"

"Yes Mary. I've never felt so miserable."Mary put on her coat and said, "I'll be right back, I'll see if Doctor Fitch can come to see you." When she came back later she said, "Doctor Fitch is out but his wife will tell him you're not feeling well and want to see him."

"I'll try to rest awhile."

Mary silently closed the door and sat staring at the wall. She told her husband that Doctor Fitch was out, but she didn't tell him that Mrs. Fitch said that the doctor was exhausted himself, caring for patients that had been stricken with the plague. Robert had all the symptoms that Mrs. Fitch had outlined as being common with her husband's patients. Mary fought back tears and prayed her husband would survive. In about an hour she silently opened the bedroom and peered in at her husband. He had his back turned and seemed to be fast asleep.

She later made some soup and thought that maybe if he had some, it would help nourish him. She slipped into his room to find him in the same position. She whispered, "Robert...Robert, I have some soup, would you like some?" There was no response.

"Robert...Robert!" She listened to see if he was still breathing. When she found out he was still alive, she tried to shake him awake. Once again she hurried to the doctor's office and found that Doctor Fitch had just arrived home after seeing his last patient. She explained about Robert's condition and said, "I think that he's in a coma."

"Mary, I'll go back with you and see what's happening."

They hurried along the sidewalk, came to the

Cushmans' house and entered. Robert was now awake, very pallid and Doctor Fitch listened to his breathing. He opened his bag and pulled out a few instruments; he looked into Robert's mouth and listened to his heart. He was hot and becoming restless. The doctor said, "He has a fever...I'll give him something to lower his temperature."

He said to Robert, "Get some rest, Robert, Mary will be right outside your room if you need her." After checking him over, the doctor went into the next room with Mary and he had a very serious look. "Mary, I think that Robert may not have been feeling well for the last week. Did you notice whether he had been restless or tired lately?"

"Well, he seemed tired but he was doing a lot of work with the Merchant Adventurers, trying to get more supplies for Plimoth and was experiencing trouble with the Pilgrims' poor financial straits. We both thought he was tired and worn out as a result of his work. He said he was going to stay home and rest but he never got around to it."

Doctor Fitch said, "We can only wait and see what happens. He seemed to be in a deep sleep not a coma. Perhaps if he sleeps for a few hours it will do him a world of good. Frankly Mary, you'll have to prepare yourself for the worst. I have to go now but I'll send my wife around to sit with you for awhile." After he left, Mary with tears in her eyes, again prayed for Robert.

In a few minutes Mrs. Fitch came to the house to visit with Mary. They discussed their life and experiences and in general, made small talk. Finally in about an hour, Mrs. Fitch said she would have to go home.

Mary said, "Before you go I'll see how Robert is doing." She tip-toed into the bedroom and found Robert sound asleep. She waited for a few seconds and then she came out and said, "He's asleep, I hope that he'll be all right."

Mrs. Fitch took Mary's hand and said, "Try not to worry Mary, we'll just have to wait and see."

When she left, Mary sat down and started a long vigil. She finally dozed off on the couch, spending a restless night, tossing and turning.

In the morning she went into the bedroom to see how Robert was feeling. He was awake but very listless and he was still running a fever. "Hello Robert, how are you feeling today? Are you feeling better?"

"I'm just about the same, I did get a little rest last night."

"Do you want something to eat?" You haven't had a thing in your stomach since yesterday morning. I can give you some soup or maybe you want a cup of tea, can you think of something you want?"

"I really don't feel like eating but I should have something in my stomach, maybe I can try a little tea." In a few minutes Mary returned with the tea and helped her husband so that he could drink. In his weakened condition he had trouble trying to handle the cup. He used both hands and slowly drank, pausing for several minutes and then he said, "I've had enough."

"Robert, do you think you'll want more later? Do you want some soup now...or anything?"

"I'll have some water, I have a splitting headache.""I'll get it for you and then I'll have Doctor Fitch come back to see you."

Later when Doctor Fitch came to the house and examined Robert he had a discouraging report for Mary. "Mary, Robert doesn't look good. As I told you before, you should be prepared for the worse. His lack of appetite, listlessness and general bearing doesn't speak well for his overall health. I have to go now but I'll drop in later to see how Robert's doing."

Mary walked with him to the door. Robert was sleeping now...he needed his rest.

The next day he was gone...dead at the age of forty-seven. Mary was again a widow. She thought, "Where do I go from here?"

Mary was in shock for a while. She stared at Robert's form in the bed and again cried out, "Robert...Robert!" She sat for a few minutes just looking at his still body and then, trying to control her weeping, she decided she should contact Doctor Fitch.

She walked the short distance to his home and knocked at the door. Doctor Fitch himself came to the door, and admitted Mary into the house. She tearfully relayed that Robert had passed away and she needed help.

Doctor Fitch, who was deeply moved by Robert's death and his friendship with the Cushmans, said that he would help her in any way that he could. He called out to his wife and when she entered the room, he explained to her that Robert was gone and he was going to Mary's house. He then suggested that maybe they could have tea when he returned.

He went to the Cushman's home and examined Robert's body. He then contacted a nearby mortician to make the arrangements to have the body picked up. He knew that Mary wasn't in any condition to think rationally in this sudden emergency, so he pitched in.

When he completed his necessary work, he returned to his house.

His wife, Lillian, said, "We were wondering why you were gone so long."

Doctor Fitch turned to Mary and said, "I hope you don't mind, but I've made arrangements with Mr. Abercrombie to bring Robert to his funeral parlor. I've also sent a message to the Merchant Adventurers advising them about Robert's demise.

"You're welcome to stay here with Lillian while the preparations are made. As for me, I have several patients I must see, but I will return as soon as possible."

Mary, who had regained most of her composure, said, "I can't thank you enough for your thoughtfulness in attending to Robert. You have been very kind."

Doctor Fitch said, "I feel a deep loss, also. Robert was my good friend and I know we've lost a good man. We will all miss him."

CHAPTER 22

Plymouth, Cape Cod

1625

J ust before Standish left for America he got a message that Robert Cushman had died. He attended the funeral and told Mary that the Pilgrims had lost a good and faithful friend. He would be missed by members of the colony and they would soon be aware, if they weren't already, of the valuable service that he had given to the colony for years.

Standish returned to Plimoth and the colony was shocked to hear of Robert Cushman's death. In addition to this news, there was also the untimely death of the Reverend John Robinson in Leyden. Both deaths had happened suddenly. The Pilgrims remembered the way they would sit at the feet of the minister and always receive solace and words of comfort and wisdom...now they were both gone. The Pilgrims were stunned at their deaths, they always held out hope that someday they would appear in their midst to join them.

Bradford told Thomas Cushman that his stepmother had sent him a letter with Standish telling about his father's death and he offered him his sympathy. He said, "You will

always have a home here, you're like another son to me."
Thomas thanked him and said that he also received a letter
telling about his father's death. He didn't know what his step-
mother would do.

The Pilgrims went on with their lives, though heart-
broken because of their loss, they couldn't mourn forever.
Cultivating their fields; hunting for beaver and muskrats,
they seemed to expand their efforts...they knew that they
would have to succeed in Robinson's memory. Building two
shallops and a lighter and working on two large ketches, the
work came to a temporary halt because of the death by fever
of the ship's carpenter and master builder. Fortunately, he
had imparted enough knowledge of his craft so the rest of the
colonists could carry on with the work.

He had proven to be a clever and ingenious builder by
cutting the original shallop in half and adding seven feet to
it's length and he completed the task by adding a deck. The
shallop's improvement had to be made because of the
increase in beaver pelt and corn trading. There were now several villages in trading competition with Plimoth. These new
villagers were trading with the Indians and were offering
twice as much for items as the Pilgrims did. To stay competitive, the Pilgrims now had to raise twice the amount of crops
to get the same revenue.

The Pilgrims heard of a fishing station which was
becoming inoperative so they went to see what bargains they
could get. Trading corn for various items at the station, they
were surprised that they earned almost £400. Exploring a
nearby French wreck, they obtained valuable rugs which they
traded to the Indians. The Pilgrims returned to the plantation with a lot of beaver pelts and several goats. They were
able to pay off Standish's debts which he had incurred while
he was in London plus several other debts.

*　　*　　*

It wasn't all business and trade at Plimoth, there was time for romance, too. Isaac Allerton had been courting Fear Brewster for several months after she came over on the *Anne*. They were married in 1626 in a civil ceremony at the fort. Isaac's children were at the wedding and they would have a new "mother" to take of them.

Bartholomew was now fourteen, six years younger than his step-mother. There would be a difficult task ahead for Fear to supervise the children even though they were well-behaved.

Fear Brewster had been a frequent visitor to the Allerton household and often looked after the children when Isaac was away on business trips. Although she had a little authority over the children then, she was now a mother to them. This would take a lot of adjustment for Fear, she was inheriting a ready-made family and she had just left her own childhood. It would require Isaac to lay down the law that they would have to accept Fear's authority. She hoped she would be successful in the transition because she loved the children and she thought it was mutual. They still held fond memories of their own mother.

Isaac had been married a month or two when he had to leave on a trip to London. He brought over a load of beaver pelts to the Merchant Adventurers and also carried a commission allowing him to handle all the plantation's business with them.

One of the first things he did was to convince the Merchant Adventurers that the plantation also had rights and claims. Once they agreed to this, he was authorized to borrow £100...then he proceeded to borrow £200, contrary to the wishes of the Pilgrims.

However, he brought home an important document that had long had the Pilgrims perplexed and now, for a change, they knew where they stood with the Merchant Adventurers. It was signed by forty-two of the Merchant Adventurers and they agreed to free the Pilgrims of all debts for a settlement of £1,000 ($50,000) and they had to pay off these debts in payments of five annual installments of £200. This reduced rate was still a great sacrifice for the Adventurers for they had already laid out £7,000; but as quoted by Captain John Smith, the First Virginia Company had spent £200,000 in building Jamestown, Virginia and hadn't received a penny in return. The Pilgrims wondered how they could pay off the debt but six or seven of the plantation leaders guaranteed they would assume the risks of the loan if the colony defaulted.

Now the Pilgrims were the owners of the plantation! It was about time for the settlers to decide how they would share in the colony. The formula they decided on, was essentially the one they had agreed to before. First came the debts that had priority over all other expenditures, and any excess was to be divided equally among the settlers. Every family was to have shares, depending on the family size. The Pilgrims could keep their homes and garden plots of flowers, which were located in the rear of the homes. If the home had more value than the neighbors, its added value had to be compensated.

There was an exception made for Governor Bradford, Brewster, Standish, Winslow and Allerton for their many years of service without compensation. They gathered all the livestock and divided it by lot according to the value.

Thirteen people formed a group and each group was given several pigs, a cow and a few goats.

Bradford and Allerton soon realized that they were

among those responsible for the debt and they should be given special consideration in picking the money-making projects. They hoped to make a little extra money that would enable them to bring over the rest of the congregation from Leyden. This was to be kept secret because they feared the shareholders would object to this, especially the Strangers. Using Allerton's plan, a monopoly was conceived whereby Bradford, Allerton and Standish were given the right to decide who would become partners or "Undertakers" in their enterprise. These Undertakers could decide what to do with all the furs, beads. corn, knives and other trading items that the Pilgrims put into the Common Store. The undertakers would have exclusive rights to the trading posts that the plantation owned. To compensate for this deal, the Undertakers would pay the debts to the Merchant Adventurers and other debts which came to about £600 a year.

The Merchant Adventurers agreed to supply the settlers with about £50 worth of shoes and stockings which could be repaid with corn that was to be valued at six shillings per bushel. The colony would need about 166 bushels of corn to repay this debt alone. This arrangement would last for six years until the debt was paid to the Merchant Adventurers.

Five partners were chosen by the Undertakers, they were; William Brewster, John Alden, John Howland, Edward Winslow and Thomas Prence. They set out at once to trade with the Indians, in all directions. They had a strong incentive to make money! Going to the north, much further than they traveled before, they opened a trading post on the Kennebec River on the site which is now Augusta, Maine. John Howland was the manager, where very active trading with the Indians went on for Otter, Beaver, Muskrat and other furs. They traded with the friendly Abnaki Indians for the furs. The traders used blankets, rugs, coats, skirts and some foodstuff as barter.

Another group went twenty miles south of the plantation on the Cape and built another trading post at Aptuxcet, now Bourne. This was followed by another trading post near Buzzards Bay at Manomet River.

The trading post was made of oak, hewn from the timber found in abundance at this spot. They kept two agents there continually during the summer and throughout the cold, harsh winter. They built a small boat with which they continued to trade and explore the coast and rivers along the southernmost part of New England.

*   *   *

Bradford received a very friendly letter that expounded the virtues of the hard working and courageous Pilgrims and their religious beliefs. The letter was from Governor Peter Minuit who inquired if the Pilgrims had any beaver or other items for sale, saying that they would pay money for them.

Minuit was now at Fort Amsterdam, a bulwark against the Indians made from logs and earthenworks on Manhattan Island. He had purchased Manhattan, all 22,000 acres, in May, 1626 from the Indians for twenty-four gold dollars or sixty Dutch guilders, along with some colorful beads for the squaws of Manhattan Indians.

Bradford replied to the Minuit letter, writing also in a friendly fashion, that some of the Pilgrims had spent several years in Holland and were always treated well and as friends. Some of their brethren were still there, he would never forget how well they were treated. He explained that at the present time they had everything they needed but certainly would deal with them in the future if the rates were satisfactory. He inquired about the price the Dutch paid for Otter and Beaver by the pound and what items they would be interested in buying; such as fish, corn, tobacco or other items and how much they would pay for each.

The Pilgrims hoped that this could be the beginning of a smooth trading relationship with the Dutch colony. However, Bradford warned the New Netherland Company that the Dutch were trading with Indians in the Plimoth neighborhood and they wanted it stopped.

Several months passed and a ship named the *Nassau* sailed around Cape Cod to the Pilgrim post at Aptuxcet. The chief trader at New Amsterdam, Isaac de Resieres, who was also the secretary at Fort Amsterdam, came ashore with great fanfare with his attendants and a flurry of trumpets. The *Nassau* was to pick him up again in a few days so they sailed off, destination unknown. Learning that he was twenty miles away from Plimoth, his original destination, and dreading the walk, the portly de Resieres contacted Bradford and inquired if he could accommodate him by sending a shallop to pick him up.

This done, he sailed comfortably into Plimoth Bay and stepped onto the pier which the Pilgrims built at Town Brook. Isaac de Resieres was impressed with Plimoth and its inhabitants with their quaint ways and likewise the Pilgrims were taken with his character and behavior.

When de Resieres related to the Dutch of hewn planks and gardens behind the houses enclosed in neat squares of planks which made for an orderly appearance. He said that they have an ample supply of fish, clams and lobsters right in their front yard; however, their farms weren't as good as ours because they have a rocky terrain. He brought fine clothes and linen from Holland and also a large chest of sugar for which the Pilgrims traded tobacco.

De Resieres offered the Pilgrims wampum and said that this was a means of trading, a convenient currency to be used with the white man and the Indians. The wampum was composed of beads, quahog and periwinkle shells on string and seemed more decorative than practical. The Pilgrims bought only a few pieces because they were skeptical about its value and high asking price. It proved to be of great value in trading with the Indian tribes on the Cape and with the Massachusetts and Maine Indians.

They no longer had to take bulky quantities of corn or other crops in trade in awkward bartering. The Indians were anxious to get the wampum (also called *sewn*) and the Pilgrims were overwhelmed at the response to it. Having wampum to trade, they practically monopolized the beaver trade because of its demand.

CHAPTER 23

Plymouth, Cape Cod

1626-1627

John Cooke, the son of Francis Cooke was with Thomas Cushman outside the Allerton's home. The Cookes had been their neighbors for years, living only two houses away. It was a fairly warm day so they searched out a cool spot where they could chat. They had done all their chores and now it was time to relax.

They had renewed their friendship when Thomas came over on the *Fortune* with his father in November 1621. Although they both had a lot of friends in the colony, Thomas was John's best friend in the colony as he had been in Leyden.

They had a jug of well water that was cool, having hauled the water up from the depths. They shared the water each taking deep gulps. John looked around and said, "Can you see anybody looking?"

Thomas also looked around and said, "No, why?"

"I'm going to light up my pipe. How about you?"

They both withdrew clay pipes and some tobacco

which they stuffed into their pipes. Using a small piece of flint and iron, they attempted to ignite some tinder and it quickly caught fire. They used the flame to light their pipes and were soon puffing away.

"Do you think we'll ever get caught?" John asked.

"Well we haven't got caught yet! Unless somebody tells on us, we probably won't. Do you have a small feeling that Governor Bradford and your father already know that we are smoking on the sly?"

"I bet that when they were our age they were smoking too! They were probably hiding from view also." John said.

Thomas said, "I think Sir Walter Raleigh brought some tobacco back to England from Virginia but I don't think there was much around."

"Maybe they didn't have any, after all."

"Maybe not." Thomas replied.

After they had exhausted the subject of smoking which didn't take too much time with their limited knowledge of the topic, John said, "What would you like to do when you're an adult?"

"Well that's easy! I'd like to follow in William Brewster's footsteps. I guess he's really my hero. He's a good man and cares for the people. He's smart too! You should see the books he owns. I'm reading some of them but I don't think I could read them all if I spent my whole life doing it. He graduated from a famous university and I know that I'll never be able to do that. I'd either like to be another William Brewster or a Governor Bradford. It's kind of hard to decide which one I'd like to be. They're both well liked by everyone in the colony. What do want to do or be when you grow up?"

John thought for a few seconds and then said, "I'd like to be like my father. He's a good man, too. He's always done his best to support our family...he's worked hard. Yes, I'd like to be as good as he."

"You're right John. He is a good father and so was mine. They have both worked hard to follow God's principles and to better the well-being of the people of the colony. I only hope that we can be as good as any of them."

There was a long pause and then John said, "I see Mary Allerton eyeing you all the time, especially when you're not looking at her. I guess she thinks you're really her hero."

"Come on John, you're trying to make sport with me, she's still a child."

"I think that if she had her way she would marry you, when she grows up."

"She's a nice girl but she can't even cook." Thomas said, laughing. "She has a lot to learn about cooking and housekeeping."

"Do you think you'll marry her some day?" John asked, jokingly.

Thomas hit John on the arm and with a smile said, "Who knows...maybe I will, when she grows up...and then again maybe I won't. Can you keep a secret John?"

"Yes, Thomas...of course I can keep a secret!"

"Me too!"

*　　*　　*

In 1625 a ship called the *Unity*, which was commanded by Captain Wollaston, landed about twenty-five miles north of the colony, beyond Wessagusset in an area which is now called Quincy. It was an arrogant intrusion upon what the Pilgrims regarded as their domain.

This intrusion was a result of an edict from the English Crown that went back to the era of Queen Elizabeth I. She was well aware that real estate in the New World was there for the taking if you had men and women of courage to claim and develop the land and a strong navy to back it up.

Unfortunately, her father Henry VIII had his problems on the European continent, along with his marital troubles and difficulty with the Pope at the time, so he was preoccupied. When Elizabeth became Queen in 1558 and really developed into a dynamic ruler in 1577 she invested her own money and that of the British Empire in exploiting the New World by turning loose the "Sea Dog" Sir Francis Drake who plundered Spanish ships and their colonies.

Merchants had seen how much money could be made by investing in the exploits. One investment of £5,000 brought in £600,000 to private investors. This investment bonanza was enough to induce Merchants to invest some of their profits in developing the colonies. Although no profit was realized from Jamestown, the Merchant Adventurers felt they would do well with the Pilgrims in Plimoth. So this thinking that started in Queen Elizabeth's reign was carried through during the Pilgrims' era.

What the Pilgrims were objecting to was the distance between the location of the new colony and their own colony. They went back to the time that the London Company, which controlled Jamestown, Virginia, collaborated with the Plymouth Company, both of whom had grants from the Crown and established a zone of one hundred miles between plantations.

The Pilgrims could see the hand of the diabolic character, Sir Ferdinando Gorges, behind the new settlement which was being established.

Fortunately, the settlement lasted for only a year when most of them departed for Virginia with Captain Wollaston. His lieutenants went along with several indentured servants which they promptly sold to the tobacco planters.

When the Pilgrims had a stroke of good luck it was usually followed by some adverse factor, which was soon to take place.

Wollaston had a partner named Thomas Morton who stayed behind in the settlement; he was to fill the vacuum created by the departure of Wollaston. Morton was a thorn in the side of the Pilgrims as time went on. Who was Thomas Morton? Thomas Morton, while in London, was a lawyer, some say a graduate of Oxford. He loved the "good life" carousing in taverns, a direct contradiction of the Spartan life of the Pilgrims. The one good thing he did in Wessagusset was to free all the remaining indentured servants. They drove the few Wollaston lieutenants out of the village and the levity and shrieks of laughter and song became commonplace. The inhabitants' role seemed to be a continual contest to see who could drink the most liquor in the shortest period of time. Morton re-founded the village on the principle that there would be no laws to infringe on the rights of the lawless.

He felt that no Justice of the Peace could touch him. His followers sold rum to the Massachusetts Indians also guns and ammunition. The Indians, using their newly acquired weapons, hunted deer and wild turkey in the woods, which they traded to the settlers. The Indians soon became quite skilled with the guns and combining that with their knowledge of the woods they were becoming a formidable threat which the villagers of Merry Mount totally ignored.

The villagers created a large Maypole eighty feet tall with deer horns on top and garlands hanging down. On the first of May, they danced around the Maypole with half naked squaws, drinking rum with the men in the village and the Indian braves shooting their guns.

The Pilgrims called the village "Merry Mount" although Morton had penned the name "Ma-re Mount" or Mountain by the Sea. It was gaining a notorious reputation among the Pilgrims who feared the settlement would corrupt the whole area with their "living for today" attitude. There was also the issue of the beaver trade which the new settlers were pursuing with reckless abandon. They were getting the beaver pelts locally and from the Indians in Maine, by trading rum, guns and ammunition. The Indians no longer wanted their corn, beads, knives and trinkets that the Pilgrims offered.

The Pilgrims were alarmed at the increase of sightings of Indian braves prowling in the woods armed with deadly muskets. Selling the Indians guns and ammunition was not done exclusively by Morton. The English fishermen and the French were also involved. Although the Pilgrims could not put a halt to their trade, they most assuredly could stop Morton's activities. They also feared that some of the younger Saints might be tempted to visit "Merry Mount" for a few days and Morton would go out of his way to make sure they were introduced to the temptation of rum and the young squaws.

Governor Bradford sent a friendly letter to Morton warning him about selling guns and rum to the Indians and the threat they could become, not only to Plimoth, but to other villages in the area. Morton replied that he never sold any liquor to the Indians but admitted to selling a few old muskets with shot and powder, but there wasn't any law against it.

Then Bradford sent a second letter that was stern and to the point; stop selling guns and rum! He had garnered support from several of the local village leaders and he acted with authority for all the villages not just Plimoth.

Morton ridiculed Bradford in his answer to the latest letter saying that King James I was dead and there was no law to prevent him for doing as he pleased and tauntingly asked Bradford what he was going to do about it.

Once again Bradford expressed his determination and authority by sending Captain Standish with nine heavily armed men in the shallop to Merry Mount. When Standish arrived with his men, Morton and his men ran to a house loaded with gun powder and shot their muskets at the raiding party. Morton's men locked themselves in and taunted Standish when he asked them to surrender. Charging into Standish and his nine men, the villagers were so drunk they couldn't even put their muskets to their shoulders to fire them. Morton also charged with an over-loaded carbine and Standish calmly took it away from him. The only casualty was a settler who, while drunk, fell on the sword of one of Standish's men and got a bloody nose.

Morton later told a different story, placing the blame on Standish and his attack on an innocent village with few people around to defend it. Morton was brought before the council to decide what they would do with him. In spite of Standish's demand for Morton's execution they decided to send him back to England with John Oldham.

John Oldham carried a letter from Bradford to the Merchant Adventurers in London giving the reason for attacking Merry Mount and the support that he got from other villagers. They said things were getting out of hand with Morton and his trading with rum and guns had just about ruined the fur trade with the Indians. They feared for their wives and children with Merry Mount so close, so they got rid of him and hoped that the Adventurers would not send people of his caliber to the New World in the future. So Morton and Oldham left for England...the Pilgrims thought, so good riddance!

When Allerton returned from England the following year he had a new secretary...Thomas Morton! The Pilgrims were dumbfounded. How dare Allerton bring this ingrate back to Plimoth. To add insult to injury, Allerton brought him back as a guest. Evidently the Adventurers paid no attention to the letter that Bradford had written to them; that is, if they really did receive it. After all, it was Oldham who was carrying a note that was also critical of himself and he really wasn't a model of virtue.

The Pilgrims immediately sent Morton out of Plimoth and he made his way back to Merry Mount. He didn't waste any time in resuming his trade with the Indians in rum and guns. The Maypole came back into service as well as the appearance of the Indian squaws. The Pilgrims knew they had no authority to rid the likes of Morton from New England...they had tried and failed.

Eventually, Governor John Endicott, whose jurisdiction in Massachusetts included Merry Mount, summoned Morton to appear in Salem to swear allegiance to the Bay Colony and to guarantee that he would mend his ways. Governor Endicott, according to Morton, wanted him as a partner in his fur trading monopoly. Morton thought he could do better working alone and he did by outmaneuvering them and trading with the Indians. He did seven times the amount of trade with the Indians as the Bay Colony did, which didn't endear him with the Massachusetts colonists.

It wasn't long before Governor Endicott came to the conclusion that Morton wasn't a very desirable person and he should be sent elsewhere. Endicott, along with the Pilgrims, agreed that Captain Littleworth would get rid of Morton once and for all. Without wasting any time, Captain Littleworth of the Bay Colony with some troops, marched to Merry Mount and burnt down Morton's house, tore down the Maypole, confiscated his supplies and induced him to change his ways. They hoped they could change the character of the town by renaming it Mount Dragon.

Thomas Morton was taken to Salem to be tried for

mistreating and alienating the friendship of the Indians. He was sent back to England where it was rumored that he was now employed by Sir Ferdinado Gorges in voiding the patents of Plimoth and the Massachusetts Bay Colony.

When the rumors filtered back to the authorities in Plimoth, they were treated with ridicule at first. Then, on second thought, they wondered if Sir Ferdinando Gorges would really do that and if he had that much authority.

Bradford contacted the Massachusetts Bay Colony with the same questions and asked Governor Endicott for his opinion. Bradford wrote that he thought little of the rumor at first, but the thought kept gnawing away and he wondered if Endicott had also heard the rumor. Ridiculous or not, if true, it could have serious implications for all the colonies in New England.

How could they argue their case in a London Court? Due to leaving England behind, they would be at a severe handicap.

In declaring their independence from England, not through written words, but by the action of leaving England without the approval of the Crown, they would be fair game in a British Court.

Governor Endicott sent a note back to Bradford saying that indeed he had heard the rumors too, and what was he going to do about it...nothing!

Either the rumors are false or they are true. If false, they had been wise in not adding credence to the lie...if true, they would sink every British ship that came to Boston to try and impose their edict. When the citizens of Britain heard what the King had done to oppress us, there would be civil turmoil all over England, once they heard the story.

They would probably feel that they might be next to be oppressed!

When Bradford read the notes, he said, "Those are my sentiments, exactly! We'll just ignore the rumors and watch for any development from our enemies...and they are our enemies. They have tried to belittle us since we gave the heave-ho to Morton in Merry Mount and Sir Ferdinado Gorges is his ally."

So they watched for a change and nothing came to their attention out of the ordinary.

CHAPTER 24

London, England

1628-1631

It was now time for Isaac Allerton to go on his annual trip to London. It was early in 1628 and among the things that he planned to handle was convincing four of the Merchant Adventurers to become Undertakers to join with the four they already had in Plimoth. The four men in London who would be recruited to be Undertakers were: James Sherley who was a goldsmith and also secretary of the Merchant Adventurers and a friend of the Saints; Richard Andrews, a haberdasher, John Beauchamp, a saltmaker and Timothy Hatherly, a feltmaker, who had been at Plimoth before.

Sherley, a modest gentleman, who helped hold the Merchant Adventurers together, was convinced by Allerton that he should represent the Pilgrims as agent in London. Sherley said that he didn't think he was up to the job, but if the Pilgrims wanted to take a chance on him, then he would do his best and he would accept the job of Undertaker.

Allerton brought many beaver pelts with him to pay

off some of the debts that the Pilgrims owed to the Adventurers. He paid the first mortgage and £200 on various debts to the creditors—who were doing well indeed. When he returned to Plimoth the Saints were jubilant when they heard that there remained a debt of only £2,000 which could be paid in five years and that he had purchased many needed supplies at a low rate of interest.

The Undertakers of Plimoth were happy that at long last they could realize their dream of bringing some of the Leyden congregation to Plimoth and the London Partners agreed to transport them free.

The Saints were also pleased to hear about their Leyden bretheren coming to Plimoth because they had waited so long.

Sherley went to Holland on business and returned with thirty-five Pilgrims. In March 1629 they embarked on another *Mayflower* with Captain William Pierce as Master of the vessel. Most of the passengers were Puritans that were bound for Salem, which had been founded the year before by Captain John Endicott who drove Conant and Reverend Lyford out. The Puritans arrived at Salem on May 15th. The Saints were eventually brought from Salem to Plimoth. Among them was Thomas Blossom, with his wife and two children. Blossom had left the *Speedwell* with Robert Cushman in Plimoth, England in 1620. Another Saint to join Plimoth Plantation was Richard Masterson who also brought his wife, Mary, and two children, Sarah and Nathaniel. Another passenger, Thomas Willet, Jr., the nineteen-year-old son of Thomas Willet, was an honest and capable youth who would become an asset to the Plantation. Kenelm Winslow, a Stranger from London, was a brother of Edward and an accomplished carpenter and cabinet maker, who would also become a welcome addition to the growing colony.

In 1630, there arrived from Leyden on the *Handmaid*,

sixty Saints from the Green Gate congregation. It took them over two months to make the trip. The passengers had trouble on board and many complained about Allerton to Sherley, who became disgusted with the continual complaints. Sherley said that he was through with the Saints in Green Gate and the only one that he could regard with any affection was Mrs. Bridget Robinson, who unfortunately, changed her mind about coming to Plimoth with her children. The Saints at Plimoth felt the same as Sherley when the latest batch of passengers arrived from Green Gate. They said that the new arrivals were the poorest, weakest group of people they had ever seen and they wouldn't help in the welfare of the Plantation.

No record was ever made of the latest arrivals and they came against the advice of the Pilgrims and the Undertakers. It cost the Pilgrims a considerable sum for those Saints including the fare aboard the *Handmaid*. Their trip wasn't free as they were told by the Adventurers, and added to this was the cost of new homes, planting crops and feeding them until the harvest was in.

The Pilgrims were a little aggravated, to say the least, when they found out the guarded secret of the Undertakers, which was that their households were taxed three bushels of corn each to bring the Saints over from Leyden. They were never repaid by the group from Green Gate for all their troubles. The Pilgrims made such a fuss over the tax whereas the Undertakers forgave them and assumed all the debts involving the newcomers.

After getting rid of Morton, which was good news, the Pilgrims now had another problem. John Billington, who was continually in trouble in Plimoth, who had also been accused of participating in the *Mayflower* mutiny, among other things, now had his most serious crime cited against him...he was being tried for murder. The court claimed that he had a violent quarrel with John Newcomen, who had recently arrived in Plimoth and was later ambushed and shot dead with a musket.

In 1630, John Billington was tried by two juries and found guilty by both of premeditated murder. The Pilgrims had the authority to form juries by a 1623 statute but they had never tried anyone for a capital crime. Upon counsel with Governor John Winthrop, the Pilgrims, who had been in a quandary about the sentencing of the accused and the punishment that would follow, had been assured that it was their right to hang John Billington, to set an example. He was executed and joined his son John who had died several years before of gangrene.

As usual the colony had a new problem to contend with. The Pilgrims had a patent for Plimoth and the surrounding area but it was always shaky and faulty because it did not have an official seal. They were dismayed when one day while sailing in the shallop, they put into shore to seek relief during a storm, and found a trader from the Bay Colony who was in their territory on the Cape. Bradford insisted that he return to Boston and keep out of the Cape area and he said we will defend our territory if we have to risk our lives. The Pilgrims hoped that the Bay Colony wouldn't try to take over.

*   *   *

Allerton, on his many trips to London came this time to see Sherley about enlarging the area for their trading post on the Kennebec River and also to see if he could get a proper grant for Plimoth and the surrounding area. Allerton reached London and after tending to some business with the ship's captain he left the ship. Other passengers had already left and he was alone.

They were lucky to reach port with the heavy fog now swirling in the cobblestoned street and visibility was now down to a few feet. They had anchored in the Thames River near Gravesend in Kent county and several miles from London. Isaac had intended to take a water taxi to London which would land him only a block away from his destination. But this plan was no longer feasible because it was nighttime and the fog limited movement.

Nothing was moving on the river but a few foolhardy souls in a rowboat and they were slowly making their way to shore.

A couple of water rats scurried away from Allerton's feet as he walked toward an Inn that he remembered was only a short distance away.

Allerton paused for a few seconds to get his bearings and he thought he heard something. He heard low voices and then it stopped...it came from ahead of him and it sounded like two men.

He was carrying two heavy suitcases and he tightened his grip on them and stood still and silent. Out of the fog came two figures, poorly dressed and their faces turned away from the flickering lamp hanging on a wooden post. One passed ahead of Allerton and the second was a few steps behind—neither spoke. Suspecting robbery to be their motive Allerton waited and out of the corner of his eye noticed a quick movement from the first stranger. His threatening gesture was soon followed by the second man closing in on Allerton.

Isaac spun around with his suitcases and connected with the first antagonist, hitting him on the arm. The other man was given a resounding blow to his head, knocking him to the pavement.Holding his injured arm, the would-be mugger shuffled off and disappeared in the darkness. The second was out cold, his face on the dirty, wet cobblestoned street.

Allerton checked to see if the man was breathing. Satisfied he was still alive and would wake up with a miserable headache, Isaac then continued on his way to the Inn.

A few minutes later he recognized the quivering lights in front of the Inn and knew he would soon be in hospitable surroundings with a warm meal under his belt, maybe he could even get some gin or wine to go with his dinner.

He went up three steps and pushed a heavy door open with one of his suitcases and entered the Inn. The manager knew Allerton because he had stayed here several times. He knew they served generous sized meals and he would also get a small room with a comfortable bed. He would welcome this change because while he was on the ship he was crowded into a small bunk for weeks on end and the meals were monotonous.

The next morning he was pleasantly surprised to see the fog had burnt off and replaced with the bright sun and clear blue sky. Isaac got out of bed, dressed and grabbing his suitcases went down the narrow staircase to the dining area. He ordered his breakfast and finished it off with a tankard of beer.

He walked back to the Thames River and boarded a barge that would take him to his destination. They sailed up the river with a small crew and several passengers. Most of the passengers were local residents who spoke to Allerton and they were especially interested when he said he was from the New World.

Allerton left the barge and made his way up the block to the offices of the Adventurers where he met Sherley and others and was well received.

Later he presented the case for getting a *bona fide* charter for Plimoth and expanding the area for the trading post on the Kennebec River. They had picked up the pelts and other items from the ship on which Allerton came to

England.

When he returned to Plimoth, Allerton and the other Pilgrims were jubilant over the success that he had made in dealing with the Merchant Adventurers. He had obtained a charter signed by Sir Ferdinando Gorges and the Earl of Warwick to give the colony of Plimoth all the land of New England up to Boston Bay to a point at Narragansett and all the land south. It gave them the authority to keep the Bay Colony from infringing in their area. It also gave them land along the Kennebec River by widening the strip fifteen miles on each side that was owned by the Plimoth Colony. It was made out to the Council of New England with Governor William Bradford being named as trustee. It was designed to name Plimoth a corporation so they could make laws that could not be questioned by any other colony. This would be great news for the Pilgrims, at last they had a charter and they would be protected from outsiders...or would they?

Unfortunately, the charter did not have the Great Seal on it, which could only be placed there by the King. It seems that to have this done they would have to pay a bribe, which according to Sherley had been done.

On closer inspection, Allerton, re-reading the charter, found several discrepancies which could cost the colony a lot of money in the future. He called Sherley's attention to the small print and they both agreed to hold it up until they added a clause specifying that the colony would not be sub-ject to custom duties for several years.

It cost the colony £500 and they still didn't have their official charter. The Pilgrims were taking a dim view of Allerton's business dealings. Allerton seemed to be undercutting his partners, the Undertakers, by bringing goods from London and selling them as an individual and not as part of a group. When Allerton appeared in Plimoth with Morton this was like pouring fat on the fire. When called upon to explain his actions he said that his private enterprise didn't compete with the Undertakers because he bought items to the colony which they didn't handle. He expanded his trade as an individual against the advice of the Undertakers who claimed that he was involved in "foreign" trade which was contrary to their agreement. They didn't like disagreeing with him because he was the son-in-law of Elder William Brewster who defended him.

Sherley was always giving high praise about Allerton saying that he knew his way around London and his dealing with the Adventurers was correct and none could do as well as he.

When Allerton returned from a trip to London in 1630, he informed the Undertakers that he got a patent to some land on the Penobscot River in Maine in conjunction with the London Undertakers, and the Plimoth Undertakers could join in if they wished. The Undertaking was the brainchild of Allerton...no wonder he was given the title "First of the Yankee Traders."

The business dealings of Allerton were beginning to hit a raw nerve with Governor Bradford and his associates. If they didn't join Allerton in his business at Penobscott, the trading post at Kennebec would suffer from unfair competition. Their only recourse was to join him and attempt to control his enterprise.

Sherley hired Edward Ashley as manager for Penobscot. He was well known to the Pilgrims as a profane young man who had lived with the Indians. The Pilgrims went along with his choice and shipped Ashley and five lusty men with corn, wampum, beans and other items to trade and build a trading post on the Penobscot River fifty miles from the one at Kennebec. They sent along Thomas Willet, a dependable young Saint, to keep Ashley in check.

Allerton now sold supplies to the Pilgrims from his

private stock to replenish their supplies, because he had brought no trading items from London for them. The next time Allerton went to London he was given explicit directions as to what he could and couldn't do for the Pilgrims as their agent.

Time went by and still no word from Allerton; the Pilgrims were anxiously awaiting their spring shipment from London. When they didn't receive any items from Ashley, stationed at Penobscot, they were forced to send corn for trading. Ashley said that he wouldn't pay for the corn and to send the bill directly to Sherley. He then sent the beaver pelts, which he received from the Indians, directly to London. He had traded the Pilgrim's corn for the pelts.

A ship called the *Friendship* landed at Boston. On board was Timothy Hatherly, a London partner. The Pilgrims assumed that at long last their spring shipment was at Boston so they sent a ship to get it. What a shock they got when they finally arrived!

There were two bundles of rugs and two empty hogsheads which had contained liquor. They were now empty. The liquor had been consumed by the ship's crew who claimed the shortage was caused by leakage.

The rest of the shipment was unloaded at Boston, no more was destined for Plimoth. Hatherly was sent to Boston to eventually go to Plimoth to check on the dealings with the Pilgrims. The Undertakers in London, although they were very active in trading, found that they were steadily losing money in the amount of £1500 ($75,000) each.

Allerton was no longer in London. He purchased a second ship called the *White Angel* and was in Maine with a drunken crew fishing for bass. Bradford, unaware of this, sent Winslow to London to check on Allerton with instructions that if he encountered any problem with Allerton's dealings, he was to terminate Allerton's job as an agent of Plimoth.

Allerton put into Boston on the *White Angel* and picked up Hatherly for the trip to Plimoth. On board was a quantity of linen, bedding, stockings, rugs, tape, pins and various other items that could be used for trading with the Indians. However, the local Undertakers would have none of it and criticized him saying that he overstepped his bounds.

Allerton convinced them that he had purchased the *White Angel* with his own money and they were not responsible for it. He also said that the things that he brought over would eventually net the Undertakers a great profit. Hatherly confirmed this and found the accounts in good shape.

Hatherly then went to visit the various trading posts at Kennebec and then to Penobscot where Ashley was the manager. Things at Kennebec were running smoothly but when he got to Penobscot he was amazed at the lack of management.

Ashley, though under bond of £500, was involved in trading guns and ammunition with the Indians. He was doing great in this illicit trade, sending over one thousand pounds of beaver and other pelts to London. The Pilgrims would have none of this illegal trade, so they sent him back to England as a prisoner.

Allerton and Hatherly went to London aboard the *White Angel* with a full load of exports that were gathered by the Pilgrims. Upon reaching London, Allerton received his death knell as an agent for Plimoth when they found the accounts in London in a mess which resulted in the plantation losing much money. Winslow, who was in London, was appointed agent for the colony and was instructed to bring some reason to the accounts.

Sherley and his associates wouldn't accept the losses incurred by the *Friendship* and the *White Angel* which was contrary to the assurances given by Allerton and Hatherly. Sherely was firm in not accepting Plimoth's debt. He said that the *Friendship* was hired by the Pilgrims and the *White Angel* was purchased by Allerton. If he had overstepped his authority as their agent, that was their problem.

Allerton had optimistically assumed that he would pay off all the debts of the Pilgrims and at the same time would realize a big profit. He was one of the richest men in Plimoth, surpassing even Bradford and Brewster. It was small wonder that Allerton was becoming affluent in Plimoth, the accounts defied imagination. It would take two years to fathom them and bring them into some sort of order. The Pilgrims found their floating debt had increased from £400 ($20,000) to £4,770 in four years and they still owed £1,000 on their mortgage. It seemed that due to poor bookkeeping or deliberate mismanagement, Allerton had charged twice on many invoices, he also had high interest rates and other expenses. He had increased his father-in-law's debt to more than £200. William Brewster assumed that the items he was being charged for were gifts to him and his children.

Allerton also invested £400 in William Collier's brewery using Sherley's name. He then demanded £300 that he claimed his partners, the Undertakers, owed him and he wanted immediate payment.

The Pilgrims were taken aback by the actions of Allerton. They had always found him to be honest and had only good intentions toward the plantation and their thoughts were amplified by Hatherly's word.

But all this activity didn't center around business, he had great affection for his wife and children. On his return from his fifth and final trip to London as agent for Plimoth he had a surprise gift.

He had hidden it from them in a wicker basket and now it was time to open the cover and show his children. "What's in the basket, Daddy?" Mary asked.

"Before I open it, you'll have to promise to take good

care of it. The gift is for all of you."

"We'll take good care it—we promise," Bartholomew said, "Won't we Mary and Remember?"

"Yes," they echoed. "Can we see what it is?"

Isaac opened the basket and out popped a young tri-colored Beagle. It was only four months old and like all healthy puppies was very lively. It had large bright eyes and a wagging tail tipped with white. It had black, white and tan smooth fur.

"What do you call it?" Mary asked. "It's so pretty!"

"Well, the man that I bought it from said her name is "Bonnie". You can rename her if you want."

"I like that name! Do you want to change it?" She looked anxiously at her brother and sister.

"I think it's all right for a girl," Bartholomew said. "What kind of dog is she?"

"They call it a Beagle. It's a fairly new breed of dog. It started about sixty years ago when Queen Elizabeth said she wanted a smaller version of a fox hound. It will be a good dog for you children because she's very gentle and friendly."

By this time Bonnie had gone to each of three children to be a patted and then she went up to Isaac Junior and Fear who put out her hand to pat her and Bonnie jumped back. She then slowly stretched and sniffed her hand. Bonnie sensed that Fear was friendly and part of the household. She licked her hand and allowed her to pat her.

"Oh, what a good little puppy you are!" Fear said. Bonnie responded by wagging her tail. Then she sat on her haunches, surveying her new family.

"I can't wait to show her to Thomas." Mary said.

Before Bonnie had joined the Allerton household, there was an incident that had created quite a stir in the colony. Early in 1632, in May to be exact, Mary and Bartholomew were walking near the woods next to the plantation. They were curious about the deafening sound that was coming from the woods.

"What's making all the noise? Do you think it's safe to explore like this?" Mary asked.

Bartholomew replied, "I think it's some kind of insects making the racket. There must be thousands of them."

When they neared the woods the sound increased. Upon closer examination they saw thousands of insects called *Cicada* eating all the vegetation.

Bartholomew saw one up close on the ground. He hit it with a stick and killed it. He picked it up and looked at it closely. It was very large, about an inch long, it was a brownish-tan color. It had a blunt head and a stout body with large transparent wings. Bartholomew said, "I've never seen anything like this before. Have you Mary?"

Mary was a little leery and replied, "How can you pick that thing up? It looks scary!"

"It certainly looks strange. I wonder where they come from?"

"Oh, Bartholomew, I wonder if they will go to the corn crop that we planted a little while ago. It's just starting to sprout and they could do a lot of damage. They could ruin the whole field!"

They ran to the cornfield to see what the cicada were doing and if they already had landed there. They were relieved to find some of the farmers looking at the corn.

Mary asked, "Are those insects eating the crops?"

"There are a few here but I guess the green leaves on the trees look more appetizing to them and there is so much more to eat." John Cooke said.

Francis Billington said to Bartholomew, "I notice that you came from the woods. Are there many insects there...they certainly are making a lot of noise!"

"Yes, there are thousands of them. I hope they don't

do too much damage. I wonder where they will go next."

Little did Mary realize that the cicada had burrowed into the ground the year before she was born and had now resurfaced after seventeen years of hibernation. The Pilgrims had never seen them before as they are common only in the New World.

In a few days the cicadas vanished into the ground after mating. They would reappear again in seventeen years to repeat the cycle.

The following year the Pilgrims thought the outbreak of disease in the colony was directly related to the onslaught of the insect attack, which of course had no bearing at all.

CHAPTER 25

Plymouth, Cape Cod

1633-1634

What a year 1634 was for Plimoth and the Allerton's...great changes were about to take place. Fear (Brewster) Allerton was stricken with small pox. She tried to fight it off, to no avail. Isaac was there with their four-year-old son, Isaac Junior and his other children, when Fear finally passed away. After her funeral, Isaac brought his son, Isaac Junior, to the Brewster's who promised to look after him.

His daughter, Remember, went to Marblehead, Massachusetts to marry Moses Maverick, a local minister. Isaac Allerton later went to Marblehead to live with Remember and her husband.

Bartholomew was quiet and depressed. He kept to himself and was moody. Mary noticed the change in her brother and was worried about his behavior.

Whenever Mary mentioned her father, Bartholomew became agitated and tried to change the subject. Mary knew the problems that her brother suffered must be caused by her father's behavior. Bartholomew said to Mary, "I'm very humiliated with the way father is acting in trying to make money. I'm afraid he has taken advantage of everybody in the Plantation. I have a chance to study to become a minister in England. I think I'll go, I can't stand the embarrassment in staying here."

Mary tried to take her father's side by saying, "I think father was blamed too harshly by the Pilgrims. I think he was trying to help them and he was also trying to help his family. He is a smart man and is willing to take a chance. He has gone to Marblehead but I know he will not accept defeat. I hope that someday our people will see that he was concerned with their future and welfare. Please don't be so unfeeling when you think of father."

Bartholomew was to leave within a month to go to England...never to return to Plimoth or to see Mary again.

Mary, now seventeen years of age, stayed with the Cooke family along with her beagle, Bonnie. She was very attentive to Thomas Cushman when he made his visits to the Brewster's to read his books and be taught. Mary used the excuse that she was visiting her brother, Isaac. Most of the time it happened to coincide with Thomas' visits.

William Brewster liked Mary and Thomas and smiled when the two were at the house. He said to his wife, "If two people were made for each other, this is it I think it's only a matter of time before they are husband and wife."

The year before, Deacon (Doctor) Samuel Fuller died, he had been the colony's respected "phystion and chirure-on." He was only forty-eight years old and left his wife, Bridget (Lee), and their two children. They had been married for sixteen years. He had been responsible for converting many Puritans to Saints at Salem and Boston during 1628 and 1630. Along with Samuel Fuller and Fear Allerton, others died, too. There was Peter Brown and Francis Eaton who had died of an infectious disease during 1633 along with six-teen others.

*   *   *

This was the year that Thomas Cushman became a Freeman, which meant that he could vote. It was a unique privilege being a voter; it required a minute scrutiny of his religious views and moral character. Also, the person selected to become a Freeman had to own a taxable estate that was worth at least £200.

Plimoth Plantation was still governed by the *Mayflower Compact*, which was unusual for its daring concept of self-government. They held town meetings...a first for America, and each head of household could stand and give his opinions. They also could oppose any decision. Although they couldn't vote in a regular election, their thoughts were known and the Freeman determined if their opinions were valid and then acted accordingly.

When he left Plimoth, Allerton went into competition against the Pilgrims. He hired the repossessed *White Angel* from Sherley under a bond of £1,000 and loaded it with supplies from London. He made his way to Maine and commenced trading with the Indians beyond Penobscot to stifle the trade north of the Pilgrim's trading post. Using unscrupulous characters that he hired, they ventured into every nook and cranny to get beaver pelts. He offered the Indians credit; he had set out to drive Pilgrims out of business.

His bitterness with the Pilgrims resulted in the way he was treated in their dispute with his trading methods. The Pilgrims could have used somebody with Allerton's ability in their desire to get economic strength. he had a knack of making money but they disagreed with his methods.

Allerton, to further stifle trade in the Pilgrim's

Kennebec Trading Post, opened up a competitive post on the river near the Canadian territory. This was very bold move because he was in the back yard of the French, and it wouldn't be long before they would try to put a halt to his trading. The French could use the Indians to harass him without involving their own troops, and while they were doing this they could also include the Pilgrims.

Allerton mastered his courage, of which he had an abundance, and was determined to visit Plimoth and see his son, Isaac Junior, and his daughter, Mary, and his friends.

On arriving at the plantation, he was greeted by the council of which he had been a member for so long. They demanded to know how he could pay off his debts to the colony. He owned a lot of property and a house and wanted a little time to raise the money. He said he had changed his ways and would make every attempt to see that the people of Plimoth would receive the money he owed. Allerton said things were progressing very well with him but he needed more time to straighten out his accounts. He said that he was being helped by a very competent accountant named Mr. Fogge and was making good progress.

Mr. Sherley of the Merchant Adventurers contacted the Pilgrims and asked them if they needed help in working on their accounts and he would send over an accountant. They refused his offer to hire a skilled accountant and instead hired an inexperienced youth, Josiah Winslow, (Edward's brother), also suggested by Sherley, who, after receiving instructions in bookkeeping, came to Plimoth to attempt what would become impossible...to restore order from chaos.

Josiah was a conscientious worker and toiled hours on end but the task was beyond him. It would have been difficult for an experienced accountant to make sense of this financial quagmire.

After losing important papers and trying to rely on memory and spending years on the project Josiah gave up...he came to the conclusion it was an impossible task.

*   *   *

Sherley who had a lot of confidence in Allerton's abilities did an incredible act. He let Allerton buy on credit! He thought that if Allerton was able to earn enough money then he could pay off all his debts. Moreover, he said the Pilgrims should have a little patience while all this was happening. Bradford was outraged at this latest development involving Allerton and Sherley.

"He should give him the *White Angel*," he fumed, "they'll never see a penny of the money he owes."

Bradford felt that Allerton "would pick the bones clean" and regain all his personal property around and in Plimoth.

*   *   *

The French regarded the trading post on the Penobscot River as an intrusion into their territory and they would make an example of the Pilgrims.

French naval officers boarded a small sailing ship with a crew intent on teaching the English a lesson that they wouldn't forget. The French had formulated a plan of deceit that would catch the English totally by surprise.

The crew put up the ship's sails and was soon in the middle of the river heading downstream. The officers were joking about what the reaction would be with the English once they put the ruse into action.

The sun was just coming up over the horizon and the early fog was slowly melting away on the river as the bow of the ship cut through the water. They had about twenty miles to go and they were making good time.

When they were about a mile from the Pilgrim's trading post and hidden from view by the bend in the river, they dropped the sails and coasted into shore.

Upon landing they sent a small scouting party to check on the English traders. They silently crept through the woods and when the French were within earshot of the trading post they observed the movement of the English. They soon found that they didn't carry guns and there were only four men around the trading post.

When they had enough information, they headed back to the ship to report their finding. They spoke to the officers and when the report was delivered the officers nodded in agreement and said, "Let's go. We will have a great surprise for the Englishmen."

They put up one sail and slowly made their way to the trading post. When they approached the pier the four men came out of the building and greeted the French. The sailors laughed and said they were lost, but really the reason they put in to shore was the ship was damaged. They said that they had hit a large rock in the river and they were taking on water. Luckily they had pulled into the pier and the crew would work on repairing the ship, if it was all right with the traders.

They assured the French that they were welcome to use the pier and if they needed any extra help, they would pitch in to help them. The French thanked the traders and said the crew could fix it.

The traders invited the officers to have refreshments. Sensing no deceit and accepting the friendly remarks and attitude of the ship's officers, the four traders lead them into the trading post.

One of the officers casually asked who was in charge.

They told the Frenchman the manager was Thomas Willett and he was back in Plimoth getting more supplies.

The officers headed for the musket rack where they were displayed in a neat row. They were admiring the muskets and ammunition and after a few minutes they pointed some of the muskets at the startled traders and said to put their hands behind their heads and not to move.

One officer went to the door and called out for the crew to come into the trading post. When they entered the building, one officer laughed at the predicament the traders now found themselves. He said, "You are about to be robbed. We have observed your ample stock of supplies and it will now change hands. We win...you lose! You learn that you will no longer trade in our territory."

To add insult to injury, the traders had to carry all their goods to the French ship. To add to their embarrassment they not only carried the loot to the ship but they had to store it away below deck, while the crew sat on the sidelines laughing at the traders.

They took everything of value; rugs, muskets, coats, blankets, foodstuff and beaver pelts that alone were worth £500.

One officer said to the traders—"we have left you some food and blankets. When your Mr. Willett returns, tell him what happened and we would advise you not to reopen. Go home to your families at Plimoth and find a new line of work." The ship, officers and crew sailed away, proverbially thumbing their noses at them.

Meanwhile, there was trouble at Plimoth! The citizens of the colony were gathered in small groups discussing the latest rumors that were coming in to them from Sowam.

The Pilgrims had established a new trading post in that Indian stronghold and things had been going along well. Four men and Captain Standish were traders in the new trading post in a rugged, oak timbered, log house. This post would be a center where they could expand their trade in several directions.

Contrary to the rumor of an Indian uprising, and an abundance of several false stories in circulation in the colony, that was one indisputable fact; there was no serious trouble with the Indians. One such story was where a few Massachusetts Indians had been in the trading post and later were walking near Sowam when they were approached by several Narragansett Indians. Although the territory borders were in dispute the Narragansetts were very firm in insisting the Massachusetts Indians were "invading" their land.

One of the Narragansett's pushed a Massachusetts Indian and he pushed back, this of course started a fight. Greatly outnumbered, the Massachusetts Indians, being near the trading post, quickly ran there and requested protection by the traders. Fearing that the Narragansett Indians would try to take over the trading post, the traders led by Captain Standish stood with loaded muskets in front of the building and waited. They said they had plenty of gunpowder and wouldn't hesitate to use it if they intruded on the post.

Upon hearing this, the Narragansetts were convinced that they should retire gracefully. There was the usual bluster and shouted insults from both sides. Standish seemed to laugh the matter off, but they increased their awareness of small incidents that might have gone unnoticed in the past.

A few days prior to the incident, the trading post was in short supply of gunpowder for their muskets and so was Plimoth. Standish sent a runner to Boston to replenish their supply and fortunately, he returned the day before with thirty pounds.

The council at Plimoth had a meeting and decided that the colony should consider expanding. The terrain at Plimoth was rocky and required an unusual amount of hard labor to remove the rocks and till the soil so they could raise crops. Bradford had heard about the fertile soil of the territory of Connecticut and considered this would be a good spot from which to start to expand. They would be able to raise a variety of crops including tobacco. The colony of Plimoth was growing larger and they were outgrowing the area where crops could be planted. They also knew they could not depend on selling beaver pelts to learn a living forever. They would have to diversify. That's why the council had used Sowam as a base and would move westward for trade and they would also try to have peace with the Narragansetts and the Pequot tribes.

Governor Bradford then contacted Governor Winthrop of the Massachusetts Bay Colony and told him about the plan to go into Connecticut and open an area for trading and farming. He wanted their colony to join in their enterprise as an equal partner and said it would be very profitable to both colonies.

Governor Winthrop's reply in essence was "thanks but no thanks". On reflection of the hate for the white man by the warring Pequots and their strength of three or four thousand battle-hardened warriors gave him pause and he wanted no part of the plan.

Time went by and Edward Winslow was now in charge as Governor of the Plimoth Colony, succeeding William Bradford. This was his first effort to revive the possibilities of expanding into Connecticut.

Several armed men went aboard with Winslow on the ships they had made. They sailed south along the coast until they reached an inlet at Sagamore and entered a stream which would bring them to Bourne and Buzzard's Bay. Then they were once again on the Atlantic Ocean and went along the coast until they reached Lyme and the Connecticut River. They sailed up the river and reached a point about thirty-five miles from their entrance point. They had stopped several times and explored the terrain. The explorers were impressed with what they saw. It was a scenic trip with lush, green forests on either side of the river. They were aware the Dutch had been there before them, but nothing would deter them from their exploration. They continued north up the river to an area later known as Middletown. They were satisfied with the evidence that Connecticut would be a profitable venture and they decided to call off the exploration and return to Plimoth with the good news.

The entire trip to Connecticut and return was about three hundred miles, and the men were a little weary from walking and sailing the boat.

Bradford and the council were anxious to learn about Connecticut from Governor Winslow and the men who accompanied him on the trip. The council was on the pier to greet them when they were alerted that their ship was coming.

Questions were answered by Winslow and the men and the council was very pleased with the results of the trip. Bradford wanted to know if Winslow was going to approach Governor Winthrop and the Massachusetts Bay Colony again to see if they would reconsider their joining in the plan.

Winslow said, "I definitely am. After seeing in person the possibility of great success, I don't know why they wouldn't want to be included."

In a few days Winslow, accompanied by five men, sailed to Boston to see Winthrop. They were warmly received when they tied up at a pier. They were led into Winthrop's home and Winslow detailed all that he learned about the Connecticut area and asked Winthrop if he could give it some thought and possibly reconsider his negative answer.

Winthrop slowly walked around the room and picked up a vase and carefully looked at the detail. He turned to

Winslow and said, "Edward, I appreciate your offer and I, too, think that it would be a profitable endeavor; however, I have given it a lot of thought since William Bradford first came up with the plan. I'm sorry, but I still can't go along with the idea and for the same reason...the Pequots. I don't know if you realize how ruthless and savage they are."

Governor Winslow, seeing that it was a lost cause and it would remain so, changed tactics by saying, "Governor, would you have any objections if we went ahead on our plan to expand into Connecticut?"

Winthrop replied, "No, of course not! But I'd be a little concerned about the risk of clashing with the Pequots or the Narragansetts. I can only wish you well in your venture."

With no objection, the Pilgrims now were free to pioneer Connecticut...in spite of the Pequot and Narragansetts.

They would have to sell the plan to the colonists and that could be very difficult. They would have to explain all the benefits they could achieve, the hardships they would have to endure and the problem with the Indians. The Pilgrims had lived with the Indians for many years and in comparative peace, now they would infringe on the territory of an unknown tribe and the Pilgrims didn't know how far a little "brotherly love" would go in dealing with them. They hoped they could have peace and live together as friends as they did with the Cape Cod tribes under Massasoit.

Winslow was a dedicated man of the colony and his skill as a diplomat was well known. He was attempting to bring a better life to the Pilgrims with his new job as Governor. He had the support of his loyal assistants who had served the colony so well in the past. The council was composed of William Bradford, John Doane, William Gilson and the late Samuel Fuller, who had recently passed away in the epidemic.

His skill as a diplomat would be called into service

when he confronted the Pilgrims. They could be a stubborn lot and they were not easily swayed, they had too many lessons on turning the other cheek.

*   *   *

Thomas Cushman was constantly accompanied by Bonnie when he walked through the woods on or around the plantation. There was always a scared rabbit or squirrel for her to chase. Usually Bonnie was unsuccessful in her hunt—she was more of a pet than a hunter. She was well-liked by the people of the plantation and the children ran up to pat her. She enjoyed every minute of the petting, too. Her tail was always wagging and if a dog could smile, Bonnie would, she certainly tried to, she seemed to be the happiest dog alive.

CHAPTER 26

Plymouth, Cape Cod

1635

"When we go into Connecticut to establish another trading post, we should plan for every eventuality," Bradford suggested to the council.

Winslow said, "I think we can prepare a house that will be ready to erect and take along with us. We won't waste any time cutting timber when we get there. It will be complete down to the last nail."

Standish said, "I think that's a good idea and while we're about it, we should also make a fort in the same manner. We can probably expect some trouble from the Dutch and we don't want to waste any time getting prepared to defend ourselves. I understand the Dutch have a small force on the Connecticut River. When we're ready to go, I'd like to send send Lieutenant Holmes to be in charge. He is a good soldier who follows orders, good at improvising and is not easily intimidated. Would there any objection to my choice?"

The group knew the abilities that Lieutenant Holmes had and there was no objection from them. They thought it was a wise choice.

The carpenters in the colony were busy preparing planks and rafters for the new house and fort they would take to Connecticut. Plans had to be followed and each plank was numbered so they could assemble it quickly on the new site.

Each plank was cut to an exact thickness by hand. The log was placed over a deep ditch, well-supported by other planks and one sawyer grasped the handle below the log and the man above held the opposing handle and in unison they rapidly sawed the length of the log creating a plank. This tiring maneuver was repeated many times until the log was completely sawed. Then a new log was placed in position and they continued sawing usually with a new team.

For days they labored on their project and then they thought that they finally finished the first stage. As a trial run they assembled the house and fort then after a few adjustments they found it was satisfactory. They dismantled both of them and packed them on a new ship that the colonists had recently built. The project was supervised by William Holmes, Chief Lieutenant to Captain Standish.

The crew had been storing food and supplies including ammunition aboard the ship and finally they were about ready to go on their trip to Connecticut.

As the day approached for their departure, excitement spread through the colony. The colonists felt as though they were all participating in the adventure and this could be a new beginning in their jump into fate.

Early in the morning the crew and Lieutenant Holmes were ready to sail to Connecticut and the whole populace was on the shore and pier to see them off.

The sun had just risen on the horizon and from all indications it was going to be a great day. The colonists said their good-byes to those aboard and the ship prepared to sail along the coast to Sagamore and retrace their last trip. The sails bellowed out from a strong north wind and they made good time.

They passed through the inlet and had gone by Bourne. This was a shortcut to Connecticut instead of going around the arm of the Cape and entering the dangerous waters in the Nantucket Sound. It also cut off about eighty-seven miles from the trip.

They finally reached the Connecticut River outlet and very cautiously sailed up the river. They sailed as far as the Dutch Trading Post to an area which would become Hartford. There they met the first opposition to their trip.

The Dutch had a well-equipped trading post and they decided that they wanted no competition. To back up their position they had a well-built fort complete with cannons.

The Pilgrims were confronted by the Dutch who had two cannons aimed directly at them and demanded they lower their flag and drop anchor at once.It was a sobering encounter. The Pilgrims could stop and give in to the Dutch and eventually retreat. They could resist with inadequate fire-power and be defeated. They had to make a decision—fast!

Finally Holmes replied, "I was told to go up the river by the Governor of Plimoth and that is what I intend to do." Ignoring the Dutch, they sailed unmolested and finally land-ed about seven miles upstream at the junction of the Farmington and Connecticut River, near what is now Windsor.

Fearing more trouble from the Dutch, they set up the fort quickly and surrounded it with a strong stockade, then they waited with their muskets at the ready. They were ready for trouble and none too soon!

Seventy armed men marched in formation from the fort at New Amsterdam and seeing Holmes and his men for-tified in a strong defensive position with muskets pointed at them, they decided to talk instead of attacking. They agreed that the Pilgrims could stay at Matianuck (Windsor).

Things were not as peaceful at the Pilgrim's trading post at Cushenoc on the Kennebec River a few months later.

One of the traders was fishing on the pier, he had just cast out the line and sat back when he happened to look up and saw a ship coming around a bend in the river. He called out to the men in the trading post and when they came out they saw it was a merchant ship from England. They anchored near the trading post. The traders soon found out the ship was under the command of Captain Hockings and they intended to stay there for awhile.

The Pilgrims feared the Indians who carried on the beaver trade with the trading post would be intimidated by the crew of the ship and stop trading. The traders were outraged and told the intruders to move on, the crew merely laughed at their suggestion.

The assistant Governors, John Howland and John Alden, who were both at Cushenoc, agreed that if they allowed Hockings to stay they might as well abandon their profitable trading post.

Howland, who was the resident agent, said, "We will have to take severe action because repeated talks with Hockings have proven fruitless." They tried to come up with a plan of action against the crew and Captain Hockings in particular.

After thinking of several possibilities Alden said, "I'll go in a canoe with a volunteer and we'll cut the ropes securing the ship."

Alden asked, "Who wants to go with me?" He didn't have to wait very long. A fellow-worker in the trading post spoke up, "I'll give it a go!" Smiling from ear to ear the young volunteer asked what they would do.

"We'll take muskets and the two of us will paddle to the

ship, cut the hawsers and the ship will drift down the river."

Howland asked, "That's all well and good but what will it actually accomplish? They'll drift down the river for a short time, they might even run ashore, but the odds for their return are great and what difference will it make?"

Alden replied, "We have to do something to get them to go away. If they stay here it will ruin our business. As a matter of fact, I don't know why they are here."

Howland said, "I guess we have to do something. I have a bad feeling about this particular action you're going to take. Right now I don't know exactly what we can do to make them move away from here. If you do go to their ship I hope there isn't any trouble."

Alden and his enthusiastic volunteer waited till early in the morning and now it was the darkest time of the day. The moon was barely visible and dark shadows cast from the trees kept the ship in shadow also.

Captain Hocking had a restless night and couldn't seem to fall asleep. Tossing and turning, he finally got up from his bunk and climbed the gangway up to the deck. He spoke to the deck watch and then slowly walked around the deck, stopped and looked over the railing at the water silently lapping at the bow. He rested his elbows on the railing and seemed mesmerized with the dark water.

Meanwhile two armed men in a canoe silently paddled up to Hockings' ship and the young man reached up with a knife and cut the hawser with great difficulty. The ship slowly turned and there was no response from the deck. The ship's lookout slowly came to realize that something was happening to the ship.

Captain Hockings looking out at the water saw the movement of the ship and he also noticed the outline of the canoe and the two figures paddling. He grabbed a loaded musket and aimed it at the figures and fired. The young man slumped to the floor of the canoe, killed instantly.

Alden reacted quickly, he noticed the flash from the barrel of the musket and fired his own musket at the source. He hit Captain Hockings in the heart and he too died, never knowing what hit him.

Alden, realizing his companion was dead, paddled rapidly back to the trading post with the body, which minutes before was so full of life. When he pulled up to the pier he was met by Howland and the men. There was much excitement both on the ship and at the trading post. Derogatory remarks were exchanged and both groups soon found the folly in the attack and the deaths.

The traders knew the reason for Alden and the traders outrage at the presence of the British. The British knew the reason that Hockings shot his musket. But was it Indians or the traders? One could question the wisdom of shooting first and finding out what the target was, later.

A few days later Alden showed up in Plimoth and was shaken up by the events. He knew that Howland was right and what started out as more of a prank turned into a tragedy.

Alden shot because he figured that he would be the next victim of Hockings. He would suffer severely as a result of this escapade.

The story of the slayings spread rapidly because Hockings was employed by the Crown although he was not part of the Royal Navy. The colonists expected retaliation by the powerful, bigoted Archbishop of Canterbury. Government was dominated by religion and they feared that the Archbishop would send a royal governor to New England and govern them with an iron fist, thus ending the colony of Plimoth.

Thomas Prence, who came to Plimoth with Robert Cushman in 1621 aboard the *Fortune*, succeeded Winslow in a new term as governor of the colony. He was either governor or acted in the capacity of assistant governor in the Plimoth Colony all the rest of his life.

Governor Winthrop wrote Governor Prence that he was concerned about the future of their colonies. On the one hand, Plimoth still didn't have the royal seal affixed to its patent and the legal standing of the Bay Colony was also in doubt.

John Alden was selected by Governor Prence to visit Boston and see Governor Winthrop to discuss business. He sailed into their bay and landed at the pier and then he went alone to a nearby tavern for a beer. While he was sitting at the bar, two militiamen came in and looked around.

The taller of the two nodded toward Alden and they came over to speak to him. "What is your name? Are you from around here?"

Smiling, John said, "I'm John Alden and I came from Plimoth. I'm going to see your governor soon...Governor Winthrop."

"John Alden you're under arrest! Put your hands behind your back."

One of the militiamen took a small length of cord from his jacket pocket and tied Alden's hands behind his back. "Why am I under arrest?"

"We were told to watch out for you. We knew you would be in Boston and were told that you murdered a British Captain in Maine. So you will come with us now."

They pushed him ahead of them and he was taken out of the tavern with the patrons silently staring at him.

"Where are you taking me?"

"You're going to be locked up in jail."

When Governor Prence heard about Alden's arrest he was outraged and sent for Myles Standish.

Captain Standish went to see Prence and the governor

explained about John Alden's arrest and imprisonment.

"Governor Winthrop knew John Alden was going to Boston and as soon as he got there he placed him under arrest. What right does he have to enforce laws against our citizens?

Will you go to Boston and demand the release of Alden and bring him back to us? Tell Winthrop the true story about what happened at our trading post in Maine. Captain Hockings shot first, killing one of our men. Alden was justified in shooting in self-defense. This is a law that goes back to the beginning of civilization."

Standish, sailed immediately with an escort, to Boston.

They arrived in a few hours and hurried to Governor Winthrop's home to explain why Alden should be released at once and allowed to return to Plimoth.

"Not so fast, Captain. John Alden will have to go to court to have this matter settled once and for all. We will have to hold you also because you have some explaining to do."

"You can't hold me. I wasn't even in Maine."

Standish was required to furnish to the court the Kennebec Patent and other important papers. Governor Prence sent a letter to Winthrop demanding to know who gave him authority over Plimoth to hold John Alden and to bring Myles Standish to court.

Replying to the letter, Assistant Governor Dudley wrote that the Bay Colony didn't mean to create anxiety over the issue but there should be a thorough investigation of the incident in Maine. Winthrop suggested a court composed of the Bay Colony, Plimoth Colony and lesser settlements that were nearby.

When the date they agreed upon arrived, they found only the Bay Colony and Plimoth represented. William Bradford and Edward Winslow were delegates from Plimoth along with Pastor Ralph Smith. The Bay Colony was represented by Governor Winthrop, Reverend John Cotton and John Wilson.

After a short trial, with heated debate, they finally agreed the primary guilt would lie with Hockings but the Pilgrims were also at fault for instigating the crisis. Bradford acknowledged the guilt of the Pilgrims and apologized to the court, which restored some harmony between the colonies. John Alden and Myles Standish were released and returned to Plimoth. Alden no longer had the loathsome stigma of being a murderer held over his head. Standish and the whole colony proved they held a legal claim on the territory on the Kennebec River.

Winthrop and Endicott of the Massachusetts Bay Colony wrote to Lords Say and Sele, who represented the Crown, and gave a lengthy explanation about the incident on behalf of Plimoth. The letter seemed to succeed in appeasing them.

Thinking the situation had not been completely resolved, the Plimoth Council decided they would send Winslow to England to represent their cause. He also was to notify the London Undertakers that their trade agreement with Plimoth had expired.

To divert attention from the experience at Cushenoc and the killing of Captain Hockings, Winslow gave the Commission for Regulating Plantations a petition. It contained a detailed account of the French attack on the Penobscot trading post and the trouble with the Dutch on the Connecticut River. In the petition they said that they couldn't defend and protect his Majesty's domain without a special warrant.

When Winthrop found out about Winslow's petition he was very angry, and justifiably so. "This petition was ill-advised," said Winthrop. "You make it appear that we have no freedom of action and everything we do now will have to be cleared with the Lord s Commissioners. We never had to make a special warrant before to deal with our enemies." Winslow was to suffer for presenting this petition.

Sir Ferdinando Gorges, always the fly-in-the-ointment, now was raising difficulties by attempting to take over all of New England and be a feudal overlord. He forced the Council of New England to give up their charter and he had himself appointed Governor General of New England. He was preparing to come over with a thousand soldiers and scores of Anglican pastors to reform the colonies and the churches according to a high doctrine established by Charles I. Sir Gorges and Archbishop Laud were assisted by George Morton of "Merry Mount fame", who had been brought into the council chamber to harass Winslow. He harangued him about Plymouth's faulty patent and about civil marriages. Archbishop Laud interested in the civil marriages asked Winslow if indeed he had performed them. "Yes", said Winslow, "I find nothing unusual about this; I was married in Holland by a burgomaster."

Outraged by this answer, the Archbishop ordered Winslow to Fleet prison for several months. Knowing that many had been sent to this prison for several years for minor religious infractions, Winslow was extremely worried about his future.

One day he was surprised to be released and he wasted no time in boarding the first ship bound for Plimoth. Leaving aside such issues as the payment of money due on the *White Angel*, the petition and other matters, he wanted out and thought he would never return. Luckily, the growing crisis in England terminated the designs of Sir Gorges on New England.

*   *   *

The courtship of Mary Allerton and Thomas

Cushman came to an end. They were entering a new stage, they planned to get married. They had loved each other for years and they wanted to spend their lives together. They had the blessings of William Bradford and William Brewster who had known Mary and Thomas all their lives. On the big day, Mary was beside herself with excitement. She looked attractive all dressed up and with her scrubbed look and neatly combed hair.

Thomas tried to look calm and collected as he got ready for the wedding but his nervousness showed through his apparent nonchalant manner. Thomas was kidded by William Bradford and his teacher William Brewster and he tried to be a man of the world. He was now twenty-eight years old, nine years older than Mary. He had spent half of his life at Plimoth and was well-liked by all.

They went to the meeting hall on the hill, surrounded by the Pilgrims, laughing and joking and in general having a good time. William Bradford, again named governor, was standing with Thomas when Mary appeared on the arm of Elder Brewster. She smiled at Thomas and Bradford when she approached and silently stood at Tom's side. Governor Bradford extolled the virtues of the prospective bride and groom to the Pilgrims in attendance and then proceeded to marry them in a civil ceremony.

They were congratulated by the townspeople of Plimoth and then they made their way to the Bradford house for a little get together. After spending an hour or two at the Bradford's they went to their new home to set up housekeeping...they were man and wife at last.

At the end of August one morning started out warm and uneventful, it would later be hot and cloudless and the people went about their chores and engaged in idle gossip. A couple of hours later it started to cloud up and the wind started to increase. The surrounding area took on an eerie look with a brownish-grey appearance. The wind grew in intensity until it reached a crescendo of an ear-splitting, howling wind. The rain fell, first in steady droplets then increasing to a terrifying downpour so that visibility was down to a few feet.

The Cushmans were walking around the plantation and they headed home and reached their house just as the downpour occurred. Mary said, "Tom, what is it? I've never seen anything like this before!"

"Mary, I think it's a hurricane, I've read about them. They usually start in the Caribbean area and work their way north. They are usually violent wind storms and create a lot of damage."

"I can't see anything out of the windows...the sound is deafening and it's dark outside. Can you see anything Tom?"

"I can just barely make out something...it looks like a tree uprooted next to the house and the leaves are partially blocking the windows."

"I'm afraid Tom, please hold me. Do you think we'll be safe here?"

Tom hugged Mary and admitted he was scared too. "I know that we're a lot safer in the house than outside, the wind can blow you away. Imagine what it's doing to the trees."

"How long do you think it will last, Tom?"

"I don't know...it will get calm, this is called the eye of the hurricane, then it will start up again for awhile then it will be over. I'm curious to see what damage has been done, but until it's over we had better stay in the house."

When the storm was over they left the house and were dismayed when they saw what destruction the storm had caused to the area. Hundreds of pine trees were uprooted and many had broken in the middle. The birch trees, although giving the appearance of being fragile, bent with the wind and most were spared. Many homes were destroyed and several had their thatched roofs blown away. Wagons and carts were broken and tossed around like kindling wood. The rain water came down the hill in great volume, flooding some of the houses in its downward path to the bay. The brook far exceeded its banks and the current was wild, carrying along some personal property of the Pilgrims. The sea rose and heavy tides broke on the shores, its fierce waves destroying everything they encountered. Luckily, no one was killed but several had been injured.

"I guess that we were pretty lucky, the hurricane seems to have done little damage to our house," Tom said.

After noting the damage done to their own property they walked through the Plantation looking at the loss suffered by others.

They stopped at Bradford's home and saw him and his wife, Alice, looking at the damage. Bradford greeted them, "Hello Mary...Tom, how did you make out with the storm?"

"Hello, Governor...Mrs. Bradford. As I was just saying to Mary, we were lucky. Our garden in the back with Mary's flowers was destroyed and we lost a tree in our front yard and a little bit of our roof...that's about all. How did you make out?"

"Well, as you can see, we've got a tree uprooted and it's leaning against the house and there seems to be a little damage, but other than that I think we're in pretty good shape. Did you notice the woods near Fort Hill? The pine trees are all uprooted and some broken in half, the storm seemed to have cut a swatch through the woods, some of the trees were two feet in diameter. It will take a long time to clean up this mess."

They were joined by other Pilgrims who discussed the storm and injuries.

They got word the next day that their trading post at

Aptuxcet on the Cape was hit hard by the hurricane. There was considerable damage to the property and it would require a lot of hard work to bring it back to its original condition. The roof of the trading post had been completely torn from the rest of the structure and blown out to sea. Such was the violence of the storm. Aptuxcet was an important trading link to the southern part of Connecticut and Long Island. They were able to navigate the narrow waterway which was to become the Cape Cod canal.

The men from Plimoth had a difficult task ahead of them trying to get things straightened out and make repairs.

Gradually, as time went on, they were progressing well and making great strides but everywhere one looked, scars from the storm were visible.

William Bradford had other things on his mind beside the hurricane. He and Elder William Brewster with a new member of the colony were discussing the problems that they had in finding a teacher and minister that would be happy to stay in Plimoth.

"Edward Winslow was unsuccessful in his attempt to find a preacher in England, as you know. He found a Mr. Glover and he spent a lot of money outfitting him and the poor fellow died just before he was to depart for Plimoth," Brewster related.

"How about Mr. Rogers, the minister who Isaac Allerton brought over from England in 1629?" Bradford asked.

"Yes, that was a sad case. We gave him every opportunity but evidently he was insane and he had to be sent back."

"Well, William Rogers, the two Rogers were not related by the way, was a good teacher but he seemed to be a renegade in regard to the Indians. He learned their language and visited with them often, but he ran into trouble with the authorities when he tried to convince the Indians not to sell their land to the English." Bradford. said.

"Yes, I remember him well. When he was banished from Plimoth and the Bay Colony he went into the wilderness with the Indians. But he was evidently a very capable fellow because he founded Providence, Rhode Island."

"How about James Norton." suggested Bradford. "He stayed about four months as a teacher then he went on to Ipswich, to be with the more affluent folks. It cost us £70 for his passage over here but he reimbursed us half before he left for Ipswich."

"It's too bad that he wasn't satisfied with Plimoth, he was very pleasant to speak to and I enjoyed many hours discussing issues with him." Brewster said.

"Well, we will see how Reverend Reyner likes us. He'll be here shortly. He's a graduate of Emmanuel College in Cambridge and I understand he is well-off financially. I hope that he can use some of his own money to supplement the salary he will receive," Bradford laughingly said.

"We've just got through with seven years of ministerial service with Reverend Ralph Smith and it was quite an experience. I remember when he first came here. He was forced out of Salem and went to Nantasket where a Pilgrim trading mission found him in a sorry plight. He was married several years ago to the widow of Deacon Richard Masterson. He was forced to resign because of complaints from the congregation," Brewster said.

"I guess we've had our share of trouble with ministers and teachers in the past. I only hope that we'll be more successful this time. Now that we've had a hurricane and the struggle to clean up after the storm, we deserve a respite from problems for awhile," Bradford commented.

"It won't happen, Governor, we're Pilgrims. When have we lived without problems since we came to the New

World? It has the power to develop character—if you survive!" Brewster laughed.

CHAPTER 27

Plymouth, Cape Cod

1636

During late August, just after the hurricane hit, the trading post at Penobscot was attacked again by the French,
wiping them out of merchandise and sending Willet
with his men and a small supply of foodstuff back to Plimoth
in their shallop.

The Pilgrims wanted to teach the French a lesson once
and for all. They figured they would need some help so they
asked the Bay Colony to help them get rid of the French or
they would be a threat to them all. As usual, the Bay Colony
refused...the Pilgrims were on their own.

The Pilgrims wouldn't accept this insult without some
form of retaliation. They met the master of a British ship,
Captain Girling, who commanded the *Great Hope*, a giant of
300 tons, well fitted with cannons. The Pilgrims agreed to
pay him 700 pounds of beaver pelts if he could recapture
their trading post and he would receive nothing if he was
unsuccessful.

Setting sail on their ship to accompany the *Great Hope*

went Captain Myles Standish with twenty men and the beaver pelts. Before they reached Penobscot, Standish tried to speak with Captain Girling about the French and their defenses and a plan of attack. He wanted the French to surrender in view of the superior forces that would be brought to bear when they launched an attack.

Girling being headstrong and rash, ignored Standish and nearing the area where the French were entrenched, opened fire at a great distance so that the cannon range was ineffective. Standish was disgusted at Girling's behavior and said that he should get within pistol range and ask for their surrender, if no answer was received or if it was negative, then open fire.

To Standish's surprise Girling said that he was out of powder. Meanwhile, the French that could have been eliminated in a very quick battle, were laughing behind their earthen breastworks.

Standish, suspecting Captain Girling would try to seize all of his supplies including the beaver pelts, offered to get more powder. Sailing with his men back to Plimoth, he put another load of powder aboard a smaller ship and it sailed, but without Standish or his men, to the Penobscot River seeking out Captain Girling.

When the ship from Plimoth reached Girling he placed the powder on board and without firing a shot at the French he sailed off without so much as a backward glance. Another embarrassment for the Pilgrims!

The Pilgrims approached the Puritans again and explained why the French should be dislodged from their position. This time the Puritans were mildly interested but they wouldn't share the cost of putting together an expedition. They probably would go if the Pilgrims put up all the money.

To make matters worse, some of the merchants in

Boston, upon hearing that the French were now running the trading post, set out to do business with them. They didn't care that the French were trading rum and guns with the Penobscot Indians, their own concern was maybe the merchants could get some bargains from the French. The French began a brisk trade with the Boston merchants. The Pilgrims wrote the trading post off and the "French Trading Post" became a seat of power in Maine.

This episode caused a rift in the relationship between the people of Plimoth and the authorities in Massachusetts. The colonists resented the fact that the authorities showed little concern about the welfare of the Pilgrims. Although the French and the Boston merchants were clearly taking advantage of the Pilgrims, and they were clearly upset, their pleas fell on deaf ears.

On the one hand, the Pilgrims felt that the Puritans didn't care what happened to them; it was up to the Pilgrims to solve their own problems. Then again, the Pilgrims had to be aware that they needed the Puritans in case of an uprising by the Indians. They could help keep them in check. If the Indians knew the Puritans would join with the Pilgrims when there was any trouble, then the British of Boston remained an important ally and a hinderance to attack.

The French were continuously trying to pit their strength against the British and divide them as allies. They were aware of the fact that they had a comparatively strong force in Canada, and this influence was felt as far away as the base of Maine. The French were allied with several Indian tribes which would gladly take up arms against the British. The French had a large fleet which put into Canadian ports often.

The British fleet was monstly absent from the New England waters and they knew they could expect little assistance from them due to their status with the Crown.

Between the French, Indians and the total lack of compassion from the Puritans, the Pilgrims felt that they were alone in the New World.

They would continue along the way that had proven so successful in the past. They would prepare for the worst but hope for the best. They believed in prayer and a high moral standard. They did not lie. It would be a sin to go back on one's word. Through faith and belief in strong family ties, they felt that nothing could harm them—but the men still carried their muskets and drilled with the militia...and most important of all, they kept an eye on all the Indians, especially those they didn't regard as friends.

CHAPTER 28

Marblehead, Massachusetts

1636

A few days after the episode in Penobscot was closed, Thomas came into the house and asked, "How would you like to visit your sister and family in Marblehead next week?"

"I'd love to go, but how will we get there?"

"Some of the men from the plantation are going to be near Marblehead on the trip with the shallop and they said they would have room for us if we wanted to go. They will drop us off and pick us up three days later."

"We can leave Bonnie with John Cooke, they like each other. I don't think John will mind."

"Yes, that sounds good. I'll ask John as soon as I see him and you're right, I don't think he'll mind, he's my friend."

"Who asked you if we wanted to go?"

"It was John Alden, he's in charge of the trip, he'll know the date and time we'll be going. You better bring some food along, so Remember and Moses won't have to feed us.

I'll be able to take a few days off work so we can go."

Mary said, "Oh Tom, I'm so glad we're going to see Remember and Moses and the little ones. I miss Remember very much. We had our arguments and little fights but we always stuck up for each other when others interfered. I miss Bartholomew, too! I wish that he hadn't gone back to England. I don't know when, or if, I'll ever see him again."

Thomas answered, "I know that you miss them all. Your brother Bartholomew is really a nice person. I remember how he was always looking out for your welfare. He took the role of a big brother very seriously...I'll be glad to see your sister and her husband and family."

Mary was excited all week about the upcoming trip. Tom had checked with John Cooke and he was happy to take care of Bonnie while they were away.

Mary said, "Well, we only have two more days to wait until we go to Marblehead."

Thomas replied, "I guess you're pretty anxious to go on this trip?"

"I haven't been any place since I came to Plymouth. At least you've been to Boston a couple of times. It will be a welcome change. As you know, I've never seen Marblehead or Salem or anyplace but the Plantation and that's not good!"

On the day they were to leave, Mary and Thomas got up early on a sunny day that was breaking and the birds were beginning to chirp to welcome early risers After eating a hasty breakfast and cleaning up, they checked and rechecked the parcels they would take along. Along with food, there were gifts they had accumulated over a period of time.

They looked around to make sure that everything they were going to take with them was in the pile. They gathered the parcels and happily walked down the hill to the pier.

John Alden greeted them. "Well, good morning to you Mr. and Mrs. Cushman...it looks like a fine day ahead for our trip. A couple of men haven't arrived yet, but they will be here soon...oh, here they come now. Good morning!"

Alden greeted them. "I guess we're about ready to go. Are you all set Tom and Mary?"

"Yes, just show us where we sit and we'll be ready."

They were all set to leave, the sail was raised and the canvas popped out in the light wind. The sun was now shining brightly as it came up on the horizon on their right. The shallop hugged the coastline and passed Gurnet Point beyond Plimoth.

"You've never seen this area before have you Mary?" Tom asked as they traveled north.

"No, but I've had my fill of ships and traveling on water since I came over on the *Mayflower*. That was quite a trip! I'll never forget the miserable time we spent on the ship. This trip will be short, so I guess I can stand it."

As time went by, some of the men were talking, others were silent, some were taking a nap. There were ten men aboard and they were used to traveling in the shallop. The boat knifed through the water steadily approaching Boston Harbor.

Thomas was pointing out general landmarks to Mary and he said, "I bet you don't know what that stretch of land is?"

"I haven't got the slightest idea!"

"That's Allerton Point...it was named after your father by the Pilgrims several years ago."

Mary was silent and a few tears ran down her cheeks. She reached for Thomas' hand, held it and looked in his eyes, her expression told it all, she was very sad.

As they went by Brewster's Islands, Thomas pointed them out to Mary and said, "I've never been on the islands but some of the men have."

They were well out to sea but they could see land a

long distance off. "How come we're going out so far from land?" Mary asked.

"We're on a direct line to Marblehead. It's much shorter this way, we'll save valuable time by taking this route." Later they passed a strip of land off to their left.

"What is that off there?" Mary inquired.

"It's a small island or rather a peninsula called Nahant." Tom said. "We're not very far from Marblehead, it's about fifty miles from Plimoth...are you getting tired?"

"Well, I am getting tired of sitting here in one spot I wish that I could walk around for awhile. I suppose I can stretch and relax my muscles."

John Alden said, "We'll be there in an hour or less if we keep up this speed. You can move around a little so that you won't be so cramped."

After traveling further they passed a couple of small islands and then they were at Marblehead Bay. Upon entering the bay they edged to a mooring spot on their right. There were a few small dwellings near the water's edge and people walking down to greet the strangers.

Thomas retrieved his parcels from the shallop and put them on the pier. He then helped Mary out of her seat onto the pier.

Mary said, "It's a relief stepping on something that's not moving."

The people from the town greeted them and asked where they were from. When they said they were from Plimoth the people were interested and asked them why they had come to such an out-of-the-way place like Marblehead.

Thomas said, "We came here to see my wife's sister and her husband, Reverend Moses Maverick. Do you know where they live?"

One of the townspeople came forward and gave detailed directions to their house. He also said that he hoped they had a good visit and would like the town of Marblehead.

Once they had directions Thomas turned to John Alden who was just getting aboard the shallop and said, "I've got the directions to their house so I guess we'll be all right, it's only a short distance away.

John Alden replied, "We'll see you here in three days, about the same time. Have a good visit and say hello to Remember for me." He turned and joined the others who were in small groups either sitting in the boat or getting ready to get aboard, finishing their conversations with the people who had greeted them. Then they boarded the shallop to continue their trip to Cape Ann up the coast.

Thomas and Mary went up a lane, looking for a house that the neighbors described. They knocked on the door and got no answer.

"Oh Tom, what if they went away for awhile."

Tom knocked on the door again, harder this time, still no answer. Tom said, "Wait here Mary, I'll go around back and see if they're home." He went to the back yard and there they were, tending to the flowers. Their backs were turned and they were extremely surprised when Tom said, "Hello Remember...Moses!

"Thomas...what a surprise!" they both said. "What are you doing here?"

"Mary and I came to see you. Mary's out front. We were wondering if you were home—we knocked, but you couldn't have heard us out here in the back yard."

Remember kissed Tom and Moses shook his hand. This certainly is a welcome surprise. Let's go and see Mary. I can't wait to see her!"

They went to the front yard and Thomas said, "Look who's here!" Mary and Remember kissed and hugged each other.

Remember said, "Am I glad to see you! How long will you stay? How did you get here?"

Mary answered, "I'll tell you about it in a minute, first I want to greet my brother-in-law!" Moses and Mary hugged and kissed each other in a warm greeting. "How's the rest of the Maverick family?"

Remember said, "Come into the house, they're taking a nap just now."

"They're awake." Remember picked up the children and said, "What do you think of Abigail and Elizabeth?"

"They're beautiful!" Mary answered. "You must be very proud of them."

Moses smiled and said, "We certainly are! By the way, you must be starved...it's a long way from Plimoth...do you want anything to eat?"

Thomas said, "We had something to eat on the way. What about you, Mary, are you hungry?"

"I'm fine. We brought enough food to last us for three days. We came with John Alden on our little boat and he had several men with him. They were bound for Cape Ann and John wanted to know if we wanted to stop off here for three days and then they would pick us up on their way back. That's why we're here and we can have a good visit in that time."

Remember said, "Oh, I wish you could stay longer. It's been such a long time since we saw you. I'm going to give John Alden a piece of my mind for not stopping in to see us."

Moses said, "You shouldn't have brought the food, Mary. We have enough to go around."

"Well we didn't want to impose on you."

"Oh Mary, you know you're family...you wouldn't impose on us! We're glad that your both here. I wish that you could stay longer." Moses said.

"Would you like to go to Moses' service on the Sabbath? His church is fairly close. I'd like to have you and Tom meet our neighbors and see the sights around Marblehead. We had a lot of damage from the hurricane but gradually we're cleaning up the wreckage. I assume that you were in its path, too. Did you have any damage? We heard that the Cape received the brunt of the storm."

Tom explained what had happened in Plimoth and the surrounding area and how lucky they were in getting little of the damage. They talked for hours, bringing each other up to date on events since they last met. Mary told about the deaths, marriages and births since Remember left.

The next day they got up early, ate breakfast and Moses said, "I'd like to show you some of the sights and damage that we had around town. Later we can go to Marblehead Neck, if you like, it's just across the bay. I have a rowboat that I want to show off. It's about a mile across to the other shore, if you would like to go."

Thomas said, "That would be great, Moses. Can we see Marblehead Neck first? What do you girls think about going?"

Mary said, "I'd like to go but how about the children?"

Remember said," I'll stay here and take care of the children. I've seen just about everything around here, including Marblehead Neck."

Mary replied, "I'll stay here with you, Remember. Maybe the men would like to be alone. I don't want to tie them down. They can climb on the rocks and walk faster."

Remember, feeding the children said, "Go ahead Mary. Why don't you go with them. I think you'll enjoy the sights. I can handle the children...I'm used to it."

Thomas insisted, "You won't tie us down. Why don't you come with us?"

Moses looked at Remember, "Would you mind very

much if Mary went with us? I'm sure she will enjoy the sights, especially the cliff...that's my favorite spot."

Remember laughed, "You and your favorite spot—it's a wonder you don't camp out in Marblehead Neck. Go ahead Mary, I'm sure you will enjoy yourself."

"Well all right, I guess that I won't be in the way."

The three of them said goodbye to Remember and went down the walk with Moses hoisting the oars to the boat on his shoulder. They retraced the way that Thomas and Mary had come the day before. Thomas said, "I asked directions to your house from a bearded gentlemen with a red hat. He was very polite and said, 'I know exactly where Reverend Maverick lives. He's the pastor of our church'."

Moses laughed, "Yes, that would be Jack Thayer. He's our local character. He's accommodating and would go out of his way to help anyone. He's a God-fearing man but a little lax in attending church. What do you say to a man like that? He abides by all the Christian values, as I said, he is ready to help others in need at any time. I guess you might say we have an understanding...I don't press him about his attendance, or lack of it, but still we're good friends. I think God looks after him. I wish all church members behaved like him...but of course, then no one would come to church."

They reached the rowboat and Mary and Thomas sat in the stern when Moses volunteered to row. Moses untied the boat and after he was seated he put the oars between the sturdy wooden pegs and then started to row. They were lucky to have another fine day. The quiet surface of the bay was disturbed by Moses taking mighty strokes and the boat moved steadily ahead to the opposite shore.

"It's a beautiful day." Mary exclaimed." I don't think we could have a nicer day if we ordered it. Look at the sun sparkling in the water...it's very calm and serene here."

Eventually they reached a sandy spot on the rocky shore and pulled the boat s bow up and tied the boat to a large rock which were plentiful on the rocky shoreline.

Moses said, "I like to come over to Marblehead Neck to relax and reflect. Remember and I came over here often before we had the children and we'll come over again when they are a little older."

Thomas said, "What if you have more children?"

Moses said, "Well I guess that will be another problem, but I'll take the children any day over a scenic view."

They went up a steep path and reached the top of a hill overlooking the ocean and they could see the waves beating themselves on the rocky coast. "See that spot up on the coast sticking out, the one that seems higher than the others?" Moses asked.

"Yes." Mary said, "Can we go over there?"

"We certainly can...that's my famous favorite spot! Remember teases me about it. We used to go there every time we visited Marblehead Neck."

They walked south down a path and came to a large rock formation towering over the landscape and extending out beyond the shoreline. The three climbed up on the rocks Mary gingerly picking her way and Tom directly behind her to make sure she didn't slip. (Moses favorite spot was later to become known as Castle Rock.)

"Can you see why I like this spot?"

"Yes I can." Thomas replied. "The waves breaking on the rocks around us, the surrounding so colorful...it's a lot different than Cape Cod with its sand dunes."

Mary said, "What's that island off there?"

"They call it Tinkers Island. I've never been there. There are several islands around here but I haven't explored them yet."

After spending a long time sitting on the rock talking,

watching the waves and the sea gulls darting down to get food from the sea, they reluctantly headed back to where they left the rowboat. On the way, Mary picked some wild flowers to give to Remember. She said, "I know that she likes flowers, she was always stopping in the fields, picking them when we were growing up."

When they reached the rowboat, Thomas offered to row back. Moses agreed. "We can go to Salem if you like, it's only about two miles away."

"I didn't know Salem was so close," Thomas said. "But I think we should go back to see Remember."

"Yes, of course. Maybe later we can go overland to look at the harbor. It's about a mile from our house. I have a telescope and we can see Salem Village from across the Salem Bay."

Thomas rowed across Marblehead Bay and when they reached shore they tied up the boat and headed back to Moses house. They met several neighbors on their way back and Moses introduced them to Mary and Thomas. Many of them had only been living here a couple of years and were surprised that Mary had been in the New World almost sixteen years. They had heard about the *Mayflower* voyage and eventual deaths in the colony. They were distressed when Mary said that she had lost her mother and step-mother, during the epidemics that occurred in 1621 and 1633.

When they got back to the house, they were laughing at a joke that Moses told. When they went up to the door it was opened by Remember who held her finger to her mouth to signal them that the children were taking their nap.

Speaking in a quiet tone, Moses said, "Tom and Mary were impressed with Marblehead Neck especially when they saw my favorite spot."

"Oh come on, Moses. They probably said it to be polite."

Mary said, "No, Remember it's true! Why even ships' captains that put into Plimoth, mention the fact that when they visit America it's always been their desire to see Marblehead Neck and be able to see Moses Maverick's favorite spot. That's the word going around Europe."

Everyone tried to muffle their laughs. Remember said in a low voice, "Mary, I see you haven't lost your sense of humor."

Remember had prepared lunch for them and they sat down to eat. They continued to speak in low tones so the children wouldn't hear them.

The conversation got around to Isaac Allerton and his stay at the Maverick household, since he left Plimoth, more or less in disgrace. He had left for New Amsterdam in 1635 at the urging of the Massachusetts Authority to leave Marblehead. This was no doubt instigated by the leaders at Plimoth. Isaac had become quite an entrepreneur in his short stay at Marblehead. He had been the owner of an eight vessel business engaged in fishing around Marblehead and Gloucester, which was renowned for an abundance of fish. He had been forced to sell the fleet at a low price to get money to move to New Amsterdam.

Remember said, "I understand that father went into business as a merchant and he's doing very well. He has also been selected to be on the council of five to guide the Dutch colony of New Amsterdam."

Moses laughingly said, "The funny part of it is, he's the only Englishman on the Dutch Council. He speaks Dutch and that's really an advantage."

Mary said, "I wish he could have come to our wedding. We haven't seen him for such a long time. Little Isaac hasn't seen his father in years and he looks upon Elder Brewster as his true father."

Just then the children woke up from their nap and

Mary and Remember went over to them. They each picked up a child and came back to the table. "I wish that we could have gone to your wedding too. It only happens once in a lifetime. It must have been nice though, being with your friends that you have known all your life. Moses and I were tied up having children. Speaking of children—you seem to be a natural to be a mother the way that you handle the children. Wouldn't you like a daughter like her? They're such company. It's fun to watch them grow, they all have their own cute habits."

"Well, we'll have our own family someday." Tom said.

Later in the day Moses and Thomas went for a walk around the neighborhood and Moses pointed out interesting locations and damage from the hurricane that still wasn't repaired. They met the nearby neighbors including Jack Thayer. Later Thomas said, "He certainly is a unique character but I agree with you, he has a lot of goodwill toward his fellow man."

Moses replied, "He claims to have been a young sailor in the British Navy and helped to defeat the Spanish Armada. He was wounded in that battle but fortunately he lost no limbs. I guess he led an interesting life. I have no reason to doubt his story, he's an honest man."

They headed back to the house and upon arrival Moses said, "I hope you folks will excuse me but I have to get ready for my service tomorrow. I have to review and write some material but I won't be too long."

After Moses completed his work they spent the evening talking about old times and Moses asked, "Mary, have you heard from your brother Bartholomew?"

"Yes, I've sent letters to him and he answered them. He is going to be a minister, too. I miss him very much. He was always playing tricks on me and was very funny telling us his jokes."

Remember joined in, "Yes, we had our arguments when we were young and like you, Mary, I love him very much. I wish he hadn't returned to England, we could all be together."

The next day was Sunday and they attended Moses' church.

He gave a very emotional sermon about the value of family and friendship. He looked at Thomas and Mary several times during the service and they felt he had written the sermon with them in mind. During the service Mary held one child, Remember the other. After the service Moses stood at the door of the church with Remember, the children and Thomas and Mary. He greeted the members of the church and introduced the Cushmans to them. He seemed to be proud to be part of the family and one could sense his affection for them.

When they returned to the house, Thomas and Moses left to see Salem Village. It wasn't very far and soon they were on the banks of Salem Harbor. Moses set the telescope on a stand and they looked through it to see the small objects that were barely discernible to the naked eye. Moses said, "The *Arabella* landed there with John Endicott in 1632, who was their leader and later became the Governor of the Massachusetts Bay Colony. (He eventually served fifteen times as governor and five times as deputy governor. Like the Pilgrims, the Puritans suffered diseases the first winter but their food situation was not as severe. John Winthrop came with his ships in 1630 but left soon after to travel to Boston where he stayed.)

Tom asked Moses questions about several landmarks and then they finally left Salem Harbor. They returned to the Maverick house and were happy to see that supper was almost ready for them. Their walk had worked up a healthy appetite for them and Thomas had seen a lot of Marblehead. The meals were typical of the ones served at Plimoth and one could find a meal being prepared, hanging in the fireplace, in a large pot most of the day. They prepared the table and sat down to a meal of venison stew which had been flavored with pork; and they had bread, cheese and pie. The beverage was milk for the children and beer for the adults.

Thomas told Mary about Salem Village and said the telescope could really bring things up close. He said he could see the houses and even make out the people walking around the village.

Moses said, "I've been over there and met some of the people. It's a good thing I have a rowboat, it's a long walk around by land to get there. You see, Marblehead is out on a peninsula."

After finishing the meal and washing and drying the eating utensils, they again sat down to talk, then Moses asked if Thomas would like to look at his collection of books. Although Thomas was not formally educated he could hold his own in cultural knowledge from his teachings by Brewster and Bradford. Moses was impressed with Tom's knowledge and asked how he came by all the facts that he was so familiar with. He said, "I owe it all to Elder William Brewster and Governor William Bradford, who so generously let me have access to their libraries and helped me wade through the complicated things."

They finally went to bed and they all realized that tomorrow would be the last day of their visit. Their future get-togethers were indeterminate, their lives were indeed insecure with threats of Indians, disease, even starvation lurking someplace in the background ready to rear its ugly head at anytime.

The next day they arose to another fine sunny day. The shallop would arrive about one in the afternoon. They prepared a hearty breakfast of bean soup, bread, hasty pudding and that old stand-by, beer.

After breakfast Mary was holding both children on her lap and looked at Thomas and smiled. The children were laughing and giggling and definitely happy with their aunt. "Thomas, look at Mary. Doesn't she seem content and happy with the children?"

"Moses, Mary always looks content and happy! I know, now you'll say there is nothing like having children...they fill a void in life."

"Yes, or words to that effect."

"I agree with you."

"Time is certainly going by fast." Remember said, as she set the table with Mary helping. "You'll just have time to eat a quick meal before you go to the boat. Mary and I prepared bean soup...again, stewed peas, boiled onions, bread, gingerbread and beer."

Moses headed for the table with Thomas, "That sounds fine, Remember, we'll just eat and run. You'll be able to go to see them off, won't you?"

"Well, I was going to say our good-byes here, the children will be taking their naps at that time."

"Come on, Remember," Moses insisted, "I don't think it will hurt the children if they take their naps a little later. The children will enjoy seeing Thomas and Mary sail off in the shallop, although I think they'll miss them."

"The children are so little I doubt if they will enjoy seeing the shallop sail away. But you're right...I do want to see them off...but we'd better hurry and eat."

After they had eaten and cleared the table, they got ready to leave for the harbor. They left the house with Thomas and Moses in the lead, each holding a child. Mary and Remember followed, engaged in a lively conversation. It didn't take them long to walk to the harbor, and the shallop was already there with the men standing on the pier. There also were several townspeople with them, talking to the men from Plimoth.

"Sorry we're late, John," Thomas said. "I thought we'd have to plenty of time to make it. I don't think you've forgotten Remember, and this is her husband Reverend Moses Maverick and their children."

"Actually we're early, you're not late! Hello, Remember, it's been quite a while since I saw you last. I can see that you've been doing quite well." Alden motioned toward the children and Moses.

Remember said, "John, you're still looking hale and hearty! Moses, this is John Alden, I've spoken of him many times, and his wife, Priscilla."

Moses said, "Yes, you have spoken of them and John, it was all flattering."

They introduced Moses and Remember to the men who were strangers. The others who knew her greeted her warmly. The townspeople looked on in silence, smiling.

They stayed for about fifteen minutes and then Alden finally said, "I guess we had better be under way, we have a long way to go. There is a good head wind blowing and we'll make good time sailing to Plimoth."

Remember and Mary hugged and kissed each other and Moses and Thomas shook hands, they didn't know when they would see each other again. They took their places in the shallop and they pushed off from the pier. The Cushmans turned to wave at the Mavericks and the others on the pier. They all waved back. Remember was dabbing at her tears. As for the children...they were sound asleep.

The wind caught the sail on the shallop and they were now underway tacking out into the harbor. Later, the boat looked tiny in the broad expanse of the sea, bobbing along.

Mary said to Thomas, "When will we see them again?"

"I don't know...I really don't know."

The trip home was uneventful but they really made good time, with a strong wind behind them. Eventually Plimoth came into sight and all the familiar things were coming into view.

"We're home, Thomas...it's nice to visit other places but I'm glad we're home again."

"I'm glad too. I'll be happy to see Bonnie. I wonder if she missed us? Do you think she'll remember us?"

John Alden and the crew, with the tired Cushmans, finally neared the pier and there were several of their neighbors there to greet them and welcome them home.

The tiny sail on the shallop attracted the attention of the colonists, and many of them rushed to see who was coming into the pier. In the Plimoth amusement level, this was an exciting event.

John Cooke, Junior, was there with Bonnie who had seen the Cushmans on the shallop and she was pacing up and down restlessly among the viewers. Within a few minutes, she was barking to greet them when they finally pulled up to the pier and secured the shallop.

Thomas and Mary exited the boat and Bonnie ran to them and jumped up and down, waiting to be petted. Afte rshe was given the necessary attention, she raced ahead of them with her tail wagging vigorously.

The Cushmans tried to keep Bonnie in sight while they greeted John Cooke and the other neighbors. It was easy to see Bonnie, she kept returning to the Cushmans to make certain they were headed in the right direction toward home.

John returned with them to their house and the Cushmans asked him if he was hungry. It seemed that they all agreed they were and the next question was...where will we find something to eat?

Everything had gone stale or rotten in this brief time away from home while they were in Marblehead visiting.

They all went to John's house, a few doors away, to see what he had available to eat. They did a little better. They had bread and jelly sandwiches and a little wine. A really hearty meal!

After eating and staying with John for a short period of time, the Cushmans headed home with Bonnie. John patted her before she left and said they could leave Bonnie anytime. She was a good dog and obeyed him with no problem.

Returning home, the Cushmans signed in relief, and Mary said, "At last we're home... really home."

CHAPTER 29

The Outpost, Connecticut

1636

Now the Pilgrims had to get ready for a new shock! The Saints that were converted by Edward Fuller in Dorchester, in the Bay Colony, were now intruding on the trading post in Connecticut. The Pilgrims bought the land from the Indians when they settled to establish the trading post. It was beginning to show a profit after a lot of hard work.

The "interlopers," coming in droves with their wagons, cattle and all their possessions, moved through the wilderness into the area and took over the fields to plant their crops. Later, they founded the town of Windsor.

The post was managed by Jonathan Brewster, William's son, who was now in his early forties. Earlier, when the Pilgrims suggested to the leaders of the Bay Colony that they become partners in the trading post, the Puritans had refused.

John Oldham once again crossed the path of the Pilgrims in Connecticut. He led ten men from the Bay Colony to a point about five miles below the Dutch position in what would become Wethersfield. They planted large fields of onions under the noses of the Dutch near their fort. Then came Pastor John Wareham with his congregation from Dorchester who settled on the doorstep of Jonathan Brewster.

The Pastor was warned by Governor Prence that they were trespassing. The Pastor and the congregation were fed by Jonathan for several days because they had little food.

Governor Prence gave Jonathan Brewster a stern warning that the settlers should be treated fair but firm and they shouldn't be there, they came without invitation.

Jonathan went to the Dutch and asked them if Pastor Wareham and his congregation could settle near them, he had other plans for the land where they were staying.

The Dutch refused and sent a note to New Amsterdam which said that the English were becoming a problem.

Governor Prence wrote to the Bay Colony explaining the problem and the Puritans seemed to enjoy the situation. They said, "They're converted Saints so the Pilgrims will have to take care of them."

More Saints were coming from Dorchester every day. Their aim seemed to be to eventually take over the trading post and all the surrounding area.

The Pilgrims wrote an angry letter to the authorities in Boston and said that if the Pilgrims hadn't gone to Connecticut the Dutch would have taken all of the land. They also said the land around Plimoth, as the Puritans knew, was almost barren while the soil in Connecticut was fertile, and now the Dutch were trying to take it away from them.

Getting nowhere with the letters the Pilgrims had to make a decision soon. The idea of using force against the Dorchester Saints was ruled out. They came to the conclusion that they would retain their trading post and the two adjoining lots and the rest of the land would go to the "intruders".

A year later, the Pilgrims were to get a strange request from the Puritans. They wanted help in fighting the Pequots in Connecticut because two men were scalped, but survived. They were two "old friends" of the Pilgrims...John Oldham and Captain Stone, who once tried to steal a ship from them and also tried to stab Edward Winslow. Later, Stone was killed along with eight men on the Connecticut River and two weeks after this incident, Oldham was struck with a hatchet thrown by an Indian and killed instantly. The Pequots were held responsible for both incidents.

Unknown to the Pilgrims or the settlers in Connecticut, a force led by Captain Endicott of Massachusetts Bay Colony was seeking revenge for the killings.

Endicott's troops attacked Block Island and the mainland of Connecticut, demanding the surrender of the guilty Indians and retribution of a quantity of wampum. Not getting the proper satisfaction from the Pequots, they set upon them and killed about twenty and took all of their supplies and destroyed everything in sight. Then they left for Boston leaving the white settlers alone and at the mercy of the Pequots and of the havoc that Endicott's troops had left behind. The Pequots raged up and down the valley, looting and killing the innocent settlers for months on end.

The Pequots were well known as fierce warriors and they hated the white men. They would give them no quarter. They thought the English were taking over their land and, unlike the Cape Cod Indians, they did not want to live in peace with the English as next door neighbors.

The young braves laughed as they painted crude warlike symbols on their bodies and clipped their hair to frighten the white women and children. They would gather near their crude huts and plan their new excursions in mayhem. They would use various weapons and with wild cries to break the silence, they would descend on an isolated home and murder all the inhabitants. To them, this was great sport.

In summer they would endure the hot days by avoiding wearing any clothing and revert to absolute savagery. They would attack aggressively and quickly fade into the background along the borders. Lying in ambush, they would rise against the white hunting parties that were unaware of their presence and instantly kill them. Isolated homes and their inhabitants would fall helpless victims to raiding parties. Entire families were methodically killed including babes-in-arms. The cattle were stolen and the homes and structures which the families had labored so hard to complete were torched and in a short time they were burned to the ground.

Laughing at the settlers' plight and distress, they would finish them off with arrows and hatchets. Farmers working in the fields near the base of the Connecticut River were put upon by gaudy, painted Pequots who yelped and gave blood-curdling screams while they attacked. Fleeing in terror, those that could escape ran aimlessly to get away.

Those unfortunate enough to remain or caught running away were quickly dispatched and their lives squelched in the midst of a scream. Soon only an occasional yelp was heard. This died out and an eerie silence fell over the blood-stained area...the Pequots moved on to their next target.

Another target was a heavily fortified settlement near the mouth of the Connecticut River. The settlers here were well-prepared to meet the threat. Although the attack was cleverly conceived and executed, the white settlers, firing their muskets, were determined that they would not be over-run by the Pequots. The Indians this time carried their dead away and realized that the opposition to their actions was strong and would become stronger as the whites organized to oppose the onslaught of the Pequots.

The word went out about the slaughter of the settlers and the populace was warned about the threat and soon weapons appeared to defend themselves and their homes.

The Pequots noticed this change in attitude and knew they would need reinforcements if they were to continue these isolated attacks on the "Newcomers" to their land.

They approached the Narragansetts and emphasized the issue that the "Foreigners"; that is, the English and the Dutch, were occupying their sacred soil and like an incoming tide would soon claim all their land. If the Narragansetts did not want to join them in their fight then they would like them to remain neutral.

The Pequots would limit their attacks of harassment of the intruders by selecting homes to be destroyed. Then the cattle from these families would be stolen and other English would be killed by ambushing them in small groups. This, they claimed, would be such a threat and aggravation the 'Foreigners" would get on their ships and vacate their land.

The Narragansetts weighed the argument that the Pequots offered and after deliberation they came to the opinion that they would choose to support the English...not the Pequots. The Pequots had caused them great harm for too many years to forgive them and become allies.

Plimoth Colony eventually heeded the request from the Bay Colony for assistance for the beleaguered settlers and they assembled a force to fight the Pequots. The group of forty-two men was commanded by Lieutenant William Holmes and accompanied by Governor Thomas Prence and was ready to move. The leaders of Plimoth received a note from Governor Winthrop of the Bay Colony stating the Plimoth men wouldn't be needed as the Pequots were practically wiped out by troops from Connecticut and the Bay Colony.

Prior to their assembly, ninety men from Connecticut, commanded by Captain John Mason and joined by forty men from the Bay Colony under the command of Captain John Underhill, went by boat to the Narragansett territory and consulted with the tribe leaders.

In collaboration with the English, the Narragansetts, using a small group of guides, quietly and under the cover of darkness led them to the Mystic River where the Pequots had their heaviest concentration of warriors in a fort.

Once they were in position to attack, the English troops opened fire on Mystic Fort and were soon to meet heavy resistance. The English set fire to the Pequot huts and were quickly in close combat with the Indians. Racing to the huts to extinguish the flames the Pequots soon found that the fire had ruined the strings of their bows and they were now useless. To add to their misery they were being engulfed by the flames of the burning huts.

The English were now attacking with muskets, swords and tomahawks and they trapped seven hundred men, women and children in a fiery holocaust. About four hundred were killed, some by battle, others perished in a scene that rivaled *Dante's Inferno*. Some were captured, others escaped to Mohawk Territory. Among those that managed to escape was the head sachem, Sassacus, who was in his late seventies. He dominated a large area which consisted of Narragansett Bay to the Hudson River and a large part of Long Island.

The Mohawks felt they could remain on friendly terms with the English with a noble gesture. They accomplished this feat by cutting off Sassacus' head.

The captured young Pequots braves were sent into slavery in the West Indies.

*   *   *

The reason for the delay in promising the use of the Plimoth troops was pure politics. When Governor Winthrop appealed to the Pilgrims for help in fighting the Pequots, Bradford reminded him about the Pilgrims requesting aid in the past which was ignored. Bradford asked several questions of Winthrop. How about the arrest of John Alden? What about the request to oust the French when they took the Pilgrims Trading Post? What about the Boston merchants that went to the captured trading post then being run by the French and engaged in trade? What will be your answer if once again we request aid?

Winthrop's reply was an epitome of double talk. Upon reading his answer one would assume that the Pilgrims were either guilty or it didn't really matter because he said they were blowing it out of proportion.

Winthrop also said, "If you desire aid in the future what will the people of the Bay Colony think of our neighbor in Plimoth if you deny us help now?"

Roger Williams, often known as a renegade, left Boston at the Puritans' request to live with the Narragansett Indians. He learned their language and customs and became a close friend.

The Puritans reluctantly admitted that it probably was his influence with the Narragansett Indians that prevented the Pequots from forming an alliance with the powerful tribe....Williams later became Governor of Rhode Island and he seemed to be admired, and respected by the citizens.

The Pilgrims replied that the situation with the Massachusetts authorities would have to change.

As time went by, more Puritans would arrive from England, and, consequently, as more immigrants came to the New World, more pressure would be put on the various Indian tribes by infringing on their land. There was a lot of resentment against the British now and there was a problem keeping things from exploding.

It would be a life-or-death matter for real cooperation

among the colonists. They would have to show a united front among the colonies to sway the Indians from provoking an attack anywhere.

Someplace, sometime, there was always the chance that a renegade Indian sachem would let his temper explode against the British and kill many of the isolated whites.

The Indians, once united against the British, could be a formidable force. They outnumbered the whites considerably.

This imminent danger was just on the horizon...a spark could set it off.

CHAPTER 30

Plymouth, Cape Cod

1638-1640

While the carnage was now over in Connecticut they still had to cope with getting supplies for the Plimoth Colony and trying to solve its financial problems. Although the Plimoth Undertakers steadfastly held that they would send no more goods to London until the accounts were finally straightened out, Winslow convinced the Pilgrims they should, to show goodwill. Privately the Pilgrims thought that Winslow's argument was weak but they sent three large shipments of beaver pelts to London. Sherley sent a note to Plimoth thanking them for the shipments but he wrote; "We still can't sell the pelts under the present conditions. There is a plague in London as well as a drought, business is at a standstill and therefore we have no money."

His business partners, Beauchamp and Andrews, would not help him out in his time of need. But there was still no word about the long overdue accounts due Plimoth.

The Pilgrims finally had their fill of Sherley and his failure to send the accounting of merchandise that the

Pilgrims had sent to the London Undertakers over the past five years. The Undertakers from Plimoth said they would no longer represent the colony and they wanted a complete accounting. When they were reviewing their books the Pilgrims were astounded when they found that over a period of five years they sent Sherley 12,530 pounds of beaver, thousands of black fox, mink, otter and other furs. They figured at the least they were owed £10,000 net, because the other furs paid all the other charges. The items they had received from London totaled £2,000. This would more than balance their account and they would send no more beaver, this was the end of their relationship.

Beauchamp and Andrews sent a letter to the Pilgrims explaining they received nothing from Sherley. They told such a heartfelt sob story and related their hardship in trying to support the Plimoth Colony. The Pilgrims thought it over and finally relented and sent a load of beaver pelts to Beauchamp and Andrews.

Beauchamp sold his share for £400 and Andrews suffered a loss. They both claimed that Isaac Allerton still owed them money, so the Pilgrims sold Allerton's cattle and sent them the money. His house had long since been seized and sold to help satisfy his debts.

The Pilgrims then sold their post on the Kennebec River along with their ship that was stationed there and sent the money from the sale to Beauchamp and Andrews...they still complained to the Pilgrims!

When Winslow was asked by Sherley to come to London to straighten out the accounts, he refused, remembering the ordeal that he went through on his last visit to London.

Captain Standish offered to go to London as a non-separatist thinking he wouldn't be subject to the same persecution.

The Pilgrims decided to contact Governor Winthrop

and get his opinion about Standish going to England and explained the situation with Sherley. He advised against the plan and said he would send a letter to Sherley suggesting they form a panel of Massachusetts merchants and other trade people that were neutral and known to the Massachusetts and London partners and Sherley. Whatever the decision, the Pilgrims would be bound by the outcome. The Pilgrims hoped that in the meantime the price of cattle would remain stable because this was now their only means of revenue.

Sherley still hadn't given up the idea that Winslow should come to London, but if it would put him in jeopardy he could meet him in Scotland, Holland or France, where he would out be of range of his enemies.

Time went on and there still wasn't a firm decision. Waiting to hear from the panel in Massachusetts, and growing impatient with the delay, Sherley said he would be forced to hire lawyers but they would end up with the money. Finally Sherley gave in and accepted the plan that Winthrop and the Pilgrims had proposed.

John Atwood, a friend of Sherley's, accepted his role as an executive with power of attorney. He had been an assistant governor of Plimoth and a religious, honest man.

Another assistant governor, William Collier, a brewer who had sold his tavern to Allerton, was named counsel to Atwood to give him advice. Collier had been a Merchant Adventurer and one of the London Undertakers before he went to Plimoth in 1633. Beauchamp's brother-in-law, Edmund Freeman who had also had been an assistant governor of Plimoth, joined with the others in making a determination.

Eventually, the Plimoth Undertakers came to an agreement with John Atwood and his assistants. The Pilgrims took an inventory of all existing items that could be counted in their joint stock; such as, the trading posts, boats, livestock, trading goods and other sundry items. The total came to £1,400, which was divided among the Plimoth Undertakers. They agreed to sign a bond that would pay the London Undertakers representing Sherley a total of £1,200; that is, £400 a year for three years.

The Plimoth Undertakers; Bradford, Brewster. Winslow, Standish, Prence and Howland were then to be absolved of all debts and claims, then due or to be become due.

Sherley and Andrews accepted the Plimoth Undertakers' word as bond and all claims were forgiven, but Beauchamp didn't sign a release. Although Sherley and Andrews emphatically denied that the Pilgrims didn't owe more to Beauchamp the Plimoth Undertakers finally paid him off to get rid of him. In order to accomplish this payment, they sold the large farms of 300 acres each, owned by Standish and Alden. Bradford and Prence sold their homes.

They hoped this was to be the end of their problems with London.

CHAPTER 31

Plymouth, Cape Cod

1637

On September 16, 1637 there was soon to be a new addition to the Cushman family. Mary, leading an active life, was in good health and looking forward to the birth. She was being attended to by Mrs. Elizabeth (Tilley) Howland and Mrs. Mary (Chilton) Winslow, close friends of Mary since childhood.

Elizabeth, sitting next to the bed, said, "How are you feeling?"

"I'm doing all right...how is Thomas?"

Elizabeth laughed, "I think he's all right, too. But a little nervous. He's waiting outside."

"Why don't you ask him in?"

Mary Winslow opened the door and said, "Thomas, your wife wants to see you."

Thomas came into the room with a serious look on his face. "Are you all right, Mary?"

"Yes, Thomas. I know this is your first baby but don't be so nervous...you'll survive."

He laughed and held her hand. "I'll try to be calm, Mary, if you will." They looked at each other and smiled. There was silence in the room until Mary let out a stifled groan.

Elizabeth went to Mary's side and said, "Mary, are you all right? How are you feeling?"

"I guess that I had a little pain...oh, there it goes again!"

"Tom, I think you'll have to go outside now. We're going to be busy soon." Mary Winslow said.

When Thomas came out of the room Bonnie came over and sat at his feet. He quietly started to pat her head. She would look toward the bedroom and cock her head when she heard Mary. She looked at Thomas with a quizzical look and then she placed her head between her two front paws, and stretched her rear legs out straight and went to sleep.

Hours went slowly by and suddenly Thomas heard a wail from the next room. Startled, he stood and waited and then he paced the floor. Later, Elizabeth came to the door and motioned to Thomas, she asked, "How would you like to see your new son?"

Thomas broke out with a broad smile and bolted into the bedroom. He greeted Mary with a hug and said, "Let's see my son."

Mary was lying in bed with their new son wrapped up and only his tiny red face with a little button nose visible.

"How do you like our new son, Thomas Junior?"

"He's so quiet." Thomas said. "Is he all right?"

"Yes, Thomas. He's fast asleep. I think he's perfect... we have a great son!"

Thomas kissed Mary and said, "Thank you for such a nice baby!"

Mary said, "I hope that he grows up just like you."

Elizabeth spoke up, "I think you should get some rest,

Mary. Giving birth to a child is tiring."

"Yes, I feel sleepy, I can use some rest."

"I'll be going, Mary. Do you think I can hold our baby soon?"

"Of course, Thomas. You'll have plenty of time for that ...I'll see you later."

He left the bedroom beaming, a smile from ear to ear. Bonnie greeted him with her tail wagging vigorously. Sensing Thomas' happiness, she jumped up on him. She looked around and grabbed a cloth between her teeth and wanted him to play tug-of-war.

Mary had no contact with her father, so she couldn't tell him about the birth of her son. She was happy with her life and whole situation.

*   *   *

Thomas was very busy on his new job as Highway Surveyor and he also held the position of Freeman. Along with working around the house and in the fields, he still had time to spend with Mary and his new son. His favorite expression was, "Mary don't you think that he looks like me?"

Mary would jokingly say, "Yes, but I think he'll grow out of it, probably he will end up being handsome."

Thomas kissed Mary and said, "You always know how to hurt a person.' He playfully hit her on the arm. "Can I hold him now?"

"Not just yet Thomas. It's feeding time and I have to take care of him."

After a few minutes Thomas said, "You look just like a mother."

"Well, that's because I am one!"

Thomas and Mary seemed to be made for each other.

301

They had small arguments, which lasted but a few minutes, and then all was forgiven or forgotten.

Thomas was given a lot of books from Brewster and Bradford which he appreciated. They were one of the ways that he could find relaxation from his arduous workday.

When their work was done, Thomas and Mary settled down in front of the fireplace. He usually read by candlelight or light from the fireplace. The flaming logs gave plenty of light and heat on cold nights.

Bonnie would usually lie at his feet and she would wag her tail when Thomas reached to pet her. She would look at Mary, who was contentedly knitting beside Thomas, and she waited for Mary to also show her gratitude that Bonnie was their dog.

CHAPTER 32

Plymouth, Cape Cod

1641

When young Thomas was old enough to be taken out of the house, he was carried by his father and accompanied by Mary. They walked around the plantation stopping at their friends' homes and introduced young Thomas, with his wobbly head and bright eyes, to their neighbors. They were proud of their new addition and took this time to show him off.

The year of Thomas' birth, the Plimoth Colony and the surrounding towns had grown to over three thousand inhabitants. The daily routine consisted of mending sails, gardening, caring for chickens, cooking codfish cakes, milking goats and cows, fishing and other duties. It was a very simple life but sometimes discouraging when they put so much effort into trying to accomplish something for the future only to find it unsuccessful and they would have to start it all over again.

This was true of their efforts at establishing trading posts and planting crops.

*   *   *

It was June 2, 1638 and Mary Cushman was putting little Thomas into his crib for an afternoon nap. He had been restless and fussy. He was only nine months old and required a lot of attention. Mary said, "Thomas, I think you're sleepy and you have to take a little rest." He couldn't understand but he liked the sound of her voice. Mary had been singing softly while she worked; she had a busy schedule, cooking, making candles and soap, and the big job of taking care of her baby... she was happy as a mother and housewife.

Bonnie started to growl quietly and became restless, she cocked her head and listened intently. She nervously went behind Mary and peeked around her. A strange sound was bothering her. Mary, who was witnessing Bonnie's unusual behavior said, "What is it Bonnie...what's the matter?"

Mary paused and listened...there was complete silence. Then she thought she heard something a long distance off...it sounded like rumbling. Mary thought, "It can't be thunder, there isn't a cloud in the sky!" The sound increased in volume. Suddenly the house began to shake and dishes began to fall from the shelves.

Mary rushed to the crib, grabbed her baby and sped outdoors where she thought she would find safety.

Mary called for Bonnie but she had already taken refuge under the bed, only the tip of her nose was visible...so much for bravery!

By this time many of the other women and children were outside hanging on fence posts and trees as the earth trembled beneath their feet. Many were hysterical, they never experienced this before. The tremors came from the Northeast and traveled Southwest rapidly.

No one knew what it was, or where it had originated. Many of the houses had been damaged slightly but the ground had not opened up. Mary held her baby tightly to her bosom and grabbed a tree, frantically holding on for dear life. She wished her husband was beside her. He had his job as Highway Surveyor and was away for the day. She wondered how he had fared; was it as bad where he was...or worse?

Gradually the tremors and shaking stopped and there was an eerie silence. Bonnie peeked around the open door and ran to Mary and young Thomas.

Then there were shouts from the townspeople, "Is anyone hurt?" There were a few minor injuries but fortunately most had escaped harm.

The townspeople roamed around the plantation to see the damage and gave thanks that they were spared. There came more rumbling in the distance, again it sounded like an approaching thunderstorm. It was the aftershock of the earthquake and it came about half and hour later. The ground shook and in its wake the houses also bore the brunt, but it was milder this time.

"I wonder if it will come again?" Mary asked a neighbor who also was hanging on a nearby fence with her children.

"I don't know...it's horrible!"

Some of the men had been at sea, fishing from the shallop near Plimoth Harbor. They had rushed to shore in the sudden turbulent sea. They had never experienced an earthquake before and they were frightened but outwardly they didn't show their fear. Their only concern was the welfare of their loved ones on shore.

Men had come from the forest where they had been chopping and sawing trees to see what damage had been done to the colony.

Several of the houses had been damaged with large cracks and many of the roofs would require repair but generally the Pilgrims had been lucky. They thought that only Plimoth had been hit but later they found that the earthquake had been felt for hundreds of miles.

After the earthquake, a new minister/teacher came to Plimoth. Mr. Charles Chauncey arrived and stayed until 1641 when he moved to another town.

Chauncey had a problem with baptism. The church approved dipping the infant but he wanted to place the child in water fully submerged—he said that dipping was unlawful.

In New England dipping was not only lawful, it was practical because of the cold weather.

They consented to his dipping and pouring on water but they would not go along with placing a child underwater.

They consulted with various churches in the Bay Colony about the problem and they all seemed to agree with Plimoth Colony. Chauncey would not accept the church's decision and there were continual arguments about his method.

After three years, he finally left to minister a church in Scituate. Soon he ran into the same trouble there when he submerged a twin son and the baby almost fainted. When he reached for the other son, the mother stopped Chauncey by grabbing his arm and almost pulled him into the basin. He was persistent in his style of baptism which created many problems during his stay at Scituate. He decided to leave for England in 1654 but he was offered a position to become Harvard's second president. He promised to forget about baptism in the future.

*　　*　　*

One day in 1639, in the great room in Governor Bradford's home, he had Elder William Brewster, Thomas Cushman, and his wife, Mary, and little Thomas as guests.

Isaac Allerton Junior, Mary's stepbrother, now nine years old, was out playing with his young friends.

William Brewster said, "I know that I am responsible for Isaac's future and that you also want Isaac to get a good education. I've taught him a lot and so has my son, Love, but he will need a formal education eventually."

Mary said, "Yes, Mr. Brewster, I know you have done him a lot of good, he has gone a long way in your teaching."

"You also did a lot for me. I've read a great amount of books and absorbed most of the material in them, although you might think otherwise," Thomas said with a smile.

Bradford laughed and remarked, "We still have hopes for you."

William Brewster went on, "I have friends in the town of Charlestown, Massachusetts that had a friend named John Harvard that passed away last year when he contracted consumption. John had a humble beginning. He was born in 1607 on High Street close to the London Bridge. His father, a butcher at Southwark, died of the plague at the same time as your father, Thomas. He left enough money so John could enter Emmanuel College in Cambridge in 1627. This was my old *alma mater*, by the way. John received his bachelor's degree in 1631 and later his master's degree in 1635.

His mother, who had two more husbands since his father passed away, also died and left John wealthy as the heir.

Harvard married and came to the New World in 1637 and was admitted as a "Townsman" in Charlestown. He had his heart set on opening a school for Christians and converted Indians. In the meantime, the Massachusetts General Court in 1636, by legislation, authorized that a college be founded and on March 13, 1639 named the college after the late clergyman, John Harvard. He left an endowment of half his estate of about £779 and a library of 320 volumes for a new college. (Harvard University now has more than five million volumes in its preeminent libraries.)

"Well, this is a first for the New World." Bradford exclaimed.

"Yes, William it is. I think Isaac should be the first in attending Harvard from Plimoth in a few years, when he is ready."

Mary replied, "I think that's wonderful that Isaac will go to college. What will they teach him?"

Brewster answered, "My friends tell me that they are going to have a varied curriculum which will consist of Latin, Greek, Hebrew, Arithmetic, Geometry, Logic and Divinity. By the way, the first class of '39 will have nine students."

Thomas said, "What will the college be like?"

Brewster explained, "Well, like Harvard himself, it has a very humble beginning. It is a white wooden structure and later they will build other buildings of brick."

Brewster, reaching for his mug of beer, answered, "The sponsors are doing all they can to make it succeed. They are soliciting funds locally and even in England. Harvard had many friends that will remember him and donate funds in his memory. They published a promotional pamphlet called *New England First Fruits* describing the aims of the institution and its hoped-for growth. One of the chief contributors was Lady Mowlson (Ann Radcliffe) who donated £100."

Bradford said, "I hope Harvard College is successful. I hate to see a dream die. However, I see that life is thriving in our colony...when are you expecting Mary?"

Mary bashfully answered, "Our daughter is going to be born in about three months."

Thomas laughed, "I keep saying, how do you know you'll have a girl and Mary says with a smile, "I just know!"

Brewster said, "Girl or boy, I know you'll be happy

with either. You're looking very healthy Mary, which foretells a strong baby."

Mary smiled and said, "I feel fine and as you say, we'll be happy with either a boy or girl...but it'll be a girl—I'm sure."

Thomas and the rest of the group laughed. Thomas said, "Now you can see what I mean!"

Finally the Cushmans said their good-byes and left and Isaac Junior, the subject of the discussion, waved to them.

*   *   *

Three months to the day, Mary had her daughter. She was healthy, pretty as babies go...and a future heart-breaker.

"She looks like her mother," Thomas observed.

Their daughter was baptized Sarah on the next Sabbath. The Cushmans had been lucky so far. The mortality rate for a mother and her newborn infant was very high. The cemeteries were full of mothers with their five or six children.

Next to be incorporated in Plimoth was something that they thought might be helpful to restore law and order and a method of insuring attendance at church services. In 1640 the General Court decreed that stocks and whipping posts be erected "in every Constablerick." This was supposed to take care of an increase in lawlessness.

There was John Holmes, a messenger to the General Court who was forced to sit in the stocks for drunkenness and fined twenty shillings. A married couple, John Thorp and his wife were adjudged guilty of having conceived a child before marriage and had to sit in the stocks and were fined forty shillings but were allowed a full year to pay the fine, because they were poor. Usually, the husband was also whipped in full sight of his shame-faced wife but John Thorp was spared. Many hapless married couples who had a premature child also suffered the embarrassment of the placed in the stocks by not having a full term baby. To be legal, the child had to be born in a minimum gestation period of nine months. They might allow a discrepancy of a few days but never over a week. The parents, embarrassed and in most cases indignant, were compelled to sit in the stocks. Eventually, the Pilgrims became more tolerant and realized that children should be born without a stigma being attached if they were born in less than the prescribed time.

The stocks had a lot of service, including being frequented by the grown children of the "Old Comers", who, having experienced the embarrassment by their children, probably said, "I wonder what's happening to the younger generation." (To quote Socrates.)

Church officials found that most of the people in Plimoth were not attending church regularly. Evidently, the threat of a fine was more compelling than suffering the embarrassment of a neighbor's belligerent looks. The recruitment for converts was carried out in many of the neighboring towns and included the Indian Villages where many had converted to Christianity. They had become devout followers and were called the "Praying Indians".

However, the Wampanoag Tribe resisted all efforts to be influenced by the missionaries when they tried to get them to join their church. Massasoit discouraged his tribes from submitting to the white man's religion and to their manner of praying. However, he still believed in keeping peace with the Pilgrims. He came to Plimoth with his son, Wamsutta, to renew his pledge of peaceful coexistence. Massasoit said he wouldn't give or sell his land to anyone without the Pilgrims' knowledge or permission.

William Bradford was again elected Governor and his

seven assistants were Myles Standish, John Alden, William Collier, William Prence, Timothy Hatherly, John Brown and John Jenny. Nathaniel Souther was chosen Secretary, and William Paddy was designated as Treasurer.

The Deacons of the First Church of Plimoth were John Doane, John Cooke along with William Paddy.

*   *   *

There was no problem with educating the young in Plimoth Colony. Most of the teaching was done at home, where parents would instill values to their children by example.Many of the original settlers couldn't read or write when they arrived, but they were blessed with an abundance of common sense and an innate ability to invent solutions to their problems. Those that could read or write taught others how to use these skills and it was then passed on to others.

To judge the success of this rudimentary teaching you have only to review the number of Pilgrims that achieved greatness. There was no doubt that William Bradford's life was a compelling story of achievement and success. Elected Governor, time after time, he was an outstanding executive for the Pilgrims and he had a humble start in adult life as a textile worker in Leyden, Holland, before his decision to go to the New World.

Bradford, however, was one of the lucky ones in Leyden. He was a prolific reader and enjoyed learning various subjects as evidenced by his large collection of books which he so treasured. They remained as "his friends" in his library during his lifetime. By today's standards, Bradford's formal education would be rated as almost non-existent. But it must have required a tremendous amount of self discipline to study on a college level at home without a tutor. Without this discipline, he could never have accomplished most of his achievements which also required an honest, rugged character, tempered with an abundance of self-esteem. He developed his self-esteem by knowing that he had nothing to hide from his neighbors and he wanted, above all else, to have his character to be considered beyond reproach.

The Pilgrims eventually opened a small private school for the children in Plimoth.

CHAPTER 33

Plymouth, Cape Cod

1643

When death came to Elder Brewster on April 18, 1643, he was seventy-seven years of age. The Pilgrims knew that it was coming, but it caused much grief and despair among them when it happened. He was surrounded by friends and relatives when he passed away. He was the father image in the colony and was loved by all and the sadness of those around him was a silent testimony of their affection toward him.

He never spoke ill of any person and was an excellent role model for the community, but few, if any, could duplicate his character or stature.

Bradford, who was Brewster's best friend, said, "He will be greatly missed by the people of Plimoth. He lived for the church and was sincerely concerned about the general welfare of all of us."

Jonathan Brewster replied, "I'm glad he had such good friends. He would be happy that he accomplished enough in life to be missed by so many."

Bradford said, "He was a private person; few knew of his problems or aspirations. His work at the college in Cambridge prepared him for his life. Did you know he served for several years as a trusted assistant to the Secretary of State? The Secretary deemed him to be the most discreet and trustworthy servant above all others. When the Secretary of State became Ambassador to the Low Countries of Europe, Brewster went with him, more as a son than a civil servant.

"When the keys of Flushing, Holland were given to the Ambassador in the name of the King of Holland, Brewster was given possession and he slept with them under his pillow.

"When they returned to England, Brewster wore them around his neck on a gold chain while they rode to the court.

"When Ambassador Davidson ran into a problem after the death of Mary, Queen of Scots, Brewster remained with him to try to serve him and the country. Eventually, he was no longer required and returned to his home in the country when he again helped his neighbors and many friends with their problems."

"Yes," Jonathan remarked, "He was always there giving a helping hand until the Bishops became more concerned about retaining their authority than in listening to the wishes of the churchgoer. It was then that he ran into trouble with many of the principles the Bishops tried to force on the parishioners, so they sent him to Boston, England, then to prison for several years. He never gave up. His courage and determination after he was released led him to Holland to avoid domination by the Anglican Church.

After returning home Thomas Cushman said to Mary, "I didn't give it much thought but Governor Bradford mentioned the longevity of many of the Pilgrims. Elder Brewster reached seventy-seven years of age which is unusually long to live. I heard that he drank large amounts of water and I know that he was always active. We have all suffered hardships that should normally shorten our lives, but maybe people like Brewster live such fruitful lives that they are immune to common disease. No doubt somebody up there was looking out for him."

"He was a great man, Thomas, it will be difficult to replace him. I wonder who will take his place?"

There was also sad news for those who knew Mrs. Bridget Robinson in Leyden, Holland. Mrs. Robinson, widow of Reverend Robinson, died in 1643. She had never made the trip to Plimoth, although in 1629 she had booked passage on another *Mayflower* along with her three children, but for some unknown reason they didn't embark.

*   *   *

This was also the year that Morton, formerly of Merry Mount, showed up in Plimoth. He was driven out of England by his inability to make enough money to buy food. He was allowed to stay in the colony over the winter. Morton tried to secretly lure some of the Pilgrims to go to New Haven, Connecticut which was recently founded as a new colony. He was unsuccessful in his attempt, so he left Plimoth in 1644 and spent a year in a Boston jail. The reason for the imprisonment was unknown to the Pilgrims. When he was released he went to the Sir Fernando Gorges Colony in Maine where he died "old and crazy" two years later.

Mary and Thomas Cushman were again parents of another child. They had a daughter named Lydia, who like Sarah before her, resembled her mother.

There was more rumbling in the colony and throughout the Bay Colony that the Narragansetts were conspiring against the English. Since the Pequots were defeated many of the Indians were whispering about the contempt that the Narragansetts held for the settlers. To provide protection, the various settlements formed a confederation with the Bay Colony to assure a collective defense against any uprising that might occur.

One day, the Cushmans were walking with their children and Bonnie when Mary said, "The children can't hear us...are we going to have trouble with the Indians."

Thomas, carrying Lydia their new baby, replied, "I don't think so...besides you shouldn't be worrying about these problems, you have enough to handle with our three children."

"Well, I am interested, besides having three children to protect, I want to know how we stand with the Indians,"

"I was talking to Governor Bradford and Edward Winslow and they said that Uncus—you know he's Chief of the Mohegans (Mohicans) and is friendly with the English and many of the surviving Pequots have become friends with him. Being friends with Uncas and in addition to having a peace treaty with Massasoit and knowing the strength of the English...I don't think we have too much to worry about."

"Well, I know it's not my place to speak out, but I think women should know the facts and the truth shouldn't be hidden from them. Especially when a threat to our lives could be in our future."

"I know, Mary, however a man's role is to protect his family."

"I guess you don't realize it Thomas, but women are exceptionally strong. There have been a lot of cases in history where women showed great courage—as much as men. Maybe they haven't had too much of a chance to display it."

"I hope that I'm always around to protect you."

Governor Bradford again spoke to Thomas Cushman about the current status of the Indians and the effect on the colony if the condition deteriorated.

Bradford said, "You know how the Narragansetts have been plotting against us since the Pequot War. Now, after defeating the Pequots they have set their sights on the Mohegans, especially their sachem Uncas. Uncas helped the English in the Pequot War and the Indians that survived went to him for safety."

Cushman replied, "Yes, I know about that, but what does the Chief of the Narragansetts, Miantonomo, feel about Uncas role in providing protection?"

Bradford said, "It all boils down to the fact that Miantonomo was jealous of the attention the colonists of Connecticut were showing Uncas. Through deception and treachery, Miantonomo attempted to get rid of Uncas by every means at his disposal. He attempted to kill him by poisoning, shooting, hitting him on the head while he slept, but to no avail. Frustrated, he attacked him by surprise with 1,000 men strictly against all written agreements between the Indian tribes. Miantonomo never said a word about starting a war; it was sudden but he ended up by being captured.

The best part of the story is that the Mohegans were outnumbered more than two to one, but they were still victorious. Now, in spite of the victory, Uncas felt they held the proverbial tiger-by-the-tail. If he released Miantonomo he knew that he would take revenge on him for his embarrassment.

"How did he solve this dilemma?"

"He didn't know whether to kill Miantonomo or keep him as hostage against any further attack. He was in a quandary so he went to the Commissioners in Connecticut for advice."

Thomas Cushman said, "I think he would be justified in putting him to death. He would be a continual threat to Uncas."

"That's exactly what they thought, but they wanted to

be sure his demise wasn't on or near any English Plantation. It was one way Uncas could rid himself of a potentially dangerous threat. They also assured Uncas that if he was to put Miantonomo to death in a humane manner and if he was attacked for his act by the Narragansetts, then the English would support him."

Cushman asked, "Did Uncas take the Commissioner's advice? Did he finally put Miantonomo to death?"

"Yes, although he said it was inhumane, it was a blow from a hatchet swung by the brother of Uncas that dispatched him to the happy hunting ground."

"Did he fight back? This seemed like an underhanded way to kill him, although he deserved to die."

"Well, the way Miantonomo was killed, was underhanded. When you consider the way the Indians resort to torture and extreme cruelty before they kill their victims. The English felt a little dismayed over the nature of his death and it bothered their conscience for years to come."

*   *   *

In 1644, Edward Winslow was elected Governor and his assistants were William Bradford, William Collier, William Prence, Timothy Hatherly and Edward Freeman.

Stephen Hopkins died this year at the age of fifty-nine years. His second wife, Elizabeth, had preceded him in death four years before. His family, now consisting of his children, Giles and Constance, mourned his passing. His two children borne by Elizabeth, Damaris and Oceanus, had died earlier around 1627. From his questionable beginning with the Plimoth colony Hopkins had become an asset. He was always ready to assist his fellow settlers. He volunteered for several exploratory missions when he was younger. He served eleven years as Assistant Governor.

John Jenny also died that year when he was fifty years old. He came to Plimoth on the *Anne* in July, 1623. He opened the first grist mill in 1636, which provided a great service to the colony by supplying a means to crush and grind the corn. He became an active member of the community and served the community in public service.

Plimoth also mourned the death of John Atwood. He served admirably by his mediation in trying to solve the financial problems with the Merchant Adventurers and later he served the colony as Assistant Governor in 1638. Another great loss in leadership was the death of the secretary of the Colony, Nathaniel Souther, who had served in this capacity for eleven years. He, like Atwood, had come to Plimoth in the 30's.

*   *   *

Life went on as usual in Plimoth Colony. There was always present the lurking threat of the Indians, but the Pilgrims' theory was that treating the Indians with respect and compassion should be the way to handle disputes should they arise and they did almost every day. It worked.

The Indians must have passed the word along that the Pilgrims were always fair and honest in their dealings with them. They enjoyed very little friction from the neighboring tribes of the Wampanoags, Massachusetts, Nipmacs and Nausets on the Cape.

They were a little suspicious of the Narragansetts and Pequots who felt that someday they could form an alliance and attach the British settlements. To do this, they would need the assistance of a huge tribe like the Wampanoags, whose territory ranged from Martha's Vineyard up to the Merrimack River beyond Boston.

The friendship with Massasoit seemed to be strong,

and nothing unforseen would break that relationship as long as he was alive. His two sons, who would inherit his reign as the most important Sachem in the area, were also friendly with the Pilgrims who would give them no excuse to feel otherwise.

The Wampanoags dealt with the Pilgrims every day, and wandered freely through the plantation, speaking with the settlers, sometimes using sign language to communicate.

Even Captain Myles Standish, who usually looked at the Indians with a jaundiced eye, came to accept their presence after a little arm-twisting by Governor Bradford, who insisted they be treated fairly.

Even the women and children of the colony, who were hesitant at first to accept the Indians in their midst, now saw them as friends. Their friendship made them more secure.

CHAPTER 34

Plymouth, Cape Cod

1645

The Connecticut Commission met in Boston on July 28, 1645 in an emergency meeting as a result of problems with the French and the Indians. The Indians had broken the several agreements that were negotiated the year before.

Once again the Narragansetts attacked Uncas in an over-whelming force in retaliation for the capture and death of Miantonomo. They killed many of his braves and wounded even more. They confiscated much war materiel which put Uncas in a most unfavorable position. This attack was accomplished without prior knowledge of the Connecticut Commission.

They sent a garrison of forty men to aid Uncas until they could come to a decision as to how to handle the Narragansetts. They decided to send three military men; Sergeant John Davis, Francis Smith and Benedict Arnold with a mission to Uncas and leaders of the Narragansetts.

They were given the task of convincing them to come

to Boston in person or to send delegates who were knowledgeable in the matter. They would meet the Commissioners of Connecticut.

They were waiting for an answer and the principals were informed that an answer was wanted immediately. If no answer was received from either party, (which was covered by prior agreements) then the Commission could assume that the English were also prime targets and they would react accordingly. An ominous sign was also seen when the Mohawks were getting friendly with the Narragansetts and offered to aid them if they were attacked.

The messengers were glum when they returned to their homes in Connecticut. They were bearing a letter from Roger Williams of Providence stating that all New England would explode into a war. To add to the problem they found that the English of Rhode Island and Aquidneck Island had signed a neutrality pact with the Narragansetts.

They allocated militia from each colony and a small force of forty men left Plimoth to go to Seekonk, near Rhode Island to act in case the Narragansetts started any belligerent action on the colonies. They had strict orders to stay in place and not invade Narragansett territory. They were to take whatever necessary measure for survival in case of attack by a hostile force. This was done while the rest of the soldiers from New Haven colony and Connecticut assembled with friendly Indians from that area. When ready, they set off on a long march to join the Plimoth force now waiting at Seekonk.

The Plimoth men had waited almost ten days for the others to join them. Now the Plimoth militia were well-equipped, carrying the new snaphaunce firing musket which replaced the cumbersome matchlock with its bothersome stand which held the musket while firing.

Captain Standish was in charge of the Plimoth contingent while Captain Mason was responsible for the Connecticut men. Major Gibbons was given overall command. There was a question of legality by the Massachusetts Court which wondered if the Commission had the legal authority to send troops to war on its neighbors. The Commission, the court decided, had been given all the official power, in case of emergency, to act as they did, circumventing the Court under the Articles of Confederation.

A message was sent to the Narragansett tribe stating reparation was sought for the attack on Uncas and to insure the future security for the colonies.

If the Narragansetts heeded this and wanted peace, then it would be available as before the trouble started. The chiefs and sagamores would come to Boston to try and settle their problems. Safe passage was assured and they would discuss future events once this situation was put to rest. If they did not accept the invitation to come to Boston then the colonists could assume they wanted war and they would then oblige them, as the troops were now in place and many more of them would follow.

Within a few days, the sagamores from the tribes of Narragansett and Niantic met with the Commissioners and concluded a treaty of peace which would act as a safety valve for the resentment that was simmering below the surface. Benedict Arnold acted as the interpreter while the Indians were represented by two Indians who spoke English.

Benedict Arnold, unfortunately a forebearer of the traitor during the Revolutionary War, bore his name but there any resemblance stopped. The first Benedict Arnold was a credit to his loyalty and his humane treatment of his fellow man.

To compensate for the travesty of justice that was shown to Miantonomo by his death, the State of Connecticut in 1819 erected a statue in his honor, one hundred and seventy years after his death.

Many United States naval vessels through the years have borne the name of Miantonomo in respect.

As for Uncas, his descendant became a hero in the battle of Fort William Henry in James Fenimore Cooper's novel, *The Last of the Mohicans.*

When Mary Cushman heard all the details that were settled in Boston, she said to Thomas, "I think the men did a very good job in settling the dispute. I don't think women would have done as well, but after all, men have had more experience in these things."

Thomas said, "I'm really glad you recognize the value of men."

On the political side, a typical male sanctuary, away from the unwelcome, inconceivable, intrusion of the so-called gentler sex, came the usual, annual, election day. William Bradford was again elected Governor, replacing Edward Winslow who served in 1644. Winslow accepted the position of Assistant Governor. Secretary William Thomas was replaced by Myles Standish.

CHAPTER 35

Plymouth, Cape Cod
London, England
1645-1647

Thomas Cushman, William Bradford and Edward Winslow were discussing a petition against intolerance toward religion and civil affairs at Winslow's home one day in September, 1645.

Bradford said, "I submitted a petition to the Massachusetts General Court and a similar one was sent in by the Boston government. William Wassall, a former judge who lives in Scituate, helped on my petition and also on the one from Boston. I'm happy that my petition was well received."

Thomas asked, "What was in the petition?"

Bradford replied, "We said civil peace and religious tolerance would be shown to all men regardless of background or origin. I think the church must hold the authority to punish the wayward who would infringe on the rights of others, we must stop the wicked and the obscene. If it continues to grow, I fear for the stability of our colony."

Edward Winslow said, "I agree with you William, in all aspects. I think our policy, like the one used in Massachusetts with the Puritans, will work out."

Cushman asked, "Don't you think that using a constable to compel the Pilgrims to attend church and fining that person ten shillings if he is absent, a little harsh?"

"I don't think so, things are getting out of hand. We could always use corporal punishment for neglect of religion as a way of life in the colony," Winslow replied.

Cushman insisted, "Maybe we're taking too conservative a view to solve the problem. I admit the liberal *laizze-faire* attitude has been responsible for a lot of problems we're getting into. I suppose we should try and reach a middle-of-the road judgment on this issue."

Bradford said, "It's pretty hard to follow a position in the center with some of the Strangers making a habit of being drunk, being vagrant and their complete lawlessness. They don't give the slightest pretense of being religious. They should lose their citizenship, because unless we take drastic action now, we won't have a colony."

Cushman agreed, "I can see your point. Something must be done. Maybe we can eliminate some of the taverns; many men stagger drunk from one tavern to another."

Bradford said, "We have had a very simplified character to our religious teaching and communication, maybe it can be changed and improved."

Cushman replied, "I think there might be some room for improvement. We have wooden benches with no backs and our congregation sits on them for hours. If it is cold we bring bricks heated in our fireplaces, wrapped in blankets and they provide heat during our sermons. We have no light other than that which seeps in from the outside. On dull days it becomes very gloomy in spite of our enlightened sermons."

Bradford said, "We'll give it a lot of thought and I know we'll come up with a solution."

*   *   *

In May, 1646, Bradford gathered his Council in an emergency meeting. They discussed the arrival and subsequent behavior of eighty crew members that came to Plimoth on three large ships.

Their leader, Thomas Cromwell, no relation to Oliver Cromwell, had plundered the Spanish in the West Indies and had taken two of his three ships from them. Under his veneer of authority he was basically a pirate and his crew were a collection of ne'er-do-wells and cutthroats. They were bound for Boston when they encountered a gale and put into Plimoth Harbor.

Bradford opened the discussion by saying, "These men are trying to corrupt the Pilgrims by their unruly behavior. They curse, drink to excess and defy authority."

Standish spoke up, "We have put many of them in jail but they still continue to act wild."

Prence said, "I understand that they will stay here about a month and a half, then they'll go on to the Bay Colony."

Freeman asked, "Where did you hear that, Thomas?"

Prence said, "One of the First Mates told me—he was sober at the time."

Collier said, "They're spending a lot of money in the taverns but we can do without their business if it effects the colony. I agree with you William, they will bear a lot of watching but Myles militia can handle them all right. Captain Thomas Cromwell, with his rough manner, seems to be able to control them but I guess they're acting on their own most of the time. He probably feels they have no ties with Plimoth so this is like a free port with no obligation and in their minds no bounds to their actions."

Bradford said, "How do you feel about the situation, Myles? Can you handle this all right? Do you have enough men?"

"Yes, William. I think we'll do just fine. The crew seems to have cooled off a bit. We just have to keep our eyes open and react at once to any violation. I don't know if you heard of an incident that happened last night? A ruffian was upset and started to fight another of the wild boys. He was told to calm down and quit fighting but he chastised Captain Cromwell in foul language. To prove his manhood, he started to draw his rapier from his scabbard and threatened Cromwell. The captain reacted quickly, knocking the rapier from his assailant's hand. Sensing no let-up in his belligerence, Cromwell used the hilt of the rapier and hit him on the head causing a skull fracture and the crew member's death."

Later, Cromwell was summoned to appear before an investigating Council to answer charges about the seaman's death. He gave his version of the unprovoked attack and his crew members were in agreement with his story. They said, on several occasions, Cromwell was forced to put the sailor in irons and other times he was locked up aboard the ship because of his erratic behavior. After some deliberation the Council attributed the death to justifiable manslaughter and Cromwell was exonerated.

The Council was formed in Boston and he left soon after with his three ships and "loyal" crews for a voyage to the West Indies which would eventually last for three years. He and his crew returned to Boston—rich.

His pirating way started, ironically enough, when he visited Boston as an apprentice seaman ten years before. He left Boston on a trading ship that was bound for the Caribbean Sea. After he arrived in the area and spent a few days visiting the nearby islands he finally ended up on Captain Jackson's ship. Probably, unknown to him, he was induced by a few seamen to go aboard the ship, as they were looking for men and they were handsomely rewarded for their service. The ship wasn't involved in merchant trading; their primary purpose was piracy!

Jackson had been practicing his trade for quite awhile and was making a bad reputation among honest captains. He used an island that was owned by the Earl of Warwick off the coast of Nicaragua as his base of operations. (This island called "Old Providence" was also used by the Pilgrims to send captured Pequots braves during the uprising in 1637.)

Cromwell rapidly adopted his new way of life and he rose in the ranks and finally branched out and became a full-blown pirate. He was unscrupulous in his treatment of prisoners and looted the islands and even Mexico.

On his return trip to Boston, after spending his three years in the West Indies, he was relaxing by riding a horse along the coast. The horse stumbled in a pothole and fell headfirst into the wet sand. Cromwell also fell, hitting his head on the hilt of his rapier and he died a short time later. This was a bizarre twist to the death of his crew member a little over three years before.

*   *   *

In 1646 Bradford and the same Plimoth Council once again served the colony, with the exception of Edward Winslow. He left Plimoth to work in England and the people of the colony found out later he was never to return. Lost to the colony was his familiar smiling, chubby face with his trim mustache and goatee. Most of all, they lost his devotion and ability which he used frequently in the service of the Pilgrims.

He was to answer a petition presented to the Commission of Foreign Plantations on May 6, 1646 and claimed by many petitioners that the Massachusetts Authority was overbearing and would soon have trouble with its troubled citizens.

The Massachusetts Bay Colony requested that Winslow represent them in this mission and he hoped that he wasn't unknowingly being forced into a situation, as he was ten years before when he was locked up in Fleet Prison.

The gist of the whole problem lay with the troublemaker Samuel Gorton who was unceremoniously expelled from Plimoth Colony in 1638. There were various reasons for his expulsion, among these were inciting some of the planters to riot against the Plimoth Council. This was the most serious of many charges.

The petition was an embarrassment to New England and was the subject of many questions to be asked by the General Court in London. Winslow was a born ambassador of goodwill in the colony but now he was representing the authority of Massachusetts as a government agent and a defense counselor for New England.

He was successful in his defense and all charges were dropped. Winslow took several critics to task and wrote several articles depicting their hypocrisy about the New England Colonies.

He was given a job by the British and became quite famous in England as the Chairman of the English-Dutch commission that assessed the damage to English ships in neutral Dutch ports.

After completion of this task, Winslow was about to board a ship to return to Plimoth when he received a letter from Oliver Cromwell which appointed him an officer of the Royal Navy to help conquer Jamaica, which was owned by the Spanish. He would be third in command following Admiral Penn and General Venable.

After a successful campaign which ended in the capture of Jamaica, Winslow was on a flagship off the island and he had contacted a deadly topical disease. After trying in vain to overcome the disease, he died on May 8, 1655. He had reached the age of sixty years and gave all the appearance of being in good health when he was struck down. His shipmates gave him full military honors and shot off a salvo of forty-four cannon rounds as he was buried at sea.

Who knows what he might have accomplished if he remained in Leyden. The experience he gained as a representative to the Pilgrims and his diplomatic skills blossomed him into a great personality that was honored by the Pilgrims and the British Crown and its subjects.

*　　*　　*

On February 8, 1647, when the snow was still on the ground and a sharp, icy wind blew from the north, with the sun just breaking in the east, there was a bustle of activity in the Cushman home.

"Thomas, I think I need help, I'm starting to feel pain." Mary said. She had been restless during the night and it seemed like her labor was about to begin.

"Wait...don't do anything! I'll get Mary Winslow and Hester Wright to help you. They said to call them when you need help."

Thomas raced out of house, donning his hat and jacket. Bracing himself against the chill wind he ran slipping and sliding through the snow. He knocked on the door of the Winslow's home and John came to see who was knocking at such an early hour.

"Sorry to bother you John, but your wife said that if Mary ever needed help she would come. I think Mary is about due and we sure could use some help."

John said, " I know how you feel Thomas. I think my wife is awake and I'll tell her about your wife and she will go right along to your house."

"Thanks John. I'm on my way to see Hester Wright

next. She also said that she will help, too."

Thomas hurried to the Wright's home, the snow making a crackling sound under his feet. When he arrived Thomas knocked, then blew on his cupped hands to warm them. The wind was brisk and he really wasn't dressed for the cold weather. Hester came to the door with her husband and invited Thomas in. Stamping the snow off his feet, Thomas entered their home and explained the problem to Hester. Seeing the concern on Thomas' face Hester tried to cheer him up and told him she'd be right over.

The Cushman children were out of bed, gathered around their mother trying to comfort her. Thomas got them out of the bedroom and told Mary that her friends would be right there.

"What can I do now?" Thomas asked.

"Calm down Thomas...we've been through this three times already. I m feeling all right. Maybe you can boil some water. That will keep you busy."

Thomas went with a bucket to get water and then he put more wood in the fireplace.

The women came and acting very businesslike they assured Thomas that they could handle the situation. They never did use the water that he boiled. Thomas was beginning to realize that the "boiling water" task was something to keep the men busy and away from the birthing scene.

A few hours passed and Thomas had fed the women and his children. Later, Mary had another son, which they were to name Isaac. Isaac later became a minister in Plympton, a town near Plimoth. He married Rebecca Rickard in 1675 when she was 21.

They had six children. He officiated in many marriages including those of his brothers and sisters.

*   *   *

Bonnie, the Cushman's pet, was feeble now, her hearing was about gone. She would no longer respond to the children's eagerness to play. She was fifteen years old and had lived a long and happy life. She was totally loyal to the family and returned their affection.

One morning when one of the children tried to rouse her for her early morning walk she did not greet them as usual with her tail wagging...she had died quietly in her sleep. The whole family was saddened and wept.

They buried Bonnie behind the house, and Elder Thomas said she would always be in our hearts and we will never forget her. They felt that she was like one of the family... they would really miss her being around.

Friends of the Cushman's were very sorry to hear that Bonnie had died. She had been around the colony for fourteen and a half years and Bonnie knew everyone by sight. She seemed to have been loved by all the Pilgrims in the colony.

She was like a member of a family that had passed away... she would be missed.

*   *   *

Thomas had a habit of reading his books whenever he wasn't involved in working or spending time with his growing family. He helped Mary with the children whenever he could.

He knew they were like all well-adjusted children— they were a handful to control!

Most of his reading was about establishing good relations with people, helping them in their time of need, and, in general, how to treat people so they will show respect toward you and you, in turn, would earn that respect.

When he was younger, he didn't show the eagerness to learn religion as he did now. As his responsibilities grew and as he reach adulthood, he was more inclined to be more serious in nature.

He had several good models in life to follow; his father, Robert, who was always fair in dealing with others and scrupulously honest. Then there was William Brewster, who devoted his whole life to being a good person, even risking his own life in the pursuit of being fair to others.

William Bradford, who had his share of problems, some personal, others involving the lives of the Pilgrims and their welfare and well-being. Unknown to the people, he spend many hours worrying about the future of the colony, but he always kept his best face forward and his optimistic outlook make the Pilgrims gain confidence.

With Thomas' attempt to make his life and that of his family more fruitful, he was preparing for what would lie ahead in his future.

CHAPTER 36

Plymouth, Cape Cod

1649-1657

One day in June, 1649, the Cushmans awoke early, their usual habit. The children were rubbing the sleep out of their eyes, and were beginning to bicker and argue. Thomas Junior, now twelve years old, said to Sarah, two years his junior, "it's your turn to get water."

"It is not! I got it yesterday."

"But we needed more and I got it!"

Thomas spoke up, "I want you children to stop arguing. Thomas you will get the water and Sarah you'll help your mother get breakfast."

Thomas Junior said, "But..."

"That s enough! You have chores to do."

Six year old Lydia said, "Father, why do Thomas and Sarah fight?"

He explained, "Children always fight, especially brothers and sisters, but they really care for each other."

Thomas turned to Mary and asked, "I wonder why Governor Bradford wants to see us today. He said it's very important and wants the whole family there."

Mary replied, "Maybe he wants you as one of his assistants. Do you think that's it?"

"No. He probably would see me alone."

"He's been asking me questions about Elder Brewster's work. He said it would take a very dedicated and intelligent man to fill his shoes. I don't think I'm ready for that yet. I really don't know what he wants."

"Well, we'll know this morning after we see him. Are we going to meet him at the Meeting House?"

"Yes. He said to dress our best."

The Cushmans had breakfast and cleared the table, and washed the dishes and all the cooking utensils. Isaac, now two years old, spoke to his father, "Where we go father?"

"We're going to get all dressed up and we're going to see the Governor."

When they were all ready to leave the house, Thomas said, " I want you children to behave yourselves and stay with your mother and me. Don't wander away and above all don't argue."

They left with Mary holding the hands of Lydia and Isaac. Thomas said, "I'll carry Isaac for awhile, it's a long trip up the hill."

Mary said, "I remember when you used to pull me up the hill on a sled in the winter. That was a long time ago. Who would have thought that we'd be married someday and have our own family?"

"John Cooke always thought we would get married. It's funny though, our children slide down the same hill...where has the time gone?"

They met several of their neighbors on the way to the Meeting house and many exclaimed, "Well, you certainly look nice this morning. You seem to be dressed for the Sabbath."

Thomas Junior proudly said, "We're going to see the Governor at the Meeting House."

By this time they neared the imposing structure and entered. They were met by Governor Bradford and his assistants; Captain Myles Standish, William Collier, Thomas Prence and Timothy Hatherly along with Deacon William Paddy, who also was the Secretary of the Colony and Nathaniel Morton, the Treasurer, and Cushman's old friend, Deacon John Cooke with Reverend John Reyner.

"Welcome Thomas, Mary and children, announced the Governor. He laughed and motioning to the gathering said, "I'm sure you know everyone here. We've saved seats for you down front."

"I'm impressed." Thomas said. "I've never seen you in one group together other than on the Sabbath."

Bradford asked. "I suppose you wonder why you're here, Thomas?"

"Well as a matter of fact, I do."

"I've asked you about the work that Elder Brewster did, his opinions and philosophy. You knew him well. You were guided and taught by William. Many times he suggested to me that you should take his place when he was no longer able to fill his job. After his death, six years ago, there was no action taken to fill his position. It was quite a loss when Elder Brewster passed on. There was always something to divert our attention from replacing him and as I have often said, he was a unique individual. Well, to get to the point, Thomas, we searched for someone to be the Elder and you were our unanimous choice. You can have the job for as long as you want. What do you say?"

"I feel pretty humble. I know that Elder Brewster was one of a kind. I'll do my best but I know that I have a lot to learn."

Bradford said, "You wouldn't have got the offer if we didn't think that you would succeed. You can be assured that you'll have our complete confidence and cooperation. Is that a definite yes?" Thomas nodded his head, he was surely humbled by this chance to become an Elder. The men gathered around Thomas and shook his hand and offered him their congratulations. Then, they offered him a toast with beer.

Mary was smiling and very happy with Thomas's new position. She juggled young Isaac from one side to another while he slept. Lydia was fidgeting in her seat and young Thomas, with his hand next to his mouth, whispered to Lydia, "I wonder when we're going home."

*   *   *

While things were going fine for the Cushman's in Plimoth, there was turmoil in England. Cromwell had succeeded in appointing a High Court, and Charles I was tried for high treason.

Cromwell now ruled with unquestioned authority and the court was convinced that Charles I had been a tyrant. He was sentenced to be put to death for his crimes against the citizenry of Great Britain.

He was beheaded in the palace yard at Whitehall where he previously held unopposed tyrannical power. The House of Lords protested against his death and Cromwell eliminated any competition by disbanding them. He called them "useless and dangerous." Becoming a Commonwealth, England was now in the hands of the protector, the Supreme Commander, Cromwell.

*   *   *

Once again, in 1650, Bradford was elected Governor and Captain Myles Standish, Collier, Prence, Hatherly and Thomas Williams were assistants. Nathaniel Morton became Secretary of the colony for the fifth time and Deacon William Paddy became the Treasurer for the fourteenth time.

Love Brewster, who had supervised Isaac Allerton, Junior as a child, died in Duxbury in 1650 leaving his widow, Sarah (Collier), and children. Sarah was remarried two years later to Richard Parks of Cambridge, Massachusetts.

Wrestling Brewster had proceeded his brother, Love, in death in 1635. He had moved to Piscataqua (Portsmouth), New Hampshire as a youth and died when he was twenty years old.

*   *   *

In 1651, it came as no surprise when William Bradford was again elected Governor. There was a change in assistants; Thomas Willet was elected for the first time. Old Timers like Standish, Alden, Collier, Prence and Hatherly stayed on to govern the colony. Nathaniel Morton was elected Secretary again and Treasurer William Paddy, a sincere, devoted man to Plimoth, died while in office. He was replaced by Myles Standish.

Some of Plimoth's citizens moved south on the Cape to found a new town called Nauset. The Charter for the town was made out to the First Church of Plimoth in June 1645. Later in June 1651, the town was renamed Eastham. This was the area where the Pilgrims first encountered the Indians while they were still on the *Mayflower* at Provincetown in 1620.

They were considering another location for a town which they were to call Rehoboth. The pilgrims had a tough time convincing the Bay Colony authorities that the Pilgrims wanted to acquire the area because it was located in the southern corner of Massachusetts and touched the north-eastern tip of Rhode Island and was well within the area which Plimoth needed for expansion.

From Rehoboth town records, evidence shows that the area was bought by Edward Winslow and John Brown. It was approximately eight square miles in area and was purchased from Massasoit in 1641 at a bargain price. The men gave Massasoit a token of sixty feet of beads and he was happy with this amount although he said he would also like a coat.

Rehoboth had no militia because it was a frontier town near Massasoit's home in Rhode Island and he and his tribe acted as a buffer or blocker to the Narragansetts to the English territory.

Rehoboth was renamed from Seacunck around June, 1645 when it became a town. The General Court accepted the name change on that date. Many of the town's inhabitants came from Weymouth and Hingham, both towns located north of Plimoth near Boston.

There were other places that became towns; Dartmouth, near Buzzard's Bay and Bridgewater. In fact, Bridgewater initially became a town to absorb the expected overflow from Duxbury. Curiously enough, Bridgewater is about twenty-six miles from Duxbury. They must have expected a tremendous population explosion! Duxbury now has less than three thousand inhabitants

*   *   *

There was another addition to the Cushman family, a son was born on June 1, 1651 and he was baptized Elkanah. Later Elkanah was to marry Elizabeth Cole on February 10, 1677 and they had three children. After her death on January 4, 1681, he married Martha Cooke in 1683. She was a descendent of Francis Cooke. They had five children. Elkanah Cushman died in Plympton, Massachusetts in 1726 at the age of 75.

*   *   *

On May 9, 1657, William Bradford died at sixty-nine and the residents of Plimoth were grief-stricken at his death. He had served the Plimoth Colony well He had assumed the governorship for thirty years and was an assistant governor four times. From his beginnings as a fustian maker in Holland he rose to become a renowned leader based on self-taught knowledge. He was devoted to the Pilgrims and their way of life. Many of his friends and relatives were with him when he died. They said they would never forget him..little did they realize how long he would be remembered, and respected for his role in the beginning of a new nation.

There wasn't a person in the colony with a dry eye when he passed away. He had touched the lives of all of them in his service to the colony. He was a trusted friend. Thomas Cushman had looked upon Bradford as a father figure. As noted, he had become his ward when his father, Robert, left to return to England on the *Fortune* in 1621.

Bradford left a large estate when he died; consisting of his library of about 300 books, a 300-acre farm, his home complete with gardens and an orchard in Plimoth and various items of glassware, pewter, and clothing.

An interesting sideline to the disposition of his heirlooms came in a recent news item which mentioned that a young man was using a pewter mug with the initial "B" on it as a convenient receptacle for pencils. His curiosity was aroused and he went to an antique collector and found to his surprise that it belonged to William Bradford and he suddenly became $70,000 richer.

There are a lot of stories floating around about the value of various articles that were "accidentally found" which traced their origin to the Pilgrims. The stories may be a little farfetched for today's sophisticated reader but even if a new owner of a Pilgrim heirloom got one-tenth of a stated proposed value it would certainly be a windfall.

Mary Cushman was saddened when she heard about the death of her sister, Remember. It was sudden and news traveled slowly. She had died at the age of forty-five, leaving behind six children and her husband, Moses Maverick. Mary wrote letters to her father and Bartholomew telling about the loss, hoping that somehow her letters would be delivered.

It seemed that more of the "Old Timers" were passing on now, as time went on. There were many that survived well beyond the normal life expectancy of that time. Unfortunately, many of the women, especially mothers, did not live long lives.

Among the others that died that year of 1655 were Edward Doty, who had been an indentured servant of Stephan Hopkins, they both came over on the *Mayflower*. And William Bassett, a Saint who contributed much to the colony after he arrived on the *Fortune* with Robert Cushman.

Bradford's son, William Junior, whose mother was the second wife of William Bradford, followed in his father's footsteps. He served twenty-three times as Assistant Governor and ten years as Deputy Governor/Treasurer.

CHAPTER 37

Plymouth-Boston, Massachusetts

1657

In 1657, there was a new development that many felt would jeopardize the whole foundation of their religion. The Pilgrims justifiable felt pride in their achievement of founding the town of Plimoth which was based on a tolerance of different beliefs. Although there was the Anglican religion of the British Isles and the Pilgrims not in total agreement, to say the least, with the Anglican beliefs, they still agreed on many principles of each others religion.

Two male strangers came to Plimoth Colony. It didn't take the Pilgrims long to find out that the strangers were Quaker missionaries or "seekers" trying to influence the settlers into accepting their religion.

The leaders of the community knew the impact that the Quakers had generated in the nearby town of Sandwich in the "Quakerisms". Then the citizens became aware that the Quakers were no longer welcome and they would have to leave.

The Council at Plimoth had two constables escort the

two Quakers out of town. After walking about six miles from Plimoth, the constables left them saying, "You're headed for Rhode Island. Keep going and don't go back to Plimoth ...you're not welcome and will only get yourselves in trouble with the authorities."

Leaving them, the Constables returned to Plimoth and said to the Council, "They know that we don't want them here so they won't be back."

Much to the Constables' dismay, the strangers returned to Plimoth, acting as though nothing had happened. They once again took people aside and started to explain what the Quaker religion consisted of that was different from their own religion. This was too much for the Constables who saw the Quakers back in town. Red faced with anger they sputtered, "Don't unpack—you're leaving!" The Constables, with little fanfare, once again left Plimoth with the two Quakers in tow. They traveled to the outskirts of Rhode Island and left them with the warning, "If you return to Plimoth, next time you'll be whipped and forced to leave."

The Pilgrims knew that Roger Williams, who had founded Providence after being banished from the Bay Colony as a radical, would probably accept the Quakers. Although Roger Williams disagreed with their religion, he was interested in their becoming settlers in his colony.

Why were the colonists at Plimoth so upset about accepting the Quakers in their midst? They thought the Quaker movement, which was started so aggressively in England by George Fox and was now making its way into the colonies, would be destructive to their way of life.

While many of the doctrines the Quakers advocated were highly moral and spiritual, there were those tenets that would never be accepted by most religions.

George Fox planned to open receptive areas for the Quakers in small towns in the New World. He had an eager group that would be recruiters or "seekers". His ambitious plan was to engulf the world with Quakerism. The Pilgrims and the Puritans regarded the Quakers as peculiar people for some of their beliefs.

There were many religions that were "on the other side of the fence" with the Anglican Church. The majority of the ones that left England to come to the Boston area were the Puritans that wanted to "purify" the Anglican religion. The Puritans wanted to form their own religious bodies and churches in England. The Anglicans wouldn't agree to this, so the Puritans left for the New World. Many times the Puritans were mistaken for the Pilgrims whose religion and philosophy were different.

The Pilgrims didn't want to stay in England and change the Anglican religion, they wanted a new start with freedom to pursue their own religion, politics and a chance to prove their own individualism.

The Presbyterians from Scotland, Baptists, Lutherans and Quakers all wanted to practice their own religion. The Anglican Church, also known as the Church of England, said the only Protestants in England must belong to their church.

After severance of the bond between the Pope and the Catholic Church in England, the state religion was the Church of England. This restriction was proclaimed by Queen Elizabeth I. The royal government persecuted Catholics and Protestants alike, for not agreeing with the new religion. To add insult to injury, no religion was allowed except the Anglican Church.

In southern Germany, Spain, Italy and France, the Pope retained control and the Catholics were in and the Protestants were persecuted. Northern Germany, Scandinavia and Holland revolted against the control by the Pope and the loyalty of the Catholics. The Protestants gaining control were now in the "drivers seat" against the out-numbered

Catholics. In England all this religious turmoil led to general immigration by religious groups into America. Catholics and Protestants were welcome to form their own communities and there was no trouble.

The majority of the populace in Virginia were members of the Church of England and the churches were supported by taxes. They tolerated other Protestants and Catholics in time, when they migrated in small numbers into their sanctuary.

It was in this mood that the Pilgrims rejected the idea of the Quakers getting a toehold in their colony. They wanted harmony and the religious differences in their community were only slight.

However, the Pilgrims agreed in principle with some of the ideas that the Quakers put forward. On gambling, the Pilgrims agreed with the Quakers that it was immoral. (On Valentine Day the Pilgrim children could not randomly select a valentine from a box...this was considered to be gambling and would not be tolerated.)

The Quakers did not believe in taking oaths. Many positions in government were lost by the Quakers because they would not bow to this requirement.

Another agreement the Pilgrims arrived at with the Quakers was their dislike for lawyers.

One thing the Pilgrims vehemently disagreed with, was the Quakers' answer to war or self-defense. The Quakers didn't believe in bearing arms to defeat an enemy but their answer was to hire a mercenary to serve for them. Therefore, if they did not serve or attempt to hire a replacement their property was seized by the government.

The Quakers also felt there should be no ministers or magistrates. They held the government in utter contempt.

The Quaker "seekers" arrived in the New World from

England between 1655 and 1662. Sandwich had an influx of Quakers in June, 1657, and they were invited to leave. All citizens of Sandwich, except servants, were instructed to take an Oath of Fidelity to the colony. They had their choice, if the oath wasn't taken they would be fined five pounds or they would have to leave the colony.

It was designed to eliminate Quakers from the colony. The Quakers were forbidden, by their religion, to take oaths and if they didn't take the Oath of Fidelity they had to leave Sandwich and either go to another town or return to their place of origin.

The Pilgrims felt that the Quakers were much more liberal in their outlook than the Puritans, so the townspeople were warned that they would be fined five pounds or were whipped if they harbored a Quaker in their homes. An exception was made if they didn't know the person was a Quaker. If they suspected a person from his actions or words then he/she would be punished for not reporting that person.

In spite of all the protests from the Pilgrims, they were still more tolerant than other colonies. In the Bay Colony, four Quakers were hung. The administrations wanted the Quakers to leave their colonies, not hurt them in any way. But, when the Quakers left the area, they would return and take up where they left off, knowing they were risking the threat of bodily harm or even death.

Two Quakers who were to appear before Governor Thomas Prence, who presided over the General Court, finally stood before him. They were arrogant, uncaring about the dignity of the Court, and immediately acting defiant, seemed to put the Governor on trial.

After a short trial, the court ordered the men whipped and they refused to pay the marshal's fee for the whipping. So they were sentenced to serve time in jail. Serving only one week, they finally came to an arrangement with the same Marshal and left Plimoth...never to return.

The first Quakers to appear in the New World were two independent, forceful women. They were, Ann Austin and Mary Fisher. Their first stop, after leaving England, to indoctrinate the people was at Barbados Island in 1655.

The Barbados residents were engaged in active trading and was a stopping-off point for immigrants that were bound for the colonies in America. The Quakers, or "Friends" as they were also known, spent many months traveling to nearby islands to seek recruits.

Mary Fisher was at this time a young, unmarried maiden of twenty-two years. Her mission in life was to extend the religion of Quakerism across the world. She had endured whippings, two years of imprisonment, and ridicule from the administrators of cities in England.

Ann Austin, was a much older woman and the mother of five children. There is no mention of her life in history books and one must assume that her children were left with her husband or with relatives. It seems that her religion took precedent over her family life.

In 1656, the two women left Barbados to sail to Boston to continue recruiting. Upon arrival and while they were still aboard, authorities questioned the ship's master and the Quakers luggage was searched and examined carefully. They found boxes loaded with books belonging to the women, which related to Quakerism. They were judged to be vile and damaging to the people of the Bay Colony.

The women were hustled off to a gloomy jail and the windows were boarded up allowing very little light to seep in. The women could not see out of their cell. There was a fine of five pounds to anyone caught talking to the women and writing material was forbidden.

When they were detained on the ship they were told to remove all their clothing and they were searched. The authorities were looking for evidence of witchcraft. They found nothing incriminating.

The master of the ship that brought them to Boston was placed under a hundred pound bond and told to return the women to England and the Quakers were forbidden to talk to anyone on the trip home.

The women left Boston, unharmed, unbowed and unshaken, but determined there would be another place...another time.

*   *   *

The Pilgrims felt that they would have to be sure that all members of their congregation would have to be fully aware of the need to adhere to their chosen religion.

If there were any short-comings, the leaders wanted to know so they could correct them. They wanted the members to be frank about the "good things" in their religion so they could continue to remind the congregation of the reason why they became Separatists.

This knowledge could defeat any infringement by any other religious group and make their members content. In their frame of mind, the Pilgrims could resist any other religion and be able to say truthfully and without reservation that they were happy with their religion and they were not interested in changing.

The church officials tried to hear from all members of the congregation about what they liked or disliked about the services. They spoke to every member, however humble in nature, and to the leaders of the community. They received many opinions and like all organizations they had to select the best suggestions and eliminate radical or unsound ideas.

Elder Thomas Cushman said that they had good suggestions from the congregation and they would attempt to put them into use. Some of the other ideas that they could never use were "put aside" and the member thanked for their participation. Some of the ideas were so impractical they would "never see the light of day". But the originator of the idea, however impractical, could brag to his neighbor that he submitted an idea that would "revitalize the church".

CHAPTER 38

New Haven, Virginia, Plymouth

1659-1661

In 1659, Isaac Allerton died at New Haven, Connecticut. He had accumulated large wealth as a result of his trading in Virginia and the West Indies, but he also had outstanding debts which depleted his savings. He left behind his third wife, Joanne. He had married Joanne in 1644 when he was a merchant in New Amsterdam, New York.

When he had gone to New Amsterdam in 1647 he continued as a merchant. Later, he was joined in business with his son, Isaac Junior, who had graduated from Harvard in 1650.

They expanded the thriving trade into Virginia and the West Indies. To handle business more efficiently, Isaac Junior moved to Virginia with his wife Elizabeth and their two children, Elizabeth and Isaac.

When Isaac Allerton Junior s wife Elizabeth died, he married a widow named Joanna (Willowby) (Overzee) Colcough. Isaac Junior became the father of four more children; Willowby, Sarah, Frances and Mary. Isaac Junior, who was living in Westmoreland County, Virginia purchased his father's home in New Haven, Connecticut. The home had four porches; the remainder of the property was an orchard, barn and two acres of meadowland which he would leave to his wife and children. He gave his stepmother the deed to the house on October 4, 1660.

Isaac Junior, in addition to being a clever merchant, had an outstanding military career. He worked his way up to major and eventually became a colonel. He was a friend and associate and was under the command of Colonel George Washington, son of Sir John Washington and great grandfather of General George Washington.

During the Indian Wars, Lieutenant Colonel Washington and Major Isaac Allerton, Junior, organized several militia officers to investigate reports of murder and stealing by the Indians in the vicinity of the Potomac River. They sent their report to the Governor, the State Council and Assembly of Virginia.

Washington and Allerton were accused of murdering some Indians. The accuser was Major Bacon, an undisciplined warrior, who wouldn't hesitate to go to great lengths to further his career. Bacon's "wild story", if believed, would end the careers of Washington and Allerton and put them in jail.

He reported that Washington and Allerton talked some Indians into coming out of their fortifications under a flag of truce to question them. Once they accomplished this, Bacon's story went on, they killed the Indians without a moment's hesitation. Major Bacon's story was finally exposed as a lie and Washington and Allerton were exonerated. Bacon was punished for lying and removed from his military position.

When John Washington was a major, he began to purchase real estate. In 1664 he bought 320 acres of untilled land. Four years later, he bought 450 acres. The next year his largest purchase was 5,000 acres beside the Potomac River. This land was later to be known as Mount Vernon, birthplace of George Washington, father of our country.

Mary Cushman had little contact with her stepbrother, Isaac, or her father before he died. Some depict her father as a money-grabber, an opportunist who would go out of his way to earn a pound regardless of how he made it. The history of Plimoth shows Allerton eventually paid all his debts. One wonders what Plimoth in its early days of formation would have been like if Allerton had been steered toward a path of economical growth for the benefit of the colony and had been given free rein.

In 1661, Thomas Prence was elected Governor again, for the fourth time. His assistants were again; Alden, Collier, Willett, Southworth and the sons of Winslow and Bradford.

This was also the year that Massasoit died. He was missed by the Pilgrims; they could always count on him as a friend. Although he was a powerful chief and his territory extended far, he was peaceful and could have wiped out the Pilgrims when they were relatively weak.

He was honored by the Pilgrims for his help when they were growing and were most vulnerable, especially when sickness decimated the colony the first year. The descendants of the Pilgrims, to honor the name of Massasoit, erected a bronze statue that stands on Cole Hill overlooking Plimoth Harbor.

Upon Massasoit's death, Wamsutta, the older son, came to Plimoth with his brother Metacomet, to renew the long-standing pledge of peace. While in Plimoth, they asked the leaders of the colony to give them English names. Wamsutta, the new chief, was given the name, Alexander, and Metacomet was now known as Philip. Everything seemed to be going along well with the new chief and the Pilgrims, until a few months later when there was a rumor adrift that Wamsutta (Alexander) was plotting against the Pilgrims. The authorities in Plimoth asked Alexander to appear before the General Court in Boston. They waited, but there was no response from him, he had completely ignored the order.

Outraged, they selected Major Josiah Winslow, an assistant to Governor Prence, to go to Sowans and bring Alexander to Plimoth Winslow, accompanied by ten armed men found that Alexander was not at Sowans but at a hunting lodge near Taunton.

Breaking into his lodge and aiming his pistol at him, Alexander was ordered to accompany them to Plimoth. Alexander refused the offer of a horse and walked with the women in his group to Major Winslow's home and was questioned exhaustively by Governor Prence. Massasoit would never have been treated this shabbily when he was alive, but then he wouldn't betray a trust as Alexander had done.

The truth behind the threat was still vague...it was still in the rumor stage. And that rumor was, that Alexander was unhappy with the English. He felt that they were infringing on his territory and everyday seemed to bring more British influence. However, the Pilgrims paid for every acre of land that they acquired. Ironically, the Indians couldn't understand real estate transactions.

They didn't know why the Pilgrims paid for land when it was all around them. They slowly came to realize the implication when they had to pack up and leave the land that the Pilgrims purchased. There were a lot of towns being chartered and there was surely no surprise that the Indians were suspicious of the white man's intention of taking all their land.

The Indians could move on and just take more territory but they found that other tribes were occupying land that they could use and they were being boxed in. This was their reason for hating the English. The English couldn't understand their reasoning, they thought that there was plenty of land for everyone.

*   *   *

Alexander became seriously ill with a fever which the Indians claimed was caused by his being treated so badly by by the colonists. Now he, with his tribe, held total resentment against the Pilgrims. His fever got worse and he died, ironically in Plimoth, two days later. The Pilgrims couldn't understand his change of heart, they always liked him. Like Massasoit, he was always willing to barter land for goods, and the Pilgrims gave him what he wanted.

Honor bearers carried his body, resting on a litter, on their shoulders, back to his final resting place among his ancestors at Sowans.

Now Chief of the Wampanoags, Philip, came once again to renew the pledge of peace with the Pilgrims. He must have heard about the false rumors of the treatment that Alexander underwent at the hands of the Pilgrims, but he gave no evidence that he thought the rumors were true.

*   *   *

Duxbury was a small area situated near the northern part of Plimoth Bay and several Pilgrims moved there from Plimoth.

Among the new citizens of Duxbury were John Alden, Elder William Brewster and his son Jonathan, Thomas Prence and Captain Myles Standish. Many of the inhabitants of Duxbury formerly attended the First Church of Plimoth, but now, especially during the cold, bitter winter, they wanted to return to Plimoth and again leave in the spring.

Taking note of the exodus from their colony, the General court of Plimoth, almost unanimously, voted that if any person left Plimoth for another town or area and this move was to be permanent, they would lose any land they owned and it would then be made available to another person who intended to stay.Ironically enough, the people that moved to Duxbury all held important posts in the Town of Plimoth.

Plimoth colony had been growing by leaps and bounds and one portion of their livelihood was raising and selling cattle. For this reason they needed land to expand. Plimoth now extended outward and encompassed many towns, including Duxbury, and eventually became Plimoth County. None of the leaders that had moved to Duxbury returned to live in the town of Plimoth.

Standish, however, continued to support the Pilgrims to his utmost ability. Although he wasn't a Separatist, he followed their principles and he really admired the Pilgrims since he joined them on the trip to America

The Pilgrims also appreciated the service and support that Captain Myles Standish gave to the community. They marveled at his cocky attitude and courage but sometimes they had to turn a blind eye to some of his actions.

Standish was rated by many Pilgrims as an intellectual. He was well-read and owned many valuable books that would be prized by many college professors. The books were of a higher quality in interest and intellectually more stimulating than those that were owned by either Bradford or Brewster.

Standish, who would live forever in the memory of future generations as an early hero of the republic, died in 1670.

A statue in his honor stands in Duxbury, not Plimoth.

CHAPTER 39

Plymouth, Cape Cod

1673-1675

Major Josiah Winslow, forty-four years old, the oldest son of Edward Winslow, was elected Governor in 1673, to replace Prence, who died in office at seventy-three. Josiah had risen steadily since his early days as an accountant in the colony. Josiah had been educated at Harvard College and married the daughter of its treasurer.

His next step was to become Assistant Governor of Plimoth, serving several terms and then he became Commander-in-Chief of the Plimoth militia. He replaced Myles Standish who had died three years before and the position had been unfilled.

To meet the new challenge brought on by King Philip of the Wampanoags, the United Colonies was formed. It consisted of the Massachusetts Bay Colony, Plimoth, Connecticut and the New Haven Colony, which at the time was an independent colony. Among the purposes for organizing this confederacy was to insure the defense of each colony. The honor of leading the force was given to Josiah Winslow, when he became Commander-in-Chief of all the colonies. The troops of Plimoth would be commanded by Major Cudworth, who was recently promoted. Plimoth was to raise a contingent of 158 soldiers, Connecticut's quota was 315 and the Massachusetts Bay Colony was to provide 517 men.

The colonies taught every boy how to handle a gun, shoot straight, and how to become a soldier in the militia. They formed a civilian army without knowledge of how to handle themselves in combat. They had never fired a shot in anger but they were ready to march when ordered.

One example of their preparedness was an urgent call that went out, saying the militia was needed, quickly. This alarm came from a town thirty miles away from Boston and within a couple of hours there was a large group of militia in place, ready to meet and hopefully defeat any enemy. Although the Pilgrims hated war, they were ready to give their lives if the cause was just.

*   *   *

The Pilgrims lived a simple life. They were totally independent and became masters of many trades through necessity. They made their own clothing, shoes, and furniture. They labored long, in the hot sun, to produce their own food.

The New Englanders, later harnessed the rapid-running rivers to give power to mills that produced lumber, grist mills, chemicals and other necessities. They spun wool from the hundreds of sheep that grazed in the quiet, green meadows. They did not believe in slavery, as every man did his own work and earned his own reward. But they did have indentured servants, who served the family who sponsored them, for payment of travel expenses, food, and clothing.

The indentured servants served for a predetermined

period of time and then went on their way. The *Mayflower* carried many of the indentured servants who were later "freed" and became some of Plimoth's renowned leaders. Each small town that dotted the landscape was composed of these sturdy, vigorous, individuals that stood unafraid and freely gave their thoughts at town meetings. The leaders quietly had to accept the accolades or the tongue-lashing of the town citizens. Ironically, many of the leaders served without compensation.

The people themselves seemed to have gained independence or a new freedom from the shackles of a demanding government in England where there were many restrictions in spite of the rights guaranteed under the *Magna Carta* written in 1215 and in effect for hundreds of years.

The Mayflower Compact still guided the Pilgrims and they were happy with the results. The Pilgrims had never experienced true freedom in England and now they took it for granted.

After the winter of 1620-21 when the pilgrims lost half of their original group, the survivors seemed to have thrived in the hostile surroundings and rugged lifestyle. They now lived on healthy food, which they grew, and from the abundant seafood taken from the ocean, which was proverbially at their doorstep. The Pilgrim fishermen labored long and hard in their daily work of fish harvesting.

It was in this atmosphere of hardworking, determined people that Philip (Metacomet) went to Plimoth Colony and said that he wouldn't wage war on his neighbors or sell land without prior agreement with the Plimoth authorities. The colonists did not want war and felt that the gesture was genuine and they could still live in peace and harmony with Philip and continue to lead fruitful lives. The decision was in the Indians' hands; if they wanted to be hostile and belligerent they would have to contend with the settlers.

One of Philip's trusted lieutenants told the Plimoth authorities that Philip was intent on starting a war with the French or Dutch in cohorts with him. Philip said the Indian who told the Pilgrim's that story was lying. When the Indian repeated the accusation to Philip's face in the presence of the authorities, Philip denied it. Philip said the Indian was paid by the Narragansett Chief to lie.

This denial by Philip was backed up by a letter that was received later by the Plimoth Court from Roger Williams stating that the Indian was an undependable person and couldn't be believed. The Court still doubted Philip's story but accepted his denial anyway.

They checked all the ammunition and guns of the militia and gave overdue promotions to all commissioned officers.

Detailed plans were made in all the colonies, for foot and horse soldiers to battle the Indians if it became necessary. Evacuation plans for the civilians were also made. Attempts were made to insure trustworthy and loyal Indian friends to become Plimoth allies. Many of those that liked the Pilgrims said they would be loyal and willing to lay down their lives, to support them.

There were problems with disarming other Indians and Philip was also called upon to give up his arms. Not having heard from him about this issue, he was summoned to Plimoth Colony to give his explanation.

Philip went instead to the Massachusetts Bay Colony and complained about the treatment he endured from the Plimoth authorities. The Plimoth Court explained to the Bay Colony that Plimoth had a written agreement with the Wampanoags of which Philip was their sachem. This agreement was about arms and the sale of land and had been effect for almost fifty years without any problems or interruptions.

The Bay Colony authorities finally concluded that Philip had given them false testimony; he was to surrender his arms. He should go to Plimoth to settle any differences and handle any complaints. The unfriendly Indians that were harbored by Philip were to leave his territory at once. Philip was fined one hundred pounds and gave his allegiance to the King of England and promised to solve any difference with Plimoth including making war on any other tribe without permission and selling land without Plimoth's knowledge.

The Bay Colony authorities reminded Philip that Plimoth was a true friend of the Wampanoags and they showed this friendship when the Wampanoag tribe had disputes with other Indians. The Narragansetts, for example, realized that the Pilgrims were friends of the Wampanoags and backed off from many arguments.

The complaints of many tribes were that they were being crowded and hemmed in by the establishment of many towns by the English. The Wampanoags said they were squeezed by the English and were limited in their space. The Narragansetts also said that the English were taking their land and Massachusetts, Rhode Island and Connecticut formed a boundary for their expansion. They were being pushed toward the Connecticut River where their bitter enemies, the Mohawks, held their ground. The Nipmuck Tribe that was situated near the Bay Colony in central Massachusetts was also being pushed out of their territory by the English in their expansion of new towns.

It was not until 1675 that a friendly Indian named Sassamon who adopted the Christian religion and was an educated Indian, was violently murdered. He had been Philip's faithful secretary. Three Indians bent on killing him, savagely beat him and broke his neck. They placed his body in a hole in the ice of a nearby pond to dispose of the evidence. Sassamon, just before his death, warned Plimoth

Colony authorities that Philip once again was determined to start a war with the English.

When they arrested the instigators of this terrible crime, the Plimoth Colony authorities installed a grand jury equally divided with English and Indians to investigate the incident. They finally arrived at an unanimous decision that all the accused Indians were guilty. Two were hanged and the third, who had meanwhile escaped from custody, met his death, a month later, by being shot by a person or persons unknown.

The Indians were becoming restless when they heard that the Indians were executed. Although it was a fair court, they thought the Indians on the jury were pawns of the English, and unrest spread.

Josias Winslow, son of Edward Winslow, was the new Governor of Plimoth when war erupted in 1675. He was assisted in his governing by John Alden and William Bradford, who was born in Plimoth and the son of William, who had been governor many times. There were other assistants; Thomas Hinckley, John Freeman, James Browne, and James Cudsworth who had been eliminated as an assistant in the past due to his friendly views toward Quakerism.

CHAPTER 40

Plymouth, Cape Cod

1675-1676

The Pilgrims were self-reliant and felt, rightfully so, that their government was established to serve the public and they were not to be bullied and subservient to their elected leaders. When the citizens held town meetings, the majority of the people participated, nothing could divert their attention. Their elected leaders could suggest solutions to problems but they were held responsible for their actions. The people were not puppets that could be manipulated but would take turns berating or congratulating, as the case warranted.

*   *   *

To this comparatively tranquil scene came the turmoil of a bloody war. It was known as the King Philip's War and would occupy a brief mention in history books, but all wars are vitally important, if you are one of the participants.

The war started after the execution of the Indians that

had brutally murdered Sassamon. There are many instances of a war starting with an incident that involved a small group of people and developing in degrees where there is raw hatred on each side, forgetting the good things that happened in the past and thinking only of the present in some cases with a wild distortion of facts and a total disregard of peace talks.

The Plimoth General Court had found no reason to implicate Philip in the murder of Sassamon. Plimoth authorities were thinking that if Philip was exonerated of the crime, then he would necessarily think that the people of Plimoth weren't as belligerent as he originally thought. Maybe he would then take a more peaceful approach in dealing with Plimoth. No such thoughts crossed his mind.

Philip, then went all out in preparing for war with the British. He evacuated all the women and children by sending them down from Mount Hope, his home ground, to the protection of the powerful Narragansetts. He welcomed Indian braves from nearby tribes to join him and eventually make war on all the colonies. He continued to build up his supply of arms and ammunition and other deadly weapons of war.

One incident at Mount Hope occurred when a "Peace Delegation" from Rehoboth tried to speak with Philip at his home. Although unarmed, they were threatened by Philip's braves, pointing their loaded muskets at them, There was no sense in trying to reason with them, the men from Rehoboth retreated safely from the area and returned home. They were lucky to escape, soon the Indians became warlike.

The next day, the same Indians looted and burned the Swansea residence of Job Winslow, brother of Josias. Two days later, braves burned and looted several homes near Swansea. The attack on homes and civilians were escalating and becoming more savage.

Troops from Plimoth, force-marched their way to

Swansea to see if they could help stem the attacks on the civilian homes and people. Before they arrived, twelve more homes were set afire and burned to the ground But this time there was resistance from the British.

One witness said that three Indians who had looted a house, ran away and one of them was shot by a twenty-year-old youth who was accompanied by his father and two other Englishmen. It wasn't too long before several Indians showed up and said that the Indian had died and asked why the youth had killed him. The youth shrugged the death away with a suggestion that "It was only an Indian". In spite of objections from other residents about the boys indifference toward the death, the angry Indians left.

The next day they returned, shot the youth and his father dead and calmly walked away. Some say, they also killed five men later but this was unverified.

That first Indian to die at the youth's hand might have been the spark that ignited the tinderbox of conflict.

Captain Benjamin Church of Plimoth marched his troops past some of the homes in Swansea that had been looted and burned and saw the results of the Indians wrath toward the youth and his father.

Later, at Mattaporset, eight more Englishman were brutally murdered, dismembered and beheaded by warpainted braves.

Church and his men marched on and saw the heads of the eight Englishmen stuck on pikes to warn other white men. The militiamen took down the heads and were determined that this savagery would be avenged. But there was still no declaration of war and where the populace wasn't involved...life went on as usual.

*   *   *

There were more incidents occurring...some equal to the worst savagery of the past. There was trouble brewing in more towns and the militia was now engaging the Indians in combat, daily.

CHAPTER 41

Taunton, Plymouth

1675-1676

Major Josiah Winslow, forty years old, the oldest son of Edward Winslow, was elected Governor in 1673, to replace Prence who died in office at seventy-three. He was now in office when trouble started with King Philip. Josiah had risen steadily since his early days as an accountant in the colony. Josiah had been educated at Harvard and married the daughter of the treasurer of the college. His next step up was to become Commander-in-Chief of the Plimoth "Army". He replaced Myles Standish who had died three years before and the post had been unfilled.

To meet the new challenge brought on by Philip, the United Colonies was formed. It consisted of the Massachusetts Bay Colony, Plimoth, Connecticut and The New Haven Colony.

The Colony of Plimoth militia would be commanded by Major Cudworth. Plimoth was to raise a contingent of 158 soldiers, Connecticut had a quota of 315 and the Bay Colony was to provide 517 men.

*　　　*　　　*

The British were now completely armed and ready for action, and they were successful in many skirmishes. They faced a foe that was furtive, and cunning which was based on their years of hunting in dense forests. They faced continual danger from hostile tribes.

Many Indians had full knowledge of handling guns and like the colonists had become expert in shooting game. The Indians owning guns seemed to be a complete reversal of the law that had been in effect for many years. The law stated that the white man could not sell or give an Indian weapons or to provide them with liquor for which the Indians seemed to have a low tolerance.

Through necessity, the acceptance of Indians owning guns just seemed to creep in, but it was still illegal.

Knowing that many guns were in Indian hands, the Plimoth Colonists had hired the Indians to assist in killing wolves that were attacking cattle herds that the Pilgrims owned and were being depleted in great numbers. The Indians were paid one-half pound of gun powder along with two pounds of shot plus a coat for bringing in a wolf's head. Now this policy, although still illegal, had came to haunt the colonists.

*　　　*　　　*

The Governor of the Colony of Connecticut, John Winthrop, Junior decided that they could no longer reason with the Wampanoags under King Philip. They would now supply man-power to Plimoth once the Assembly in Connecticut found the authorities in Plimoth correct in denouncing Philip.

The Plimoth Council had sent a letter to Philip complaining of his belligerent behavior and requested a meeting to discuss a cooling-off period in the heated exchange and wanton brutal measures taken by the Wampanoags and their allies. The message was ignored by the Indians.

The main thrust of the Plimoth Colony was to prevent the Narragansetts and the Nipmucks of Central Massachusetts from becoming allies of Philip's. They wouldn't necessarily have to become allies with Plimoth, although that would help, but not to take sides but stay neutral.

This argument did not prevent the Wampanoags from moving into the Nipmuck area when they escaped from the Plimoth troops When they tried to trap the Indians after they had destroyed the town of Dartmouth.

Savage Indian attacks were spread over a large area of Massachusetts and were soon occurring in the outskirts of Connecticut and Rhode Island.

The Niantic, Mohegans and the Mohawks, long time enemies of the Wampanoags and their allies sided with the English to fight against them. The Narragansetts were undecided with their loyalty...was it with the Wampanoags or the English.

Should they join the Wampanoags? Meanwhile, using hit and run tactics and quickly running from trouble-spots the Indians suffered minor casualties. They hadn't stayed to fight the English. Right now they were calling the shots.

*   *   *

The Cushmans were seated in the great room in their home and the conversation was centered around the ongoing war with King Philip, son of the late Massasoit, who the Pilgrims had admired for being a close friend. It was 1675 and the war had been going on for a couple of months

The group was composed of Mary Cushman, Elder

Thomas, Elkanah and his wife Martha (Cooke) and Eleazer and wife Elizabeth (Coombs).

Elder Cushman raised a question to the gathering; "Why did Philip start this war? We've always been friends with the Wampanoags and for over fifty years we had a treaty of peace."

Eleazer spoke up, "I think that they felt they were being hemmed in, they were losing land left and right."

"Well. we always paid for the land that we got. I don't know about the other colonies, but we never took an inch of land from them." Elkanah replied.

Mary added, "From what I hear the Narragansett tribe also felt the same pressure from the English. They are surrounded on three sides by Connecticut, Rhode Island and Massachusetts. In addition, the Mohawks, sworn enemies of the Narragansetts, are on the Connecticut River right next to them. They haven't been belligerent yet."

Eleazar raised his eyebrows and laughed, "You sound just like a military man, mother."

"Well, it's very serious Eleazer. I hope that you boys won't have to go to war. I also wish that it gets over with soon."

Elkanah said, "Well, I'm ready to go."

Eleazar put up his hand, "Me too. I've never fought the Indians before, but I'm ready to go."

Elizabeth said, "I don't want anything to happen to either of you. You're both married and have children. I'm afraid that if the war goes on you'll be forced to go because all our lives will be in jeopardy."

Martha, Mary and Elizabeth went to the kitchen to prepare some food and when they were gone Thomas said, "Maybe we shouldn't dwell on the war...let's talk about something happy for a change. We're stronger now then when we first came from England. When I think of how weak we really were in the first few years, it's a wonder we weren't all wiped out by the Indians. The Indians numbered in the thousands."

Eleazar said, "Before we change the subject, do you know what happened close by...it was only two miles from here. I heard the story the other day. Six Indian braves, covered with war paint and painted symbols, sneaked up with bows and arrows and silently surrounded the Clarke's small farm house. They broke the front door in and rushed into the house with wild whoops. Mrs. Clarke and her young son were paralyzed with fear momentarily then she tried to get her son behind her. One of the braves grabbed her by the hair and with his sharp tomahawk hit her repeatedly and her loud shrieks were silenced as she slumped to the floor.

Her son, seeing his mother lying dead, yelled and flailing with his thin arms hit one of the braves. The brave held him off with one hand. Suddenly, the boy hit the brave in the eye with his fist. The Indian angrily hit the boy a glancing blow with his tomahawk and the boy fell unconscious beside the motionless body of his mother, who had died where she fell.

The boy didn't moan and the Indians assumed that he too was dead. They began looting and took everything of value and ran out of the house. They brought the stolen articles back to their village and proudly displayed the loot to the other young braves. Many of them were envious and said that they too would loot the English but get better things.

Mr. William Clarke, who had been away from home attending a meeting, was devastated upon seeing his wife and son covered with blood and the havoc that the Indians caused.

Thinking that both his wife and son had been killed, he ran out of the house, yelling in rage at the top of his voice. As the Indians had stolen his musket, he grabbed a club and headed in the direction of the nearest Indian village.

Fortunately, he was stopped as he ran by several neighbors, who grabbed his club from his hand and tried to offer him some solace once they found the reason for his rage.

They persuaded Mr. Clarke to return home and the neighbors accompanied him. They were surprised to see the boy sitting up, holding his bloodied head. His father ran to hold him while his friends attended to his wound. Clarke looked at his wife and sobbed and blamed himself for not being at home to protect his family. Under the circumstances he too would have become a victim.

The injured boy was finally able to give all the details of the Indian raid. They reported the incident to the local authorities and they later found that the residents of the village where Mr. Clarke was headed were friends and would never allow any local brave to harm the friendship with the English.

Two Indians, who were responsible for the raid, came from another village and they were apprehended after an unhappy squaw had overheard a conversation by two boasting Indians. The two braves mentioned that a group of six were responsible for killing a married couple named Mitchell and a neighbor named John Pope and they also mentioned the Clarkes. The two Indians implicated and then named the other four braves that were part of the raiding party that killed the others and then went to Clarkes' home, looted it and killed Mrs. Clarke.

The Indians were all found guilty of the several murders and were hanged.

Thomas said, "I'm glad that justice was done. But it getting pretty close to home. I doubt that Plimoth itself will be attacked. The Indians respect our power and overall defensive position.

Elkanah said, "I heard a story that was going around, you probably heard it too. We had a victory of sorts when Captain Michael Pierce with a force of fifty-five English and twenty friendly Indians chased about five belligerent Indians into some woods near Rhode Island They had gone a short distance when suddenly there were over a thousand Indians surrounding them."

"Were they overpowered and slain?" Thomas asked.

"Well, they drew into a small tight circle, practically back to back and fought them for two hours. The Indians they were fighting were thirty feet deep in places. The English and their allies managed to escape with eight soldiers and ten Indians. They were all seriously wounded. They had killed over three hundred and wounded many of the enemy. The belligerent Indians caught up to them and the weary soldiers and their allies fought desperately and valiantly until in total exhaustion Captain Pierce and his men gained immortality, ground down by the sheer weight of numbers. From the beginning of the battle they were outnumbered over thirteen to one."

"I heard the story also and it was verified by an Indian that was at the battle. Did you know that these Indians were on their way to Plimoth when they decided on ambushing Captain Pierce? We really owe a lot to Captain Pierce and to his brave men. With all the savagery of the war going on, I guess it's pretty hard not to talk about it or to find happy things to talk about these days," Thomas said.

Eleazar commented, "It's really a shame to hear about men dying like this. I guess we have to face stark reality. You know the men called up for service are now fined ten pounds for not reporting for duty. If they don't have the ten pounds for the fine they will be sent to jail for six months. Constables are pressed into service into rounding up the resisters, and they in turn are fined for selecting those unfit for service."

Eleazar said, "I was talking to some of the men that saw action against the Indians and they said the tactics that were used on the plains of Europe using massed troops were eliminated when they fought the Indians. Our Indian allies taught them how to ambush the enemy and fight behind trees and rocks or use whatever was handy to afford protection and surprise the enemy. The soldiers soon changed their tactics by hitting the Indians before they could mobilize to attack the settlers. The Indians would attack weak points, kill the civilians then disappear into the nearby woods."

Elkanah agreeing with Eleazar went on, "Yes, I heard about the new training they're getting. It's practical and should save many lives. I also hear that the scales are beginning to tip in our favor. There are more Indians fighting on our side now and they are masters in the art of ambush. We have an ample supply of ammunition but the food supply is touch and go. I understand that the soldiers are capturing large, hidden supplies from the Indians."

Thomas replied, "I've heard that, too. The Indians are getting desperate in searching for food but they are self-sufficient in finding roots and herbs to eat. That's why the harvesting of our crops is very critical. It's almost as important as sending men to fight. If we don't tend the crops and get them in, they will rot in the ground and the people will starve to death. It's going to be a close call, to send more men or have them remain here as farmers."

After a pleasant afternoon together and having dispensed finally with the worries of war, they departed, leaving Mary and Thomas in the doorway, waving to them. The war would continue, and life still had to go on.

Many of towns had garrison houses which were constructed of solid oak. The upper floor was extended so that the inhabitants could shoot downward at the Indians if they tried to rush the door to break in. The door was heavily barricaded from within but in spite of all precautions they were vulnerable to one simple fact...the Indians could place a large quantity of dried brush against the walls and set it afire or used a loaded wagon with flaming debris and run it into the house. The only hope in defeating these ideas was to either shoot the Indians before these ideas were put into effect, or with foresight, the English would have water filled buckets upstairs to put out the fires once they occurred, but this was not always the case. Many garrison houses were destroyed and the towns were destroyed. Once captured, all of the inhabitants of the town were massacred.

When the English troops met the Indians in force, even on rare occasions when they were barricaded behind strong positions, the English had remarkable success. Many of the Indians were captured and along with most of the women and children were sold into slavery.

The Indians that lived near Plimoth were looked upon with some suspicion even though they came to the colony unarmed and had befriended the Pilgrims for many years.

The "Praying Indians", those that had chosen to be Christians, were likewise treated. Many Pilgrims, speaking in defense of the Indians, were putting their friendship with the other colonists in question.

The captured Indians were put into perpetual slavery, other Indians were held on Clarke's Island, away from the colony. The colonists in their present frame of mind, couldn't tell friend from foe, and in a life and death struggle one couldn't take a chance.

The colonists were put in a bind by the critical need for available men to fight the Indians and those needed to harvest the dwindling crops. The food supply was being exhausted with the army using a great quantity and the reserve stock was running low for the civilians. It was becoming a struggle to balance both needs.

The English were superior to the Indians in manpower, firepower and food. The food situation with the Indians was desperate. The colonists soldiers raided Indian strongholds and seized large quantities of their food supply. To avoid starvation, many of the belligerent Indians soon found themselves fighting their friends, they deserted their ranks and joined the English.

*   *   *

John Winthrop, Senior, who had been Governor of the Bay Colony in Massachusetts for several terms during the development of Plimoth had long passed from the scene. Both of the Governors, John Winthrop Senior and his son John, who had inherited the position were revered by succeeding generations for their devotion to the society and for the general welfare of the citizens.

Winthrop, Senior had called out the militia years before in 1635, to deal with an obstinate "would be" Governor General of New England, Sir Fernando Gorges.

After four years of work, Gorges and the Archbishop of Canterbury seemed to have defeated the Massachusetts Bay Colony by attempting to recall its Charter. The attempt to eliminate the Charter for Plimoth was also underway. Winthrop, Senior made an effort to fortify Castle Island outside Boston harbor, he feared a British invasion. He also strengthened the defensive network by raising taxes to build forts at Salem, Dorchester and Charlestown.

As time went on, there was no hostile ship on the horizon. They were to realize that the English would not fight fellow Englishmen, in spite of the reward of new land.

Later in 1638, John Winthrop wrote to Archbishop Laud stating, "If our Charter is removed, we shall either return to England or relocate to another place and become independent."

Once again, Sir Edmund Andros, who had planned on taking control of all of New England, same as Gorges, came on the scene John Winthrop, Junior, stood shoulder to shoulder with the citizens of Connecticut against the tyranny of Andros. Unfortunately, Winthrop was at the end of his time on earth. His wife of forty years had died in 1672 and this led to his general melancholy. He wanted to visit England again, to see it for last time, but it would also be a business trip, and for health purposes. But he didn't have the money for the trip

In 1674, the Connecticut Assembly voted to give Winthrop, Junior a small amount of tax money to help him with his debts. They said it was to repay the Winthrop family for using their own money to help gain the Connecticut Charter, back in the 1630's. However, when Winthrop suggested again in 1675, before the trouble developed with King Philip, he asked that he be relieved of his duties as Governor to travel to England, the Assembly agreed and suggested that he represent them in addressing the British Government in protesting the behavior of Sir Edmund Andros and in effect tell them he's not wanted in Connecticut.

It was in early 1675 that Andros tried to annex the western part of Connecticut to the eastern section of Long island. The citizens of eastern Long Island had signed a petition requesting that they be taken over by Connecticut.

As a military man with the rank of Major, Andros thought that he would give them a military show of force in Saybrook, Connecticut. He would take their fort and the citizens would bolt and run fearfully in the opposite direction.

The Connecticut Assembly was in a quandary, they heard rumors that Sir Andros was planning something to harm the residents of Connecticut. Now they had two problems to solve in haste...first, there was the Andros affair, second, the Indians were beginning to trouble the Pilgrims around the colony of Plimoth

They found that Andros destination was indeed to be Saybrook, a small town in Connecticut.

They assumed that Andros, instead of helping the English settle the Plimoth problem, would attack the town thinking that the militia had gone to Plimoth to help them out.

The citizens of Saybrook were determined to defend their town and fort then defeat Andros and save the colony of Connecticut in the name of his Majesty's government.

Captain Thomas Bull, with a company of militia, was given orders to hold the fort under all circumstances, regardless of the enemy...Indian or Redcoat.

Bull and his militia tried to reach Saybrook before Andros, who had two boatloads of soldiers that were headed for Saybrook and was now at the mouth of the Connecticut River. Bull had stopped at several towns and their militia soon joined him and before long they were at Saybrook watching Andros come ashore. All of the militia were eager to stop Andros, based on the stories they heard about his arrogance and his unpopular grab for power.

The Connecticut militia was maneuvering the cannon in the direction of the Andros troops. He remained in his boat, now a primary target for the threatening artillery. Andros had fully expected that there would be few people to oppose him and the fort would be an easy target.

Captain Bull had been given two sets of instructions by the Assembly. He was to invite Andros to go to Plimoth and offer his help. If this invitation was not accepted by Andros, then Bull was to take command and resist all efforts by Andros to land at Saybrook.

Before Sir Andros debarked from his boat, he said to

Captain Bull that he wanted the western half of Connecticut. Bull handed him a note from the Connecticut Assembly.

The note was blunt and to the point. It said that Connecticut would defend any intrusion on its territory by anyone.

Andros immediately knew that he would have a battle on his hands if he attempted to take the fort from the armed and angry civilians now gathered on the shore.

Taking a new tack, he inquired about Winthrop's health and tried to appear friendly with the crowd. There was no fooling the Connecticut men on the beach angrily threatening him with muskets. They saw through Andros feeble attempt at appeasement and ridiculed him.

He finally sailed away and was dismayed about his ill treatment when he was only trying to be friendly.

John Winthrop, Junior, had two sons, Fitz and Wait. Fitz was thirty-eight years old and Wait was four years older than he, when John died in April, 1676.

Fitz was deathly ill at his home in June 1675, recovering from a virulent fever. He was the Commander of the County Militia and with the King Philip War erupting and involving New London, Connecticut, the Council appointed Wait Winthrop to take Fitz's place.

King Philip had attacked Taunton, Middleborough and other smaller towns, then he struck at the outskirts of Plimoth and sacked and burned Scituate, then he expanded his attacks into Connecticut. It was into this situation that Wait Winthrop with sixty militiamen and sixty friendly Indians marched to met the Narragansetts to make sure they remained neutral.

The neutrality did not last long. The Narragansetts, the most powerful tribe in New England, joined Philip's Wampanoags tribe in their fight against the English.

In Massachusetts, "Praying Indians", two hundred converts, went with Philip. For revenge, their fields were ravaged and many put into close confinement, some were put to death. Some Indians could go no nearer than Sandwich in a zone that protected Plimoth. If they came closer than the restricted area allowed then they were confined to Plimoth or were herded onto Clarke's Island.

Philip went to New York where he was headquartered at Hoosick, about thirty-five miles from Albany. He was accompanied by a large force of braves. He met with a powerful sachem near Canada and together they planned to destroy Connecticut in the spring and later Boston in the fall. Meanwhile, brutal strife continued in Massachusetts and Connecticut.

The colonists were very fortunate in having staunch allies in the Pequots and Mohicans. They helped clear the woods of the enemy and captured many of them. The women and the children of the enemy were held hostage while the braves were forced to help in trying to round up and influence other belligerent Indians into surrendering.

By February the war with Philip against Plimoth was enlarged into the Algonquin campaign against the people of New England. Sir Andros of New York attempted to introduce the Mohawks into the battle. The Mohawks would deprive the enemy of food by destroying their corn crop. When Sir Andros proposed this plan to Boston the magistrate refused and they found later that Andros kept a powerful garrison of soldiers in their barracks when they could have helped Plimoth and nearby towns fight the Indians.

The Algonquins, who were busy in Virginia and Maryland, had burned eight towns and wiped out a garrison of militia in New England. The twenty-one hundred Algonquins, now armed to the teeth, joined with five hundred Canadian Indians and King Philip's force along with the

Narragansetts Indians and all this was done in two month's time.

The English were also active during this period. On one occasion Captain George Denison with a Connecticut force of one hundred men and equally supplied with a hundred Indians from the Pequots, Niantic and Mohicans attacked a party of Narragansetts. The Indian allies were commanded by the Christian son of Uncas and they captured a bloodthirsty and cruel sachem called Quononshot, the son of Miatonomo. (How ironic that these two would meet, once more history was repeating itself.)

When Quononshot was captured he was with several other notorious sachems and sagamores. They were brought, hands bound, back to authorities in Connecticut. Proud and arrogant, Quononshot said, "I am a Prince and I won't be questioned by commoners. If somebody of equal rank would come to me, then, and then only, will I consent to speak."

The authorities had quite enough of his arrogance. They were all too familiar with his heartless and diabolic nature. His reckless murder of helpless civilians and wanton destruction of property and plundering, left no mercy in the souls of the colonists. They left the final disposition of Quononshot in the hands of their allies, who were also aware of his character. They now sat in judgment. Quononshot then threatened the Indians by saying that if they decided on his death he would send word to his 2,000 braves and they would attack his killers at once.

He didn't have time to send his message. He was shot by the Pequots, the Mohicans cut off his head and quartered his body. The Niantics finished the job by starting a bonfire and burned his body. The job was over. They had saved his head and it was sent to the authorities in Hartford, Connecticut as a gesture of their love and loyalty.

Several months later, during the war, Captain

Benjamin Church became a hero to the Plimoth colonists. He knew the habits of the Indians and their method of fighting guerrilla style and he adopted this practice soon after he entered battle. He was able to persuade the Indians to switch sides, even the surly type that seemed to hate the white men, were convinced and almost on the spot, became allies and fought Philip's braves. Things went well for Captain Church and he persuaded a female sachem named Queen Awashun-eke to surrender her tribe and to go to Plimoth.

King Philip finally went to his home at Mount Hope in Rhode Island accompanied by his remaining force, now down to ten braves. One brave that was disgusted with Philip's downfall, left Mount Hope and sought out Captain Church.

Trying to find Philip was Captain Church's main purpose now, and he was very happy when the Indian brave provided him with the information about Philip's whereabouts. The brave guided the English troops and soon they were nearing the place where Philip had taken refuge.

They entered a swamp and experienced great difficulty in trying in trying to make any headway. Some of the soldiers were up to their waists in the muddy water. The soldiers struggled and finally got to dry ground. They found well-worn, dry paths which crisscrossed the swamp and then they were able to make some progress.

Suddenly, two of the men, a friendly Indian and a Plimoth soldier, scouting together, heard and then saw an Indian running down one of the paths. The soldier was urged to shoot at once. The gun misfired with a loud click and the running Indian was alerted and in turn attempted to aim his gun at the pair. The allied Indian was faster and shot the on-coming Indian in the stomach and he died in seconds.

They approached the fallen Indian, turned him over on his back, and realized that they had bagged the ringleader of the Indian War.

Hearing the shots, the main body of troops soon reached the scene. It was King Philip himself...a great prize that would go a long way in settling the dispute. Captain Church, after praising the pair on a job well done, nodded to the Indian brave who defected to the English, and the guide then cut off Philip's head and hands and they were dispatched to headquarters in Rhode Island. Later the head ended up in Plimoth. A couple of Philip's lieutenants surrendered and soon the rest of his men turned themselves in to Captain Church.

Hunger was also a great stimulus for the rest of the tribes in giving up. Soon, after so many had given up, for all intents and purposes the war was over.

The people of Massachusetts, Connecticut and Rhode Island were getting back to their usual routine. However, there was still some sporadic fighting in Maine and New York, but this ended with the resisting Indians in their desperate attempt to find food to prevent starvation. They finally gave up to the British.

The thirteen month King Philip's War extracted a large toll of killing and suffering for the English settlers and the Indians.

The cost to the Algonquins alone was the death of six thousand braves, women and children. It decimated the tribe, both with the deaths and those sold into slavery.

The personal property of houses, livestock, corn and military material were eliminated. The settlers didn't come out of this unscathed, they lost twenty-five towns which were plundered, seventeen had been burned to the ground and the fields which were the heart of their agricultural life were destroyed, hundreds of helpless civilians were killed.

*   *   *

The whole war was brutal and it took a long time for the wounds to heal. The Indians could not accept the whole blame for starting the conflict. All they could see was their land rapidly disappearing and more white men assuming control over their lives. One thing the Indians cherished above all else was freedom. They wanted the freedom to run their own lives, to fish and hunt on their own land. Some of the nations of Indians were well governed. They had strict laws that were welcomed by the Indians but they never would accept anything less than complete independence. They had knowledge of herbs and medicinal organic material which was effective in healing and to this day one hundred seventy of their remedies are accepted by the medical profession and listed in the *United States Pharmacopoeia*.

Most of the Indians on Cape Cod were friendly to the Pilgrims and they proved their loyalty by being allies. However, they were naive in their dealings with the white man. They did not understand the buying and selling of land and they did not know that to sell the land was to forever lose their rights of possession. They thought that the white man was foolish in buying the land because there was so much land around. If they moved to another area they soon found that their new land was occupied by others who would not give them access to it. In fact they were to find that their neighbors would become hostile and belligerent if they wanted to move in. This was the sorry plight that the Indians now found themselves.

*　　*　　*

In England, the typical Englishmen, who were farmers, tilled the soil and earned low wages. Their lives depended on their jobs and lack of money made it impossible to take time out to seek other opportunities. The government found that by raising sheep and selling the wool to the Europeans they could realize more money and the labor involved would be sharply curtailed.

Thousands of acres were converted to graze land and the farmers were out of work. The people were desperate in their search for work.

The land was owned by a few landlords and it was next to impossible to buy a farm. The cities were unsuitable places to look for employment as there was strong competition for the low paying jobs that might be found. Poverty was found in various areas of England and families that made living wages felt that their children would fall into the same economic trap eventually.

Showing limited tolerance, Protestants that did not agree with the policy under the reign of James I and Charles I, were considering moving to America. No wonder then, when the down-trodden heard the words; "Free Land in America", they wanted to hear more. There was the promise that if they were to be indentured as a servant for five years, they would be fed, clothed and then given land up to fifty acres free! Given the promise of a job and an end to religious persecution was a welcome incentive to the unemployed, especially when they could become a landowner in five years.

They also learned that the leaders of the colonies, on the most part, were educated men with experience in government, ability to make compacts, were cultured and had various skills and were on a par with the best brains of Europe. Over a hundred men who came to Massachusetts in the early years had graduated, with honors, from Oxford and Cambridge Universities. They had majored in law, religion, philosophy, medicine and in every conceivable science, known in the seventeen century, that would prove invaluable to a blossoming nation.

From evidence of the earliest arrivals, especially Brewster, Bradford and Standish, they were all well read. They enjoyed their libraries and ranged in a wide variety of books from Greek to Silkworms.

The immigrants from England were intelligent, determined people that were on self-government and held high hopes for their future and a better life for their descendants. They brought high morals and a work ethic that is still envied but seldom duplicated. There was still instilled a certain quality of patriotism, valor and respect for neighbors. A man could be an indentured servant and end up owning a large estate, living like an English squire. They came to believe that anything that they set their minds on, they could eventually accomplish.

CHAPTER 42

England-Canada

1676-1691

When James II assumed power, he secretly hid his idea of promoting Catholicism and returning the land into the hands of the Pope in Rome. He allowed the Catholics to organize, for a year or two, by convincing his enemies that he had become tolerant of all religions. Once the Catholics would become the dominant religion he wouldn't have hesitated in his grand strategy. Being Catholic himself, he could see a certain advantage in his act, but the Pope rejected his plan and it was abandoned.

This was not the only scheme that King James II tried to put into effect. He sent Sir Edmund Andros, who had been Governor of New York for years, to Boston to be named Governor-in-Chief to dominate the whole territory of New England. Later, there was to come under his control, an area which would include all English settlements north and east of the Delaware River. Sir Edmund Andros had from birth an aristocratic, military background that had roots in the Dutch and English societies. He spoke Dutch fluently and this fit into his executive ability and success in New Amsterdam, New York. He had been commissioned a major in the Barbados infantry and saw service in the Leeward Islands. His infantry regiment was converted to a regiment of Dragoons (mounted) much to his delight because he liked horses. The experience that he gained dealing with the natives in and around Barbados Island was a great asset to him later in negotiating with the Algonquins and Iroquois in 1676.

During the reign of James II the monarchy was determined that they would control all the English speaking area in the New World, thus Sir Andros was given experienced redcoats who immediately set about to demoralize the Puritans by urging them to drink to excess, to become lackadaisical about their work, to curse and other ways tried to end their religious standards. Andros planned to abolish all forms of governments and he placed all areas under his vise-like grip. When this was done, he invited various magistrates to sit on his governing councils.

He summoned the governing body of Plimoth to Boston, which was the seat of power. Governor Thomas Hinckley with Major William Bradford his deputy, along with his assistants Thomas Freeman, Daniel Smith, John Walley and Nathaniel Clarke who was now the Secretary of Plimoth since the death of Nathaniel Morton, were invited to sit on the governing council. Under the circumstances it was an offer they couldn't refuse.

The first thing on the agenda for Sir Andros was to increase taxes. The Selectmen of Taunton objected, stating that the citizens of their town didn't desire to be taxed without knowledge of where the tax money was going, or who would benefit from it. (The first example of taxation without representation.) The selectmen took an unusual bold step when they said they couldn't accept this taxation without discussing the matter in assembly.

Sir Andros had no time or sympathy for the "impudent colonists". He sent the Taunton Town Clerk to jail for several months for his audacity in sending him a document criticizing his actions.

His next action was to challenge the validity of their title to the lands from the English government and the deeds obtained from the Indians. This made the colonists from all areas very uneasy; they didn't know what he would do next.

The colonists at Plimoth were dismayed and shocked when they found their Secretary Nathaniel Clarke, in favor with Sir Andros as a result of his sneaky deeds against the colony. His reward for the betrayal of Plimoth was the gift of Clarke Island; a valuable piece of real estate. It provided wood for the pastor and the poor of the colony, its salt mill and pasturage were valuable assets.

Nathaniel Clarke was the son of Thomas Clarke, the sailor from the *Mayflower* who was the first to land on the island during early expeditions. He returned from England to live in Plimoth in August, 1623 as a passenger on the *Anne*.

When the Town Clerk of Taunton was released from jail he wanted to fight Sir Andros treatment of his fellow citizens. Deacon John Faunce, the Duxbury Town Clerk, joined with Pastor Wiswell, also of Duxbury and started to collect money from the citizens as a fund to fight Sir Andros and to let the courts decide. They were immediately squelched in this effort by being arrested for "imposing taxes" on his Majesty's subjects without the proper authority.

Sir Edmund Andros in his arrogance and animosity toward the citizens didn't realize they were independent of the Crown's authority.

Wiswell was ordered to stand trial in Boston and he objected saying that severe gout made the trip impossible and he wanted a delay. His complaint was to no avail, he had to make the tiresome trip three times resulting in his near death. Wiswell also complained to the court that he couldn't die because his small pension would result in his family starving to death. His complaints and urging for a respite in the trial fell on deaf ears. He was found guilty and paid a fine.

In early 1689, John Winslow, son of John and Mary (Chilton) Winslow sailed from England into Boston Harbor with the unconfirmed story that King James II had been overthrown and replaced by William and Mary. The story, although vague at the time, proved to be true. William, Prince of Orange and his wife Mary, the elder daughter of James II were called to London, England. Under an act of Parliament they were crowned King and Queen of Great Britain in late 1688. After the coronation, the rivalry between France and England which had been contained for a hundred and fifty years came to a boiling point.

Official word came to the colonies and suddenly there was a rumble and excitement began to fill the air. Small groups were discussing the news and then crowds appeared in towns. The Town Criers soon came out with the announcements that one of Sir Andros' lieutenants was in jail in Boston and then came the news that Sir Edmund Andros was himself taken prisoner. They were sent back to England along with the traitor Nathaniel Clarke, to answer to William and Mary for their crimes.

With much rejoicing, the Plimoth colonists finally eliminated the "reign" of Sir Edmund Andros and once again Thomas Hinkley resumed his governing role and was assisted by his Deputy Governor ,William Bradford, Junior, and his other assistants, Daniel Smith, Barnabas Lothrop, John Thacher, John Walley and John Cushing. The position of Secretary was taken by Samuel Sprague replacing Nathaniel Clarke.

The French wasted no time in seeking revenge against

the British. The French in Canada solicited the Indians from wide spread tribes to become their allies in once again beginning a war between the Indians and the British. The French bribed the Algonquins, who lived near the Quebec Territory, with whiskey and guns. They eventually talked them into becoming Catholics. The French sought the friendship of the Hurons, whose territory was in the western section of New York and would help them fight their bitter enemies, the Iroquois. The French soon found the folly of irritating the Iroquois Confederation.

The warlike Iroquois wouldn't stand idly by while the French instigated friction between the tribes. They soon attacked the French settlements and this in turn acted as a buffer for the British and the Dutch colonies in Hudson Valley in the New York territory.

It was inevitable that there would be friction between the two countries in the colonies. They had not declared war in Europe, but in the colonies there was a fierce rivalry in the fur trade between the British and French and the Indians were placed in the middle. Both the British and the French now supplied the Indians with weapons and liquor although they knew that this would probably come back to haunt them. The French Catholic missionaries taught the Indians to hate the Protestant British.

*   *   *

After several minor skirmishes, eventually France and England fought three wars. They were the King William's War, 1690-1697; Queen Anne's War, 1701-1703; and the King George's War, 1744-1748. These were mainly hit-and-run or guerrilla tactics introduced in the King Philip's War.

*   *   *

391

In 1691, Massachusetts obtained a Charter to take over more land. Plimoth fell under its grasp. The authorities in Massachusetts claimed that Plimoth was a little colony and quite weak with few people and very poor. The colony of Plimoth was to donate £500 to the Bay Colony to retain its independence. Governor Hinckly gave a half-hearted effort to stymie their move but in the end the Bay Horse threw its rider. Plimoth became part of the Massachusetts Bay Colony.

There was no explanation of why they had the authority other than their own General Court which could authorize Charters and charge fees. Massachusetts had its hand out in all directions. They wanted to take over New Hampshire, Maine and Nova Scotia. They gave the reason that New York had Plimoth on their list of colonies they wanted to take over and Massachusetts wanted to beat them to it.

It was unclear why Rhode Island, at the time, was smaller than Plimoth Colony but was able to keep its independence

The Bay Colony taking over Plimoth must have been a hard blow to Elder Cushman in his dwindling years. He died in December, 1691 to a lingering illness that had gone on for eleven weeks. He was eighty-three years old and he had been married to Mary for fifty-six years. They had eight children, seven had married, and one had died early.

Mary was at his bedside with many friends and relatives when he passed away. He had accomplished much during his forty-two years of service as Elder of the First Church of Plimoth. Only once in his life had he shirked his duty, this is when he was a Highway Surveyor and was accused of non-performance of his duty.

He helped Isaac Allerton, his father-in-law, by appearing in court on March 3, 1645, to enable Allerton to have a year's grace period to try and collect money owed to him by private citizens in the colony. Thomas was successful and

Allerton again sought his help on October 27, 1646 by assigning him to collect a debt of £100 owed by John Coombs.

Thomas Senior, was a simple, easy going person who enjoyed his family and was happy to help others in his work or at church. Many descendants of Thomas achieved greatness in many fields, among them were educational and judicial. (President Roosevelt was related to Thomas and Mary as a descendant of their son, Eleazer. Roosevelt was a ninth generation descendant from Robert Cushman.)

Some historians claim that Thomas Cushman was responsible for starting it all. They say that anyone named Cushman was directly related to him. There are many towns named after the Cushman brood.

Like Isaac Cushman, Thomas' son, there are many descendants that have followed in his religious profession as ministers. Isaac performed many marriage ceremonies for his brothers, who carried the name along and there are thousands of families with the Cushman name.

*   *   *

With Plimoth now falling under the influence of Massachusetts Bay Colony, the Colony was still able to extend its own influence to a range of towns and eventually would be the hub of Plymouth County.

The Colony was steadily increasing in size and the economy, while always struggling in its early years, had now stabilized and was performing well.

The moral factor, which had been imbedded in the minds of the early settlers, was still in evidence although there were few left of the original Mayflower passengers. Many of their offspring had left Plimoth with their families to live in other regions of the country which were now opening up for settlement.

They still had the pioneering instinct; they would go where opportunity was still offered. These settlers seemed to be a restless lot, they left to form towns which later became cities. The cities would become capitals of States.

As the population increased and the families started their westward trek, many of these "restless people," descendants of the original Pilgrims, headed in their wagons to new lands.

They battled hunger, disease and even the Indians, as their ancestors had when they first arrived in the New World.

Many never finished the trip west. On every wagon trail would be the silent testimony to their courage in the form of simple grave markers, known only to a few.

CHAPTER 43

Salem, Plymouth

1692

In 1692, at the age of seventy-six, Mary Cushman was thinking about the Witch Trials in Salem, Massachusetts. Her sons, Elkanah and Eleazar, were visiting her with their wives.Mary said, "Have you heard the news from Salem?"

Elkanah replied, "I guess you mean the Witch trials and the executions that are taking place?"

"Yes, isn't it terrible?"

Eleazar said, "I've heard about them, too. The reports are quite grim. I heard that twenty people were executed. Nineteen were hanged in a place called "Gallows Hill", another was "pressed to death" under a pile of stones. The claim of witchcraft, no doubt, was made up by people with gripes against the accused."

Elkanah replied, "The cause of all this hysteria was Reverend Cotton Mather. He continually urged the people on to persecute these poor unfortunates. Panic seized the town, the townspeople wondered who would be next to be revealed as a witch. Unfortunately, it is an age of superstition that effects many countries and it is estimated that about 40,000 people were put to death in England alone during the past forty years."

Elkanah's wife, Martha said, "Well, there was an earlier execution for witchcraft in 1648 at Boston and two more were executed in Connecticut a couple of years later."

Elkanah said, "Do you know who started all the executions in Europe?" Getting a blank stare from all present, he went on, "If my history is correct, in 1484 one of Pope Innocent VIII's agents boasted that he personally burned at least nine hundred people that were condemned as witches."

Eleazar commented, "It started even before then. It was around 1348 when they got rid of cats because the authorities thought they were possessed by witches. The rats really began to flourish. The rats infected the populace and one-third of the people of Europe died a horrible death. They called it the "Black Plague" or black death. Whole families were wiped out."

Eleazer's wife, Elizabeth (Coombs) spoke up, "I suppose that witchcraft started when people began to communicate in the dark ages. I heard that in the 13th Century, the inquisition was beginning and they attempted to end sorcery and witchcraft and unfortunately thousands were questioned and tortured and then executed."

Mary said, "Well, it was not only England that was involved. During the 16th Century, the Romanists and the Protestants competed in their persecution of witchcraft. In Hamburg, Germany, they executed six hundred "witches"; five hundred perished in Geneva, Switzerland, in Toulouse, France, four hundred died in one execution. Not to be outdone, in Nancy, France a judge condemned eight hundred in sixteen years. In Como, Italy, a thousand died in a single year."

Eleazer got up and hugged his mother. Laughing he said, "Mother, where did you get all that information?"

Mary replied, "Your father read a lot and we used to talk about many subjects and that was one of them. If he were here now and heard about the witchcraft trials, I know that it would bother him deeply."

Elkanah said, "I guess that I am a little more involved with Salem than most of you. I have a friend in Salem that corresponds with me and he said that all this started with some girls going to Reverend Samuel Parris house to hear his servant tell folklore of the West Indies. The girls are Elizabeth Parris and Abigail Williams and they were only nine and eleven years old, when they started the stories.

"Shortly, more girls joined the two and they were soon influenced emotionally by the woman's stories and superstition and they even went into convulsions. This was the spark that set the flame of witchcraft in Salem."

Mary asked," How could such a small group, that age, influence adults including judges in such a story?"

Elkanah said, "Mother, that was only the beginning. They were doing wild things. They laughed, then threw books across the room, ranted and raved. Eventually, thirteen girls were involved, the oldest was twenty. They soon became celebrities, people would watch them from a distance and to their shame, many began to believe the stories. The girls actually named eccentric women as witches. One of the first named in this category was a pipe-smoking beggar. She was a poor crippled Negro, wedded three times, and was the mother of an illegitimate half-caste son. She, along with the others all falsely accused, were tortured and subjected to many unspeakable punishments to force them to admit causing harm to the young girls. The girls had put on an act, crying out, supposedly in pain, being bitten and paralyzed."

Eleazar asked, "Did your friend say why the court didn't see through their antics and call a halt to this madness?"

Elkanah replied, "No, they didn't stop it. In fact, the harassment increased during the summer and now the girls were accusing neighbors they might have disliked for some unexplained reasons. The girls collaborated in these stories and showed signs of torment when they approached the accused. This travesty was upheld by Judge Hawthorne, an ancestor of Nathaniel Hawthorne. The judge was a firm believer in witchcraft and was impressed by the girls' performance."

Mary said, "I still don't know how the adults would believe them. Weren't they suspicious.?"

Elkanah answered, "Yes, all of the victims said the girls were lying. The girls would then answer, 'The accused themselves are lying and it proves that they are unbalanced and not sound of mind because they don't agree with us, this is due to witchcraft.' Many other people who knew the victims' character and lifestyle, could attest to their innocence, were a little reluctant to speak in their defense because they in turn would be accused of also being a witch. To add to both the victims and their friends desperation, Judge Hawthorne was convinced the girls would not lie. To show the insanity of the whole situation, if they were accused of witchcraft and said, 'Yes, I'm guilty,' they wouldn't be hung. If they were accused and said, 'I'm not a witch, it's a complete lie,' then chances are you would be hanged. The trouble was, none of the innocent would claim they were guilty."

Eleazer replied, "When you analyze the situation I can't understand their thinking if indeed they were thinking. I still can't see why the girls had such influence.

Elkanah said, "Well, my friend mentioned that two of the girls who were then a part of the "Witch Bitches", as they were known around town, admitted that the trials were a farce. Two other collaborators put up such a spectacle that the two girls recanted their stories. They were fearful that their "friends" might claim that they were also witches and would be hanged. The term "Witch Bitches" was coined for the girls but not echoed within earshot of the them. It was used discreetly with trusted friends."

Eleazer said, "It certainly seems that the people were frightened to death to even speak. Were the people spying for the girls thinking that they wouldn't be included on their list if they appeared friendly toward them.?"

Elkanah replied, "I guess that it's almost impossible to imagine what went on in Salem. Some neighbors of my friend who were very good people and were always ready to help others, unfortunately fell prey to the accusers. Their names were John and Elizabeth Proctor and were actually well liked in the community. They were accused of being witches by their maid, Mary Warren, who was easily intimidated by the girls and she was soon collaborating with them. The Proctors were thrown in jail and their five children then became the wards of Mary Warren. The sheriff came to their house and seized all assets, including cattle, and disposed of them, long before the trial. The sheriff left nothing to support the children, even throwing out the broth in a pot.

"Finding that she couldn't appear in court because of the children, the girls became terrified that Mary Warren would admit her hoax and become the weak link in the chain. The girls solved the problem by saying that Mary Warren was herself a witch."

Elizabeth said, "Why didn't the neighbors all get together and testify to the character of the Proctors, if they really liked them? It seems that they were too quiet about it."

Elkanah replied, "The people were beginning to come to the conclusion that they would have to do something about the trials and they would stick together and protest. In fact they were very brave about it when you consider the danger that they faced in defying the girls. They could find themselves accused. About fifty-two neighbors testified to the Proctors innocence and in spite of the number that was involved, the court accepted Mary Warren's word and the Proctors were hanged. Mary Warren said that she had signed the devil's book and made her mark. The girls had no regrets that people were dying due to the absurd stories they were telling in court. They thought that it was great sport! Ironically, many of the people that went along with the girls and their stories, were themselves pointed out as witches, due to their slightest whims. It wasn't only the eccentric that were earmarked for condemnation, it could be a laborer, a businessman; anyone could fall victim."

Elizabeth said, "Surely, there must have been somebody in authority that would question the trials that were taking place. Why was so much faith put in the girls statements and antics?"

Elkanah said, "My friend wrote that one constable from Salem Village realizing that the girls tales were false, said, 'Hang them instead of the others.' He fled the village but was picked up ten days later and within twenty days was hanged, being accused by the "Witch Bitches" of several murders, which of course was a lie."

"I can't understand why they had such credibility—I agree with mother, there must have been some suspicion. How could they accuse others so easily?" Eleazer said.

lkanah replied, "The girls claimed that they could spot witchcraft at great distances, that s why some of the victims came from faraway towns and villages."

Eleazar questioned, "Just how would they go about it? How would they pick out their victims and then accuse them?"

Elkanah said, "If a person, on the slightest pretense, was accused of being a witch, one or more of the girls would face the accused and the girl would pretend to be in an uncontrolled fit. The victim was forced to touch the girl and if the fit ceased the unfortunate victim was adjudged to be a witch and was then hung."

A descendant of John Alden, an army captain who bore the same name, had fought in the Indian Wars with great distinction was also hauled into court. He was also accused of being a witch. When the girls erroneously faced the wrong person they were told of their mistake and then turned to Alden. He was ordered to stand on a chair in front of the girls and face them. Immediately, they all fell flat on their faces, supposedly writhing in pain. He was then told to place his hand on each of them, miraculously they all regained their normal pose. Alden then asked the judges, "When I faced you, why didn't you fall? Can you give me a good reason why you weren't effected too?"

"He was found guilty, sent to prison in Boston and escaped fifteen weeks later."

Mary said, "Good for John Alden for speaking up! His father would have been proud of him. John, Senior was never a timid one and I guess his son takes after him."

Elkanah said, "I remember them both and I agree with you."

Elizabeth asked, "Did your friend tell you how long this kept up without the girls realizing how much damage was being done?"

Elkanah said, "Yes, finally the people began to doubt the stories that the girls were telling. Many of the accused were set free and the girls stories simply ignored."

"The trials and the imprisonment must have a cost a lot of money," Eleazer said.

Elkanah said, "This is the most ironic part of the whole story, you'll never guess what the victims were forced to do. If they were hanged, the grieving relatives had to pay for the executioners services plus the food that the accused ate and the cost of the cell accommodations. Typical of the insanity at the time, one victim who was acquitted of the 'crime' was still in jail. All of her family's assets had been taken and she had no money to pay her expenses to buy her way out due to the heavy debts that had accumulated while she was in jail. A wealthy stranger happened to hear of her plight and paid her way to freedom. In spite of her innocence, the Negro that had been imprisoned, fortunately wasn't hanged but she had spent thirteen months in jail. She was supposed to be released but having no money to pay the expenses she was then sold as a slave.

Two women that were declared innocent, 'by reason of pregnancy', now found themselves pronounced dead and all their property had been seized. To show you how ridiculous the whole affair had become; in Andover, Massachusetts, the judge signed forty warrants for witchcraft. When he stopped signing them, he was accused of being a witch. He left town to avoid arrest but unfortunately his dog which was left behind was hanged for being a witch."

Well over one hundred and fifty people had been accused by the girls, fifty-five had confessed and therefore were released from jail.

Fourteen years after the trials, the girls confessed that they lied...they received no punishment.

CHAPTER 44

Plymouth, Cape Cod

1695-1699

John Cooke died in 1695 at the age of eighty-one years old. He had been a resident of Dartmouth, (now New Bedford) Massachusetts. He was the father of four children and his wife, Sarah, was the daughter of Richard Warren who came on the *Mayflower*. After he was excommunicated from the church at Plimoth for being a Baptist, he went to Dartmouth. He had served as a Deacon at the First Church of Plimoth for seventeen years In 1684, at the age of seventy, he and his associates formed a Baptist church in Dartmouth with John Cooke as its preacher. He kept that position until his death eleven years later.

He was the last male survivor of the original *Mayflower* passengers. There was only one left that came on that eventful voyage... Mary Cushman.

Mary was in her eighty-third year in 1699, when she passed away. Her sons, daughters and their spouses with her grandchildren and great grandchildren, had visited her within a month of the time of her death. It seemed that she had a premonition of her impending death, she wanted to see them at least once more.

She had been a good mother and grandmother with a good mixture of life and discipline. She had left a legacy of helping others in need and inspired others with her courage and optimism despite the hardships she had endured during her lifetime. What a life she had lived! She had lead a wondrous life...although most of the time she and her family lived a frugal life. With seven children to raise there wasn't much money to spread around.

She met death with dignity. She closed her eyes and with a seemingly contented smile passed away with peace and serenity. Her family was at her bedside...weeping.

*　　*　　*

> *"This last, this seventieth year,*
> *two persons living that came in the first ship*
> *of the old stock...the old stock*
> *there are two...there are none at last*
> *...of the old stock...the old stock..."*

Western Star by: Stephen Vincent Benet